The New World

Hannah,

Best Wishes

Doug Felten

The New World

Book One in the New World Trilogy

Doug Felton

First paperback edition October 2019

Cover design by Matthew West

www.dougfelton.net

For Linda, God's gift to me.

"Since it has pleased Providence to place me in this station, I shall do my utmost to fulfil my duty towards my country; I am very young and perhaps in many, though not in all things, inexperienced, but I am sure that very few have more real good will and more real desire to do what is fit and right than I have."

- Queen Victoria

Prologue

July 6, 2060

Ella took three long deep breaths before gripping the sides of her bed and crying out in pain.

"Push!" Nate said.

"I *am* pushing," she said in a low growl.

"And you're doing great. You're almost there."

How does someone endure that kind of pain? He would have done anything to take it for his wife, but all he could do was help her through it. That didn't feel like nearly enough. There must be something for him to do besides yelling push. Maybe not, but he knew when it was all over, he'd be her hero. At least he hoped so.

The contraction passed, and Ella collapsed on the bed, exhausted. "I can't do this. I can't do it anymore."

"Yes, you can." Nate used his best calming tone, despite the storm brewing in his gut. There would be plenty of time later to think about everything that could have gone wrong. Right now, his wife needed him.

"I can't. I can't," Ella moaned.

Nate was firm. "Yes, you can."

What he wouldn't give right now for a doctor, but all the doctors within driving distance were either dead or treating the infected. Nate was on his own. Still, he worried, what if something went wrong? What if the baby was too big for a natural delivery? Nate had been over eleven pounds at birth and would never have made it into the world without the help of a surgeon. Was that kind of thing genetic? What if she *couldn't* deliver this baby?

Another wave of pain hit Ella, causing her body to tense. Despite her claim to the contrary, she was able to push again. Nate was amazed at the strength of his wife. He loved her, and he would take the pain for her if he could. But watching her, he wondered

1

whether he could handle it. Another cry escaped her throat, piercing the night in their tiny apartment. For a moment, Nate considered what the neighbors might be thinking. Then again, they had bigger things to worry about than a woman crying out in the night. The threshold of normal shifted over the last ten months, and most people were only concerned with staying alive. Everything else was secondary, including whatever might be going on in the apartment next door. No one would be checking on them tonight.

Ella had been pushing for an hour. This was their first baby, and Nate had no idea how long the labor was supposed to take. He did know if Ella could keep going like this without any meds. Heck, he didn't know if he could.

"You're doing great, babe. Just a little more. You need to push again."

She took three more breaths and pushed hard. Then something breathtaking happened. The crown of a tiny head begins to emerge.

"I see it," he cried. They didn't know the sex of the baby, so he or she was just *it* for now. "Oh, Ella, this is amazing. Keep pushing. You're almost there." His heart rate shot up, and his body tingled with adrenaline at the sight of his child entering the world.

As Ella pushed again, the baby's head slowly appeared. Another push and the rest of the tiny body slipped out in one motion, resting in Nate's hands on the bed. The room filled with the squeaky cry of a newborn. Nate smiled.

I'd be angry too if someone just pulled me from a warm Jacuzzi.

He reached for the knife he had sterilized for the occasion and carefully cut the umbilical cord. Nate controlled his breathing – in through his nose, out through the mouth, holding his nausea at bay. As a Ph.D. student in history, cutting flesh wasn't exactly his thing, but he managed to get it done. Tying off what was left of the cord, he lifted the little pink squirmy body and brought the baby to Ella.

"Say hello to your daughter," he said, half laughing, half crying. "You did it, babe. I can't believe it, but you did it. We have a baby girl."

Ella took the baby, placing their daughter on her chest, skin to skin. "Hey there, sweetheart," she said.

"So?" Nate asked, sliding next to his wife on the bed and kissing her softly on the lips.

"So, what?"

"So, what are we going to call her? You did all the work; I figure you get first dibs on the name."

"Is that right?" Ella said, mustering a smile. "How about Jamie Elizabeth Corson, after your dad and my mom?"

Their parents who'd been lost to the virus.

Nate kissed his little girl on the forehead. "That's perfect."

Chapter One

Eighteen Years Later – Present Day

Jamie and her brother Ben were the only two people left in the visitor's gallery of the United States Senate. She peered down at her father. He sat at his desk in the now empty chamber staring at the flag that stood to the left of the rostrum. She was glad she had gone for a run that morning to clear her head. He would need her to be thinking clearly tonight.

How long would her dad sit there, she wondered, his coat draped over the chair and his tie hanging loose around his neck? A picture of his wife and two kids stared back at him from the small Senate desk. Jamie had seen that picture a thousand times in his office. It was a picture from four years ago, the three of them posing on some occasion that Jamie couldn't remember. Her mom was laughing at something, Ben wore his little league baseball cap, and Jamie had her ballet toe shoes slung over one shoulder. Her dad loved the picture because he said it captured who they really were, but it saddened Jamie every time she saw it. She wished her father hadn't brought it with him tonight.

Outside of the chamber, in the hall, the click-clack of someone's high heels on the marble floor punctuated the silence. Not twenty minutes earlier, when the Senate had voted, the chamber was abuzz with frenetic activity, nearly chaotic. Why wouldn't it be, since that was the most important vote the U.S. Senate had ever taken.

The Vice President stood at the podium. He didn't need to be there. No one expected this to be a close vote, but he had come to execute his official duty as the President of the Senate, nonetheless. A "Yea" and "Nay" vote would be taken, adding to the drama. Every senator present would individually voice his or her vote. One by one, they sounded off until they had all voted.

"Are there any senators who wish to vote or change their vote?" the Vice President followed the script, decorum to the last. "Seeing none, the 'Yeas' are eighty and the 'Nays' nineteen. The joint resolution passes."

Every senator was present for the vote except one, Senator Franklin. He had committed suicide the night before. Jamie couldn't blame him for not wanting to cast a vote, but suicide? She didn't understand giving up. That's what cowards did. Even so, the Senate convened that evening with a moment of silence on his behalf, adding to the somber atmosphere in the room. The Vice President's face drained of color as he lifted the gavel after the vote. He looked like he might be sick. The crack of the gavel dislodged frozen senators and set off an explosion in the chamber of shouting voices, angry voices. Men and women confronted one another with an urgency that bordered on hysteria. For a moment it looked like there might be a brawl. Jamie was ready to make a quick exit with Ben if the scene turned ugly, but it didn't. In fact, after the initial outburst, the chamber cleared remarkably fast. Senators scurried from the building like rats from a sinking ship. After all, the Senate had just voted to dissolve the Federal Government of the United States of America.

It was July 4, 2078.

America had lived to the ripe old age of three hundred, two, and died on her birthday. Actually, in the history of the world, America was still an adolescent. She died too young. Some would take offense that the Senate scheduled the vote on Independence Day, but what difference did it make? Dead was dead. Jamie didn't mourn any more on the anniversary of her mother's death than any other day. Every day hurt the same. A date was just a date. Just another day. It made no difference if they voted on the fourth or the fifth or the fifteenth. If anything, the irony of taking the vote on

Independence Day would play out well in the history books, giving the historians something to talk about.

She wondered, *do other teenagers think about these things?*

Probably not. Maybe it was because she was the daughter of a history professor turned senator.

"You think he'll be okay?" Ben asked.

"I think so, once we get out of D.C."

"Did he really say you could go to Harvard?"

"Yeah." Despite everything, Jamie couldn't help but smile. Her dad had surprised her that morning with an early birthday surprise. He'd arranged for her to go to Harvard.

Ben leaned his head on her shoulder. "What am I going to do without you?"

"I won't be far, and I think after this, dad will be okay." Jamie didn't know if she believed that, but she wanted to with all her heart.

It was getting late, and she couldn't let her father sit and mourn the death of his country all night, at least not here. It was time to go. She motioned to her brother, and Ben got up and made his way toward the gallery exit. A day shy of eighteen, Jamie was no stranger to taking charge of her family, and Ben had learned to follow her lead. He was ten when their mother died three years earlier, and Jamie looked after him from that moment on. She had to. Her mother was gone, and her father was emotionally unavailable. Maybe, it was because of his stressful job as a U.S. Senator, but it probably had more to do with the results of mixing grief and alcohol. Whatever. They needed a dad, and he wasn't there for them. Even when he was home, he wasn't really there.

"He's not doing it on purpose," her best friend Raven said one night as Jamie sat on her bed crying. "He's hurting, and he's lonely, and he's under a lot of pressure with all the government stuff he's gotta deal with. You know he loves you guys."

No doubt Raven was right, but Ben was hurting too, and he needed the attention of his dad. But Jamie was all he had, so she took care of him. She had earned his trust, which earned her the right to tell him what to do, even though he was a teenager now. Sometimes she overdid it, but she was trying. If he minded her bossiness, he didn't show it. He was a good kid.

Down on the chamber floor, Jamie quietly approached her father and put a hand on his shoulder. "Time to go."

Senator Nathan Andrew Corson turned his head and smiled at his daughter with a weary smile, "You're probably right."

"It didn't fail, you know," Jamie said, "the Great Experiment." Her father frequently referred to America as the Great Experiment.

"No," Nate said, "It didn't fail. It just didn't last. And now it's over." He sighed deeply and wiped a tear from his cheek. "What have I done?"

Jamie didn't answer. He did what he had to do to; he pulled the life support on a dead patient. It was his joint resolution they had voted on that evening. Authoring it was an act of courage, as far as Jamie was concerned, but he didn't see it that way. The history professor had become a part of history, and he might never get over it.

Jamie looked at Ben, who stood wide-eyed. They had never seen their father look so small and weak, and she felt for him. She drew her athletic frame to its full height, pulling her blond hair into a ponytail with a hairband. Everyone was hurting, but someone had to make a decision.

"Dad, we should go."

"I know, Peanut." He stood and slipped a hand into his pocket, a casual pose that he often used to signal confidence. Was it an act for their benefit? Maybe. But if so, she appreciated the effort. As her dad looked around the chamber for the last time, Jamie's eyes followed his to the chaos in front of them; chairs misplaced and paper strewn about. It was a good picture of her heart right now, but she had to keep herself together. She had a family to look after, and they had plans for a new life.

"We'll be alright," she said. "We'll get out of the city, and we'll start over. It'll be okay."

He nodded and picked up the picture on his desk, tucking it under his arm. As they turned to leave, her father put his arm around Ben, something he hadn't done nearly enough in the last three years. Jamie smiled at the tender gesture and then steeled herself for the New World that awaited them.

• • • • •

"Senator!" a woman's voice called out.

Halfway down the Capitol steps, Jamie looked at their waiting car and then turned with her father to face the voice calling him.

"Not anymore," he said.

"Right. Sorry," replied an Asian woman in a blue and red uniform. Jamie read her name badge – Commander Song of the New World army.

So, this is Commander Song.

The commander opened her mouth to speak again but hesitated.

"It's alright to call me Nate," he said. "What can I do for you, Commander?"

Her father's posture was uncharacteristically stiff toward the woman. Was it due to his general mood at the moment, or was there something more going on? Maybe Jamie was projecting her dislike for the lady onto her father's body language. She didn't have a good reason to dislike her, but she did anyway. Was it because the commander was closer to Jamie's age than her father's and very attractive? Or was it because they had spent so much time working together? Song was the New World liaison to the U.S. Senate. Her father was the chairman of the Committee on Governmental Affairs, which meant he was the Senate's point man dealing with the New World. As a result, the commander and her father were thrown together in a close working relationship. Commander Song's name had been spoken frequently at home in recent months, a little too frequently for Jamie's taste. Now that she'd met her, dark hair, fair skin and all, she was definitely worried.

Or maybe I'm paranoid.

"I wanted to say I'm sorry about all of this." The Commander's words were kind, but her stance was all business. The sidearm strapped to her waist and the crisp uniform told Jamie that even if she was sorry, she was New World through and through.

Her father ran a hand through his thick dark hair as he looked at the New World transports parked around the Capitol, the drones flying overhead, the guards lining the steps, and the New World banners ready to be unfurled on the front of the building.

"Thank you, but I think we are way past that now," Nate said. Then he added, "What are you doing here, Commander? I mean tonight?"

"My role as liaison to the Senate was temporary, just until the vote. I've been assigned to the Capitol reclamation team. We wanted to secure the Capitol building and get started on our project as soon as possible."

"Your project?"

"The New World has decided that the building will no longer serve to house the legislative branch of government. We have something different in mind."

"Reclamation is an interesting word," Jamie said, inserting herself into the conversation. "You have to own something at one time to reclaim it. Native Americans could make that case, maybe, but the New World?" She narrowed her eyes, "I don't think so."

"You must be Jamie," Song said with a smile. "Your father has told me so much about you. And I must say, he was spot on. It's good to finally meet you." She turned to Ben. "And that would make you Ben."

Heard so much about me? Like what?

What was her father doing telling a New World commander about his family?

"I see. Well . . ." Nate looked back at the waiting car. He obviously wanted to end this conversation, but Commander Song was not through.

"This isn't our fault, Nate. It was *your* resolution. We didn't do this. We're just here to pick up the pieces."

Nate, who had started angling himself toward the car, turned back to the commander with a suddenness that surprised Jamie. "You're kidding, right? *My* resolution? I had no choice. Once the president signed the London Accords, and we lost control of our nukes . . . I had no choice."

Jamie could see that Nate was struggling to get his words out through his emotions. "And yes, the New World has their fingerprints all over this," he said. "You could have helped heal this nation, brought us together, but that's not what you did, is it?"

Jamie knew what her dad was thinking. The New World and the other provinces had acted like looters in a blackout when America was at its weakest, crippling and eventually killing the once-great nation. She couldn't help but think of how barbarian tribes had carved up the Roman Empire after it had been overrun. History did repeat itself.

Commander Song didn't respond. Nor did she offer a further apology. Instead, she closed the gap between them with a few steps and lowered her voice just enough to catch their attention. "You need to leave the city," she said in a flat tone.

Jamie was confused by her statement. Leave the city? Why?

Nate gave a measured response. "We have plans to go north in the fall. I have a teaching job lined up. It's not much, but we'll get by."

"You might not want to wait that long." The commander kept her gaze fixed on Jamie's father but showed no emotion on her face. "Just to be on the safe side."

"What are you talking about, Elaine?" Nate shot a furtive glance at a nearby soldier. And then in a harsh whisper, "Are you telling me the New World is planning to take action against U.S. government officials? We had an arrangement with the Council. They said they'd protect us. They said we could leave the city."

As a student of history, Jamie knew that leaders ousted from power were often treated harshly by those who had assumed power. In ancient times, a new king would wipe out the family members of the former king, eliminating at least one set of highly motivated rivals for the throne. That's why the transition of power in America was so remarkable for more than three centuries.

But this wasn't America anymore. Panic began to grip her chest. It was then that she realized how many New World soldiers had positioned themselves around the Capitol.

So many guns.

She looked to their waiting car and saw the uneasy expression of her father's chief of staff who was sitting behind the wheel. Commander Song stood like a statue. Her posture and silence told them she had said all she would say.

Jamie felt her father slowly pull her and Ben in front of him as they turned away from Commander Song and descended the steps. It took everything she had to keep her body loose and her gait even. Was the commander trying to warn them? Was she protecting them? If so, why would they be in danger? The New World had won. America was dead. Her father wasn't a threat.

"Why would the New World keep us from leaving?" she asked. "They said they wouldn't stop us."

"I don't know, Peanut. They're kind of paranoid. Maybe they're worried we'll oppose the monarchy somehow."

Of all the ideas the New World had embraced, Jamie thought, this was the dumbest. She couldn't envision a monarchy here, even if it were no longer America. The very idea of a monarchy would be laughable to most citizens, but for the well-funded PACs that promoted its virtues, while at the same time highlighting the failures of American democracy. Thanks to the corruption rampant among Washington politicians, they had plenty of material from which to draw. Public support for the ruling political class was at an all-time low. All the New World had to do was offer an alternative. Something that looked new and sounded noble. Something that didn't involve greedy politicians.

That's exactly what they did, and voila, after a decade of good PR, a monarchy was starting to sound like a real alternative to a lot of people. But what was the difference between politicians who acted like royalty and an actual king on the throne? Not much.

"I don't understand why they'd worry about you. I mean, who would listen to you?" Jamie said. "The New World already controls the media."

"I don't know. Maybe this is about Ashwill making life hard for me. Maybe it's personal."

Jamie had no use for Creighton Ashwill, the leader of the New World, but whatever was going on, she needed him to keep his promise. Her family had to get out of the city.

As they descended the steps, Jamie watched the blue and red-clad soldiers, guns held at ease. She reached the car as her dad opened the passenger doors and they all piled into the sagging sedan. Jamie slammed the door.

Her father turned to his chief of staff. "We need to get home."

Chapter Two

Jamie watched the beleaguered city pass by outside her window on their way home. Victor Campo, her father's chief of staff, had turned off the car's auto-navigate system and was negotiating the streets himself. At a dozen years younger than his boss, Victor didn't look his age. His wiry frame suggested a younger man than he was. As the car's electric motor purred, abandoned buildings, boarded-up windows, and dirty streets provided the backdrop for their journey. Armored transport vehicles pulled into position at major intersections, where New World troops poured out of them. They were securing the city. Just like that, the New World Province was transforming itself into a nation.

Even without the overbearing presence of the New World military, the city was nothing like the Washington, D.C., Jamie's grandfather had visited as a child. Then again, America was nothing like the country her grandfather had once told her about. Jamie wondered what America would be like if it hadn't been for the virus. Would there still be a United States? Like her father, she loved history, but that was a part of history she would rather forget.

Nearly two decades earlier, a deadly viral outbreak began in Pittsburgh, Pennsylvania. It triggered a wave of panic, sending people fleeing west ahead of the threat, and, in some cases, taking the virus with them. Flights in and out of the area were canceled, following protocols developed in the mid-twenty-first century after several pandemics threatened populations around the globe. That was the first time the protocols had been implemented in America, causing widespread panic throughout the region with particularly devastating effects in New York City. The protocols were effective in preventing the virus from spreading through air travel, but they didn't prevent infected people from getting into their cars and driving. As the death toll rose and the epidemic spread, so did the panic, and so did the wave of people moving west.

It was nearly impossible to stop the surge of frightened humanity until it hit the Mississippi River. At the river, bridges and ferries were closed, backing up cars and angry drivers for miles. The impulse to flee the growing epidemic had collided with a desperate attempt to contain it. The collision of those two forces created a violent reaction. As word spread, local governments and communities hurried to reinforce the containment by blocking every Mississippi River crossing. Seemingly overnight, a nearly two-thousand-mile border materialized, right down the middle of the United States. It would never be removed. Tennessee and North Carolina moved quickly to establish a containment border to stop those who had turned south. That was more difficult without the natural boundary of a river. But the governors of those states were desperate enough to put sufficient resources and manpower behind the effort. Kentucky didn't move quickly enough and became part of the quarantined states.

Nineteen states lost more than fifty-eight million people to the virus. Supplies and aid sent from neighboring states weeks after the initial outbreak could not heal the acrimony. Nothing could change the course that had been set by their callous disregard. As a result, flint struck steel, and the New World sparked to life.

"What'd Commander Song have to say?" Victor asked.

"She told us to leave the city."

"You *are* leaving. Right?" He ignored a red light at an empty intersection. Most of the streets were void of civilian traffic these days. It had been a while since Washington, D.C., was a bustling city.

"Yeah, but something's wrong."

"That's a little vague, Senator. I need you to tell me what's going on. I want to help, but I can't if you don't keep me informed."

"I don't know what's going on, and I'm not a senator anymore."

Jamie, who was sitting in the back seat with Ben, could see the growing concern on her father's face as he turned toward Victor. What did he think might happen?

"Dad, they can't stop us from leaving," Jamie said.

"They can. It's their country now, and the rules are different."

Jamie knew he was right, but she didn't want to admit it. The New World had been gobbling up more and more power, taking excessive liberty, and assuming responsibility for the wellbeing of the people, and no one in the federal government had the political will to stop them.

Nate continued, "But I think it's me they're interested in. Ashwill doesn't let anything go. I'm sure he'll come up with some reason to have me arrested or detained." He looked at his chief of staff again. "Listen to me, Victor. You've got to make sure my kids get out of the city. I've got a few connections left, political supporters. They'll help you."

Victor was single and had been fiercely loyal to Nate, first as a campaign worker and later as his chief of staff. Over the years, Nate and Ella had treated him like a favorite nephew. Jamie knew how much her father had counted on him.

"You know I would do anything," Victor said, "but don't go there. Not yet. The New World Council will honor the agreement. I mean, after everything you've done to broker a deal and keep them out of a war, what would they gain by stopping you now?"

Nate didn't respond as he looked out the window, but Jamie could guess what he was thinking. Tensions between the federal government and the New World had been on the rise for years. The New World leadership had taken on an authoritarian tone, proposing to fix everything through government edicts. In the absence of real leadership from Washington, scores of people had joined the movement. Momentum was on their side, and now, drunk with newly acquired power, it was not at all clear what the New World might do.

Military drones streaked by overhead, and Jamie got a glimpse of blue and red-clad soldiers lowering the American flag at some nondescript government building, then raising one of their own. For the first time in more than three hundred years, Washington, D.C., was in the hands of someone other than a constitutionally-elected American government. Tension worked its way up the back of Jamie's neck.

Victor turned onto Twenty-Third Street as they approached George Washington University Hospital. The facility loomed dark and ominous with no lights or activity. It had closed down a year ago and was now a derelict complex of buildings. When Washington, D.C., no longer provided access to money and power, it became less attractive to most people, and many of them left. The hospital was one of the many casualties of the exodus.

From the shadows of the large building on the right, Jamie could see movement. Somebody was there. Several people actually. She was still trying to make out the shadowy figures when two of them stepped out of the darkness and into the lighted street. She could see them more clearly now. One was tall and broadly built. His red hair receded slightly, and his red beard was full and bushy. He had his hands in the pockets of his overcoat. The other, shorter and rounder, had a large brick in his hand.

"Traitor," the man with the brick yelled as he hurled it at the windshield of their car. It smashed into the glass, creating a spider web of cracks. Thanks to the auto insurance lobby, the tech on these windshields was top rate, even the older ones, making them virtually impenetrable. The brick hit Nate's side, leaving most of Victor's view unobstructed.

"Damn," Victor yelled as he swerved. To avoid the man in the road, he veered closer to the hospital complex. Other people began to emerge out of the shadows with a brick or rock or an empty glass bottle in hand. As the various objects pelted the car, both windows on the passenger's side shattered, raining glass in on Nate and Ben.

Ben screamed as a bottle flew through the open window, hitting him in the head. Victor accelerated past the attackers narrowly missing several of them.

Jamie grabbed Ben, shielding him from any more objects thrown at the car. As they passed the hospital, she sat him back up and began checking his wounds. Fortunately, they were superficial – tiny cuts across the right side of his face, and a welt on his forehead. The whole thing had lasted only a few seconds but left Jamie shaken and Ben crying as he held his head.

"They were waiting for us," Victor said. "Maybe we should've taken another way home. Is everyone okay?"

"I'm fine," Nate said, twisting in his seat to see Jamie and Ben. "Are you guys, okay?"

"I think so," Jamie said with a shaky voice. "Ben?"

"He's okay, Dad," Jamie answered for Ben, who was still sniffing. She knew he would be embarrassed that he had cried and didn't want him to have to choke out an answer to their father.

For a moment, none of them spoke. All they heard was the sound of tires on the pavement and the purr of the engine. Then Nate said, "They have a right to be angry, but they don't have a right to throw bricks at my kids."

"Who are *they*?" Jamie asked.

"And why are they mad at us?" Ben added brushing glass from his hair.

"They're mad at your dad for daring to suggest that the country they loved was dead and should be buried," Victor answered.

"They were angry before tonight," Nate said. "They've been angry for a long time. They were angry when the rest of the country turned on us. They were angry when the president signed the London Accords. They were angry when Creighton Ashwill started talking about a monarchy. The vote tonight just gave them a reason to be angry at me. And I don't blame them. I'm angry too. But I swear to God, if they attack my kids again, there will be hell to pay."

Jamie appreciated the thought, but she was a realist. What could her father do to anyone? As a senator, he had some pull, some influence. But now? She knew he was blowing off steam, but this was exactly why they needed to get far away from this place.

"You think it was Return?" Victor asked, looking at her father.

"Maybe," Nate said.

"Return?" Jamie asked. "You mean the resistance group?"

"Could be."

"And they think they can overthrow the new government throwing rocks?"

"This wasn't about overthrowing the government," Nate said. "It was more personal than that. But after tonight, it will be. They'll use the vote to recruit supporters. They'll get organized, and they won't be throwing rocks anymore."

"If they're going to be mad at anyone, it should be at Creighton Ashwill, not you."

"Oh, they're mad at Ashwill, all right. But as far as they can tell, he and I aren't all that different; two sides of the same coin."

"Can't they understand why you had to do it? I mean, what choice did you have?"

"Yeah," her father said tiredly, "what choice did I have?"

• • • • •

Victor pulled to a stop at the curb outside of the Corson's Georgetown home. It was still one of the nicer neighborhoods in D.C., and there were not many of those left. Even here, half of the units were unoccupied, and it was beginning to show. Jamie followed Ben out of the car as her dad hurried to the door. She had half expected soldiers to be waiting for them when they got home, but all was quiet. Maybe they had misread Commander Song. Maybe there was no threat. Her father hadn't received any messages from his fellow senators or their staffers, suggesting that they had run into trouble. With the stress of the last few months leading up to the vote, maybe they had lost perspective, and they were reading more into Song's message than she intended. A demon under every rock and all that.

Maybe.

At any rate, nothing was happening on their street right now. That was a good sign.

Inside the house, her father did a quick inspection. Seeing that nothing had been disturbed, he went to the liquor cabinet and poured himself a drink.

"Dad," Jamie said softly, "do you think that's a good idea right now?" About a year earlier, she'd snuck a taste of his liquor, and hated it. More than that, she hated what it was doing to her father. He wasn't violent or abusive, he would never do anything to hurt them, but he had become distant, turning in on himself and shutting everyone else out.

Nate ignored her question. "I think we should move up our plans to leave town," he said after letting the drink take effect. "I don't know what Elaine was talking about, but something spooked her."

"You trust her?" Jamie asked.

"I do. We don't always agree, and she drives me nuts sometimes, but I trust her." He took another swallow, and the tension on his face began to ease.

"And you think she was warning us to get out?"

"I think so," Nate said. "Let's not take a chance. We can head out in the morning. You two go upstairs and get your things together. Pack what you need most right now. We'll send for the rest later. Jamie, help your brother get his stuff together."

"I don't need help," Ben said defiantly.

Jamie knew he was right; he didn't need help. But more than that, Ben needed his dad to treat him like a young man and not a little kid. It frustrated Jamie her that her dad couldn't see that.

At the top of the stairs, she told Ben, "Dad's under a lot of pressure, you know."

"That's what you always say. He doesn't think I can do anything."

"I know," she said. "Things will be different when we leave."

In Ben's room, they sat next to each other on the bed.

"You knew I couldn't stay forever," she said, beginning to feel guilty about her plans to go to Harvard. "In a few weeks, you'll be turning fourteen, and you're ready to step up."

"He doesn't think so."

"But I do," Jamie said. "I know you're ready."

Ben sulked. "I guess. I'll be glad to be out of here."

"Me too," Jamie said, her stiff-upper-lip-smile fading as she left Ben's room.

She wanted nothing more than to leave Washington. For Jamie, this would always be the place that took her mother from her. She knew it was a car accident and it could have happened anywhere, but it happened here, and that stained the city for Jamie. The man who had hit her mom and dad that night died in the accident. If he hadn't, she might have pinned her feelings on him. But he was gone, and the city was still here, so it was the city she loathed.

Downstairs, someone turned on the news feed. As she pulled essential items out of her closet, she could hear a talking head announcing Ashwill's upcoming speech. He must be full of himself tonight, she thought. The commentator droned on about what a great day this was for the New World, filling in the time until finally Ashwill was introduced. Despite herself, Jamie switched on the video feed in her room. There, staring back at her, was the face of Creighton Ashwill. In his late fifties, he was a handsome man for an older guy. His black hair was touched by gray at the temples, giving him a distinguished look. But Jamie thought his eyes screamed insincerity. *How can anyone believe a word this man says*? She turned back to her packing as he spoke.

22

"Citizens, a New World has dawned. It is a world forged in the trials of the past and armed with a bold vision for the future. Together we will make it safe and secure and prosperous, not only for us and our children but for their children and for generations to come. Earlier this evening, following the vote of the United States Senate to dissolve the federal government, the New World Council swore me in as the President of the Council. I know that the transition of power on such a large scale can be unsettling and even frightening, but I assure you that you can rest easy tonight. The New World government has led this province for years in the absence of strong leadership from the United States, and we will continue to do so. We led the way to recovery after the Pittsburgh Virus. We protected our citizens against those who tried to take advantage of us. We forged relationships with foreign companies, encouraging them to once again invest in us. And they have. They took a chance and have begun investing in you, my fellow citizens, and you have not let them down. The United States has ceased to exist, but we will continue as we have, supporting one another, looking out for one another, and standing strong against those who would seek to do us harm."

Ashwill paused for a moment before continuing. "If you are like me, you grew up here, in America. And saying goodbye to this once great nation cannot be done without sadness. It has had a rich history, a history that we can appreciate and from which we can learn. The failures of recent decades are not the whole story. We do ourselves a disservice if we don't remember and honor the successes and triumphs of the past. But looking back should never keep us from moving forward. We will not repeat the mistakes of the past, but rather we will become who we are meant to be. And so, it is the future that I wish to address tonight.

"Recent polls have indicated growing support for a new kind of leadership in our country."

"You think," Jamie said as she hoisted a stack of clothes into a suitcase. "And how much did that cost?"

23

"Many of you have voiced your opinion in favor of a monarchy to lead our nation. And so, as its first official act, the New World Council has voted to establish a constitutional monarchy as our new form of government. For some of you, this decision will be met with skepticism and confusion. I understand, but if you permit me, I will explain how we came to this very important determination.

"The New World Council is made up of elected officials, the governors of our nineteen states, me included. Several of these governors have also served as congressmen or senators. We are politicians, and therefore we are a part of the system, a system we've discovered to be wholly corrupt. What started as a noble idea, the American system of representative democracy became poisoned by the inevitable lure of money and power. Elections have become little more than popularity contests in which the winner enriches himself by peddling his influence and taking advantage of the taxpayer. In the meantime, the needs of the people are left unmet.

"We intend to correct that by removing both the contest for power and the lure of wealth. The masses will not pick our monarch from among a small group of people who are fortunate to raise enough money for a national campaign. Instead, she will be chosen for her character and intelligence as well as her ability to provide lasting, stable leadership. She will have all her material needs met in a style befitting the leader of the New World, eliminating the need for her to use her power to enrich herself.

"The people will still have a voice," he continued, "but it will be a different kind of voice. The governors of each state will be elected, as they have always been, and will still serve as members of the New World Council overseeing the daily operation of our government. The president of the council, the role I have assumed tonight, will function as the head of the government and our monarch's chief political advisor. Our monarch, as head of state, will determine the policies that guide our nation. Until she has been chosen and installed, I will provide additional leadership and guidance to our nation."

Creighton Ashwill paused again before continuing. "My fellow citizens, I am optimistic about our future, but it will not come without its challenges, challenges that will require our resolve. Right now, I am told, the Constitutional Republic of America is building up its military presence along our border. Like us, they too have become a nation this evening. And like us, they've been planning for this evening for a long time. Unlike us, their plans have included aggressive action against their neighbors. These are the same states that left us to die eighteen years ago, and now they plan to take us by force. We will not allow this. Together we will stand strong and forge the way for a new kind of nation on the American continent.

"I am optimistic, for the first time in a long time. Our future is bright with possibilities that we will realize as we commit ourselves to a common vision of a great and prosperous New World."

The image of a smiling Creighton Ashwill was replaced by two news commentators who were giddy with joy over the speech. Jamie wondered if they had ever had an original thought in their lives. Downstairs she could hear Victor react to the speech.

"You must be out of your freaking mind," he yelled. Victor was vocal about most things, but especially politics. Jamie had grown used to his passionate rants over the years, and she thought she might even miss them.

She finished arranging her clothes in her suitcases and walked next door to check on Ben. "How's it coming?"

"Good," Ben said. Two large suitcases lay open, stuffed with clothes. He had emptied the shelves in his room. The stuff he wasn't taking lay strewn about on his bed. The stuff he was taking filled a box on the floor. "I think I'm almost ready."

Jamie was halfway down the stairs with her suitcases when a knock on the front door stopped her. Her father opened the door, and two men in blue and red uniforms stepped into their house.

Chapter Three

This can't be happening.

Song was right; they should have left already. She backed up the stairs and made her way to her room, sliding both suitcases under her bed. If the soldiers were there to keep them from leaving town, she didn't want to give them the impression that they were planning to go anytime soon. Maybe that would buy them some time.

Jamie went into the hallway, ready to tell Ben to stow his stuff, and instead ran smack into a soldier standing just outside her bedroom door. "Jim-i-ny Cricket!" she said with a start. It was not much in the way of cursing, but it was Jamie's go-to phrase when she was startled.

The soldier was young, not too much older than Jamie, maybe twenty or twenty-one, but he had a poise that made him look older. "Planning a trip?"

"What are you doing up here?" she said, trying to hide her fear. Being so close to a New World soldier, especially in such tight quarters, triggered something like a feeling of claustrophobia in Jamie. She didn't like soldiers. It was a thing with her.

He looked around as if searching for an answer. "Securing the premises," he said casually.

"The premises were secure before you showed up."

"There's a lot going on tonight, a lot of changes. And there are a few people upset about it. You can't be too careful."

"And you think they might be up here in my bedroom?" Jamie had retreated into her room to put some distance between them. It wasn't enough.

He smiled. "Like I said, can't be too careful."

"Well, now that you see I'm safe and sound, you can go." Jamie kept her hands clasped behind her back so he couldn't see them shake.

"Actually, Jamie, why don't you and Ben come downstairs." *How does he know our names?*

27

He used them so casually as if he knew who they were. As if he'd been watching them or reading about their lives in some file. Were they the subjects of someone's briefing? Did soldier boy sit around with his buddies and talk about them? About her?

Creep.

She looked at the name plaque on his uniform. "Listen up, Second Lieutenant A. King. I'm not in your army, so I'm not taking orders." Jamie knew she should keep her mouth shut, but when she got nervous, she became overly aggressive. It was kind of like the strategy she had read about to fend off a bear in the woods – make yourself as big and scary and noisy as possible. Right now, Lieutenant King was the closest thing to a bear in her life. In theory, the bear would run away. The young lieutenant stood his ground.

"Why make this any more difficult than it needs to be?" the soldier said. "You and I both know you're going downstairs. My orders are to bring you downstairs, and I got a VIP down there waiting for us. You think I'm going to leave him waiting? No. So, either I throw you over my shoulder and carry you down, or you can walk. Your choice."

Everything in Jamie wanted to call his bluff, but she wasn't sure he was bluffing, and there was no way she was letting this New World thug put his hands on her. She pushed past him into the doorway. "Ben, let's go," she called.

Ben, who had been watching the confrontation from the hallway, followed her to the living room.

Downstairs, her father was wearing an *everything will be okay* expression. She doubted that was true, considering who the VIP was standing in her living room.

"Governor Ashwill," Jamie stammered, "W-what…"

"Ah, Miss Corson, Ben, so good to see you again. It's been too long."

The last time Jamie had seen Creighton Ashwill was at her mom's funeral three years earlier, and even then, the relationship between the Corson family and Ashwill had been strained. Before they had a falling out, Ashwill had helped her dad win his first campaign for the U.S. House and then later for the Senate. They had become friends, but Jamie didn't know him in any personal way.

Her dad didn't bring Creighton around his family the way he did with some of his other political allies. Maybe it was because he sensed the governor's true nature, even back then. More likely, it was her mom who told Jamie's dad that Ashwill wasn't welcome in their home. If either one of them had sensed that Ashwill couldn't be trusted, they were right. As it turned out, his political expertise and connections came with a price tag. Jamie didn't know all the details, but snippets gathered from conversations over the years told her that Creighton had asked her father to do something unethical, and he refused. Nate's refusal had angered Ashwill and ended their friendship, as well as their political alliance. And now he was the man with all the power. Not good.

"Weren't you just giving a speech?" Ben asked.

"Yes," Ashwill responded with a broad smile. "How'd I do?"

"You weren't wearing that. How'd you get here so fast?"

"It was recorded in advance. Wanted to make sure I got it just right. What'd you think?"

Ben shrugged.

Ashwill turned to Nate. "Senator," he said in a loud, confident voice, "I forgot to say congratulations on the vote. I didn't think anyone could convince the U.S. Senate to commit hari-kari, but you did it. That's impressive."

"Thank you, Creighton. But as you know, I didn't have much of a choice."

"Oh, there are always choices," Ashwill said, "But I'll agree, they're not always good ones. You choose wisely."

Jamie could see her father growing impatient the longer they talked. Or was it fear? She couldn't tell.

"To what do we owe the pleasure of your visit?" he asked. "I'm sure you're a busy man on a night like this."

"Indeed, but I thought it would be prudent to ensure that senior government officials were," he paused as if searching for the right word, "tended to during the transition."

"You're personally tending to each government leader?"

As her father spoke, Jamie's eyes shifted to Lieutenant King, standing just to her left. He was right-handed, she noticed, which meant his sidearm was within her reach. Being so close made Jamie uncomfortable. They didn't keep any guns in the house for a reason. She felt dizzy. It had been a long time since she had had a panic attack. She was doing her best not to have one now.

"Were you planning to leave the city?" Ashwill asked.

"Yes," Nate said tentatively, "that's the plan. My family and I are heading to Lewiston, Maine. I'll be teaching there at Truett College."

So many of the colleges and universities across the nineteen states had closed after the outbreak of the Pittsburgh Virus. There were too many dead professors and administrators to continue, not to mention the dead among the student body. Scores of students in close quarters accelerated the spread of the virus on most campuses, turning them into zones of death. It took months to clear out the bodies left in the dorms and years to clean up the mess created by death and looting. Some schools never reopened. Although Truett College had fared better than most, it still took three years to start issuing degrees again, and then only a limited number were awarded. That was fifteen years ago. The academic dean was a friend of Jamie's dad, and he'd offered him the teaching position.

"Teaching has always been your first love, hasn't it?" Ashwill said.

Jamie's eyes shifted from the soldier to Victor, who had been standing silently at the entryway to the kitchen behind her father. He followed her gaze to the soldier, and now he was looking at her. He gave the slightest shake of his head.

No!

If Victor was like a favorite nephew to Nate and Ella, he was like the cool older cousin to Jamie and her brother. Endless nights of playing games at the family table had given them a certain kind of bond. After all, when you need your partner to guess the right word based on a very minimalist pencil drawing, you begin to get inside each other's heads.

She narrowed her eyes.

Why not?

Jamie suspected that Victor knew what she was thinking: *This is about to go south real fast.* If Ashwill himself showed up, something was terribly wrong. She also knew that Victor didn't trust her judgment. He thought she was impulsive and worried about how she might react to a soldier in her own house.

He widened his eyes and clenched his jaw.

Stay put!

Jamie broke eye contact with him. She hated it when he bossed her around. Since she couldn't talk to him at the moment, she couldn't make her case or explain her plan. She had thought it through, and it was the only real option. This wasn't just about getting out of the city and starting over anymore. Her dad was in real danger. She could feel the tension in the air as if gas permeated the room, and a match was about to be struck. Ashwill was toying with her father, feigning politeness, but that was all pretense. Something was about to happen, Jamie was sure of it, and somebody had to do something.

Ashwill smiled again. "I'm sure you can't wait to get back to the classroom, but there's been a change of plans. The Corson family will be staying right here, for the time being."

"But Dad," Ben said, "You said we'd leave once you took the vote."

"Hang tight, buddy," Nate said, "We're working it out."

Jamie could see the fear beginning to etch itself into her father's features. "We negotiated with you people in good faith. The Council said you'd let us go without any reprisals."

Jamie shifted her eyes to the soldier one more time. He wasn't paying any attention to her. It had been a mistake to bring just one, she thought. Her dad wasn't close enough to catch him by surprise, but she was, and hopefully, it would only take a moment of distraction for her dad to get there. He'd been on the track team in college, but that was a while ago, and tonight he had been drinking. Still, with any luck, the two of them could overpower one soldier not paying attention.

Jamie tensed and shifted her stance, ready to launch herself, but her dad dropped his gaze. It looked as if he were examining his shoes. He did that sometimes when he was working out a problem in his head. Jamie stared at the top of her dad's head, willing him to look up.

"I'm afraid you've misunderstood me," Ashwill said. "Your family is not being punished. We need you on our leadership team."

Nate shook his head slightly. He'd been approached two years earlier about joining the New World leadership, and he'd declined. "I'm afraid I can't possibly be of any use to you now."

"Not you," Ashwill said to her father. "I mean you." He was looking at Jamie.

"Me?"

"Yes, you."

"What are you talking about?" Victor said as he moved to stand next to Jamie. "She's seventeen."

"Yes, and Joan of Arc was eighteen when she led the French army to victory over the English. Cleopatra helped rule Egypt as a teenager. Queen Victoria was eighteen when she assumed the throne. By comparison, Elizabeth was an old lady at twenty-five when she became the queen of a country that had been ravaged by war. And

32

how old was Pocahontas when she saved John Smith? Senator, you're a historian, you should know these things. People love young, female leaders."

"What does any of that have to do with Jamie?" Nate asked.

"The New World needs a fresh young face to lead its people. It's one thing for an old man like me to govern a province, but if we're going to build something lasting here, we need a vision for a new kind of future. We need a queen."

"So I've heard," Nate said. "If you asked me, I would have told you that you've lost your mind!"

"Open your eyes, Senator. America's been a monarchy for some time now, but without any of the benefits of a true monarchy."

"That's absurd."

"Really?" Ashwill shot back. "Supreme Court Justice Antonin Scalia said that our presidents were, and I quote, 'more George III than George Washington.'"

Nate knew the quote well. "That was a criticism, not a recommendation," he said.

Ashwill pressed on. "Jefferson said our constitution 'wears a mixed aspect of monarchy and republicanism.' Patrick Henry said it 'squints toward monarchy,' and John Adams called it a 'limited monarchy.' But here's the problem, Senator. Because our American kings and queens are chosen in a contest that pits one side against the other, they cannot provide the stable center we need. They can only divide us. Scalia's criticism was right; our presidents are more like George III, but not enough like him. They are elected, and that is their weakness. We need a head of state who represents all the people. Ashwill slowed himself down, emphasizing his words. "The Pittsburgh Virus didn't divide us, Nate. It just revealed the division that had already torn us apart."

Jamie knew he was right. The virus had pushed the country over the brink, but it hadn't led them there. Since the early part of the century, long before the virus, political observers had recognized the country's growing divide, and some had even begun calling for a monarchy to unify America. "We need a king or something like one" one political analyst had written. She knew her dad would concede this point. He wouldn't revise history to support his argument.

President Ashwill continued, "Besides, nothing captures the imagination like royalty. People need someone larger than life to rally around. They won't give themselves to a bureaucracy, and they're done with politicians, but they will cherish their pretty young queen. They will be fascinated by her. She will inspire them. And they will follow her."

Nate shook his head, looking for the right words. "This city is named for a man who refused to be king. It will never work."

"Have you looked around this city named for a man who refused to be king?" Ashwill said. "Have you looked around what's left of this country? Are you okay with tent cities for the homeless? Are you okay with towns and whole regions run by local militias? Are you okay with what happened at the river? People are hurting. They're suffering. They're scared, and they need something to have hope in."

"You and your corporate buddies are doing all right," Nate said. "All this misery has been good for business."

"My 'corporate buddies' are making our New World vision a reality. They will help us create a country that is good for everyone."

"But better for some than for others."

"Yes, Nate, that's how it works," Ashwill said as if he were lecturing a grade-schooler. "You can fight it, or you can use it. I plan to use it."

"But you can't be the face of it, can you?" Jamie said, realizing for the first time why he didn't appoint himself king.

"No. Not entirely. People are sick of politicians. We need a queen. Somebody who didn't get bloodied in a nasty campaign. Somebody of beauty and strength and power who stands with them, not with a party, not with special interests."

"You call yourselves the *New World* for crying out loud," Nate said. "People came to the New World to escape the monarchies of the old world."

"Yes, well, perhaps we should have called ourselves the New, New World." Ashwill waved a dismissive hand. "At any rate, what we are building here is not a warmed-over version of the old republic. It's something new, and I'd like Jamie to be a part of it."

Jamie was stunned. Her legs no longer felt sure beneath her. The vote had seemed like a bad dream, but this, this just seemed like a bad joke. She half expected Ashwill to burst out laughing and slap his knee with a "gotcha" expression. He did not.

"Why me?" she said.

"*Ducunt volentem fata, nolentem trahunt,*" President Ashwill said in Latin. "Translate."

"The fates lead the willing, but drag the unwilling," Jamie said.

He smiled and tilted his head toward her. "It is your destiny."

"I don't believe in destiny."

"Fair enough. But the fact that you speak fluent Latin says something about why you were a candidate. That and the fact that you are well-read in the classics, you know history, you can articulate more than a few thoughts without saying 'um,' and you look like a million dollars in a dress."

Second Lieutenant A. King never took his gaze off of Nate, but Jamie could swear she saw the trace of a grin on his face.

Nate pulled himself up to his full height. "You are not taking my daughter to fulfill some royal fantasy you have." And then, as if to create a more conciliatory tone, he added, "I think Jamie's great, but she's not Joan of Arc."

"We don't need Joan of Arc," Ashwill said. "We just need someone strong enough to capture the attention of the people and bright enough to learn."

"Yeah, and there's got to be a lot of people out there like that. Why her? Of all the people you could choose . . ."

Creighton locked eyes with Nate and slowly said, "She's the one."

Jamie saw her dad's face morph into a mask of incredulity as if a deep secret had been unearthed. He turned his gaze back to the lieutenant, who stood relaxed in his stance. And then his face changed again. This time it was a look of resignation.

"If you take her, where will she go?" Nate said. "Can we see her?"

"Dad?" Ben looked confused.

Jamie couldn't believe what she was hearing. Her heart began to beat wildly in her chest. The adrenaline which had dissipated a few moments ago was back. Why would her dad give her up without a fight? He'd always protected his family, but over the last three years, she had seen her father fade like a dwindling campfire. His heart was not in his work or his family as it had been. But she never thought he would give up like this. Even if he failed, he needed to try to stop Ashwill. Couldn't he see that?

If he wouldn't try, she would. Without a plan or any warning, Jamie launched herself at the young soldier who stood like a statue to her left. The impact knocked him off his footing, but he didn't fall. She took his momentary imbalance as an opportunity to reach for his gun as she fell against him. Nate never moved.

"Scorpion," Ashwill blurted out.

The lieutenant grabbed Jamie's wrist and pulled her hand away from his gun while wrapping his arms around her flailing body. He may not have been much older than her, but he was much stronger.

Crap.

She didn't know exactly how she expected this would go, but this wasn't it. She could feel the panic rise as Lieutenant King held her in a tight grip, the heat from his chest radiating against her back.

Three seconds later, security forces flooded the house from the front and the back doors, guns drawn. "I told you she'd try something," Creighton said to the soldier as he released Jamie. "That's the kind of fire we need in our queen."

"I'm not your queen," Jamie protested.

"*Dulce et decorum est pro patria mori*," Ashwill said. He put a hand on Ben's head.

Jamie's face went pale. She squeezed her eyes shut, breathing heavily now, trying to block out the echo of gunfire sounding in her head. A memory she worked hard to keep buried. *Bang! Bang! Bang!*

"What does that mean?" Victor asked.

"It's sweet and fitting to die for your country," Nate said through a clenched jaw.

"You son of a –"

"I'm afraid it's time to go," Ashwill said, cutting Victor off. He motioned for the lieutenant to escort her out.

"Wait, no!" Ben screamed.

"It's okay," Jamie told her brother, as she cried and pulled against the soldier who guided her out the door. "I'll be back for you."

Ben tried to follow, but another soldier blocked his path.

"At least let us say goodbye to her," Nate barked. "You of all people should –" he faltered, unable to finish his sentence.

Ashwill nodded to the soldier. Nate and Ben ran to her and embraced her, both of them crying. As her dad hugged her, he whispered in her ear, "We'll come for you. Stay strong. We'll come."

Jamie could smell the whiskey on his breath and wondered if he really would. She knew he meant it, but he wasn't the man he'd once been, and it would take every bit of that man to keep his promise.

"Time to go," Council President Ashwill said.

The New World

Jamie worried that she would never see her family again. As the soldiers pushed her out the door, she craned her head to see them one more time. "I love you," she mouthed silently.

Chapter Four

Well that isn't what I expected.

Of course, Jamie wasn't sure what to expect. She hadn't had much time to consider what being queen would be like, but she had thought there would be more pomp. Was there precedent for a queen who started her reign as the victim of a kidnapping?

As it was, there were no red carpets and no press conferences, no trumpeters. Instead, Jamie founder herself in a very nice suite somewhere, not royalty nice, but nice. It didn't look like a prison – most prisons didn't have a jacuzzi, a spacious living area with fancy sofas and tables, and a huge bedroom with incredibly soft sheets – but the guard outside the door was quick to remind her that she was not free to go. Also, unlike most prisoners, Jamie was given an attendant who offered to get her anything she needed or wanted.

"How about a disguise?" Jamie asked. The attendant, Allegra or Laura or something, just smiled.

Most of the week Jamie spent there had been like one long, extensive job interview. But not for a normal job. More like applying to be an astronaut. Or a queen. And it wasn't an interview. Jamie did answer some questions, personality, and psychological profile-type questions, but it was more as if they were making sure she wasn't defective. They drew blood and ran tests. Two floors down, one of the rooms had been converted into a medical testing suite with scanners and other equipment. They would take her down there and lay her on the narrow platform, run her through a machine, and bring her back. All the while saying please and thank you and calling her ma'am. Some of the folks calling her ma'am were old enough to be her parents. *Kinda weird.*

"Ma'am, your lunch has arrived," what's her name, the attendant, said. "Would you like me to bring it in for you?"

Somewhere nearby someone was cooking all of Jamie's meals, and they were good, really good. Toward the end of the week, she figured out why they didn't prepare them in her suite. Her kitchen had very few utensils, no knives or forks, nothing that could she could use as a weapon.

"Sure. Thanks," she said to the lunch offer.

Jamie smiled. Her attendant smiled. The guard at the door, letting the guy with the food in, smiled. Everybody smiled. Jamie figured they were smiling because they were told to be as polite and professional and helpful as possible. She was smiling because she wanted to put them at ease. If she were tense, they would be tense. If she chilled, she hoped they would chill, and if they chilled, maybe she'd have a shot at getting out of here. *Maybe.*

That was a lot of ifs, but one thing she knew for sure, letting her anger dictate her behavior was a losing strategy. She learned that the first night.

They had brought her directly to the suite that night, but thanks to her emotional outburst, she had no idea where they were. If she'd paid attention on the way, she might have had a clue. Fat chance of that, though, once Lieutenant King got into the transport vehicle with her. Having his smug face staring back at her was all the invitation she needed to unload on him with a full verbal assault, which she did. That was a mistake. She hurled her anger all over the lieutenant who, by the way, seemed to be completely unaffected by it. Meanwhile, she lost any sense of which direction they were heading or, for that matter, how long they had been heading that way.

Stupid. Stupid. Stupid.

Jamie was smart enough to know that any little bit of information might make the difference, and now, that was a bit of information she didn't have. Since then, she had become determined to keep her mouth shut, and her eyes and ears open.

Then there was Ashwill's threat. *Dulce et decorum est pro patria mori.* She had to consider that. Did she believe he would hurt her or her family? She had never thought of Ashwill as a dangerous man. Arrogant perhaps. Misguided certainly. Vengeful for sure. But dangerous? A killer? She didn't know. Anyway, who recruits someone to their cause by kidnapping and threatening them? If she had had any thought of supporting the New World, and she had not, but if she had, she wouldn't anymore. Ashwill was smart enough to know that. So why do it? Jamie could only think of two reasons. He needed her, and he needed her now. But why?

"She's the one." That's what Ashwill said to her father. But the one what? Jamie didn't have a clue, but her dad seemed to know. Maybe. It was hard to tell, but when Ashwill said it, her father acted as if they shared a secret.

By the sixth day in her luxury prison suite, Jamie had cycled through several emotional responses. Anger gave way to vigilance, which had been no match for the boredom that soon set in. Hard to be vigilant when you're stuck in a suite with nothing to do and no one to do it with. She had not heard from her family or her best friend, Raven since she arrived, and there was no way for her to contact them. The only connection to the outside world was the news feed. It felt like being dropped into a hole. From boredom, it was a small step to loneliness and then from loneliness to fear. Too much time to herself meant too much time to think. For a few days, she convinced herself that this was all some sort of cruel joke or a mistake, or at the very least, a bad decision which would soon be rectified when the powers-that-be came to their senses. Or maybe she'd be rescued. She fantasized about her father breaking down the door with a group of commandos and whisking her away. But, like most fantasies, this one had no relationship to reality, and for the first time, Jamie considered that maybe this was her new reality, whatever *this* was. That scared her.

Three short knocks on the door to her suite, and then the guard opened it and announced a visitor. She liked this guard. He was tall with dark skin and dark hair and, unlike the others, he seemed genuine. The other guards smiled at her as everyone did, but his smile wasn't fake; it was warm and friendly. Why couldn't he be stationed on her side of the door? Maybe then she would have someone interesting to talk to. He looked interesting and not unattractive. Something else to fantasize about. His name badge identified him as E. Jackson.

I wonder what the E stands for. If only he weren't in uniform.

"Ma'am, there's someone here to see you," Lieutenant Jackson said.

Jamie stood and faced the door, wide-eyed. Her mouth hung open in anticipation. But then her mouth closed and her eyes relaxed as a woman entered whom she had never seen before. The young lady who had been attending Jamie followed the other woman into the room.

The woman was all business in heels and a stylish suit, carrying a leather attaché case. She walked briskly across the floor, long dark hair flowing behind her, hand outstretched. "Good morning. You must be Jamie. I'm Nikole Saizarbitoria, Special Assistant to Council President Ashwill. It's so good to meet you. Of course, you know Alora," she said, shaking Jamie's hand while simultaneously motioning to Jamie's attendant.

Alora, that's it.

"May we sit?"

"Sure," Jamie said. "Your game, your rules."

"Great," Nikole said, either unaware of Jamie's terse attitude or unwilling to acknowledge it. "I'm guessing this hasn't been the best week of your life, but I'm here to talk about your future in the New World. It's my job to see to it that you have a bright future with us."

"As queen." The word felt strange coming out of Jamie's mouth.

"As queen," Nikole confirmed.

"Look, I'm sure you've thought through this and everything, but what if I don't want to be queen? I didn't exactly apply for the job, and I'm not a big fan of the New World."

"Of course," Nikole said with a look of genuine empathy. She set her attaché case aside and met Jamie's gaze. "When my grandmother married my grandfather, she didn't love him. They met at the university in Spain, and since they were both Basque, it was a good match, so she agreed to the courtship. It was expected of her. They were married for seventy-one years, and she often told me that it was after they got married that she fell in love with my grandfather."

"I'm guessing he didn't kidnap her and drag her off to a wedding chapel," Jamie said.

Nikole laughed as if they were two friends catching up over tea. "Point well taken. It's not exactly the same, is it? But you understand what I'm saying. Sometimes duty comes before desire, but that doesn't rule out desire altogether. You might actually like being queen."

"But what if I don't? Then what?"

"Then it's just about duty," Nikole said pleasantly. "Did you know that every young person in the New World, age eighteen to twenty-five, will soon be required to serve a year of active duty in the military, and then five years in the reserve army? And each year to follow, every able-bodied citizen turning eighteen will attend Basic Combat Training and give a year of active duty to our armed forces. Drafting citizens into military service is a practice employed around the world and has been for centuries." Nikole paused, and Jamie finished the thought for her.

"And I've been drafted into service."

"Yes. I think that's a good way to look at it. Don't you, Alora?"

Alora smiled but said nothing.

"Just like a soldier, you've been drafted to serve your country."

"But my tour of duty never ends," Jamie said.

"No," Nikole agreed. "Now let's talk about how this will all work itself out."

"But I haven't agreed to anything."

"That's the nature of being drafted, dear. You don't really get a choice."

"I understand, but that seems like a strange way to pick a monarch. Aren't there a lot of well-qualified people who would *want* to be king or queen?"

"Council President Ashwill has made his choice. It is my job to make it a reality."

Jamie couldn't bring herself to return Nikole's smile.

What about my family? Who's gonna take care of my family?

For the last three years, Jamie had been the one holding them together. Late nights helping Ben work through his homework or work through his feelings, whichever was the most pressing at the time. Early mornings getting her dad up, reminding him of a meeting or an appointment he couldn't afford to miss.

"You're the fishbowl," Raven told her. Jamie had no idea what she was talking about. "You know, the fishbowl? It's what keeps all the water in place so the fishies can swim around. No fishbowl and they just flop around on the ground."

Yeah. I'm the fishbowl. And now Ashwill wants me to be the fishbowl for the whole country.

Nikole pressed on. "I understand what you're feeling..."

I don't think so.

"...but think of this as an opportunity to make a difference. You are a bright, gifted young lady, and you have a lot to offer. The New World needs someone to look to, someone to follow, someone to rally around. You can be that person."

"A figurehead," Jamie said.

"Yes, maybe at first. But you will grow and learn and become a queen who leads her people."

"I want something," Jamie said, cutting Nikole's sales pitch short. She was bright enough to see that for the moment she had no way out of this. So why not trade her cooperation for a favor? "I want to see my dad and my brother."

"Easy enough, but it will have to be soon. You start Basic Combat Training in two days."

Chapter Five

Nate Corson held Jamie's hand as the two walked home from school. Her eight-year-old legs worked hard to keep up with Nate's longer stride. The route they took was their usual, past the abandoned grocery store and then an entire housing development that had been cordoned off with a chain-link fence. At first, Nate tried to find a less depressing route, but this was the shortest, and the others were not all that much better. Eight years after the virus and parts of the New World Province still looked like a war zone, albeit an overgrown war zone. This neighborhood in Charlotte was one of those parts.

Life had returned to normal in the sense that they'd started doing some of the routine things they used to do before the virus, such as going to work and going to school. But it was like the kind of normal you celebrate when a patient comes out of a coma and starts to take a few tentative steps. Everybody is elated because yesterday he couldn't even do that. But after a few days you realize that he's not who he was, the sickness has changed him, and you worry that if he tries to do too many normal things, it might set him back. That's how Nate felt every day. They were doing normal things, things they did before the virus, but the routines felt fragile as if one small tragedy would cause everything to come crashing down again. New York City was an example of just how bad it could get; a whole city rendered uninhabitable.

Nate hoped no such tragedy would revisit the New World. The Corson family had, at last, started on their road back to normal. His wife, Ella, was working part-time for New World Renewal, the relief agency formed out of a partnership among the states of the New World Province. NWR had kept his family afloat in the early days of the epidemic, and Ella wanted to be a part of helping other families survive. It didn't pay much, but it gave her a sense of purpose, and every little bit helped.

Nate was in his third-year teaching history at UNC Charlotte. The university had reopened only three years earlier on a limited basis, but thankfully, they needed a history professor. The pay wasn't great, and he wore several hats including Dean of Judicial Affairs and Housing, as well as Assistant Registrar, but he was doing what he loved, teaching history to college students. Maybe someday soon, he'd be doing what he dreamed of, writing about history — one step at a time.

Even Ben was enjoying life as a normal three-year-old in daycare.

Once they got past the boarded-up grocery store and the abandoned housing development, the street began to show some signs of life. New construction punched holes in the tapestry of devastation like rays of sunlight through storm clouds. Some cities and towns of the New World states had fared better than others during the crisis. In too many places, panicked citizens had overwhelmed local governments which were barely keeping up with the rising death toll. Once the police and emergency services collapsed under the tsunami of desperate residents, the baser side of human nature fed on the chaos, and life became hell on earth. Nate hadn't lived in Charlotte during the virus, and no one who had lived there talked about those days. He was fine with that. He'd seen enough on his own to last the rest of his life.

Nate and Jamie turned the corner at the end of the block heading toward their apartment. Nate felt no apprehension walking with his eight-year-old daughter along the streets. These days, the city knew nothing of the chaos and depravity it had during the darkest hours of the crisis. The physical damage remained in many places, but peace and order had been restored here, as it had throughout the region. Restoring order had been the first step to ending the epidemic. New World security forces and local law enforcement took positions at every major intersection of the city so that everybody knew chaos was no longer an option.

The New World security forces were under the jurisdiction of the New World Province which was collectively overseen by the governors of the nineteen states. The New World province was, in theory, under the authority of the federal government. *In theory*, because the federal government had lost credibility in this part of the country.

They should never have abandoned us during the crisis, even for a while. To Texas of all places, Nate thought.

Most people Nate knew trusted the New World leadership more than the American government. With momentum on their side, the New World Council began assuming more authority as the federal government grew weaker and increasingly distracted by other issues. In a daring move, the New World began funding the collective National Guard troops of the nineteen states. They assumed full control of the troops after Washington had slashed their budgets. The federal government was too weak to stop them and too poor to challenge them. And just like that, the New World had its very own army.

Nate and Jamie were nearing a newly opened market when Jamie said, "I got an A on my math quiz from yesterday."

"Did you now?" Nate said. "That's very good." He knew exactly what Jamie was angling for, but he was going to make her say it.

"It was a hard quiz too. The teacher didn't even tell us we were going to have one."

"Well, I'm very proud of you," Nate said with a smile.

Jamie began to slow her pace as they passed in front of the market, forcing her father to slow down.

"Don't you think it's a good idea to celebrate victories?"

Nate could hardly contain himself. What eight-year-old talks like that? She needed to read more books written for kids her age.

"I think that's an excellent idea," he said. "When we get home, mommy and I will sing you a victory song."

"Dad!" Jamie had stopped and put her hands on her hips. "You don't celebrate with a song; you celebrate with ice cream."

"Oh, right. If only we knew where to get some."

Jamie added a *really?* expression to her hands-on-hips pose.

"Okay, we can get some ice cream," Nate said, ending the little charade. And why not? Jamie didn't just get an A on this quiz; she got an A on everything. A little ice cream was in order.

Inside the market, shoppers scurried up and down the aisles gathering the ingredients for the evening meal.

Coffee beans!

Nate saw them almost immediately as if his eyes contained a set of coffee bean radar detectors. Coffee was something of a luxury these days, and so he bought it any time he could find it.

"Why don't you go get the ice cream, *one pint only this time,* and I'll go grab some coffee. Meet you back here in two minutes."

Jamie headed toward the ice cream like a guided missile. Nate walked across the front of the store to the coffee display where beans waited to be bagged, taken home, ground, brewed, and enjoyed by a desperate coffee addict. And Nate was a desperate coffee addict. It had been too long since he had had a decent cup.

A strange bang, bang, bang noise slowed his stride as he looked around trying to place it. Other shoppers also stopped, looking at each other with the same curious expression. His mind had almost processed the sound when a woman's scream jolted him, followed by two more bangs. Gunfire.

Jamie!

By now most everybody had deciphered the sounds and were heading toward the exit in a hurry, making it almost impossible to get to the ice cream aisle. He wove his way through streams of shoppers, some still pushing their carts, as he made his way across the front of the store. He didn't bother yelling Jamie's name. She'd never hear him in the commotion. He only needed to get his eyes on her and get her out.

New World soldiers stationed outside fought their way in, against the tide of frightened market-goers. Nate watched as four of them moved toward an aisle that fleeing shoppers pointed out to them. Not the ice cream aisle, Nate noticed with cautious relief. It had been years since he'd prayed, but he couldn't help himself. *Oh, dear God, please. Not my little girl.*

The soldiers disappeared down the aisle, raising their guns as Nate lost sight of them. He came to the freezer section where Jamie would have gotten her ice cream, which was two aisles short of where the soldiers had disappeared. Jamie was nowhere in sight. Nate backed up, looking down each aisle that he had run past. Still no sign of her.

Where are you?

"Sir, put your gun down and let the girl go," a voice boomed.

Was that one of the soldiers? Nate ran toward the voice two aisles over, a sick feeling brewing in his gut. Rounding the corner, he saw that it wasn't an aisle at all, but an open area filled with produce on display. Backed against a cooler filled with lettuce and carrots was a man with a gun. And Jamie. He was holding her tight against his chest as a shield, waving the gun around. In one hand she held a pint of ice cream and in the other an apple. The four soldiers were fanned out in front of the man, guns trained on him. Jamie looked terrified. On the floor was a store employee lying in a pool of blood.

Nate's sudden appearance caused one soldier to swing his weapon away from the man and point it at Nate.

"Sir, stop right there," he yelled.

Nate brought himself up short holding both hands out in a conciliatory gesture. "That's my daughter."

"Daddy," Jamie cried.

"Sir, I need you to leave now."

Nate hesitated, looking at the man holding his daughter. He looked strung out. His breathing was irregular, and his eyes were red and watery. His expression was that of a wounded animal getting ready to claw his way out.

Nate looked past the soldier and spoke to the man. "Sir, please. She's eight. She's just a little girl."

"I need you to leave now," the soldier said again, this time louder.

The man with the gun began breathing heavier, his face contorting as if he was in pain. He moved the gun from Jamie's temple to his own and then back as if he couldn't decide who to shoot, himself or Nate's daughter. As he raised the gun from her head once again, Nate heard someone call out, "Viper," and immediately a shot rang out. The man and Jamie both dropped to the floor, blood spraying the glass case behind where they had stood. The soldiers sprang from their positions, converging on the two, guns still trained on their target.

Nate was frozen. It had happened so fast, and now time stood still. The image of a soldier firing at his daughter burned into Nate's brain, rendering him paralyzed. He wanted to run. He wanted to be sick. He wanted to call out to her. But he couldn't do anything. Frozen time gripped him in an eternal second. Why had they fired at an eight-year-old girl?

Time began moving again with a rush of sound as Nate realized he could hear voices shouting and sirens growing closer. "Get her out. Get her out," someone said.

He ran to the place where his daughter had fallen in time to see them pulling Jamie from beneath the man and helping her to her feet. Blood and ice cream mixed on her dress, but she was unharmed. The blood was not hers. In her left hand, she still held the apple.

"Jamie," Nate said kneeling and pulling her tight against his chest. He held her for a long time and then pulled her away from the hug to look at her. She wasn't crying. Instead of tears, he saw fear in her eyes. "It's okay, Peanut. It's over."

He could see that it wasn't over. Not for her. "Is she in shock?" he asked one of the soldiers nearby.

As the man approached, gun still in hand, Jamie recoiled and pressed herself into Nate's side.

"Hey, sweetheart, it's okay," Nate said, stroking her hair, "this man is here to help us. He's a good guy."

Jamie relaxed a bit but kept a wary eye on the soldier in the blue and red uniform.

"I think it would be good for her to get checked out at the hospital," said the soldier.

He was right. Jamie slept well that night at the hospital with the help of sedatives. The next night, at home, she woke Nate and Ella, screaming. It was the first of many nights they would have to calm her down after a nightmare about the soldiers with guns.

Chapter Six

Ten Years Later – Present Day

Jamie had never been in the Pentagon before. She knew it had housed the Defense Department for the United States for many years, but that was before her birth. Before the virus. It hadn't been nearly that important for a long time. For a while, it sat abandoned until the U.S. government sold it to the New World.

Twenty years earlier when the Pittsburgh Virus began to spread, and people started freaking out, most of the federal government had temporarily moved to Dallas, including the Defense Department. Jamie's dad had always chalked it up to incredibly good luck that Congress was in recess when the outbreak began so that most of the senators and members of Congress were in their home states, safe from the epidemic. The same was true of many cabinet secretaries. They were gone, doing the business of the government. Lucky them.

As fear spread, states untouched by the virus began closing their borders, effectively creating a quarantine of all the unlucky ones. Federal officials safe on the outside decided that a provisional government needed to be established to ensure stability in the nation. Having been medically cleared, the president evacuated Washington and went to Dallas, which happened to be in his home state. Once the epidemic was under control and order had been restored, the government returned to Washington, nothing ever returned to normal. The Mississippi River might as well have been the Pacific Ocean.

While in Texas, the president had stupidly suggested that Dallas become the nation's permanent capital. Several states in the South and Midwest supported the idea. Several states in the West and Northwest did not, nor did the quarantined states. The idea never went anywhere, but it did increase the amount of yelling across the river, as well as the volume. The President and Congress eventually returned to Washington, but the Defense Department never did. As if foreseeing the future, they had left the bulk of their operations in Dallas, which left the Pentagon mostly empty. The New World was all too eager to assume control of the building, turning it into a training facility for their armed forces.

"Combat training," Jamie asked Nikole, "What for? You want me to be a queen, not a soldier."

"No one expects you to lead troops into battle if that's what you're thinking," Nikole explained, "but there's something endearing about a monarch who trains with her soldiers. And if every other person your age will be doing their mandatory service, you can't exactly skip out. Besides, you'll have a new respect for them once you've experienced what they go through to become soldiers."

A new respect. That would be helpful. I'd settle for not freaking out when I'm around guys in uniform with guns.

She knew that her feelings toward New World soldiers were irrational, but they were her feelings. It had been ten years, and she could still conjure the fear of facing four soldiers pointing their guns at her as if it were yesterday. She never really saw the man who grabbed her, so it wasn't his face she pulled from the file folder of her mind. And no matter how much her head told her the soldiers were there to help, that's not what her heart told her. The yelling. The confusion. The deafening shot. The blood. The weight of the man they killed falling on her, smothering her. In her eight-year-old mind, the men in blue and red had done this.

"Six weeks of basic combat training," Nikole was saying, "and then we move onto the real work of transforming you into a queen."

And yet, I haven't agreed to a thing. What kind of queen serves with a gun to her head?

"Okay," Jamie said because she couldn't think of anything else to say. At the moment it was like being in a car heading down a hill with no brakes. Try as she might, she couldn't stop it. But cars careening down hills usually ended in a heap of twisted metal.

"Now, about your name," Nikole said.

"What about my name?"

"It's a lovely name, it really is, but we're going to have to change it."

"Why?"

"Well, you don't want anyone in combat training to know who you are, and by that, I mean whose daughter you are. The old and the new might not mix so well."

"You don't want people loyal to the New World to know that my father was a U.S. Senator?"

"Exactly."

"Because they might see me as . . . what? The enemy?"

Nikole nodded. "Maybe. Your father was a very public figure in the months leading up to the vote. At any rate, let's not take that chance. But here's the real reason. You will be queen soon, and Jamie, while a very fine name, just isn't regal enough. Queen Jamie," she said, wrinkling her nose as if to demonstrate how silly it sounded.

"You're kidding, right?"

"No, I'm afraid not."

"Okay. So who am I?"

"Raisa."

"Why, Raisa?" Jamie asked.

"A lot of thought went into this," Nikole said with a hint of pride, suggesting that she had had a part in it. "First, it is a beautiful name, very regal. Second, it is unique. Third, and this is my favorite, it has two possible meanings, *rose* and *leader*. And what's more perfect than that for a beautiful, strong, young queen?"

"Just Raisa?"

"Yes. Once you become queen, you will be known simply as Raisa, Queen of the New World. But for your full name will officially be Raisa Cordova. Cordova is a name dating back to when the Romans occupied Spain. Interestingly, it is also one of the first surnames introduced into the New World of the Americas. Mexico, not America, but still, we thought it was fitting."

"Don't you think someone might notice that I don't look like a Raisa Cordova?" Jamie asked.

"Not really. We see what we are told to see. Most people don't think about it."

The next day Nikole had arranged for Jamie to meet with her dad and brother. The visit hadn't gone as she'd expected. Jamie's hope of a joyful reunion soon gave way to a quiet conversation of despair. Nate told her that he'd exhausted the few options he had, with little to show for it. Exhausted was the right word, Jamie thought – he looked terrible. It had only been a week, but she wondered if he'd slept or eaten at all. Bloodshot eyes and three days of stubble rounded out his desperate look. Ben was uncharacteristically quiet. When he first got to her suite, he hugged Jamie tightly, for a long time, but he hadn't said much.

"We're so glad you're okay," Nate said. "We had no idea how you were. No one would tell us anything."

Jamie had never considered how worried they would be. They had no idea where she was, or that she'd been taken to a luxury suite, given a personal assistant, a professional chef, and been tended to by a team of physicians. She could tell by the look on their faces when they walked in that this wasn't what they expected.

"What do you do all day?" Ben asked as he wandered from room to room, checking it out.

"It's pretty boring. I read some when I'm not getting tested. They have a great selection of books."

58

"Tested?" Nate asked.

"Yeah. They draw blood, take scans, do exams, that kind of thing."

"They tell you why?"

"No."

"They find anything?" Nate said.

"No. I don't know – no one tells me. Like what?"

"Doesn't matter."

Jamie eyed her father. "I figured they just wanted to make sure I wasn't diseased or had some genetic problem before they spent too much time or money on me."

"That's probably it."

The two of them sat silently for a moment while Ben continued to inspect the suite.

Nate broke the silence between them. "I knew Ashwill had more soldiers outside. I knew he wasn't going to leave there without you one way or another. That's why I didn't try to stop him."

"How'd you know?"

"Just a hunch. The way the lieutenant with him held himself. Confident. Relaxed. Like he knew he had back-up if he needed it. I want you to know; I didn't just let them take you, Jamie. There was nothing I could do."

"I know. It was stupid to attack him."

"Yeah, pretty stupid," Nate said with a tired smile, "but I've got to tell you, I was kind of proud of you, since . . . you know, you and soldiers and all."

Nate's smile brought tears to Jamie's eyes. She longed for happier days away from this godforsaken city where her dad would have a reason to smile every day, where they could put their lives back together.

"What are we going to do, Dad?"

Nate lowered his voice even though no one else was in the room. "I've talked to Jimbo. He's going to see what he can do."

Jimbo Haynes was the former Speaker of the House who, years before, had been forced out of office and currently owned and operated a diner. He and Nate had become good friends after they moved to Washington, but Jamie didn't like the man. Maybe that's because her mom never liked him or maybe it was because Jamie had good instincts. She wasn't sure, but she knew she didn't want to put her future in the hands of Jimbo Haynes.

Nate said, "I know what you are thinking. I know you don't like Jimbo, but I'm not a senator anymore. I've got no pull, no political favors to call in, no influence to leverage. No one wants to talk to me. I'm worse than a nobody. I'm a liability. And the only person who doesn't care that I'm a liability is someone who has nothing to lose."

"Someone like Jimbo Haynes."

"Yeah. Someone like Jimbo Haynes," Nate agreed.

"Well, great," Jamie said. "I hope I look good in a tiara."

That conversation had been two days earlier, and Jamie found herself waking up, not in a luxury suite with designer sheets, a personal attendant, and a professional chef, but on a cot in a room that smelled like sweat and was filled with fifty other people roughly her age. She had arrived at the Pentagon late the night before, having been escorted there by Lieutenant Jackson and Nikole, who introduced her to Commander Linch, the man in charge of training new cadets, as Raisa Cordova, a late arrival. No more explanation was given, and none was asked for. She was told that the day began at 0500 and that she was expected to keep up even though she was starting a week late.

Great. Sauntering into Basic Training a week after everyone else ought to make me the most popular girl here.

True to the commander's word, lights came on at 5:00 a.m. and everyone came to life with groans and quiet cursing. The night before, when Jamie arrived and was assigned a cot, it had been dark.

Now, in the light, she could see that most of the people in the room were boys. In fact, of the fifty, only six were girls, including her. She watched as the guys headed to one door off the main room and the girls to another, with their clothes and various personal items in hand. At least she didn't have to change out here in the open. Looking down, she saw a container at the foot of her cot. It had everything she needed, including a change of clothes identical to the set everyone else was carrying.

As she gathered her things, Jamie felt the *who's the new girl* stares from most of the guys and all of the girls as they passed by.

Here we go. Raisa Cordova, reporting for duty.

Jamie kept saying her new name over and over in her head so that if someone asked, she'd be ready. *Rai-sah, Rai-sah.* Nothing like stumbling over your name to look conspicuous. As it turned out, none of the girls asked her as she changed and brushed her teeth. None of them even talked to her.

Jamie dressed quickly. Her only hope of being where she needed to be was following the five snobs in the girls' dressing room as they left. As Jamie emerged, one of the boys in the group was waiting for her.

"Hold up, new girl."

Jamie stopped.

"I'm Cadet Kendrick. I'm the squad leader." Cadet Kendrick was tall and broad and definitely a man, not a boy. He was probably twenty-one or twenty-two and very military. He did not extend his hand, and nothing about him suggested that this was a social contact. He just stood there waiting.

Your name. He wants your name. "Um, I'm uh, Cadet Cor- uh, Cordova."

Jamie couldn't believe she screwed it up. Of course, they would go by last names. She should have spent more time rehearsing that in her head.

"Here's the deal, Cadet Cordova, I don't know who you are or why you showed up a week late, but this squad is in second place right now, and I intend to finish in first. That means that you're going to pull your weight. Understood?"

"Understood," Jamie said, even though she had no idea what pulling her weight meant.

"That would be, 'Yes, Cadet Kendrick.'" Kendrick corrected.

"Yes, Cadet Kendrick," she said, already hating the military. Jamie liked being at the top of her class, but that was in the classroom where she knew the rules. In the world of combat and uniforms and protocol, she had no idea what counted for a passing grade. "It would be really helpful," she said, "if someone could tell me what in the world I am supposed to do."

"0500, formation, and morning PT."

"PT?"

"Physical training. Push-ups, sit-ups, running. Don't be late."

"We lose points for being late?"

"Don't be late," Kendrick repeated. "Each squad is evaluated on PT, physical combat skills, marksmanship, and team challenges. The better we perform in each of these areas, the higher our ranking. The better you perform, the better we perform. Understood?"

"Yes, Cadet Kendrick."

"The highest-ranked class is granted privileges after graduation. I intend to win." Cadet Kendrick looked at his watch. "We're due at formation. Stand behind Cadet Penly when we get out there and do exactly what she does." He pointed to one of the other five girls.

Jamie followed Cadet Kendrick and the others out of their sleeping quarters into a large hallway that intersected with another large hallway which led to a five-sided open courtyard. In the courtyard, Jamie watched four other squads gathering into formation, each wearing the distinct colors of their squad.

Why do the other squads have so many girls?

Unlike the Gamma Squad, the others were a more even mix of guys and girls. The guys still outnumbered them, but not in an eight-to-one ratio like her squad.

"Hey, new girl," Cadet Penly called. "Behind me. Now!"

Jamie's squad had organized into ten rows of five as had the other squads, one on each side of the pentagon-shaped courtyard. She quickly took her place at the back of one of the rows behind Penly, as Commander Linch stepped out of the building. Every Cadet snapped to attention. Jamie followed half-second behind the rest, but it felt like an impossibly long delay.

Two other officers joined commander Linch in the center of the five squads. She recognized one, Lieutenant King.

Great.

The Commander spoke in a loud voice. "Good morning, cadets. Are you ready to work?"

"Yes, Commander Linch," came the booming response from the two hundred, fifty cadets. Jamie flinched at the sudden explosion of voices.

"Good, because if I think you're slacking off, just a little bit, we'll ratchet it up so far you'll think you died and went to hell. Am I clear?"

"Yes, Commander Linch."

Jamie managed to get in on at least part of that one.

"As of this morning, Beta squad is leading the pack. Gamma Squad is a close second, even though they've been a man down. I can't decide if that's because Gamma's so good, or the rest of you are so sorry. Speaking of Gamma Squad, they're no longer a man down."

Don't call me out. Don't call me out.

Jamie wasn't thrilled about being in a military complex filled with soldiers, but anonymity in the crowd was helping her cope.

Linch turned toward her squad. "Cadet Cordova is a late arrival, joining the squad today. Cadet, I need you front and center."

Jamie looked left toward Kendrick for some help, but he remained frozen, at attention.

It was only a second or two, but apparently, that was a second or two too long, because Linch said, "Cadet Kendrick, can you explain to Cadet Cordova what I expect when I give an order."

"The commander expects full and immediate compliance," came the full and immediate response from Kendrick.

Put the gun down, now," Jamie heard Commander Linch's voice bark the order. She knew that's not what he said, but that's what she heard. Figuring that he had probably repeated his original command, she stepped out of formation and walked slowly to the commander. Every eye was on her, watching her, judging her, sizing her up. Would she help Gamma Squad or hurt it? Would she be tough competition or easy pickin's? Would she excel under pressure or fall apart? Would she end up crying in front of them all?

Looking down at her, the commander said, "I need you at attention, Cadet."

Jamie stiffened.

"Because you're a late arrival, you don't know this, but every one of these cadets was evaluated when they got here. Do you think it is fair that you skip the evaluation process?"

Jamie choked down the acid rising in her throat. "No, Commander Linch," she said quietly.

"I'm sorry; I didn't quite hear that," Linch said.

"No, Commander Linch," she said again with as much volume as her wobbly voice could muster.

"I agree, but we'll make it easy for you. We'll make this a one-exercise evaluation."

Did Kendrick mention squats? She couldn't remember. *Is that an option? Please pick squats. I can do squats all day.*

"Lieutenant King," the commander said, "what do you think we should ask Cadet Cordova to do for us this morning?"

Jamie held her breath. The lieutenant had experienced her upper-body strength when she attacked him at her house. He knew how weak she was. What he didn't know was that she was a runner. Her legs were strong. She wouldn't embarrass herself with her legs. She could even do a decent number of sit-ups if she had to. Just not –

"Push-ups, sir," King said. "I think she should show us how many pushups she can do in a minute."

I hate you.

"Alrighty then," the commander said. "Down you go."

Jamie had no idea how many push-ups any of the other girls could do, or how many they expected her to do, but it didn't matter because she knew she would be a miserable failure. She just didn't know by how much. Getting down on the ground, she assumed a push-up position; back straight, arms fully extended.

"Go," Linch said, looking at a device in his hand.

Down. Up.

That's one.

Down. Up.

Two.

Down. Up.

Three.

Jamie kept her pace as even as possible, trying to fill the full sixty seconds. If nothing else, she wanted to go the distance. At ten, she started to panic. Her arms started to feel shaky. She hesitated on the next one, wondering, if she went down, would she be able to push herself back up?

Down. Up.

Eleven.

How much time had passed? She couldn't stop before Linch called it. Down. Up.

Twelve.

She was pretty sure that the other cadets weren't evaluated in front of everyone like this. So this wasn't really easier, was it?

Down.

Oh, crap.

She couldn't stay down. She had to make it back up, but she didn't know if she could. Jamie pushed with everything she had in her soul. Every eye was on her, and she would show them she was not a quitter.

Push!

Halfway up, Jamie's arms gave out, and she slammed down on the concrete walkway beneath her, striking her forehead against the hard surface.

"Twelve," Linch said. "Not exactly what we're looking for in a soldier. You have some work to do. Return to your squad."

Jamie rose to her feet, thankful that at full attention, the other cadets couldn't laugh at her or make snide comments. That would come later, she was sure. She could feel a trickle of blood on her forehead, but she resisted the temptation to wipe it away.

As Jamie passed Lieutenant King, she kept her face straight ahead, but cut her eyes to him, expecting to see a smug look of satisfaction. She did not. He had a furrowed brow and a downturned mouth. It looked more like concern than anything. Maybe pity.

Once Jamie was back in the formation, Linch dismissed the squads to morning PT, which would be followed by breakfast. The nicely formed groups of cadets melted into a mishmash of people heading to the next thing.

"Jamie," a voice called out from behind her.

At first, Jamie didn't think anything of it. But before she could turn around, she realized that there, she was supposed to be Raisa Cordova.

So much for going incognito. Options?

She could keep walking and get lost in the crowd, but that wouldn't solve anything. She would have to face this person at some point. She wasn't sure how she would explain her mysterious name change, but what choice did she have?

"Jamie," the voice called out again.

What a minute, I know that voice. Jamie turned around. "Raven?"

Chapter Seven

Cadets scurried in every direction, heading to morning PT assignments. Raven and Jamie stood out like statues among the flurry of activity, drawing the attention of Commander Linch, who was watching them.

"Raven, what are you doing here?" Jamie asked. "You joined the army?"

"That's a strange question coming from you . . . Cadet Cordova." Raven shot a glance at the commander. "We don't have time to talk right now. I'll see you at breakfast."

Before Jamie could protest, Raven was gone.

"New girl," Cadet Penly called. "This isn't social hour. Get over here."

Jamie jogged toward the rest of her squad, as they entered one of the doors off of the courtyard. Inside she followed them to the third of five corridors that ran parallel to the five-sided courtyard.

"You suck at push-ups," Kendrick said, pulling his foot up behind him as he stretched his leg. "Can you run?"

"Yeah. Why?"

"Cuz morning PT is all about running," he said.

"Okay." Jamie was excited to find something she could do to earn her keep with the squad. "So what do we do?"

"We run until we puke."

"No. I mean, how does this work? Is it a race against the other squads?"

"I wish," Kendrick said.

"It's our fastest runner against every other squad's fastest runner," Penly explained. "And we've been getting our butts kicked all week long by Beta Squad."

Jamie joined the rest of the group and began stretching out her muscles. "So the fastest runner wins for the whole squad?"

"As long as the rest of the squad makes regulation time, yeah, the fastest runner wins."

"Can the rest of you make regulation time?"

"Yes. But none of us is fast enough to beat Samuels from Beta."

For the second time today, Jamie could feel everyone's eyes on her. She didn't know if they were pinning their hopes on her or just hoping she didn't blow it. After her pathetic push-up performance, she knew that she had to prove herself. She hadn't lied when she said she could run. She was built like her dad, who ran in college, and for the last three years, she had taken up running to replace ballet in her life. But she hadn't been on a good run since the morning of the vote, more than a week earlier.

Jamie looked around and noticed that Gamma Squad was the only one in the corridor. "Where's everyone else?"

"Each squad is in a different corridor," Kendrick explained. "We all run eight kilometers, so for the Epsilon Squad in the last corridor, that's about five and a half times around. For us, it's about eight-and-a-quarter times. The guys in the shortest corridor closest to the courtyard have got to make, like, fifteen rounds. They time us, and the fastest runner wins."

Eight kilometers!

Jamie could feel her hopes dim. Eight kilometers wasn't a lot to run during track season, but for someone who had not been running every day, eight kilometers would be a challenge.

A training officer showed up with a stopwatch and a datapad. "Alright, Gamma Squad; ready for a nice morning stroll?"

"Yes, Lieutenant Franks."

Everyone lined up at a spot marked in the corridor. Fifty people were a crowd, so Jamie pushed her way to the front, where Kendrick stood poised, ready to go. He looked at her.

"You can run?"

"Yeah."

Lieutenant Franks held his hand in the air and called out, "Three, two, one, go" dropping his hand on the word "go."

Jamie took off. Fast. Too fast. *Pace yourself, girl; this isn't a sprint.*

Pacing herself was hard when her competition wasn't in front of her, or behind her for that matter. She couldn't allow herself to compete against the fastest runner in Gamma Squad. That wasn't her competition. Somewhere in the building was someone faster. That was her competition. But how fast was he? Was he fast like lightning or just milliseconds ahead of everyone else? Could she be competitive or was it already over and everyone knew it but Jamie?

And what was Raven doing here?

No. Concentrate on your pace. You can think about Raven later.

Rounding the fifth corner, Jamie crossed the starting line, completing her first lap but didn't see Franks, the officer who had started them. It wasn't until she had turned two more corners that she saw him checking his watch as she passed him. He held up one finger.

Seven laps to go.

Jamie settled into the best pace she could, trying to balance pushing herself to win with surviving the run. Office doors and bay windows whizzed past as she found her stride. Somewhere around lap four or five, she felt a release. Heavy legs got lighter — burning lungs filled with life-giving air. The chore turned into a pleasure, and every worry seemed to fade into the background like blurry images of another world. Endorphins flooded her brain, prompting the memory of her mother arguing with her. It wasn't a heated argument, but a pleasant memory of Jamie and her mother sparring over some social issue. Arguing, for Jamie, was the mental version of running. It stretched her thinking and toned her mind. Jamie recalled her mother challenging her to defend her position. *"Don't be a sloppy thinker, Jay. Convince me why I should agree with you."* The memory-filled Jamie with a strange sense of hope and made her feel lighter than air. She couldn't stop herself now if she tried. And she knew she was going to win.

• • • • •

The cafeteria was alive with the tinkering of silverware on plates. Jamie stood in the doorway for a moment, getting her bearings, as other cadets pushed past her. She hated the new-kid-at-school feeling that she was having at the moment. A feeling made worse by the fact that everyone in the cafeteria knew her as the girl who'd smacked her head on the ground trying to do a push-up. But that wasn't her biggest worry. Her real concern was finding Raven before she called out her name again. Her real name. Yoohoo. Jamie, Jamie, Jamie.

I don't need to be explaining to everyone why I have two identities.

The problem was that she didn't see Raven among the couple of hundred cadets and officers in the room. Jamie decided she had two options; move forward or go back.

Stepping out of the doorway into the cafeteria, she headed toward the food line. A couple of cadets snickered at her as she passed. The goose egg on her forehead didn't help. It stood out like a billboard saying, "Remember me? I'm the girl who had a sudden and unfortunate encounter with the ground." She'd done her best to clean it up after the run, but there was no hiding it.

Halfway to the food line, Jamie heard Raven's nasally voice behind her. "Yoohoo…"

Oh, no.

"Cadet Cordova."

Jamie turned as Raven ran to her and hugged her. Raven was tall for a girl. Not freakishly tall, but taller than average. Her jet-black hair and dark eyes complemented her name.

"I don't know what's going on with your name," she said in a whisper, "or what you are doing here, but I'm glad to see you."

Raven and Jamie got their food, which looked amazingly good, and found two seats as far from anybody else as possible. It wasn't as far as she would have liked, but they did their best to talk quietly. Thankfully, the din of noise in the room helped camouflage their conversation.

"I don't know where to start," Raven said, shoving a fork full of eggs into her mouth. "Do I ask how someone afraid of soldiers and opposed to guns ends up volunteering for the army, or do I ask why your name is now R. Cordova?"

"Raisa," Jamie said. "The R stands for Raisa."

"Great. That clears it up."

Jamie looked at her friend, wondering how much to tell her. It's not that she didn't trust her, but she didn't want to complicate an already complicated situation. Plus, this could get dangerous. Ashwill had already threatened her once. Jamie didn't know how this would play out. The fewer people involved, the better. On the other hand, she had no reasonable story to tell that did not involve her explaining exactly what she was doing there.

"Why don't we start with why *you're* here?" Jamie said, buying herself some time. "You never told me you were going to join the army."

"What? Are you kidding me? That's the biggest freaking question on the table? Why *I* joined the army? Okay, let's start there. I joined the army because my dad told me to. In a couple of months, the New World will enact mandatory military service for everyone eighteen to twenty-five, and my dad said it would be in my best interest to join on my own before then. So, here I am."

Raven didn't need to say *how* it would be in her best interest. It was enough that her dad had said it. As an official in the New World government, he was in the know about most things regarding the New World. It never bothered Jamie that Raven's father was New World, and Raven didn't care that Jamie's dad was a U.S. senator. They had both come to Washington around the same time, both uprooted from their homes and sucked into the world of Washington politics, a world neither one of them wanted to be a part of. It was their shared experience, albeit from different sides of the fence that drew them together.

"Why didn't you tell me?" Jamie asked.

"I was going to, but I kept putting it off. I know how you feel about the military and the New World, and I didn't want things to get weird between us. And then, the night of the vote, you just disappeared, and your dad wouldn't tell me where you were." Raven caught Jamie's eye before adding, "Where did you go, Jamie?"

As Jamie opened her mouth to respond, a chorus of hoots and hollers arose from the crowd in the cafeteria. Jamie looked at Raven, who pointed to a digital display board on the wall in the cafeteria. The board showed the day's scores in bright yellow numbers. Jamie knew the results before she looked.

LEADER: CORDOVA – 25.5 MINUTES
SECOND: SAMUELS – 25.8 MINUTES
THIRD: NAJJAR – 26.3 MINUTES
FOURTH: QUINN – 26.9 MINUTES
FIFTH: LIU – 27.0 MINUTES

"Yeah! About freaking time," Jamie heard Kendrick yell from across the cafeteria.

The overall squad scores still showed Gamma Squad in second place, but Jamie knew that if she could keep this speed up, they would take first place eventually.

Penly walked by with her tray offering an approving smile. "Hey, new girl," she said, "do that again tomorrow, and I might stop calling you new girl."

Others offered a *way to go* and *about time*.

"Samuels is ultra-cocky, and everyone except Beta Squad is happy to see him lose at least once," Raven explained.

One cadet suggested that it was a good thing Jamie didn't fall while she was running since she might have a hard time pushing herself back up. Very funny, probably Beta Squad.

"Why does the fastest runner win for the whole squad?" Jamie asked. "That hardly seems like a team effort."

"It forces the squad leader to identify and develop someone to compete on that level. He's got to decide if he's got someone like that, or if he needs to put his efforts into preparing his team to compete in other areas." Raven quickly redirected the conversation. "But tell me now – what are you doing here, Jamie? I thought you were getting out of the city?"

Jamie hated the idea of being anything less than truthful with Raven. They shared everything. Raven was her rock. No one in the world knew Jamie as she did. Not her father. Not Ben. No one since her mom had died. But Jamie's secret was too big to put on her as if it were some adolescent fear that a guy wouldn't like her or even worries that her dad was slipping away. This wasn't that. Not even close. But what could she say that wasn't a lie?

"I was drafted."

"Drafted? That doesn't make any sense."

"It's true," Jamie said. "I didn't volunteer. The night of the vote, I was drafted."

"To be a soldier?" Raven screwed up her face. "Why you?"

Jamie shrugged. "I'm just telling you what happened."

"No offense, but you're not exactly the soldiering type." Raven laughed. "Let's face it, girl, you're more suited for a ball gown than a pair of fatigues."

Jamie held her gaze but didn't respond. She could feel her face blush as Raven swerved near the truth. Raven stared at her for a moment and then whispered, "Oh. My. Word. They chose you to be the queen."

Chapter Eight

"It makes perfect sense," Raven said, talking fast as she did when she got excited. "They want somebody young and smart they can groom, not a politician made over to look like a queen. They want someone attractive who can present herself as an assertive leader when it's time to inspire the nation for war. How am I doing so far?"

"Raven, you can't say anything to anyone! This isn't a game. And how could you possibly guess all of that? And by the way, what war are you talking about?"

"It was an educated guess. Don't forget who my father works for. He's been almost giddy the last few weeks about the new queen, dropping little hints that didn't make any sense until now. He told my mom that Ashwill has been quietly vetting prospects for months and had come down to six finalists, but he was leaning toward a girl here in D.C."

Ashwill was considering other girls? Why didn't this give Jamie a sense of relief? Wasn't that just what she'd hoped for, a way out? Was Nikole working with the other girls, telling them what she had told Jamie? Or did they each get their own Nikole?

"What war?" Jamie asked again.

"My dad thinks the CRA is going to attack, try to destroy the New World before it gets on its feet. That's probably why you're here. They want you to identify with the soldiers, and they want the soldiers to respect you."

"Wow, if they were looking for someone smart, they should have considered you."

"Nah," Raven said, "I look terrible in a tiara."

The rest of the day passed in a hectic blur. Jamie did her best to keep up with her squad. As it turned out, she was a miserable failure in hand-to-hand combat. One of the girls in her squad, Cadet Elliot, put Jamie on the mat more than once. Or twice. Or three times.

Every time she went down, Penly coached her on what she did wrong and how to fix it. "New Girl, don't attack in straight lines. She's right-handed – move counterclockwise in a circle. Move away from her strong hand." Jamie did everything she said. The problem was that when she fixed one thing, Elliot changed her approach, and down she'd go. It wouldn't have been so bad except that every time she found herself on her back looking up, Lieutenant King was looking at her. The few times she got a good shot in, he seemed to be otherwise occupied. Who cared? It didn't matter what he thought.

Weapons training followed personal combat — weapons, as in guns. Jamie had been putting up with the sight of soldiers everywhere, mostly because they were unarmed in the building. But weapons, that was a different story.

"Is there a problem, cadet?" Kendrick asked as he passed Jamie standing outside the weapons training room looking in. It was a large room, maybe forty thousand square feet, equipped with various training centers for different kinds of weapons.

Jamie shrugged. "I'm not a big fan of guns." Acid tore at her stomach and worked its way into her chest.

"You joined the army, but you don't like guns?"

Stupid. Think before you speak. "Yeah. Kinda weird, right?"

"Kinda. But honestly, I don't care if you have a hang-up about guns as long as you get in there and shoot some. And it'd be nice if you hit the target."

"This wouldn't happen to be the best shooter wins for the whole squad kind of competition, would it?" Jamie asked.

"Negative."

Figures.

Entering the room, Jamie got a pair of ear guards that filtered out the high decibel sound of the gunfire while allowing her to hear conversations. Unfortunately, she could still hear the guns, albeit not as loud. Her squad split into four groups, one for each kind of weapon– pistols, rifles, shoulder-mounted weapons, and grenades.

Jamie followed her group to the pistol range where Lieutenant King was instructing. He seemed to be migrating with her squad from one training session to another.

After extensive instructions on how to efficiently use the weapon, the cadets took up positions in front of their targets, and each received a pistol. The guns were loaded with training ammo that allowed the cadet to feel the recoil of the gun and allowed the target to register a hit, all without any actual projectile. That didn't stop Lieutenant King from going over every safety feather in detail. "They won't always have target ammo," he said.

Jamie left her gun on the counter in front of her, looking at it. The other cadets had picked theirs up and were firing. Each bang caused her to flinch, tears welling up in her eyes.

I can do this. It's been ten years already. Get ahold of yourself and pick up the gun.

She did. It was heavier than she expected, more substantial. Holding it in her right hand, she followed the training, using her left hand to cup it. Extending her arms, Jamie squeezed the trigger, and the gun lurched upward. The target didn't register a hit. Images of soldiers pointing their guns at her danced in front of her eyes. She blinked hard and forced herself to point the gun downrange. Another explosion in her hand pushed the gun back hard against her palm. This time the target registered a hit in the lower-left corner. Another shot gave the same results.

"If you use the pad of your finger on the trigger instead of your knuckle, it will help you not to pull down when you fire."

Jamie turned around to see Lieutenant King standing behind her. "Also, you're anticipating the recoil," he said.

Jamie returned to her target without responding, but she was listening. She adjusted and pulled the trigger — better, but still lower left.

"Try to keep your elbow fully extended." The lieutenant reached around her, putting his hand under her elbow. His other hand rested on her shoulder as he adjusted her stance. Jamie could feel the warmth of his chest against her back. "Okay, watch your finger, keep your elbow straight, legs slightly apart, take a breath and let it out slowly as you squeeze the trigger."

The chant reverberated in her mind. *Finger. Elbow. Stance. Breath. Squeeze.*

Another boom and the target registered a hit a few inches to the left of the bullseye.

"There you go," King said. "Piece of cake."

Jamie looked at the gun in her hand as if it were Aladdin's lamp. *That was amazing.*

She pointed at the target again, walking through her mental steps, then squeezed off two quick rounds. The first hit the bullseye; the second just left of the big red circle. The final nine shots jumped around a bit, with four registering in the center of the target and the others nearby. Jamie tightened her grip around the gun, rubbing her thumb along the smooth metal. So much power from something so small. The power to take a life in the palm of her hand. The glowing red dots on the target told her she could hit it, but could she pull the trigger if it were for real? Jamie turned around, expecting a nod from Lieutenant King, but he had moved down the line, monitoring the other cadets.

She reloaded and delivered another fifteen rounds, walking deliberately through every step in her mind and scoring high. She reloaded the gun and again lit up the target, moving her aim from the large circle in the center to smaller ones in the four corners. As the echoes of the last shot faded, Jamie laid the gun on the counter and looked at it for a long time. She closed her eyes, allowing the image of the soldier pointing his gun at her to float to the surface of her conscious mind. But this time her reaction was different. The soldier was there, and the gun was there, but Jamie's heart wasn't racing, her palms weren't sweating. She was not a frightened eight-year-old anymore. She was a shooter, and that made a difference. She inspected the memory more carefully, without emotion, this time. The soldier's gun wasn't pointed at her at all that day in the grocery store. Why hadn't she noticed that before? It was aimed at least a foot above her head. The soldier's eyes were clear, his breathing even. He was in control. He was never a threat. Jamie opened her eyes, and the sound of guns firing down the line returned to her. Bang, bang, bang. She looked at the cadet next to her, arms stretched out, gun jerking with shot after shot, and she smiled.

"Good shooting."

• • • • •

Day one gave way to day two, which gave way to day three, and Jamie found herself settling into the circadian routine of basic combat training. If it wasn't for afternoon PT, she could even learn to enjoy most of it. But it was that ninety minutes every afternoon that took her to the edge of the cliff and threatened to throw her off. The lion's share of it was working her upper body. Not good. Her trainer, Major Burke, didn't seem to care what Jamie's limitations were, only what her potential was. As far as Jamie could tell, he was in a hurry for her to reach it. He didn't seem to care if she died in the process. Dinner followed PT every afternoon, but Jamie's arms were so wobbly at first that she could hardly get the fork to her mouth.

"You okay?" Penly asked, sitting next to her in the cafeteria.

"I don't think my arms work anymore."

"That's cool, as long as your legs still work."

Thankfully they did. Most days Jamie managed to beat Cadet Samuels in the eight-kilometer morning run, pushing Gamma Squad narrowly into the lead and raising her status considerably among the cadets. Penly stopped calling her "new girl" and instead anointed her with a new nickname, "Wings," after Hermes, the god with wings on his feet. The winning trend didn't last forever, though. Word reached the Gamma Squad that Samuels had started training more intensely for the morning runs. As a result, he started winning some of them again. This setback prompted Kendrick to cut back on Jamie's nightly chores so that she could increase her training schedule. No problem. Running beat cleaning toilets and mopping floors any day. But running with the hopes of the squad resting on her shoulders did add a bit of pressure. It was more than just pride at stake. Kendrick didn't give her the details, but the top squad had a distinct advantage once commissioned. If she were an ordinary cadet, like everyone else, Jamie's hopes would be riding on this too. But she wasn't, and they weren't.

• • • • •

The nights were the hardest. Without the rush of the day to distract her, her father and her brother inhabited her thoughts. They haunted her. Why hadn't she asked her dad how he was supporting himself and Ben when she last talked to him? His teaching job was gone. How would he survive? Would Ben go to school in the city? What kind of education would he get with a dead mother, an emotionally distant father, and an absent sister? Sure, they were in the same city, but they might as well have been a million miles away. The promise she made to take care of them might as well have been a million years ago. It was all so far out of reach. Running to them in her dreams only left her further away.

Jamie tried, but couldn't arrange a scenario in her mind that would get her back home. A thousand possibilities floated around her brain, but they all ended with the New World holding the winning cards unless Jamie played the one card she held that they couldn't take away. But that would require an act of desperation and defiance beyond anything she had ever known before.

If the time came, could I do it?

If she couldn't, her life would never be the same. Either Jamie ended her life, or she accepted one that wasn't hers at all. So the question came down to this: Would she be a real person in a coffin or a shadow in a dress?

The darkness pressed in on Jamie, suffocating her. Why was it always worse at night, as if hope only lived in the light? Surrounded by sleeping cadets, Jamie wiped the tears from her cheek.

"What's wrong, Wings?"

Apparently, not everyone was asleep. Penly pushed herself up on one elbow.

"Don't worry about it," Jamie whispered

"Hey, we're on the same team here. I got your back."

"I'm crying," Jamie said, "not fighting off commandos."

"Yeah, well, I gotta make sure you don't go flippin' out on us, lose your will to run and all that."

"Your concern is heartwarming."

"For real, what's going on? My cot has been next to yours for more than a week, and you've cried every night."

Jamie wiped her nose on the back of her hand. "I didn't choose to be here. It wasn't my choice."

"Family thing? Dad force you to come, or something like that?"

"Something like that," Jamie said. "There's just someplace else I'd rather be."

Penly didn't say anything for several minutes, long enough that Jamie thought she might have fallen asleep. Then she said, "Can I tell you something?"

"Sure."

"I joined the army to get away from my father. He beat my mother, treated her like dirt. When my brother finally stood up to him, my dad broke his arm. He was sixteen. Don't ask me why, but even then, my mom wouldn't leave my old man. She just kept making excuses. So, when the recruiter took an interest in me at school, I was willing to listen."

"Why are you telling me this?" Jamie asked.

"Because you don't want to be here, but for me, this is my family. And it's safe. I know what the rules are here. I know what to expect. If some officer is in my face yelling at me, I know it's mostly for show – he isn't going to hit me. For the first time in my life, I'm not afraid. It's a good feeling."

"What happened to your brother?"

"He ran away. My dad wouldn't take him to a doctor to fix his arm because he said it would toughen him up. So, one night, he just left. I heard from him about a month later. He wouldn't tell me where he was, but he said he was okay. So, when I say I got your back, it's because we're on the same team, Wings. I got your back, and I know you got mine. Right?"

"I got your back," Jamie said. Penly fell silent, and Jamie checked off another day of Basic Training in her mind.

Day twenty-one. Thirty-one days since she'd been taken from her home.

Chapter Nine

Jamie hadn't ventured above the first floor of the massive building that had been her home for the past three weeks. None of the cadets were granted access, since all training facilities, sleeping quarters, and the cafeteria were located on the first floor.

But the first morning of her fourth week in Basic Training was different. As Jamie followed her squad toward morning PT, Lieutenant King pulled her out of the flow and directed her down another corridor to an elevator.

The fifth floor, where they exited, was noticeably different from the first. Gone were the drab institutional features that made it feel as if it were a government building. Carpeted floors offered Jamie's feet a cushioned walk down the hall. Artwork dressed the walls with color.

"In here, ma'am," the Lieutenant said as he opened a door that was more suited to a high-end apartment than a military office complex.

Ma'am? Jamie bit back a smirk.

"I'm not Cadet Cordova anymore?"

"Not up here."

She stepped through the door into a plush residential apartment. In front of her stood Nikole, Alora, and Lieutenant Jackson. Jamie smiled. And Ashwill. Her smile faded. It had been a month since she'd last seen him, but the bitterness was fresh. Lieutenant King was standing to her left, much as he had been the last time she encountered Creighton Ashwill. But this wasn't like the last time, was it? Her body was toned. Her muscles were stronger. Her mind was clearer. If she got hold of the lieutenant's gun now, she'd know what to do with it.

"Welcome," Ashwill said, raising his cup of tea in greeting. "You haven't had breakfast." He turned and motioned toward a buffet of breakfast food. "Please."

"No, thanks. I'm good."

"Suit yourself." Ashwill took a sip of tea. "We've been watching you. You're doing very well."

Watching? That would explain the shadowy figures occasionally peering down from second-floor windows that overlooked many of the training facilities.

"That's kind of creepy," Jamie said. "I'm curious, are you watching just me or all six of your girls?" She'd finally put it together. Raven said Ashwill was considering six other girls, and there were six girls in Jamie's squad. None of the other squads had such a mismatched ratio. The girls in her squad had to be the other five under consideration to be queen. It made sense. Why hadn't she seen it before now? Did they know? If so, did they know that *she* knew?

Ashwill was not pleased. "Ah, someone's been talking. No matter, you've always been our choice. The others are contingencies."

Jamie's eyes narrowed in thought, but she kept her mouth shut. If the others were only contingencies, why did he put them in the same squad? The only reason for them being together was to observe all six at the same time, to see how they would respond differently to the same situation? So, what had happened in the last three weeks that would show them the metal of these girls? Jamie thought through the events of the previous weeks. There had been an unannounced drill in which shots were fired during morning formation three days earlier, creating a panic among the cadets. Later, they found out it was an exercise designed to evaluate their leadership reflexes in a crisis. With all six of them in the same formation, it also allowed Ashwill and his gang to compare their responses.

Had one of them demonstrated better reflexes than the others during the drill? Had one of them emerged as the dominant leader in the group over the past three weeks? Jamie's money was on Penly as the group leader. She had a strong, confident personality and consistently scored high across the board in the various training regimens. Was she also in an apartment somewhere on the fifth floor? Had Ashwill just come from talking to her?

Ashwill set his cup down and clapped his hands together. "Now, onto more pleasant things. We have something to show you. Think of it as a demonstration of our commitment to a new kind of political order. But to do that we'll need to take you on a bit of a field trip. Nikole will explain everything. I have other matters to attend to." With that, he left.

"I'm leaving the building?"

"Yes," Nikole said.

"Won't my squad miss me?"

"Not today," King interjected. "The squads are being broken up today for their initial round of officer training. They'll all assume you were with a different group. If anyone asks, say you were bored, and they'll think you were there. "

"So, I'm leaving the building," Jamie said again.

"Yes."

Alora, who had left the main living area of the apartment, returned with three dresses in hand.

"Now, since you can't go out looking like that," Nikole gave a dismissive wave to Jamie's PT gear, "we've arranged three options for you to choose from."

"Great, but can it wait? I think I'll have some breakfast after all. Then we can pick out dresses."

Jamie approached the breakfast table, keeping her back to the group and found what she was looking for, a knife. She picked up a bagel and cut it in half. When she finished, she put the bagel on a plate and slid the knife into the waistband of her running pants, pulling her shirt over the handle. She took in a deep breath to steady her nerves. Her mouth was dry and her stomach tight, but she had to eat the bagel now that she had cut it. Jamie slathered on a healthy dose of cream cheese and choked it down with a smile, using orange juice to make sure it didn't get stuck in her throat.

"Now," Nikole said when Jamie finished, "let's find a dress that works for you."

Jamie chose a simple but classic dress with straight lines and solid, bold colors. It came to just above her knees. Her mom, the senator's wife, had owned plenty of nice dresses, and, like those, the one she wore was beautifully made. She pulled her blond hair back into a ponytail. An elegant necklace, matching earrings, and a pair of low heels finished the look. Simple but elegant.

No doubt her every move would be choreographed from here on out, including her attire. At least Nikole seemed pleased by her choice. Good, let her think everything was copacetic.

Jamie looked at herself in the full-length mirror in the bedroom. She had insisted on changing by herself to keep her knife a secret. Only a month after her eighteenth birthday and the image staring back at her could pass for someone in her twenties. The clothes changed her. They weren't her style, but she had to admit, she looked great. They probably had a whole wing of the building filled with clothes just for her. Too bad she wouldn't be sticking around to try them all on.

As she stepped out of the bedroom into the living area, her entourage awaited. Lieutenant King was smiling at her. "You look nice. Ma'am."

Jamie didn't respond. Instead, she looked at Nikole. "I'm ready to go."

They traveled down an elevator to a part of the building Jamie had not seen before. A corridor led to a large room with several New World transport vehicles and large bay doors that stood open.

Lieutenant King held the door to one of the vehicles open for Jamie. She didn't acknowledge him or take the hand offered in assistance as she stepped up into the vehicle. She wasn't a cadet at the moment, and he wasn't her instructor. He was the guy who dragged her out of her house. Who cared if he thought she could shoot, or fight, or do a dozen push-ups? For all his politeness, he was

Ashwill's lackey, and that made him her enemy. He walked around the back of the black-armored transport and opened the opposite door, preparing to get in next to her.

"What are you doing?" Jamie asked.

"I'm getting in," he answered.

"I don't think so. I don't want you sitting next to me."

King looked at Nikole who was sitting in front of her, and then looked back at Jamie. "You're the boss," he said.

"Really? Then give me your gun," she shot back.

He smiled but didn't offer his gun.

"Then how about your name?" she said.

"I'm sorry?"

"You can sit next to me if you tell me your first name. You too." Jamie looked at Lieutenant Jackson. "We're not going anywhere until I get some first names."

Dial it back, girl. They want assertive, not rabid.

Nikole nodded her approval before Lieutenant King spoke. "I'm Alexander, and the handsome guy in the front seat is Eli."

"See, that wasn't so hard. We can go now."

Nikole forced a smiled. "Right. Let's go then."

The three auto-driving transport vehicles pulled out of the Pentagon grounds onto I-395 heading east.

"I'd like to go to Georgetown," Jamie said.

Nikole didn't bother looking up from her notes. "We have a tight schedule to keep."

"I want to see my house," Jamie insisted.

Nikole turned in her seat to face Jamie. "I don't think that would be a good idea. Your father and your brother don't live there anymore."

Of course, they don't. Jamie hadn't thought about it, but they probably couldn't afford to live there anymore. "Where are they?" she asked.

"I'm not at liberty to say," Nikole said flatly.

Jamie said, "If you want me to cooperate with you, you might want to cooperate with me."

"When I say, 'I am not at liberty to say,' do not confuse that with, 'we don't know where they are.'" Nikole said.

Was that a warning? Jamie eyed her handler but said nothing.

"Raisa, dear," Nikole continued, "I'm trying to help you. You have a wonderful opportunity here to be an inspiration, to make a difference, to help shape a nation. Isn't that worth the sacrifice?"

Jamie looked out the window, but Nikole kept talking. "I know this all started very badly, you being taken from your home and all. Believe me, if it were up to me, I would have done things differently. Too much testosterone involved in that decision, I'm afraid. But are you going to throw away the chance of a lifetime so you can protest the poor choices of a few?"

Jamie didn't respond, and Nikole didn't press it any further. As she looked out the window, Jamie saw a digital billboard along the street. She had seen a few others along the way but hadn't paid enough attention to read them. This one caught her eye, though. It was blue and red and had words in bold letters: **Who Will Be Queen?** Below the message was a generic silhouette of a woman wearing a tiara.

Nikole said, "People are excited about their new queen. They're depending on you."

Really? Was Jamie supposed to believe that if she didn't go through with this, she'd be letting the people of the New World down? How could anyone be so gullible as to put their faith in a person they had never met? After everything they'd witnessed over the last twenty years, they still trusted the government to save the day? Had Ashwill bought himself so much credibility, taking on the role of a hero in the crisis, that people would blindly follow him? The masses might have faith in the government's choice, but Jamie did not. Playing soldier was one thing, but being queen was something entirely different. But, she hadn't been playing soldier. She'd enjoyed her training, and she was good at it. In another life, that might be a career she'd choose for herself. But none of that mattered because her father and her brother were her life. They were her purpose. No one told her they had to be, least of all her family, but she wouldn't be content chasing any other dream if she couldn't protect them.

Jamie put her hand on her leg and felt the knife concealed in the pocket of her dress. She had cut a small hole in the bottom of the pocket so the blade would slide down against her leg and the handle would rest in the interior of the pocket. She'd taken a gamble that they would not search her as she left the Pentagon, and she'd been right.

As the motorcade turned on Maryland Avenue, their destination came into full view: The U.S. Capitol Building. The caravan proceeded around Garfield Circle onto First Street, past the Peace Monument, and onto Northwest Drive.

Suddenly, Jamie said, "Wait, can we stop?"

"We've got a schedule to keep," Nikole answered.

"Please, just for a moment. I'd like to visit the Summerhouse. Just a quick stop."

Nikole looked at her watch. "Okay," she said. "You can have fifteen minutes, but Alexander's going with you."

Alexander opened her door and extended his hand, which Jamie ignored again. He walked behind her as she made her way to the Summerhouse, a small hexagon-shaped open-air brick building set on the west front lawn of the Capitol. It had three arched doorways and three windows with benches that could accommodate about twenty. Without a roof, it was more like a walled-in courtyard than a building. It had been built in 1880 to provide travelers coming to see the Capitol with a place to rest and get water. The fountain in the middle was merely decorative now, but it was still a good spot for people to pause and rest.

When they reached the Summerhouse, Alexander stopped at the doorway, staying just outside. Jamie descended the steps and looked at the familiar surroundings, touching the walls as she walked the perimeter.

"I love this place," she said.

Alexander nodded. Jamie didn't really want to talk to him, but so many memories were welling up inside, and she was a talker, so it was him or no one.

"When my dad first became a congressman, he brought me here. I was probably ten and being here, just me and my dad; it was like our special place. Whenever I came to visit him at the Capitol, we'd sneak off to the Summerhouse. Sometimes we'd have a picnic lunch." Jamie sat down on one of the benches. Alexander seemed to realize he wasn't expected to say anything in response because he stood silently, watching her.

"He used to tell me that if I wrote down a wish and put it in the notch on the wall, it would come true." She pointed with her chin to a crevasse deep enough to hold a folded-up piece of paper. "Kind of like throwing a penny in the fountain. I never noticed that the wishes didn't come true. I believed they would someday, so I always had that hope to hold onto until I grew up."

Fairytales could be a useful delusion for kids, Jamie thought. Even if they weren't true, they cast the world in a different kind of light, a magical light, something everyone needed to survive. Secretly she hoped there was something to all those wishes she had placed in the wall. Maybe there was some force out there guiding the course of her life.

"When he wanted to tell me something really important, he'd bring me here. This is where he told me my mom lost the baby, it was after Ben, and that my grandad had cancer. This is where he told me about his resolution to dissolve the federal government. This is where we cried about my mom, more than once. Being here . . . it's like being with him."

That was more than she intended to say. Alexander watched her intently. For the second time since she'd known him, he looked sad on her behalf.

The knife pressing against her skin reminded Jamie of her goal that day. She realized that there was just one soldier with her now. Maybe this was her chance to escape. From Constitution Avenue, where the transport vehicles sat idling, the Summerhouse was barely visible through the trees. If she walked south, keeping the building between her and the vehicles, she could get several hundred feet away without being noticed by her entourage.

Several large construction and supply vehicles were parked outside the west entrance of the Senate wing. Drones were swooping in and out, delivering supplies. All the activity and equipment was, no doubt, part of the Capitol renovation project. The surroundings bustled with people coming and going. She could use the activity as cover and maybe hide in one of the transports. It was not much of a plan, but it was the only one she had.

To pull it off, Jamie would need to catch Alexander by surprise and neutralize him as she'd learned to do in personal combat training. She already knew how quick and strong he was, but this time she was armed. Maybe she could capitalize on his sympathy. Would a few tears cause him to drop his guard before . . . Before what? Before she plunged a knife into his chest? Is that what it would take? Could she do it?

If it weren't for Alexander standing in the doorway, the choice would be simple. Walk away. But it wasn't simple. He was there, and he was the one person standing between her and freedom. If Jamie had a piece of paper, she would've put her wish in the notch and wished him away. In one last effort to reconnect with the magic of her childhood, she wrote her wish on her hand as if it were an imaginary piece of paper. She was a little girl again, hoping something out there would make her wish come true.

She stood to put her imaginary paper in the notch. But as she did, she noticed a piece of paper was already there. Had someone else picked up on the tradition of the magic notch? Not likely. She looked at Alexander. He had turned partially away from her and taken a step away from the Summerhouse.

Jamie pulled the small, rolled-up piece of paper from the hole and slowly unrolled it. She tried to stifle a gasp, unsuccessfully.

It was a note to her from her father.

Chapter Ten

Alexander turned at the sound of her gasp. Jamie looked away, hoping it sounded as if she were crying.

"Are you okay?"

"Yes, I'm sorry," she said, steadying herself, "I'm ready to go now."

Alexander hesitated.

Jamie added, "I'm okay. Just a little emotional."

They walked back to the transport vehicle, Alexander sweeping his gaze back and forth. As they walked, other New World soldiers headed back from a perimeter they had set up around her location. She never knew they were there. Had she tried to run; she wouldn't have gotten far. She wondered if they had set up this perimeter to contain her or to protect her?

Back at their caravan, Alexander opened her door and once again offered her his hand. Jamie didn't look at him or acknowledge him, but she did take his hand. She wondered if he could feel her hand trembling in his.

Pulling around to the east entrance of the Capitol, the motorcade stopped at the base of the steps. Commander Song and a small delegation of soldiers awaited Jamie.

Before getting out, Nikole said, "We briefed Commander Song on your status as the presumptive monarch. The others only know that this is a VIP tour."

"Okay. But I've seen the Capitol," Jamie said.

Nikole smiled but didn't respond. Stepping out of the vehicle with Alexander's help, Jamie was greeted by Commander Song, whom she'd met on these steps a month earlier. "It's a pleasure to see you again," the commander said. "Imagine how surprised I was to hear that you would be coming for a tour today, ma'am."

Again, with the ma'am. "Surprised?" Jamie asked, watching Song's expression stiffen. If Song knew what Ashwill had been planning on the night of the vote, and had tried to warn Jamie's father, she would be guilty of treason. That little secret gave Jamie an advantage. Not wanting the moment to become awkward, she added, "To be honest, I don't know why I'm here today, but I'd love to find out. I understand you have something to show me in the Capitol building."

The group ascended the steps, entered the building, and made their way down a short entryway lined with plastic construction sheets.

"Yes," Song said, "but we no longer call it the Capitol building. We are referring to it as the Palace."

"The Palace? Why?"

They stepped into the Rotunda. The vast circular room had been stripped of its old stuffy museum feeling. The blotchy sandstone walls had given way to gleaming white paint with gold trim. New lighting hung from the perimeter of the dome, brightening the room considerably. Workers were busy removing the brownish marble flooring.

"The Palace," Song repeated. "As in a royal residence."

Fit for a queen. Of course. What is a monarchy without a palace? Turning the Capitol into a royal mansion was a bold move, but then, so was trying to establish a monarchy in what had been the United States of America. Jamie had to give it to Ashwill; he wasn't a timid leader. And maybe that was the point of all of this, taking bold steps away from what America had been.

Song called one of the soldiers over, and Jamie saw that he was carrying a metallic case. He held it open for Song, and she removed three pairs of glasses with thick frames and dark lenses, handing a pair to Jamie and Nikole and keeping one pair for herself.

"These are Augmented Reality glasses. We've programmed with the architect's design for this room. Put them on, and you'll get a vision of the future."

Jamie slid the glasses on, and before her, she saw the room in it' finished form. Most striking was a white semi-translucent marble floor with rose tinting and tiny lights embedded in it. It was brilliant.

"I've never seen anything like this. What is it?" Jamie asked, pointing to the virtual reality floor in front of her.

"They tell me it's the latest thing in Euro-Asia," Song said. "It's very expensive, but it was a gift from the Russian Czar. It will make this room look magical, like walking on stars shining through a fog."

The Commander explained that her goal was to complete the rotunda quickly. As the centerpiece, they would use it to show off the Palace while the rest of the building was being transformed. Through the glasses, Jamie could even see the elegant furniture that would encircle the perimeter, creating intimate seating areas to offset the grand expansiveness of the space. Except for the shape and size of the room, it bore no resemblance to the capitol rotunda that she had known.

Plans had been finalized for the rest of the building as well. Song told Jamie the north wing, including the old Senate chamber, would become the official residence of the royal family.

Family? There's supposed to be a royal family?

It turned out that, among her other duties, a queen was expected to produce heirs. Jamie wasn't sure she was ready to think about that. She didn't even have a boyfriend.

The east wing would be used for official state business and would include a large room for royal balls and state dinners. The Capitol Visitor's Center would become apartment-like residences for visiting dignitaries and other guests. Hallways would be widened and ceilings raised where necessary to give the whole building a regal appearance.

As Song played tour guide, Jamie looked up into the dome. *The Apotheosis of Washington* was gone. In its place was a sheet of gold foil. In fact, all the artwork had been removed.

"Where are the paintings and sculptures? You haven't destroyed them, have you?"

"No, of course not. They've all been carefully removed and stored in a safe place. You have my word; they are secure. At the appropriate time, they'll be available for display. But that may be a while."

As a student of history, Jamie couldn't bear to think of losing the artwork that told a story of its own. With her mind at ease, she allowed the beauty of the room to draw her attention once again. "This is stunning," she said.

"The next phase is the royal residence in the north wing," Song explained. "We have an army of workers on it right now, but it'll take some time. It's still in the demolition stage, but I can show it to you if you'd like."

That was a good question. Would she like to see it? The Senate chamber wasn't just a place where history played out. It was more personal than that. Jamie's father had been a part of that history, and it had cost him dearly. Did she want to go to that stately room and see it laid bare by a demolition crew?

Nikole answered for her. "She would love to see it."

Jamie would have been angry with Nikole for interjecting, except she was right. She did want to see it. Maybe it was morbid curiosity, or maybe it was a weakening of her resistance, but whatever it was, she didn't object when Commander Song led her through the north entryway.

"The royal residence will begin here," she said, "in what was the small Senate rotunda, and it will encompass the entire north wing. It's not as big as Buckingham, but it won't be cozy either."

Jamie was just about to ask how they planned to incorporate the smaller rotunda into their architectural plans when Commander

Song said, "We have something special that I'd like you to see," and continued walking to the north wing of the building.

As they approached the narrow doors to the Senate chamber, the wake of demolition could be seen lying all around – rolls of carpet that had been ripped up, pieces of wood and plaster. Jamie and the Commander walked ahead through the mess as the rest of the entourage stayed back.

"Most of this will be gutted so that we can start fresh with a new design," the Commander said. "It's a shame really; there's so much here that's really beautiful, but we can't use it." She stopped outside the chamber. "There is something we did save." She pulled a cover from a piece of furniture that had been removed from the chamber and placed in the hallway. "It was your father's Senate desk. We hope to use it in the final interior design of the residence."

Jamie stared at the desk for several moments, tears threatening to spill over her cheeks.

"We don't have to be enemies, you know," Song said. "Your father and I weren't. We were on opposite sides, and we hardly ever agreed, but I never thought of him as the enemy, and I don't think he thought of me that way either." She gestured to the desk. "This is my way of honoring him and everything he did for his country. With your permission, we'll make sure it has a place in the residence.

"I would love that," Jamie said softly, running her hand across the mahogany surface. She would make sure it was preserved forever in the Palace. Her Palace. It was her decision to make. It was the first she had made in her role as the future queen, and it was about her father's Senate desk. Jamie wasn't sure if that made her decision poignant or offensive. And, she wondered, had Ashwill set this up so that saving the desk required her to tacitly accept her role as queen? Just how manipulative was he?

The note she had found at Summerhouse now felt like a bonfire in her pocket. It was a declaration of her father's intent to rescue her. Somehow, he had discovered that she'd be at the Capitol and left a note in the one place where she might find it. He was devoting his life to getting her back, and here she was touring her next prison. But it didn't have to be a prison. Not if she embraced it as a part of her new life.

What's wrong with me?

"Demolition in the chamber is almost finished," Song said, leading Jamie through the partially open doors. Inside, the chamber was almost completely gutted. The rostrum was gone, as were the desk and chairs that had once populated it. Scaffolding reached to the ceiling two stories above as workers removed the gallery seating area that surrounded the chamber. So much history, so much tradition, and it was all gone. Could something so firmly established be so easily dismantled?

Without warning, the building shook, and the lights flickered. Everyone froze for a split second.

"What the hell?" Alexander closed the gap between himself and Jamie as a second explosion shook the building. Song immediately pressed her fingers to her ear along with the other soldiers, listening to their comms.

"There's been an attack outside. Get her to the safe room."

As Alexander grabbed Jamie's arm to lead her out, the sound of twisting metal grabbed her attention. She turned to see scaffolding as tall as the ceiling collapse, taking several workers down with it. The sound of the crash was deafening. Two of the workers lay on the floor, moaning. One of the men's legs bent at an unnatural angle. Jamie sucked in a breath at the sight and looked away. Another man was pinned under the large metal structure. He lay with his arms stretched out, his face alabaster white.

Commander Song ran to the man with the broken leg. Everyone else was momentarily stunned, but they all flew into action as soon as they regained their senses. Jamie pulled away from Alexander and ran to the man pinned under the scaffolding. He wasn't moaning like the other man, and Jamie didn't know if that was a good thing or not. His eyes were open, and he fixed his gaze on her as she knelt next to him. Foamy blood oozed out of his mouth. The man was about her dad's age, maybe a little older. Others rushed over and grabbed hold of the scaffolding.

"Hey," she said sweetly. "We got some guys working on getting you out. Stay with me, okay?"

The man didn't smile or react in any way except to look at Jamie with blinking eyes. It was as if he could hear her, but he couldn't understand what she was saying. A single tear ran down the side of his face toward his ear, and Jamie bit her lip.

Nikole and the others in her entourage had made it to the chamber now, and Alexander joined the crew trying to lift the structure off the man. She looked up at him from her crouched position with pleading eyes.

Turning back to the man, she asked, "What's your name?"

His eyes bore into her with a desperation she had never before experienced. He held her in his gaze, and his lips moved, but only a whisper came from his mouth. Jamie leaned in to try to hear what he was saying.

"What is it?" she said. "Tell me again."

He moved his lips again, but nothing came.

She grabbed his hand and squeezed it. Tears streamed down her cheeks. She could see the life fading from his face.

No, no, no.

"Listen to me," she said, "I'm not leaving you, so you can't leave me. Deal? You can't leave me here!"

Jamie's words seemed to calm the man, and he stopped trying to talk. By now, enough workers had gathered to lift the bulky structure off him. Raising it a few feet, they shifted it to the left and carefully put it on the floor. Jamie could now see the full extent of the man's injuries. She gasped, despite her best effort not to. Had the man seen her reaction? *Please, God, no.* She looked back at his eyes. They were open but vacant. He was dead.

Jaimie backed away, eyes wide in horror. The man's lifeless stare locked on her; he wouldn't let go. She forced herself to turn away. Where was Alexander? She could use the kind expression she'd seen from him in the Summerhouse. Twenty feet away, she saw him looking at her; his face gripped in panic. He was yelling something, reaching toward her.

Before he could reach her, searing pain shot through Jamie's back, knocking her to the floor, face first.

I broke my nose.

What a funny thing to think of as the weight of a scaffolding pressed her to the floor. Feet rushed over to her, then knees hit the floor, and then a face was in front of hers. Alexander. Jamie smiled, and everything went black.

Chapter Eleven

Summer 2070

Nate held Ella as she sobbed into his shoulder. Her cries came in short staccato shudders. A perimeter formed around them as people steered clear. There was not much privacy in the hospital corridor, but that was as far as they got before she broke down. They'd have to work through it right there. Working through it was all about having an emotional release. No words would do. That would come later. Crying wouldn't fix anything, but it could treat the wound with a temporary anesthetic, enough for them to get home where they could fall apart.

The day had started good, great even. What could be better than a day at the beach? For the Corson's, not much. They were born to have sand between their toes and the sun in their eyes. At five, Ben was all about building the perfect sandcastle. Ten-year-old Jamie was content spending the whole day on her boogie board, paddling out and riding the waves back in. Ella always had a good book, and Nate split his time between them; a little bit of sitting under the umbrella, a little bit of packing sand, a little bit of frolicking in the water.

Today had been like so many other beach days, perfect, until Nate couldn't see Jamie on her board anymore. He got up from his chair and started toward the water. He didn't say anything to Ella at first. No need to alarm her. Jamie was a good swimmer. She was probably all right. His eyes swept back and forth, looking for some sign that she was there. Bodies bobbed up and down in the surf, but no Jamie. Nate stood at the edge of the water, watching, waiting. *Where are you?* A beach ball flew back and forth between two half-submerged swimmers. As the ball cleared his field of vision, a hand jetted out of the water and then disappeared beneath the surface about fifty yards out.

Nate turned to Ella and yelled, "Get a lifeguard!" Then he dove into the waves. As he rose and fell with the whitecaps, Nate caught sight of Jamie's boogie board. It was tethered to her, so if he could get to it, he'd find Jamie. It took him three or four minutes to swim to the board. He grabbed it and found the strap. It was pulled taut into the water. Nate put one arm over the board and pulled up on the strap with the other. Jamie's limp body rose to the surface, and Nate hoisted her onto the board, pushing it towards the shore as he swam. Halfway back, two lifeguards met him, transferring Jamie to the back of a jet ski and rushing her back to the beach.

Exhausted, Nate used the board to get himself to shore. He staggered onto the sand, where a team of lifeguards knelt around his daughter. Ella stood next to them, hands over her mouth, terror etched into her eyes. Ben had abandoned his sandcastle and was watching without expression. He probably didn't understand what his five-year-old eyes were seeing.

"Babe, it was only a second. I only looked away for a second." Nate had his hands on his knees, trying to catch his breath. "It was only a second."

Ella didn't say anything. She stood frozen; hands affixed to her mouth.

A distant siren drew closer and stopped fifty yards away, where the pavement ended, and the beach began. The lifeguards lifted Jamie, after strapping her to a board, and ran with her to the ambulance.

"Go with her," Nate yelled to Ella. "I'll get the car and Ben, and I will meet you there."

Nate flew to Ben, grabbing him on the run as he sprinted to his car.

Outside the emergency department, he screeched to a stop. No time to look for parking. He was entering the double doors when he stopped and threw his keys to a valet who was waving at him with both hands.

"You can't leave it there."

Nate was already inside as the valet continued to yell at him about getting a ticket.

He ran to the desk. "My daughter's here. Jamie Corson. I need to find her."

The lady at the desk checked her display. "She just arrived. Go through that door, and I'll take you back."

She led them back to a room where a team was working feverishly in a crowded trauma bay. It was so quiet. How could so many people working so urgently be so quiet? Ella stood just outside, watching. She was pale. Her eyes met Nate's, and she shook her head. Nate caught a sob in his throat and denied it life. Ben shouldn't be here. He shouldn't see this. The lady from the desk was still there, looking as if she might cry, too.

"Um, can you possibly take my son somewhere else? I contacted our neighbors who are on the way, and I think it would be good for Ben to wait for them . . . somewhere else."

"I want to stay with you," Ben protested.

"Uncle Bill and Aunt Carolyn will be here soon. They'll hang out with you until we get this taken care of." Nate held out his fist for a fist bump, which was Nate and Ben's man-to-man way of agreeing on something. Ben reluctantly held out his fist.

As the desk lady led him back to the waiting room, a doctor came out of the trauma bay and approached Nate and Ella. A few of the others who had been working on Jamie left, walking somberly past them.

"Mr. and Mrs. Corson, I'm Doctor Wyatt. I'm afraid I don't have very good news. Jamie suffered severe oxygen deprivation that, I am afraid, has damaged her brain. We've done the best we can, and she is on life support right now, but I can't guarantee that she'll ever come off of it. As much as we know about the human body, the brain is still a mystery. I can't say for sure how she might respond."

"But you have a pretty good idea," Nate said.

"I do."

"We would appreciate it if you would tell us what to expect."

"I'm very sorry, but I don't think Jamie will ever recover. You're going to need to go home and talk about how long you want to keep her on life support. We have counselors who can help you make that decision and answer any questions you might have. Again, I'm very sorry."

Dr. Wyatt walked away, leaving Nate and Ella alone. In the trauma bay, everyone was gone except a couple of nurses who checked the displays and tended to Jamie. Nate could see his daughter, ghostly white, a ventilator breathing tube extending out of her mouth. It didn't look like her.

"I don't want to leave," Ella said.

"I know, but we need to go home, just for a while. We can't do anything for her here. We need to talk and get some things together before we come back."

I can't feel anything.

Nate and Ella made their way out of the trauma unit. In the corridor, Ella broke down. Nate held her as she cried.

I can't afford to feel anything. Not yet.

Bill and Carolyn had left word that they took Ben to their house. Ella exhausted her tears for the moment, and they made their way outside. The same agitated valet was there, but he had enough good sense not to say anything about Nates' hasty parking job. The car was gone, so he must have parked it for them. When he saw Nate, he got the keys and ran toward a parking garage.

How can we live without our little girl? Nate thought.

"Mr. and Mrs. Corson!" a voice behind them called. It was one of the trauma nurses.

"Yes?"

The nurse said, "We need you to come back inside."

"What's wrong. What happened?" Ella didn't look as if she could take more bad news.

"Jamie's awake."

Chapter Twelve

Eight Years Later - Present Day

A soft glow penetrated Jamie's closed eyelids. The sun was shining in from somewhere. She was lying down, but this wasn't her cot at the Pentagon. The bed hugged her in a way the cot never could, and the sheets caressed her skin.

I know these sheets. She thought back to the luxury apartment-prison she'd lived in before Basic Training.

Memories began to push their way to the surface of her mind. There was an accident. Jamie had been in an accident. No, an attack. She touched her nose. She'd been hurt. The memory of being pierced inched its way into her mind. Her hand moved down her abdomen and found the spot where a piece of scaffolding had skewered her. With her eyes still closed, Jamie took a deep breath as she touched her fingers to the wound. Why wasn't it bandaged? The skin was tender, and the muscles sore, but there was no open gash or stitches. She pressed the spot. That hurt, but not like it should. Maybe she was wrong. Maybe her injury wasn't as bad as she thought. She might have landed on something which jabbed her in the stomach when the scaffolding struck her in the back. That might account for the impression she had that she'd been run through by something.

With great effort, Jamie pried her eyes open. This wasn't the Pentagon, and it wasn't the apartment. It was an older, more elegant room. A large four-poster bed coddled her in a spacious master suite. An exquisite chandelier hung just beyond the foot of the bed. The window letting in the light was to her right. She would have lifted her head to look, but it weighed a thousand pounds. So did her arms and legs. An IV tower stood next to the bed with a line running down to her arm.

Jamie's eyes worked, but nothing else seemed to. Being paralyzed like that should have triggered runaway panic, but it didn't. Her body was doing exactly what it needed to, how she knew that she didn't know.

"Well, look who's awake," a voice came from the foot of the bed. A nurse with a kind, round face made her way into Jamie's field of vision. "How do you feel?"

"Like a transport hit me."

"I don't doubt it, but you're doing very well. Remarkably well, considering your injuries."

"What are my injuries?" Jamie asked.

"Someone will be in to talk to you soon." The nurse finished whatever it was that she was doing in a flurry of activity and left the room.

Jamie's eyelids were as heavy as the rest of her, too heavy to fight.

When she opened her eyes again, the light from the window had shifted, casting a shadow across the room. Her head, arms, and legs were no longer made of lead, but they were still too heavy to move easily. A presence stirred next to the bed. Jamie sucked in a startled breath and turned her head to see Alexander sitting in a chair, head back, sound asleep. A smile found its way to her lips. She closed her eyes, and Morpheus reclaimed her.

Later, she woke again and found the room was dark and her IV was gone. Her body was as light as a feather. She pushed herself to a sitting position, feet hanging over the side of the bed. A light showed through under the door. Voices mingled from the other side.

Jamie stood and surveyed the room in the dim light. At the far end, two chairs, a couch, and a couple of end tables fashioned a seating area in front of a fireplace. She stood and made her way around the bed to the large window that had let in the sunlight earlier. Jamie pulled open the heavy drapes and stepped back, putting her hand over her mouth. Before her, gleaming bright in the night sky, like a sword thrust into the air, was the Washington Monument. Jamie was standing in the residence of the White House.

Outside the room, Jamie found Eli talking to Alora. Based on their body language, it was a social conversation and a slightly awkward one at that. *Hmm, never would have put those two together.*

Jamie stood in the doorway of the darkened room for several seconds before either of them noticed her. When they did, they both looked at her as if she were an alien. Jamie looked down at herself. She was wearing silk pajamas, but that couldn't be why they were staring.

Alora lost the girl-meets-boy expression she'd had with Eli and assumed a professional pose. "Ma'am, it's good to see you up. Can I get you anything?"

"I'm starving. Something to eat would be great."

"Of course, I'll have Chef prepare something right away."

Alora left, and Eli smiled at her. "We thought we'd lost you. But look at you. You look great."

Lost me? "How long have I been out of it?"

"It's been a day-and-a-half."

Jamie tallied the days in her head; thirty-three days since she'd been taken from her home. "What happened?" she asked.

"I'll let someone else fill you in."

"Why does everybody keep saying that?"

A sliced chicken sandwich on pressed Panini bread with a pasta salad arrived in the main living area of the residence. Jamie finished half of the sandwich and most of the pasta salad before Creighton Ashwill arrived. His presence always filled a room. He smiled as he sat across from her in a wingback chair.

"You did a good thing yesterday."

"I watched a man die. How's that a good thing?"

"You helped a man die. That's different. I know you wish you could've saved him, but sometimes helping someone die well is just as important. The last thing he saw was your caring face. The last thing he heard was your reassuring voice. Perhaps you are too young to fully realize it, but that's worth something." He looked down at his hands for just a moment. "I was proud of you."

Proud? He delivered the words as if he had said them before. Did Creighton Ashwill have children? He'd been married, but his wife had died during the outbreak. A lot of people died.

"Do you have any children of your own?" Jamie blurted out.

"Of my own? No," he said. "I had a daughter once, but she died a long time ago."

He smiled, but sadness etched the furrow of his brow and the corners of his eyes. How sad to lose a child. But if he knew that kind of pain, how could he take her from her father?

"Can I tell you something?" he said, leaning back in the chair and unbuttoning his outer coat. "I never wanted to be the leader of a country."

"I know the feeling," Jamie said.

"I wanted to be a concert pianist. I love music."

"You play the piano?" Jamie was genuinely surprised.

"Oh, yes. And I'm very good." He looked around until he saw the baby grand piano behind him. He stood, walked to it, and sat down on the bench. After adjusting it to his liking, he put his hands on the keys and began to play. It was beautiful, played with such passion and grace.

"Chopin," Jamie said.

"You're a musician?"

"I play the clarinet, nothing like that, but I do know classical music. My mom insisted."

Ashwill sat with his hands on the bench, staring at the floor as if lost in a memory or thought. He looked as relaxed at the piano as she had ever seen him.

"So why didn't you become a concert pianist?" she asked.

"Like you, my mother was the musical force in my life. And, like you, she died when I was young. My father lacked an appreciation for the arts. He was a hard man, even when she was alive, but he was harder on me after she was gone."

Why was Creighton Ashwill baring his soul? Whatever the reason, he had opened a window, showing himself to be more complex than Jamie had realized.

"He thought life in the military would better suit me, and here I am – soldier turned politician, turned national leader."

"Your fate?" Jamie said, remembering the conversation in her kitchen.

"My duty. My father was hard on me, but he wasn't wrong. The military did suit me. I found a calling to be a part of something bigger than myself. It took me a while to appreciate it the way I appreciated music, but I came to value it even more. Jamie, leadership is a calling."

Jamie wasn't willing to go down that road yet. "What happened yesterday?" she asked.

Ashwill stood and made his way back to the chair. "There was an attack. A week ago, we lost a drone. It was hacked. They loaded it with explosives and planned to fly it into the Palace. They almost did, but one of our fighters intercepted it and shot it down. Another sixty seconds and we might not be having this conversation. As it was, several military personnel and civilians on the ground died."

"Who hacked it?"

"We think it was Return, probably working with the support of the CRA, but I haven't confirmed that, yet." He paused and leaned toward her. "Jamie, we think they knew you would be there."

That should have generated a whole new list of questions. *How would anyone know where she'd be? Why would they try to kill her?* But Jamie had a more mystifying puzzle to solve. "What happened to me? No one will tell me."

"You, my dear, were impaled by a falling scaffold."

"I feel fine, a little sore, and really tired, but not like someone who was impaled." She touched her nose. "Even my nose is better."

"Your parents never told you how you're different?" Ashwill looked genuinely surprised.

"Different?" Jamie asked. She studied Ashwill's face, but he showed no sign of deception. He was either a pathological liar, and a good one, or he knew something about her that she didn't. "How am I different?"

Council President Ashwill didn't answer at first. He seemed to be weighing his options. Then he said, "You deserve a better answer than I can give you. You need to talk to Dr. Sidney Forrester. She's a geneticist who can answer all your questions. She's very familiar with your case."

I'm a case?

Ashwill continued. "I'll have her brought here tomorrow. She'll explain your situation."

I have a situation?

He stood to leave and then turned to her. "When you hear what she has to say, you'll understand." And then, with a smile, he added, "Trust me."

The door shut behind him, leaving Jamie with yet another unanswered question. Was Creighton Ashwill a man who could be trusted?

Leaving the White House wasn't an option after the attack, but Jamie needed some fresh air. Eli, who was on duty in the central hall just outside the living area, suggested she go to the promenade on the third floor of the residence, one floor up. He escorted her up the stairs but stayed inside as she went out onto the open-air walkway that encompassed the floor. It was a warm night, but a breeze made it pleasant. Too much bed rest had made Jamie stiff. The walk loosened her muscles. Washington, D.C., spread out in front of her. Large sections of it were still dark, waiting for people and money to move back in.

"A New World credit for your thoughts."

Jamie turned to see Alexander standing behind her. "You're kidding, right? That's the best we can come up with for our new currency? New World credits?"

Alexander shrugged.

"What are you doing up here?" Jamie asked.

"Checking on you."

"Don't you have cadets to train?"

"They'll get along without me," he said.

"Guess they figured out I wasn't coming back."

"Yeah, the cat's out of the bag on that one."

"What'd you tell them?" Jamie asked.

"The truth. That you were injured while on a special assignment. Unfortunately, you won't be able to go back. There will be too many questions you can't answer."

"Something's been bothering me about my first day at Basic," Jamie said. "Why did you make me do push-ups in front of everybody? You had to know I'd fail miserably."

"Linch expected me to be hard on you. Basic is about pushing people to their limit. It's about tearing them down and building them back up. That's why in personal combat, we started you off with Cadet Elliot. We knew she'd kick your butt. It's important to get knocked down a few times."

"So, who kicked Cadet Elliot's butt?"

Alexander laughed. "If I had let you run for your evaluation, Linch would have suspected something." He leaned on the chest-high cement wall that enclosed the promenade. "Next question."

What were her other questions? She lost them when Alexander said, "Linch would have suspected something." What was there to suspect?

When she didn't say anything, Alexander filled in the silence. "How does your kingdom look from up here?"

"I'm not a queen."

"No one is until they are."

"Well, that settles it, sign me up. And by the way, *my kingdom* looks as if it's seen better days."

"The city has been through a lot," Alexander said, "but the Council is working on re-populating it with loyal New World citizens."

Jamie made a scoffing sound.

"You don't approve?"

"Loyal citizens?"

"Don't you think it's important to reward loyalty and that the capital city be a model for the rest of the nation?"

"A model of what? People toting the party line, afraid to speak their minds? Whatever can be granted as a reward can also be used as a weapon. You want to see fear and paranoia, make loyalty a litmus test."

"Then say something. Take a seat at the table and say something."

Jamie was tempted. How many times had she argued with Raven or her father about an issue, knowing that it was purely academic? Now she was being offered a chance to have a voice where it mattered.

"Who would listen to me?"

"A lot of people."

"Just because I was picked to sit in a chair?"

"No, because you're smart and good. Because you don't have to win a popularity contest every couple of years. Because you don't have to please one political party while you're trying to destroy another." Alexander suddenly took both of Jamie's hands in his. "You can lead from someplace deeper, purer. People will follow."

Alexander's passion was intoxicating, his touch warm against her skin. For a moment, she was short of breath. Would he try to kiss her? What an odd thought.

"I can't," she said, pulling her hands away. "When my mom died, I made a promise to myself that I wouldn't let my family fall apart. And they *are* falling apart."

Alexander returned to leaning on the wall. "I know. I found the note in the pocket of your dress, along with a knife."

Jamie's eyes went wide, but she kept them forward-looking out over the city. The knife, how could she have forgotten about the knife? What did Alexander think of her? And what about the note – had he told anyone? If Return was responsible for the bombing, any hint that her father was involved with them would be devastating. The note didn't exactly say that, but someone could infer it.

"Alexander, please . . . I didn't –"

He gestured for her to stop. Pulling the note out of his pocket and handed it to her. "No one saw it, or the knife."

Relief, gratitude, confusion – pick one. They all swirled in Jamie's heart. She threw her arms around Alexander. "Thank you." He held her in his embrace for the second time. But this was nothing like the first.

After a long moment, he pulled her back. With his hands on her shoulders, he said, "I would follow you." And then, with a wink, "ma'am."

Chapter Thirteen

Jamie slept better than she had in a long time. When she woke, pleasant memories of the evening before greeted her. The lingering impression of Alexander's embrace pushed concerns for her family and her future out of the spotlight. At least for the moment.

A knock at the living room door told Jamie that her breakfast had arrived.

"Come on in," she called from the bedroom as she headed for the dressing room. Dishes clanked as they were being set out on the table. "Thank you," she yelled, standing among the clothes. There were a couple of outfits that had caught her eye. Today was a perfect day to try one on.

The meeting took place in the Green Room of the residence. At 9:45 sharp, Alora showed up and escorted her downstairs. When she arrived, Nikole surveyed the room, making sure everything was properly arranged for the meeting. Several bottles of water sat on a table as well as some fresh fruit.

The room lived up to its name with emerald and gold wallpaper. The furniture displayed various shades of green, and a rug with a rich green pattern lay atop the hardwood floors. Many of the pieces in the room were old, like antique-old. A crystal chandelier illuminated several impressive works of art that hung on the walls. This was Jamie's first time in that room, and it was very much old U.S.A. The New World didn't seem as bent on ushering out the old world at the White House as they had been at the Capitol Building.

Both Nikole and Alora left a moment later when President Ashwill entered, escorting a woman into the room. He introduced her as Dr. Sidney Forrester. She was short and squat with a bright face and intelligent eyes. The doctor carried herself with the confidence of a woman who didn't mind telling you what was on her mind. She smiled as she shook Jamie's hand.

"It's good to finally meet you," she said. "You don't look anything like your cells under a microscope." The doctor laughed at her joke.

Jamie chuckled to be polite, but then said, "How long exactly have you been looking at my cells?"

"For some time," Dr. Forrester said, but offered no further details.

President Ashwill motioned for them to sit and began the conversation. "Dr. Forrester is familiar with your cells because she's been consulted regarding your genetic make-up."

Jamie closed her mouth, trying not to look dumbfounded.

Dr. Forrester took up the explanation. "I was contacted by a colleague a number of years ago who had been asked to run a DNA test on a fetus. What he found was perplexing, to say the least. He asked me for my professional opinion, which I gave him. I've wanted to study that DNA sample ever since then, but until recently, I haven't had the opportunity."

"You want to study my DNA? Why?"

"How much do you know about how viruses work?" Dr. Forrester asked.

"I know enough," Jamie replied. "I know that viruses need a host to survive because they can't make the proteins they need without the chemistry of the host cell." Biology, like most subjects, came easily to Jamie. "When viruses invade host cells to replicate, they end up killing them or disrupting them, and that's what makes us sick."

"Yes," the doctor said, "but retroviruses do more than that. They not only invade a host cell, but they will transcribe their RNA, their genetic instructions, into the DNA of a host cell. They can change the chromosomal DNA of the host," she said for emphasis.

"What are you saying; I have a virus?"

"Had," Dr. Forrester corrected.

"I don't remember having a virus," Jamie protested.

"No," Ashwill interjected, "in fact, you don't remember being sick at all, do you?"

Jamie squinted, searching her memory. It was true; she couldn't remember ever being sick. She had gone to the doctor several times as a kid to get blood drawn, but she never felt bad. Outside of the accident that day at the beach, she had never gone to the hospital or even needed a doctor. Why had she never noticed that before? Her brother got sick, but she never did.

"This virus changed your DNA making you . . ." the doctor looked around the room as if she were searching for the right word, "healthier."

"So, I'm special because I'm healthy? How does that make any sense?"

"You're not special because you're healthy," Ashwill corrected. "You're healthy because you're special." He said the words slowly as if treading on uncertain ground.

"Special how?" Could it be that her parents had kept something from her? She'd much rather believe that Ashwill and the doctor were lying to her, but the truth wasn't about what she *wanted* to believe.

Ashwill said, "Nearly nineteen years ago, a man named Thomas Walker checked himself into the UPMC Mercy Hospital Emergency Room in Pittsburgh. He had flu-like symptoms – fatigue, low-grade fever, headache, sore throat. When they ran tests, they discovered a viral infection no one had seen before. It was an exogenous retrovirus, meaning –"

Jamie, remembering her biology class, cut in, "– one that could be transmitted horizontally between human beings."

"That's right. But unlike other exogenous retroviruses, this one was airborne; it wasn't transmitted solely through contact with blood or sex. By the time they discovered that fact, thirty people at the hospital had been infected, and it would infect many more, very quickly."

"I already know about the Pittsburgh virus," Jamie said. "Everybody does."

Ashwill nodded, then said, "But not everyone knows this; one of the thirty people infected at the hospital by Mr. Walker was a nurse practitioner named Nelly Campbell. She also worked two days a week at a fertility clinic. She was working at that office the day after she was infected when your mother came for an appointment. She discussed your mother's fertility treatments with her and, without knowing it, infected her with the virus."

"She was pregnant with me, wasn't she?" Jamie asked.

"She was not, but she was about to be. The fertility treatments were successful, but not before the retrovirus in her body invaded the egg that would become fertilized and transcribed viral RNA into it."

Ashwill stopped there. This was not at all what Jamie expected to hear.

"I'm the product of a viral mutation?" It sounded worse coming out of her mouth than it did in her head.

"Yes," Dr. Forrester jumped in, "but don't get too worked up about it, bits of viral DNA has been woven into the human genome from millions of years ago. We're all carrying around a little viral mutation."

"But not like me."

"No," the doctor said, "not quite like you. In your case, the viral mutations made you healthier. I know it sounds counter-intuitive, but the virus gave you an amazing ability to fight off infections. And when I say amazing, I mean it. You have been genetically altered to have an indefinite life span."

"How is that even possible?" Jamie asked, approaching the conversation like a biology tutoring session. Her strategy was simple; keep the emotions at bay and figure out what the doc was saying. There'd be time to freak out later.

"It gets rather complicated," Dr. Forrester said, "but essentially a hormone receptor in your cells has been mutated in such a way that it doesn't receive certain hormones which cause aging in a cell. When this happens, other hormones or proteins are turned on that go to work, protecting the cell and even repairing it when the damage occurs. In particular, a protein called Foxo activates specific genes, genes that promote renewal at the cellular level and maintain healthy stem cell growth, which promotes tissue regeneration and suppresses the formation of tumors. If aging is the breakdown of the body on a cellular level, the Foxo gene is what keeps it from breaking down."

Jamie looked from Dr. Forrester to President Ashwill and back again. She opened her mouth to say something but closed it again.

"Think of it this way," Dr. Forrester tried again. "Imagine a city that is completely surrounded by a wall. It is one big circle and inside live all the residents of the city. Now, this city has one gate for anyone who wants to come in. At that gate is the gatekeeper. But this gatekeeper is not very good, because he lets in the wrong kind of people. The people he lets in dirty up the city and don't clean up after themselves. They tear things up and don't fix them. And the city gets worse and worse. The bad people dirty it up and the good people who could fix it stay home.

"But then imagine that a good gatekeeper kicks out the bad gatekeeper and takes over. And this gatekeeper no longer lets in the people who tear up the city. Instead, he lets in a building contractor who goes into the city and begins to hire painters and carpenters and masons and puts them to work cleaning up and repairing the city. Not only that, but he has connections with suppliers who provide all the materials they need to keep the city in tip-top shape. That's the Foxo gene."

Now Jamie did have a question. "So why not genetically alter human beings so that their hormone receptors do that all the time?"

"We've known about Foxo for a long time," the doctor answered, "but we've never figured out a way to genetically alter the cell to receive the Foxo protein without causing other unintended and detrimental consequences. We can't turn these hormone receptors off completely, because then the cell won't get the right amount of certain hormones they do need. In other words, we can't figure out how to let only good people in the city while keeping only bad people out. It's like trying to balance a pin on its tip. Theoretically, it's possible, but we've never done it."

"And this virus did all that?"

"Yes."

"Why didn't the virus kill me or destroy the egg or something?" Jamie pressed.

"We don't know," Dr. Forrester admitted. "There's a lot about this virus we still don't know. It may be that you have a unique genetic marker that changed the way the virus interacted with your DNA. It may be that others have were affected like you. But what makes your case unique is that it was the egg into which the virus transcribed it's RNA. You were *shaped* by this mutation, not just affected by it."

"You're making this up," Jamie said.

Dr. Forrester shook her head.

"So, what? I'm going to live to be really old?"

"Something like that. We call it conditional immortality. That's a bit of an overstatement, but, genetically speaking, you could live for an indefinite length of time."

"I can't die?" Jamie asked incredulously.

"No, you *can* die," Ashwill said, "but it won't be from a disease or the normal aging process, at least not for a long time. It would be from extreme physical trauma or malnutrition. But even then, your body has a remarkable ability to heal itself, if too many vital organs aren't irreparably damaged."

Creighton Ashwill's words arrived in slow motion, unfolding one at a time as if scrolling by on a display suspended in front of her, until she grasped their full meaning – you're not who you thought you were. She stood and began pacing. A swarm of questions buzzed around her head. Was it true? Of course, it was true. Two days ago, she'd been impaled by a metal pole, and there she stood without a wound in to be found. And then there was that day at the beach. That made a lot more sense now. But why keep it from her?

Jamie stopped her pacing and faced Ashwill. "How did my parents find out about this?"

"Your mom was one of the lucky ones. She survived the Pittsburgh Virus, maybe because of a genetic marker she had as well. When your parents discovered she was pregnant, they worried about what the virus might do to you, so they had some testing done."

"And that's when my colleague called to consult with me on what he had found," Dr. Forrester added.

"It seems to me that that would have been a big deal," Jamie said tracing down all the possible holes in this fantastic story. "Wouldn't someone with that kind of DNA be in a lab all the time under a microscope?"

"Yes," Ashwill said, "but not if they had your parents. Your mom and dad worked very hard to keep you and your condition out of the spotlight. They had your blood drawn and tested over the years, but always in a very controlled environment. Dr. Forrester was cut out of the process very early on and only recently did she gain access to your DNA to study."

"So how do *you* know all this?"

"Your dad and I were friends, once," he said. "We had some things in common. He confided in me."

"I bet he regrets that now," Jamie said.

"Perhaps, but now you know, and now you have a decision to make."

"I don't know how this qualifies me to lead a nation."

At that, President Ashwill stood and thanked Dr. Forrester for her time and insight.

The doctor stood to leave but looked at Jamie before going. "You have a gift; I hope you realize that."

Once she was out of the room, Jamie sat on a sofa. Ashwill sat next to her. "Of course, this doesn't qualify you to lead a nation, not by itself. But imagine the knowledge and wisdom someone like you could amass over what would be several lifetimes. Imagine the good you could do with that kind of experience."

Something sparked inside of Jamie at Ashwill's words, a kind of hunger.

He continued, "But it's more than just being smart or good. Imagine the dynasty that will follow you. A line of royal kings and queens with superhuman lifespans. Think of the hope that will give to a nation that has been marked by sickness and death."

"Wait. What?" Jamie stammered. "My kids will be like this?"

Ashwill nodded. "Dr. Forrester assures me that these genetic changes will pass onto future generations. The virus shaped you, and it will shape your offspring. Over time, the effects will diminish as other DNA joins to the mix, but that will take some time."

Superhuman? Was this a nightmare or a dream? Didn't everybody want a long, healthy life? Wasn't the search for immortality a basic human quest? So why did it feel like a curse? Was it because everything she'd ever imagined about her life had just been upended? Was it because she knew the burden and responsibility that would come with such a gift? If this were true, Jamie could never settle for an ordinary life. Her parents had instilled in her the importance of using her gifts for something bigger than herself. That was why, after her mother's death, she made sure her family survived. Wasn't that something big and important, and worthwhile? She wasn't sure it was big enough anymore.

Jamie stood, and the room began to spin. She might have conditional immortality, but she was still an eighteen-year-old girl, and this was a lot to handle. Jamie put one hand on her stomach, and one on the table next to her, and tears began to race down her cheeks.

"I need some time alone," she managed to say. "I need to think."

"Of course," President Ashwill said as he stood to leave. He opened the door and looked back at Jamie. "Raisa," he said, "you would make a wonderful queen." He stepped out and shut the door.

Chapter Fourteen

"I need to get out of here!" Jamie put both hands on the wall surrounding the promenade. She was outside on the third-floor walkway again, but she might as well have been suffocating in an airtight room. Jamie breathed air into her lungs as if it were a rare and precious commodity.

If only jumping were an option.

It was nine hours since Ashwill had introduced her to who she really was. A freak of nature. An anomaly. A scientific curiosity. Nine hours to try to convince herself that conditional immortality was a gift. Nine hours to wrestle into submission the emotions flooding her heart. Nine hours to make excuses for her parents. But it wasn't enough. All the self-talk and rationalizations in the world couldn't begin to set her right. Four weeks of tension, anger, and fear brewed below the surface and pierced the fragile boundary of her psyche that had held them at bay.

Ashwill hadn't been joking when he said the fates drag the unwilling. Fate had trapped her in a body destined for virtual immortality. How long, nobody knew. But more than that, it had trapped her on a course she couldn't unchoose. A course that had taken her from her family and forced her father to make desperate choices. Choices that would forever separate them if she were queen.

"Ahhh!" she screamed.

"Are you okay?"

Jamie turned to see Alexander. "What are you, my guardian angel?" She turned back to the view of the city.

"Lieutenant Jackson said he thought you had a rough day. Would it help to talk about it?"

No. Definitely not. "I'm fine."

"You don't sound fine."

"Now you're a psychologist?"

"I hope I'm a friend, but if you'd rather be alone, I can leave."

127

Jamie didn't look at Alexander or answer him until his footsteps retreated toward the Solarium. "Wait," she called. The footsteps stopped. "What are the chances you could take me out tonight? I need one normal night out before . . ."

"Take you out, like you and me alone? No protective detail?"

Jamie turned to face Alexander. "That's the idea. It's not like I'm a celebrity, yet, and since it's spontaneous, who out there's gonna find out?"

"Even so, I don't think we could get this approved," Alexander said.

"So your answer is no?"

"I didn't say that. There is a way, but we'd have to sneak out. Are you up for that?"

"What are they going to do? Fire me?" Jamie said. "Wait a minute; they could fire you, or worse."

"I'll take my chances."

Alexander came up with a plan remarkably fast. Together they would go to the residence on the second floor where Jamie would change into something for going out. Alexander would explain to Eli that he and Jamie would be having dinner together in the Solarium on the third floor. Eli needn't come up with them since Alexander would be there. They would take the stairs up to the third floor where they would then take the elevator to the basement. In the basement was a little-known tunnel Alexander knew of that led from the East Wing to the Treasury Annex Building on H Street two blocks away. Alexander explained that the tunnel had been excavated in the 1940s as a bomb shelter for President Franklin D. Roosevelt, and later connected to an existing tunnel between the Treasury Annex and department headquarters across the street. The tunnel ultimately led to a well-fortified door in an alley. Alexander didn't explain how he knew this, but he assured Jamie it was true.

"How will we get into the tunnel?" she asked. "I'm sure there's no key under the mat."

"I'm a part of your security detail. Don't worry about it."

• • • • •

Standing on H Street, Jamie could have flung her arms open and spun in circles like a little girl experiencing her first snowfall. What an amazing feeling. Had it only been a little more than a month? This was the right call. She needed this — all of it. The crowds of people coming and going. The traffic. Life. Normal life. People walked past her without giving her a second look. Anonymity –what a beautiful thing.

She grabbed Alexander's hand, "Okay, where to?"

"How about some dinner and dancing?"

Dinner and dancing sounded like heaven. Jamie didn't date much, so she couldn't very well claim that this was her favorite thing to do when she went out, but she was willing to find out. "That sounds nice."

"There's a great Thai restaurant not far from here," Alexander said. "You like Thai food?"

"Do you mind if I pick the restaurant?"

"Sure. What do you have in mind?"

"Ever been to The Speaker?"

Alexander had never even heard of The Speaker, much less eaten there, so Jamie filled him in with all the details as they walked. It was a diner owned and operated by a former Speaker of the House who had a short but colorful career as the most powerful man in the U.S. House of Representatives. Unlike so many of his colleagues, who had been forced to resign because of sexual or financial malfeasance, Jimbo Haynes packed up his office for a very different reason. He brought a gun to the floor of the House during a debate and brandished it to make a point about forest preservation. No one was quite sure how the gun was supposed to fit into his floor speech about forest preservation because he never had the chance to finish. Capitol police responded quickly when he pulled the gun, a Smith and Wesson .357 Magnum revolver, from his briefcase. Jimbo was known for his attention-getting stunts and was wildly popular with his constituents because of it, but everyone agreed that the gun stunt had crossed a line. In his defense, Jimbo claimed the gun wasn't loaded, but when the optics were that bad, statements like "the gun wasn't loaded" didn't help.

Also, unlike many of his colleagues, even those who had resigned in disgrace, Jimbo didn't get a career in one of a dozen lobbying firms making a boatload of money. Instead, true to form, he did something different. He opened a diner which became two diners and then three. Jimbo spent most of his time at the original shop where he'd built up a clientele of politicians and regular joes alike. Behind the counter, in a protective case for customers to gawk at, was the gun that made him famous.

"You're kidding?" Alexander said when she finished.

"Nope. One hundred percent true. A tiny but weird slice of American history."

"I got to be honest; I wasn't crazy about eating at a diner. But after that, we gotta go. I want to see the gun."

A short cab ride later, Jamie and Alexander walked into the diner. She paused inside the front door, scanning the restaurant for Jimbo. He wasn't hard to find. He stood out, dressed in coral pink pants, an untucked, long-sleeved, multi-colored shirt, and sandals, he stood out. Anyone who didn't know would never have guessed that he'd once been the Speaker of the House. His election to that post had been the result of the perfect political storm, but the storm had passed, and now he looked more like someone who had washed up on the nearest beach. Deeply etched crow's feet stretched from his eyes, and a gray beard hid the features of his face. With his hair pulled back in a sloppy ponytail, he could have passed as anything but a once-powerful man. As Alexander gawked at the gun, Jamie kept her eyes on Jimbo until he noticed her. When he did, she shook her head slightly.

You don't know me, she signaled.

A large American flag hung on the wall, and next to the gun was the gavel Jimbo had used as Speaker. The place was packed, and Alexander was the only one wearing a blue and red uniform. If he felt out of place, he didn't show it. "Looks like the vote didn't hurt business," he said. "Probably got a bounce from the pro-America crowd."

They sat at a booth as a waitress took their order and delivered their food. Alexander sat where he could see most of what was going on in the restaurant.

Jamie laughed at him. "You're never off duty, are you?"

Halfway through the meal, she stood. "I'm going to use the restroom. Do I need an escort?" she said with a grin.

Don't come.

"I've got things pretty well covered from here."

Good.

Jamie made her way to the bathroom where she stood at the sink, looking at herself in the mirror. Less than a minute later, Jimbo Haynes walked in.

He said, "I wish you'd let me know you were coming, I could have made some plans. But I think we can still get you out. Is Mr. New World out there the only security?"

"I don't want you to get me out, Jimbo. I want you to get a message to my dad."

"You can take your own message, Jamie. Let me help you."

"Like you helped my dad by hooking him up with Return? That's how he knew I'd be going to the Capitol, isn't it?"

Jimbo was an imposing figure who didn't back down easily. "Your dad was getting nowhere. He'd run through all of his contacts in and out of the New World government. No one would tell him anything. Jamie, he was desperate. He'd lost Ella, and he didn't want to lose you. So, yes, I hooked him up with the Return because they have information from someone on the inside."

"Which they used to try to kill me," Jamie said.

"We didn't know that's what they were planning."

"Alright, Einstein, where's my dad now?"

"He's in hiding with your brother. I can take you to them."

"They're in hiding? Why?"

"Return is afraid that your dad is desperate enough to use the information he has on them as leverage with the New World; he helps the New World root out Return, and they give him access to you. That kind of thing." Jimbo leaned against one of the sinks and crossed his arms. "So, they set him up by creating a video in which he appears to be giving his support to Return. If he rats them out, they use him in a PR campaign claiming that the great Senator Corson now supports the resistance."

"Are they safe? Jamie asked.

"For now."

Time was running out. Alexander would come looking for her if she didn't get back soon.

"Tell my dad that I'm okay. Tell him that I'm going to be the queen. Tell him I'm going to fix this."

Jamie didn't wait for Jimbo to respond. She pushed past him, exiting the ladies' room and nearly ran into Alexander.

"Got a little worried about you," he said.

"I'm good," she said, slipping by him and heading back to their table.

Not far from The Speaker was Meridian Hill Park, a twelve-acre landscaped urban park tucked between two neighborhoods. Jamie and Alexander took their time after dinner walking to the park, known for its dramatic thirteen-basin cascade fountain and formal garden.

"I think Jimbo found his calling," Alexander said. "I wouldn't expect to get Jambalaya at a diner, but I gotta say, it was good. And I can't remember the last time I saw a revolver. Very old school."

Jamie listened as Alexander did most of the talking. He seemed to be especially chatty after dinner, going on about the best places to get various dishes. That was fine with her. She enjoyed hearing him talk, and she needed time to think. Talking to Jimbo at the restaurant was the first time Jamie had admitted to herself or anyone else that she was willing to be queen. When had she decided that? Somewhere between being taken from her home, thrown into Basic Training, almost killed in an attack, and being told she would live nearly forever.

Alexander stopped at the cascading fountain, and they sat on a bench under a large red maple tree. The sound of the water was soothing. Alexander's stream of words seemed to dry up, and a moment of silence followed, which should have been awkward, but wasn't. Instead, it was freeing. Jamie had never been around a guy, other than her dad and her brother, who she could just sit with and not have to say anything. She always felt too self-conscious for that. Why was it so different with Alexander? She didn't know him, after all, not really. Why did it feel as if she did?

"I need to tell you something," she said.

Alexander turned toward her.

"I did have a bad day today. I found out something about myself, from Ashwill of all people, that I didn't know. Something life-changing." She paused, watching his reaction. So far, nothing. "I have a condition that keeps me from getting sick and allows me to heal very fast."

"That would explain your recovery."

"Yeah. It kind of shook my world." Jamie said.

"Why? It sounds like a good thing."

Jamie told him what she'd learned about the virus and conditional immortality. As she talked, his expression changed to a

133

look of sympathy she'd seen from him twice before. A look that drew her in deeper.

"What bothers me more than anything," she said, "is that my parents never told me. How do you keep something like that from a person? Maybe you don't tell a kid, I get that, but by fifteen I should have known." Tears welled up in her eyes. "I don't know how to live that long."

"I don't either, but it's not something you should have to do alone."

Alexander couldn't have given a more perfect answer. Jamie shifted her body to lean against him, her head on his shoulder. His chest rose and fell with a deep sigh. "I think there is probably something I should tell you at this point," Alexander said.

Jamie didn't move, but she stiffened against him.

"I'm not Alexander King."

She sat up and faced him.

"My name's Seth Bridges."

Chapter Fifteen

Who the heck is Seth Bridges?

Alexander must have read the panic in Jamie's eyes.

"Before you freak out, let me explain. If you still want to freak out when I'm finished, fine."

Jamie fought the impulse to run.

"My name is Seth Bridges, and I am a Second Lieutenant in the New World Army. When I graduated from the military academy, I was assigned to work with Governor Ashwill's unit, preparing for a transition after the vote. Shortly after I arrived, he picked me for a special assignment. You."

"Me?"

"He wanted me to get close to you."

"I'm sorry? Close to me?"

"I was to endear myself to you," he said slowly. "They were concerned that you wouldn't have a chance to meet a lot of guys as a monarch, so they wanted me to be the guy. A single queen with no heirs won't do, and they don't leave anything to chance."

Jamie stood and took a few steps away from him. "Why are you telling me this?"

"Because you deserve to know. Because you stopped being an assignment the moment I knew I liked you."

"Yeah. When was that?" Jamie said.

"The first time you tried to throw me down and take my gun. That was *so* romantic."

Jamie kept her back turned to him and her arms crossed. He wasn't going to get out of this by being cute. She had a right to be mad. But, despite her best effort to cling to it, her anger ebbed away. Nothing about this man felt fake. He didn't have to tell her this. In fact, he was probably defying an order. But he did it anyway, and wasn't that the kind of thing the Alexander she knew would do? Or whatever his name was.

"Look, I didn't set this up. I was just following orders, for the good of the country and all that, so if you want me to walk away, I will. But I like you, and I don't want to walk away."

Jamie turned around. Alexander stood in front of her, looking serious with his brow furrowed. She stepped closer.

"I don't want you to walk away, either."

Jamie put her arms around his neck and kissed him on the lips for a long wonderful moment. She lost her breath when he pulled her close and leaned into the kiss.

When she pulled away, he said, "You're going to have to still call me Alexander."

"I don't get it. What's wrong with Seth?"

"Same reason they want to change your name. I guess Seth and Jamie didn't sound as regal as Alexander and Raisa."

"Wow. They were really counting on you to win me over."

"Well ..." he said with an air of exaggerated confidence.

Jamie kissed him again and then laughed.

"They named you King? Was that supposed to be funny?"

"I think they were shooting for ironic."

Jamie had never heard of a century club before, but that was their destination as they left the park. Alexander assured her that century clubs were the latest thing, not only in the New World but across the continent. If she wanted to go dancing, this was the place.

"So why is it called a century club?"

"Everything there is a century old. The music. The drinks. The decor. You'll love it."

The club was in the Union Market warehouse district. The depression-era warehouses had nearly been torn down sixty years earlier when a non-profit preservation group intervened and suggested that the area could be remade into a mixture of stylish apartments and shopping. Many of the old buildings had been renovated, giving the area a new-meets-old kind of sophistication. The posh character of the renovated warehouses had not survived the upheaval of the last couple of decades, and many of them sat abandoned and deteriorating — the perfect place for a club harkening back a century.

Inside the hanger-like building music pulsed and lights flashed while a mass of people moved as one to the beat. A trio of male falsetto voices belted out the song.

Above the heads of the crowd floated holographic images of actors and singers long gone. Jamie picked out the personalities she recognized, just a handful. World history was one thing, she got that. But the history of pop culture, not so much. At the front of the room, a DJ pumped out music from vinyl records. He was a black man with a large afro and sideburns. He wore a white suit and a red shirt with an oversized collar and cuffs.

Alexander led Jamie to the bar. "What'll it be?"

The drink menu might as well have been in Russian; Blue Lagoon, Long Island Iced Tea, wine coolers of various flavors, The B-52, Alabama Slammer, light beer . . .

"I don't know what any of that is," she said.

"Unless you were a heavy drinker in the 1980's you wouldn't," Alexander laughed.

"You know, I've never been drunk," Jamie admitted.

"How did you make it to eighteen without getting drunk at least once?"

"I don't know. Growing up, my parents didn't drink much, not until we moved here. Then my dad started drinking to fit in. After my mom died, it got worse, and I guess seeing what it did to him just turned me off to it."

"Got it. So, I can assume you're not planning to get smashed tonight?" Alexander looked at the bartender. "How about two wine coolers. I dare you to get drunk on a wine cooler."

They took their drinks to a small table on the edge of the dance floor. Overhead the sound of synthesizers accompanied a woman singing about someone named Gloria. They watched people for a while and laughed at the odd clothes.

"I like the skinny ties, and the poofy pants," Jamie said.

Talking over the crowd and the music was a challenge, but after people-watching lost its appeal, Alexander took her by the hand. "I have something to say to you," he pushed his words above the noise. "You are the master of your fate. Your future should be the one *you* choose."

"Maybe the future I choose is the one I was destined to choose. Maybe at the end of the day, you can't control fate."

"That's a lot of maybes. Just don't let Ashwill dictate your life. That's all I'm saying."

"This coming from his hand-picked Prince Charming," Jamie said.

Alexander smiled, "So I ought to know, right? I want you to be happy."

"Happiness is overrated. But that doesn't mean life can't be satisfying." Jamie had heard her mom say that a thousand times. It was starting to make sense.

The song changed again, this time to something slow and romantic. Couples paired up, arms around each other, swaying to the melody. A man began to sing in a nasal tone. It was a song about the fate of two lovers.

"Master of my fate, huh?" Jamie laughed. "How do you explain that?" She waved her hand at the music.

"Maybe you're right; I think this is a sign. The universe is telling us we should dance."

Alexander held out his hand, and Jamie took it, following him onto the dance floor. Being in Alexander's arms was fast becoming one of Jamie's favorite places to be. The song couldn't have lasted more than a few minutes, but in those minutes, she abandoned herself to his embrace. The world could have ended, and she would have felt completely secure, her head resting on his shoulder.

The song drew out its final chords and gave way to the iconic voice of Michael Jackson, much to the delight of the crowd. Finally, someone Jamie knew. *Wanna Be Startin' Somethin'* didn't lend itself to holding and swaying, but Jamie was reluctant to let go until the irresistible beat of the music pulled her away. She had come to dance, and she was going to dance. She reveled in the freedom to let herself go and move to the music. It was cathartic. To her delight, Alexander could dance, and he appeared to be enjoying himself as much as she was.

Michael Jackson gave way to a Latin beat. Alexander told her this was a band called the *Miami Sound Machine*. Whoever they were, the song fueled the frenzy of the crowd. Jamie could have danced like this all night, and might have, if Alexander hadn't said over the music, "We've got company."

"Wings?"

Jamie turned. Cadet Penly! Behind her was Kendrick, Elliot and what looked like half of the Gamma squad. A sea of red and blue worked its way into the crowd. Was every cadet from Basic there?

"Hey, guys." Jamie fidgeted with her dress.

Penly appeared stunned. She looked at Alexander with a nod. "Lieutenant."

"Cadet."

Jamie's face got hot.

Penly looked her up and down. "You look nice, Wings. We heard you were injured."

"Turns out I heal fast." That sounded lame.

"Or you weren't really injured all that bad?" Kendrick said. "You abandoned your squad to do what, seduce an officer?"

"That's enough, Cadet," Alexander barked.

Jamie was uncomfortably aware of how close Alexander was standing behind her.

"You let your squad down, Cordova."

Alexander stepped forward. "Stand down and step away, Cadet."

"Sir. Yes, sir," Kendrick said without a hint of respect.

He and several members of Gamma squad pushed their way through the crowd. Penly didn't leave.

Jamie said, "Alexan . . . Lieutenant King, can you give me a minute?"

She and Penly found a spot away from the frenetic motion of the dance floor.

"I don't get it, Wings. You go on some secret assignment where you are injured so bad you can't finish Basic, and two days later you show up at a club? Dancing? With an officer?"

"It wasn't my choice to leave," Jamie said.

"You didn't choose to join the Army. You didn't choose to leave." She looked at Alexander. "You gonna tell me this wasn't your idea either?"

Penly was right. This didn't look good. "It's complicated."

"Tell me you did not just say that."

"It's true. I wish I could explain everything to you, but I can't, okay? It's bigger than you and me and the squad."

Penly made a scoffing sound and shook her head. "You got quite an ego, Wings. You know, you are the only person I ever told about my father and why I joined the army. I thought we had a thing going – part of a team – I got your back and you got mine. I thought I could trust you. But it looks like you've got your own team. Congratulations."

"You don't have any idea what you're talking about," Jamie yelled over the music. "I didn't ask to join the army, and I didn't ask you to tell me about your father. My family's my team, and the only thing I want is to be with them. But that's not going to happen because somebody has got to be the freaking queen."

Penly's mouth fell open.

"Wait," Jamie said quickly. "I need to explain that."

Penly waited.

"Okay, so-"

Before Jamie could get her words out, the music suddenly stopped. The crowd responded with a collective, "Ah." As the echo of the silenced music faded, the overhead lights came on, flooding the darkened room with a harsh brightness. Again, the crowd responded. "Agh."

Jamie followed Penly's eyes to the front of the room. A soldier stood at the DJ's rig, holding a microphone.

"Ladies and gentlemen, my name is Major Wilkins. Thirty minutes ago, the Constitutional Republic of America launched an attack against the New World."

Angst rippled through the crowd.

"Everyone needs to stay calm. A curfew has been imposed for your safety. You will need to return home immediately. Cadets, you will report to your commanding officers at headquarters."

Someone yelled from the crowd, "What happened?"

"Our southern border was breached south of Norfolk. It looks like they're trying to take the Naval Station and the Chesapeake Bay."

Another ripple of noise from the crowd.

"And there has been an aerial attack in the city." The major paused. "The White House has been hit."

Someone screamed. Jamie's legs turned to rubber. She reached out for Penly to steady herself.

The crowd began to shift uncomfortably as if any sudden movement might trigger panic. Alexander must have sensed the tension because he looked at Jamie, but didn't rush to her. Instead, he moved slowly, almost imperceptibly, in her direction.

"If there was an aerial attack, why didn't we hear anything?" Penly asked.

Jamie looked around and said, "With the decibel level in here? I couldn't hear myself think."

The major continued. "Our airspace is secure, but we need everyone to calmly exit the building and return home. Folks, if we remain calm, everything will be alright."

People began to make their way toward the exits, eyes shifting to one another as if each were wondering if the other would make a break for it. Alexander was moving with the crowd toward Jamie when someone near the back began pushing people out of the way. Others began pushing back. Voices were raised. Shoving turned into fighting, and the peaceful flow of humanity toward the exits turned into whitewater rapids. Those who were slower or weaker got knocked to the floor. Alexander had to work his way across the angry current to reach Jamie.

"Alexander . . ." Tears choked out her words. If they hadn't snuck out, they would have been at the White House during the attack, as Alora and Eli had been. Jamie couldn't bear to think about the people she knew who might have died.

"I know," he said, as he embraced her. "We can't worry about that yet. We need to get you somewhere safe." Alexander searched the crowd as if he were looking for something. People continued to stream toward the exits in a chaotic mess. "I don't think I can get us any support. Looks like we're on our own. Cadet Penly, you're with us." Alexander pulled a small gun from an ankle holster and handed it to her. "Keep this out of sight, until we clear the building. You're taking the lead. We're heading to the Pentagon." Alexander put his hand on the gun on his hip.

Desperate people pushed against them, even though they flattened themselves against the far wall. Cadet Penly looked at the gun in her hand. "Excuse me, sir, what are we doing?"

"You and I are going to get our future queen to safety."

Chapter Sixteen

Christmas 2075

There's nothing quite like the sound of a sold-out audience awaiting a live performance. Nate hadn't performed live on stage since high school, but the murmur of the crowd and the discordant sounds of the orchestra warming up brought back memories as if it were yesterday. He had butterflies in his stomach, and he wasn't even the one going on stage tonight. This was Jamie's night. At fifteen, she was dancing in the Nutcracker.

Nate had been to the Warner Theater on a couple of occasions, but never to watch his daughter perform. Usually, it was about schmoozing with dignitaries of some sort or another. This time it was personal, and that made him nervous. He could use a scotch. Nate headed to the VIP lounge for a drink, while Ella found her way backstage to check on Jamie.

Jamie had been dancing for ten years and had been in dozens of performances, but this was, without a doubt, the biggest night of her young life. The lead ballerina playing Clara had gotten sick, and Jamie was her understudy. She had all of twelve hours to prepare for the performance tonight. She knew the part backward and forward, but still. And, of all nights for her to debut as the lead dancer, tonight the new Russian Czar would be in attendance.

Nate lifted the glass of amber liquid to his lips, eager to feel the familiar burn. How the heck had the Russians ended up with a Czar? Again? Nate thought about the tectonic shifts that had taken place in the world order over the last century. No one could have guessed the world would look the way it did, although some people had warned about Russia. Of course, this Czar was not exactly like Nicholas Romanov – it was a different world after all – but he was close enough. The President had invited the new Russian leader to Washington, eager to maintain relations with Russia. And now here he was, at the Warner Theater, ready to watch Nate's daughter dance in a role for the very first time on stage. He'd read that Governor Ashwill would accompany the Czar and his wife to the theater that night. That made sense. Ashwill had long advocated a monarchy in America. He was probably salivating over the chance to sit with the new leader in public. That meant there was no way around seeing Creighton tonight, even though Nate would rather not. But a sitting U.S. Senator could not very well ignore the Russian head of state at such a public event, and it wasn't likely that Ashwill would leave the Czar's side, even for a minute. Nate put his glass on the bar.

"I'll need one more," he said to the bartender.

As Nate made his way back to his seat, an usher approached him. "Senator Corson?"

"Yes."

"Your wife has asked that you join her backstage."

That couldn't be good. Nate followed the usher who led him out of the beautifully ornate auditorium and into the unattractive and somewhat chaotic realm of the backstage. Ella was waiting for him.

"She's freaking out."

"Why? She knows the part."

"I know that, and so does she. But she hasn't been given a lot of time to process this, and you know Jamie. She needs time to process things, or this is what happens."

Nate let out a long sigh. "So what can I do?"

"Talk to her," Ella said. "She listens to you. You need to calm her down and get her to where she needs to be emotionally."

"She listens to you too," Nate said defensively.

Ella pursed her lips and raised her eyebrows.

"Well, she does. Just not in the same way."

Ella pointed to the door where Jamie was hiding. Nate knocked on it. "Jamie, it's dad."

"You can come in."

144

Inside, Jamie was in costume with her hair and makeup done. Everything was ready except her.

"You look fantastic," he said. She'd been crying.

"I don't know if I can do this, dad. Yesterday I was the Sugar Plum Fairy, and today I'm Clara. I don't know if I'm ready."

There were all kinds of logical arguments Nate could make or inspirational quotes he could give Jamie, but none of them would make a dent in the wall of fear she had erected.

"Okay. So what are your options?" Nate asked, matter-of-factly.

"I quit and let everyone down and embarrass the troupe. I go on, fail miserably, let everyone down, and embarrass the troupe."

Typical Jamie under stress, all doom, and gloom.

"Or?" Nate prompted.

"I go on and do a decent job, and everyone's happy," she said reluctantly.

"Yes. Especially you." Nate turned toward the door. "The choice is yours, Peanut, but you need to know something; you'll get over a failure. You'll never get over quitting."

Nate read his daughter's features and body language. She was processing. She could never be pushed to do something. It had to be her choice. He had to present her with the options and be willing to walk away.

"Is it true that the Russian Czar is here tonight?" she asked.

"It is. He's in for a treat."

Jamie smiled.

"Knock 'em dead."

"You're supposed to say, 'Break a leg.'"

"That too," he said with a grin.

Outside, Ella looked worried.

"I think she'll be fine," Nate said. "We just have to give her some space."

"I'm a nervous wreck," Ella asked. "You?"

145

"Steady like a rock," Nate said with a wink. The two drinks hadn't hurt.

As the curtain went up, the crowd grew silent. The familiar Christmas Eve party at the Von Stahlbaum home unfolded on stage, Jamie in the midst of it smiling and greeting guests as they arrived. Nate squeezed Ella's hand.

Halfway through the evening, Ella whispered, "We should have made Ben come. She's wonderful."

The audience laughed and clapped in all the right places. Jamie grew more confident as the night progressed. Maybe no one else noticed, but Nate knew his little girl. His heart swelled with pride as the dancers made their way out for the final curtain call. Jamie bowed gracefully and beamed with joy.

In the crowded VIP lounge after the performance, the Russian Czar attracted quite a bit of attention. Some of the dancers had made their way there and were mingling with the guests, eager to meet the colorful Russian leader.

When Jamie entered the room, Nate and Ella made their way to her. Nate wrapped her in his arms. "I always thought option three was the best," he said.

Jamie smiled. "Your advice was all it took. Oh, and one round of throwing up in the bathroom."

Ella hugged her. She took Jamie's face in her hands. "You are beautiful and graceful."

Behind them, Nate hears the voice of Creighton Ashwill. "Excuse me."

He turned to see Creighton and the Russian Czar.

"If you would permit me, I'd like to introduce you to the Emperor of All Russia, Viktor Vasiliev. Your Excellency, this is Senator Nathan Corson and his wife, Ella."

"Pleased to meet you," the Russian said with a heavy accent and a hearty handshake.

"And, of course, the one you really want to meet," Ashwill continued, "the beautiful and gifted Jamie Corson."

Vasiliev took Jamie's hand, kissing it lightly. She blushed. "Young lady, you-." He stopped and turned to his interpreter. "Kak ti skazhyeshv Vi preyekrasno tantsuyetye."

The interpreter said something quietly to the Czar.

He turned back to Jamie, still holding her hand. "You are a world-class dancer. You come and dance in Russia."

Jamie's blush grew deeper, and her smile wider. "Sure. If my parents let me."

The Czar laughed loudly, "Yes. I make them let you."

The evening couldn't have gone any better. As the crowd started thinning out, Nate signaled that he was ready to go.

Jamie approached Nate with a question that he could see she was reluctant to ask. "I thought that maybe I could go out with some of my friends for a little while. You know, to celebrate. It's kind of a big night for me."

"How will you get home?"

"Logan will bring me."

"Who's Logan?" Nate asked.

"One of the dancers. He's seventeen. Mom's met him."

Nate looked at Ella, who was nodding her head.

"You two have already worked this out, haven't you?"

Both of them smiled.

"Okay, fine. But I want you home by eleven."

"But dad –"

"Aahh," Nate interrupted. "The city can be dangerous late at night. Eleven. Understood?"

Jamie nodded. "Understood."

Nate and Ella left the theater, got into their car, and headed toward home.

Chapter Seventeen

Three-And-A-Half Years Later – Present Day

"Come in, Raisa." Creighton Ashwill waved Jamie over as she entered the large conference room. Around the table were a number of advisors and high-level military officers. On the walls were monitors allowing the other New World Council members to participate in the meeting. As she entered, everyone in the room stood.

"It's a little soon for that," Jamie said. "I haven't been crowned yet."

"Yes, ma'am, but that's a formality," one of the generals said. "You have been officially named Queen of the New Word by the Council, and therefore you deserve the respect of that position."

Jamie didn't argue. She took the open seat next to Ashwill. Her seat.

It had been two weeks since the incursion at the border and the attack on Washington. The residence of the executive mansion had been targeted, leaving much of the west and east wings undamaged. Nonetheless, Ashwill moved the center of government operations to the larger and more secure Pentagon. Jamie also moved there, occupying a suite on the top floor. The accommodations at the Pentagon were very nice, but it wasn't the White House. There was something about being in that building; the history and feel of it. Jamie had had two whole days to enjoy it, and most of that was spent unconscious.

Four days after the attack, funerals had started for those who died. Several White House staff and military personnel died during the attack, and Jamie attended as many of the services as possible. She wasn't crazy about how Ashwill appeared to be using the funerals as a soft rollout for the big announcement about her. After only the second service, she learned that people began speculating about who the elegant young woman seated next to him might be. It seemed Ashwill had a way of making everything political. When she protested, he said that's why she'd be an excellent queen, because she didn't have a political bone in her body.

The hardest funeral was Eli's. Jamie and Alexander had lied to him that night so that she could sneak out and escape her problems. That detail was left unscrutinized by those who knew about it since it had saved her life, but Jamie carried the guilt with her. Eli was there because he thought *she* was there. After the attack, New World officials naturally assumed Jamie was in residence and had died at the hands of the CRA. When she showed up with Alexander at the Pentagon several hours later, their relief outweighed whatever questions they might have had about that night.

Getting back to the Pentagon from the club had proved more challenging than any of them expected. With Penly leading the way, they made it out of the building and into the night. Above them, drones patrolled close to the ground while New World airships secured their airspace at higher altitudes. Even though they were friendly forces, the presence of so many aircraft only reinforced the reality that they were under attack — people scattered in every direction. Vehicles jammed the streets as pedestrians spilled off the sidewalks between the cars. Getting an automated cab was out of the question.

"How are we supposed to get to the Pentagon?" Penly asked.

"How'd you get here?" Alexander replied.

"Linch provided transports and drivers, but I don't see any of them now."

He touched the comm in his ear. "My guess is that communications are down, or someone's jamming them."

"Why don't we just hitch a ride?" Jamie asked. "There's got to be somebody here who'll take us to the Pentagon."

"You're on the right track, but I was thinking more like 'borrow' a car. If Return is working with the CRA, there may be more to this before it's over, and I'm not getting in a car that I'm not in control of."

He made his way to the closest car, which was trying to work its way out into the traffic from a side street.

"Excuse me, ma'am," he said, "we need to borrow your car."

The twenty-something behind the wheel gave him an *I don't think so* look.

"Listen, lady; I'm with the Army. We've got a situation here, and I need to borrow your car."

"Don't you guys have your own?"

Alexander holstered his gun and opened her door. "I'm going to need you to step out of the vehicle. You can come with us or not, but I'm taking this vehicle for official government use."

He was about to reach in when her car and every other vehicle on the road began to move randomly without regard for the other cars or the people in the street. As they lurched forward, out of control, they pinned people between them; others were knocked down and crushed under their weight. The sound of crunching metal and screams filled the air. Alexander pushed Penly out of the way of an oncoming vehicle and grabbed Jamie's hand, pulling her out of the road. On the sidewalk, Jamie put both hands over her mouth in horror.

"Someone's hacked the auto navigation systems," Alexander yelled over the commotion. "We need to get out of here."

Jamie followed Penly as she ran back toward the warehouse they had just left. They stayed close to the building and away from the cars careening out of control. Alexander was behind her with one hand on her back, the other holding his gun.

"Turn left between these buildings," he directed, "we need to get to get to the train tracks."

Running south along the warehouse district were tracks that led to Union Station. Getting to them meant safe travel, at least for part of their journey. There should be no cars on the tracks. Penly took a left as instructed, and Jamie followed as they worked their way under the New York Avenue overpass. Several cars had driven themselves off the overpass and landed in heaps on the tracks below. Jamie gasped as they approached the first one. The car was lying on its roof, steam hissing from under the hood. She pulled away from Alexander and ran to the car, falling on her knees and looking in the driver's side window. Broken glass cut her knees and palms as she peered in.

Don't be dead.

The driver's body was twisted unnaturally, causing Jamie to recoil and fall back. Alexander rushed to her, grabbing her shoulders and lifting her to her feet.

"We can't help them," he said. "Right now, our priority is getting you to safety. If we stop at every crisis, we'll never make it."

Jamie nodded her head. A wave of nausea hit her, and she turned to the side, vomiting. "No more stopping," she said. "Let's get home." *Home.* Home used to be the place her family lived. Now it was wherever her duty lay.

It took about a half-hour to make it to Union Station on the tracks. Then it was time to hit the streets again. Thankfully, most of the cars that were going to crash had crashed. The scene was dreamlike – cars piled in heaps, people staggering around in a daze while others helped the injured. Now and then, someone would see the uniform worn by Alexander and Penly and beg for help. There was no way to help – no supplies, no communication – but that didn't matter. The uniform represented the government, and that meant help.

One man was insistent to the point of being threatening. Alexander drew his gun when the man persisted, following them for

Doug Felton

several blocks, yelling and cursing the New World. He held a bat in his right hand.

"Sir, you need to step back."

"Go to hell!"

The man was either high, in shock, or just plain mad. Whatever the reason, he hurled the bat, end over end, at them. He was probably aiming at Alexander, but it hit Jamie in the forehead. She went down hard. Penly ran to her. Alexander holstered his gun and charged the assailant, lowering his shoulder. The man, who was at least fifty pounds heavier, crumbled in a heap upon impact. Alexander pinned him to the ground, punching him in the face.

From the shadows of a nearby building, two other men quickly appeared and joined the fight. One kicked Alexander hard in the ribs, knocking him off the bat-man. Alexander made it to his feet quickly, ready to defend himself. The two newcomers attacked Alexander in tandem, but he easily knocked one to the ground, improving the odds for the moment. Bat-man was still shaking out the cobwebs from his beating and trying unsuccessfully to get to his feet.

Penly then joined the fight, kicking the man Alexander had just put down as he tried to get up. The assailant went down again, but as he fell, he grabbed her leg, putting her on her back with a loud thud. He moved quickly to jump on her, pinning her to the ground. Alexander launched the heel of his foot into the chest of his opponent, crumpling him and then ran to help Penly.

Jamie sat helpless on the ground, watching the fight. She pushed herself to her knees slowly. The world spun for a moment, making her sick to her stomach, and her head pounded, but she found her feet and planted them a shoulder-length apart for balance. Penly took several blows to the face before Alexander got to her attacker. He tackled the man, and the two rolled several feet, ending with Alexander on top. He had delivered two punches to the face when the bat-man finally got to his feet. The man quickly picked up his baseball bat and started toward Alexander. Jamie couldn't get there in time, and she was in no condition to help even if she could. She looked around for something, anything she could use, and saw the gun Penly had laid on the ground when she knelt to help Jamie. She picked it up and aimed it at the bat-man's chest. He raised the bat high above his head, ready to bring it down on Alexander when Jamie squeezed the trigger.

The roar of the gun was deafening. The man fell backward with a crimson stain spreading on his shirt. She held the gun on the fallen man for several seconds before meeting Alexander's gaze. He stood slowly, walked to her and took the gun, before looking back at the man she had shot. Penly was on her feet, surveying the scene. The two other men staggered away as quickly as they could.

"Who were these guys? Return?"

"I don't think so," Alexander said. "A crisis just brings out the worst in some people." He looked around. "We can't stay here. I'll report this as soon as we get to the Pentagon." He put his hands on either side of Jamie's face. "Hey, you did what you had to do. You saved my life."

"I know."

"I'm serious. You're not at fault. You did the right thing."

Jamie put a hand on one of his. "I know."

Two hours later, a floodlight pierced the darkness and stabbed Jamie's eyes as they approached the Potomac River. On the Fourteenth Street Bridge, a group of soldiers, maybe a platoon, and several armored vehicles lay between them and the Pentagon. Jamie stepped past Alexander and Cadet Penly and stood before the soldiers. She called out, "I'm Raisa Cordova. Council President Ashwill will be looking for me."

In the conference room, Jamie listened intently to the discussion. This was the third high-level meeting she had attended in two weeks. Now that she knew the drill, it wasn't as overwhelming as it had been at first. The people sitting around the table were serious men and women dealing with serious issues, but no one questioned her presence there. Apparently, being a part of the New World government meant buying into the idea of a monarchy. She couldn't' imagine that Aswhill accepted anything but complete loyalty. They welcomed her questions, and everyone did their part to educate Jamie about the issues at hand. She had to give credit to Ashwill; he had his team in order. Jamie took copious notes and spent the evenings researching questions not answered in the meetings. A team of advisors was also assigned to brief her on domestic and international policy, although, at the moment, international affairs took center stage.

The night of the attack, after walking back to the Pentagon, Jamie sought out Creighton Ashwill. Bloodied and dirty, she burst into his office and told him that she was ready to serve her nation as their queen. He looked at her as a proud father might look at his favorite child. Jamie thought he might even hug her, but he didn't. Instead, he told her that an emergency meeting of his top advisors was about to begin, and he wanted her there.

"I need to change first and get cleaned up," Jamie protested.

"No. They need to see this. They need to see what you've endured."

And so she went, torn and bruised and bleeding. Ashwill introduced her as Raisa Cordova, the Council's choice to be the queen of the New World. As he relayed what she had been through that evening, Jamie surveyed the expressions of those around the table. Some looked shocked, others angered, and some had tears in their eyes. Jamie watched them watching her, and the weight of responsibility settled on her like a heavy blanket. Each minute that ticked by pressed into her heart the sobering reality of leadership. This was her life. It was who she was meant to be. Nothing had ever been more certain.

As the meeting started, Jamie asked Ashwill for a favor. He agreed, and a messenger was sent out. He soon returned with Alexander, who was also still disheveled. Alexander took a seat with the other advisors sitting around the room against the wall.

"Each of you has the person you trust the most in the room this evening," she said, "and now so do I."

Alexander had been at each of the meetings since, taking notes and discussing them with Jamie. He had a knack for this kind of thing and learned the issues remarkably fast. He became a valuable resource, decoding policy language for her in a way that only someone not in it up to their eyeballs could. Soon, she added Raven and Cadet Penly to her staff. She had a lot of experts around her, but she needed people she knew and trusted. People who could remember her as she was and tell her if she was becoming someone she wasn't. Anchors, she called them. After finishing Basic, both Raven and Cadet Penly were commissioned as second lieutenants. Having been promoted to first lieutenant, Alexander still outranked them and didn't hesitate to remind them of that fact.

The first three meetings Jamie attended were contentious and emotional. Passions ran high as the council, and their advisors tried to make sense of the attack and formulate a response.

"I'll tell you what it means," a man named Colonel Gregory said in the second meeting. "It means they intend to defeat us and add our territory to the Constitutional Republic of America. They've been clear about their intentions to reunite the nation. Why else attack Norfolk? It's a close, high-value target, that gives them a military installation and strategic control of the Chesapeake Bay." Gregory's intense style and close-cropped white hair added to the force of his argument. "What we do now will set the stage for generations to come. We can either play defense and deal with this for years, or we can end it now with a decisive attack."

Some people nodded their agreement. Jamie looked at Ashwill, whose face remained impassive.

"Assuming we can end it with an attack of our own," the Secretary of International Affairs countered. "We could end up in a prolonged war that does nothing but cost lives, drains resources, and leaves us with the same threat we face today."

"We have a right to exist as a sovereign nation, and a duty to protect that sovereignty."

"Of course, we do. That's not disputed. The question is, how do we get to that goal? A defensive strategy might be a more prudent option at this point."

Jamie shook her head slightly and made a slight grunting sound.

"You have something to say, Miss Cordova?" Ashwill asked.

Through the first meeting and up to this point in the second one, Jamie had sat quietly, taking it all in. But her mind was spinning with too many questions for her to keep them all to herself. "What about trying to talk to them? I haven't heard anyone suggest that. If an all-out attack is too risky, and a defensive strategy is too passive, wouldn't diplomacy be the obvious choice?"

Sitting next to Jamie, Ashwill shook his head. "You may be right," he said, "but it's hard to negotiate with a country bent on conquest, especially when they see it as their moral imperative."

And that was that; the final word. No one challenged Ashwill, and the discussion moved on.

When the meeting adjourned, Jamie returned to her suite with Alexander. They sat on the couch, she leaning against him, as they both decompressed and processed what they had just heard. Since the attack, they'd been nearly inseparable, often talking late into the night. Jamie had barely had time to process the news about her condition before the attack, and Alexander had become the sounding board she needed. It wasn't unusual for her to wake up on the couch and find herself curled up next to him, sound asleep. Was this love?

"I don't understand why Ashwill shot down diplomacy so quickly," she said. "If it doesn't work, it doesn't work. But isn't it worth the effort? There are a lot of examples in history where two sides talking prevented a war."

"You've got to understand that there's bad blood between most of the people in that room and most of the people in the CRA's administration," Alexander explained. "Council President Ashwill and President Kaine knew each other years ago, before the virus. Same with the other council members. There's a lot of pent up anger and hatred, and that's never good when everyone is pointing a gun at everyone else."

"There's got to be a way to get past that. *'It's hard to negotiate with those kinds of people,'* doesn't cut it."

"Good luck finding someone who has a heart for it. Anyone over thirty remembers how those states left us to die after the outbreak. People want revenge. After all these years, they want someone to pay for fifty-eight million deaths."

"What if it's not somebody over thirty?" Jamie said.

Chapter Eighteen

Jamie sat quietly as General Keller, the ranking general in the room, presented three options for an attack on the CRA. Each one included an estimate of casualties. They were not insignificant.

"Thank you, General," Ashwill said. "In your opinion, which contingency would most efficiently achieve our goal of crippling the CRA's military strike capacity?"

"I believe the first plan would achieve that objective, sir."

"It would also create the highest number of civilian casualties in the CRA," Jamie said.

"Yes, Ma'am," Keller replied. "To cripple the CRA's military capacity long-term, we will need to destroy key infrastructure. This plan will yield a higher civilian casualty rate than striking military targets alone."

"A diplomatic option would yield no casualties at all."

"Unless it failed," General Keller answered.

"In which case, you can execute whatever military plan you like," Jamie said.

"It's a fool's errand."

"Then send me," Jamie insisted. A murmur made its way around the table. She added, "If I appear to be a fool for the sake of peace, I can live with that."

"With all due respect, Ma'am, they tried to kill you."

"So who better to go? Only Nixon could go to China, right? We've got to give them the chance to walk the attack back. I'll let them tell me they were shooting at Creighton."

That brought a tiny smile to the general's face.

Jamie's hands were sweating, and her stomach was in knots, but she kept her voice even. "Look, everyone in this room knows that I'm not opposed to using deadly force when necessary." Alexander had suggested she use that line. He said the military types respected her for saving one of their own and she would need to remind them of that. "But if I thought I could have talked that man instead of shooting him, I would have. You're right, Colonel Gregory. What we do now will set the stage for generations to come. So let's set the stage with our best effort for peace."

Jamie finished with a deep sigh, and no one spoke. She wished her dad was there to hear her. As she spoke, she could hear his voice in her head, saying the words that came out of her mouth. He would have been proud.

Ashwill let the room sit in silence for a moment, and then polled the council members. Six favored the military plan recommended by the general. Two opted for one of the other plans with less collateral damage. Seven wanted to explore a diplomatic solution.

"I am of the opinion that the seventeenth-century historian Thomas Fuller was right," Ashwill said. "It's madness for sheep to talk peace with a wolf. But for the sake of peace, I am willing to entertain the idea that the CRA is not as wolfish as I might imagine. The only way to find out is for you to go and talk if they will have you."

Did Creighton Ashwill just sign off on sending her on a diplomatic mission? Was it really that easy? The old saying, *be careful what you wish for*, suddenly left the realm of theory. Jamie had never been outside of the New World territory, and now she was going to negotiate peace with the CRA.

Wait. I can't do this alone.

As if reading her mind, Ashwill looked at the Secretary of International Affairs and said, "Secretary Paulson, I'd like you to accompany Miss Cordova with whatever staff you need. She will take the lead, but you will advise her. But first, contact your counterpart in the CRA and see if they are willing to meet with our special envoy."

Later in her suite, Jamie said to Raven, "Close your mouth."

Raven snapped her mouth shut. "I can't believe you talked them into letting you go."

"Letting *us* go," Jamie said.

They sat at a table eating lunch, just the two of them. Lieutenant Penly was down in the training center, honing her hand-to-hand combat skills. Alexander and Nikole were meeting with Ashwill's staff on the big announcement that would be happening the next day. The New World Council decided that the best time to unveil Jamie as Raisa Cordova, Queen of the New World, was at the already scheduled ratification ceremony for the New World constitution. Nikole and Alexander were hammering out the logistics and staging.

Raven put her fork down and dabbed her mouth with a napkin. "Did you ever imagine any of this when we were in high school? We're going to Texas. Texas! I wonder if people there wear cowboy hats like in all the old pictures."

"No," Jamie said. "I didn't imagine this, even this morning."

"Alexander said you gave one heck of a speech."

"I guess, but still. I didn't push that hard." Jamie had been kicking these thoughts around since the meeting but hadn't verbalized them until now. "It seems strange they would pick me. I mean, wouldn't it make more sense to send Secretary Paulson?"

Raven smiled. "He'll be there, whispering sweet nothings in your ear."

"More like diplomatic strategies, but that's the point. He doesn't need me there. I'm going because I volunteered. Why would they go with the understudy?"

"You're overthinking this. Maybe you've got something to offer that Paulson doesn't. You know, like the X-factor – you're young and fresh and all that. Stop worrying and eat your salad."

A knock at the door interrupted their conversation. Alora stepped in. Her eyes had lost something since Eli's death. They were sadder, and Jamie couldn't quite meet her gaze. Did she blame Jamie for his death?

"President Ashwill is on his way to see you."

"Thank you, Alora. How are you doing?"

"I'm fine. Thank you, ma'am," Alora said quickly, stepping out of the room, closing the door.

"I guess that's my cue to finish lunch," Raven said.

A few minutes later, Ashwill entered the suite with a man Jamie had never seen. Raven saluted him.

"Lieutenant Ramirez," Ashwill acknowledged while returning the salute.

As Raven left, Jamie directed Ashwill and his guest to the formal living area of the suite. "President Ashwill, what can I do for you?"

"I wanted to talk about your trip to the CRA," he said. "I'm not as optimistic as you are about the diplomatic solution."

"I'll admit, I was surprised that you supported the idea so quickly."

"Yes, well, I think it is important that I support you openly. People in the administration and in the public need to have confidence in you. That won't happen if I don't show it myself first."

Jamie tried to take his words at face value, but she didn't trust Creighton Ashwill completely. He didn't exude transparency, not like Alexander. Jamie couldn't pin it down, but there was always something more behind his words.

He continued. "You need to let me know what you're thinking before you suggest something of that magnitude in a meeting."

"Absolutely. My apologies." Jamie was surprised at her own words. Since when did she say things like "my apologies?" Not too long ago, her response would have been, "Right. Sorry."

"We have some unsubstantiated intelligence reports that the CRA is planning to use biological warfare against the New World."

"Unsubstantiated?"

"One asset reported a conversation with some mid-level government officials in the CRA who suggested that was an option."

"Asset, as in spy?"

"Yes," Ashwill confirmed.

"Do we have any idea what kind of biological warfare we're talking about?"

"We think it's the Pittsburgh virus."

Jamie stood and walked to the window overlooking the Potomac River. So many people had died from the virus. How could anyone with any shred of decency think of unleashing something so deadly on a civilian population? It made the civilian casualty statistics from earlier seem hardly worth noting. "How would they have access to the Pittsburgh virus?"

"The CDC in Atlanta. They've had vials of it stored for twenty years. This was my underlying concern with the diplomatic mission. I don't trust them. They could infect you and everyone with you. You, our olive branch, could become the delivery system for their weapon."

Jamie turned to Ashwill and his guest. "I don't understand. If they infect us while we're there, don't they run the risk of being infected themselves?"

Ashwill pointed to the man who had come with him. "This is Dr. Zurich. He's an epidemiologist. I'll let him explain."

The man stood, and awkwardly attempted a bow. Jamie smiled. "That's not necessary. Please have a seat." She sat down nearby, hoping he'd relax a little.

"Thank you, ma'am." He was a short, skinny, balding man with a scruffy goatee that was mostly white. "President Ashwill is quite right. If they have the Pittsburgh virus, they could weaponize it and deliver it to you in any number of ways."

"Give me an example."

"They could deliver it through polymeric nanoparticles."

Jamie shook her head, looking confused

"Fullerenes," he said.

She still had no idea what he was talking about. "I'm afraid I'm not up to speed on nanotechnology."

"These are soccer-ball-shaped nano-cages that deliver treatment to targeted cells. Most often they're used to deliver treatment to cancer cells, but in this case, they'd deliver the virus. They could introduce them to your system in any number of ways. And that's just one possibility. They could go old school and plant it on your airship in an aerosol form. It wouldn't be hard to time its release. Or they could go low tech and recruit several viral hosts to function as your departure team when you return home. As long as they tightly control their interactions and dispose of them quickly once you've gone, they could pull it off."

"That's insane."

"One-hundred-and-thirty-seven years ago, it was insane to fly military aircraft into naval ships. Seventy-five years ago, it was insane to fly commercial planes into buildings, but don't forget where your standing."

Jamie looked out the window at the 9-11 memorial below. He was right that the world had gone mad. Or maybe it had always been mad, but some invisible force had kept the madness at bay, regulating how much seeped into the world at any given time. If that were true, the last quarter of a century didn't bode well for the effectiveness of the madness regulator. Maybe it had just stopped working altogether.

The doctor continued. "Twenty years ago, it was insane for one part of a nation to quarantine another part and leave them to die. And yet, here we are."

"So, what's the bottom line?" Jamie asked. "We cancel the trip to the CRA?"

"Not necessarily," Ashwill said. "We can take steps to protect you and the rest of the team with nanotechnology we've developed."

Dr. Zurich continued the explanation. "The CDC isn't the only organization with vials of the Pittsburgh virus. Ever since the outbreak, we've had scientists working on technology to prevent that from happening again." He held up a small device. "This is the product of that research. It's implanted just under your skin, say below your collarbone, and it monitors your body for the presence of the virus. If the virus is detected, it immediately releases an army of nanobots programmed to attack and destroy the virus as well as the host cells the virus has infected before they can fully replicate."

"I thought I was immune?"

"You won't suffer the effects of the virus, but you can carry the virus and infect others. This technology reduces the chance of that happening by destroying the virus before it can be transmitted."

"Sounds simple."

"It's not. It's taken a lot of time and money to get it right."

"And it works?"

Dr. Zurich looked to Ashwill before answering. "We've tested it extensively. With some fine-tuning, we've had a high rate of success in both animal and human trials."

"You experimented on humans? With the Pittsburgh virus?"

"The final stages of clinical trials required human subjects," Ashwill said. "It's an unpleasant reality, but we couldn't avoid it, and we can't change it now."

Jamie didn't appreciate the lecturing tone in his voice. "Let's not lose sight of the issue at hand," Ashwill said. "We can say with a high level of certainty that this device will protect you in the event you contract the virus. Are you still willing to go under those conditions?"

Jamie stiffened at Ashwill's pointed questions. Why was he pressing so hard? She had just learned that the Pittsburgh Virus was likely being weaponized, and the New World had experimented on human beings with the very same deadly virus. A girl needed time to process.

But she was determined to prove to him that she was unafraid. She smiled. "Of course I'll go."

Chapter Nineteen

Jamie shook Dr. Zurich's hand as he and President Ashwill stood to leave. "Thank you for coming, doctor, and thank you for your work. I'm putting my life in your hands," Jamie said sweetly.

She waited for the door to shut before calling for Alora. "I need a transport."

"Ma'am?"

"I'd like to go see Dr. Sidney Forrester, the geneticist who met with me at the White House. Can you set that up?"

"Yes, ma'am. You'll need a security detail to travel with you."

"Get Alexander to set it up. Also, would you ask Lieutenant Penly to give one of the medics a blood sample? Tell her I asked for it. And Alora, let's keep this between us for now."

"Yes, ma'am."

Alexander arranged for two means of transportation. One for Jamie, Alora and him, another for four soldiers he'd personally picked for the job.

"Okay, so what's up?" he said once they were on the road. "Why the field trip?"

"Tomorrow my life's gonna get hectic, and I never had a chance to follow-up with Dr. Forrester about my condition, not after I had time to think about it. I wanted to do that, talk to her, before everything gets crazy."

There was more to this visit than just what she'd told him, but with Alora in the car, Jamie couldn't say so. She had questions dancing around the edge of her consciousness, close enough to know they were there, but distant enough that she couldn't put them into words yet. Maybe talking to Dr. Forrester would help her shake away the fog.

Alora, who was sitting in the front seat by herself, tilted her head when Jamie mentioned her condition, but she didn't say anything.

Jamie addressed Alora's obvious curiosity. "I have a genetic condition, but it's not bad. I'm not going to die or anything. Actually, it kind of helps me stay healthy. Not a lot of people know about it."

"Is that why you healed so quickly after the attack at the Palace?"

The Palace. Jamie was amazed at how quickly people adapted to the language of the New World. "Yes," she answered. "It's kind of handy, but I've got some questions, and I'm hoping Dr. Forrester can answer them."

Alora smiled at her. "I hope so."

"Alora, I'm sorry about Eli."

Her gaze dropped. "Thanks, but it's not like we were a couple or anything."

"But you were hoping," Jamie said.

Alora nodded. "I liked him a lot. And I think he liked me, and I allowed myself to hope that maybe it was real."

Jamie waited a moment before saying, "I want you to come with me on the diplomatic mission to the CRA. I need people around me that I can trust. I trust you."

"I'd be honored. Thank you."

Jamie looked at Alexander sitting next to her in the second row of seats. He was grinning. He mouthed the words, "Nice job."

Dr. Forrester's office was in a complex of buildings housing several biotech and genetic research companies. Two soldiers stayed in front of the building with the transports near the entrance. Two stood guard in the hallway. Alexander and Alora waited in the outer office while Jamie talked with Dr. Forrester privately.

"I can't tell you how glad I am that you're okay," Dr. Forrester said. "When I heard about the attack, well, I feared the worst."

"Thank you, and thank you for meeting with me on such short notice."

"I must say, I'm curious as to why you wanted to meet again," Forrester said.

"You told me that my DNA has been altered so that I can't get sick and I heal quickly."

"That's right. The retrovirus changed the chromosomal DNA of the fertilized egg when you were conceived."

"Have you ever seen that before or heard of that happening to anyone else?"

"No, although I suppose it is possible. There are any number of factors that would have to coincide for it to happen, but it's not out of the realm of possibility, especially given how many people were infected. Why do you ask?"

"If I left a blood sample with you, could you analyze its DNA and tell me if this person has the same condition I do?"

Dr. Forrester leaned back in her chair, appearing to weigh her options. Finally, she said, "This is an unusual request. There are certain ethical issues involved. Where did you get this sample? Did this person give consent to having their DNA examined? You understand?"

"I do," Jamie said. "And I can't answer those questions. But I would consider it a personal favor if you would do this for me. A favor I will not soon forget." Manipulation didn't suit Jamie, but she needed answers, so she was willing to set aside her scruples for the moment. She was certain Ashwill knew more than he was saying and she couldn't afford to be in the dark, not with so much at stake.

"Look, I like you," Dr. Forrester said. "I feel like I've known you for a very long time, and in a way I have. Under normal circumstances, I would have to decline your request. But these aren't normal circumstances, are they? I'll have a look."

"Thank you. I have one other question." This was the bigger question Jamie came to get answered, but she couldn't just come out and ask it. She had to beat around the bush and see what was stirred up. "Is it possible to create a nanoparticle that could be programmed to destroy the Pittsburgh Virus in a host?"

"May I ask why you're asking?"

Jamie chose her words carefully. "There have been discussions about using nanotechnology to protect me from biological warfare. I wanted to learn more about it."

"But you can't be infected."

"No, but I can be a carrier, and those around me could be infected."

"So why talk to me? I'm a geneticist, not an epidemiologist, and I have no expertise in nanotechnology."

Good point. How much did she dare tell Dr. Forrester about what she wanted to know? That all depended on how much Jamie trusted her. Her gut said to trust the doctor, that she wasn't an Ashwill loyalist, but her head wasn't so sure.

Jamie was ready to end the interview, opting to follow her head when Dr. Forrester spoke. She talked like a woman who wanted to get something off her chest. "Six weeks ago, the day after the vote, I was contacted by a scientist who was researching the use of nanotechnology to prevent viral epidemics for the New World. I was asked to look at a specific DNA sample, yours."

"Was that Dr. Zurich?"

"Yes."

"I don't understand," Jamie said. "Why would they need to know about my genetic makeup? I thought the nanotechnology was designed to interact with the virus, not a person's DNA."

"I would assume the same thing. But Zurich said there were issues with how the nanobots could affect DNA on a cellular level. Evidently, they could handle those issues with normal genetic code, but they needed additional information about your particular DNA."

"What kind of information?"

"Everything from how it was altered to how it was able to resist an infectious agent like the Pittsburgh Virus."

"Did that make sense to you?"

"There were some holes in their explanation, but I was so excited to be able to study your DNA again after all these years that I didn't press them too hard."

Every answer generated new questions, but Jamie hadn't asked the one question she needed answering. "Dr. Forrester, is there any ethical way to conduct human trials for this kind of research?"

"It would be very hard. The primary role of human beings in clinic trails is to provide sources for data. In this case, data on how nanotechnology affects the virus in a human host. In most clinical trials involving humans, the subjects already have whatever condition is the researchers are treating; diabetes, cancer, and so on. The main ethical concerns, then, are those of beneficence and non-maleficence; doing good and preventing harm."

"But there are no cases of the Pittsburgh Virus to use in a clinical trial," Jamie said.

"That's correct. Infecting a patient with the virus in order to treat them is unethical and immoral. But you need to understand something. If this technology went to human trials, it wouldn't involve one patient or even dozens. They would need thousands to reach any reliable conclusions."

On the way back to the Pentagon, Jamie sat quietly, lost in her thoughts, while Alexander and Alora chatted away. Was it possible that Ashwill was a moral monster, experimenting on human beings? And if so, were they willing volunteers? Were the people already sick with some other terminal disease? No, that didn't make any sense, they'd need healthy patients for clear results. What person in their right mind would volunteer for something like this? A fresh wave of nausea hit her as her thoughts traced down the possibilities.

Whoever they were, they didn't volunteer. That was the only thing that made sense.

Tears welled up in Jamie's eyes. Alexander and Alora grew quiet.

"I need to tell you something," she said to both of them, "and then I need you to help me find the truth."

Chapter Twenty

Nikole was busy with last-minute details, getting ready for the announcement later in the day. The busier, the better. Jamie didn't need her paying too much attention to the fact that Alexander wasn't there. When she asked, Jamie told her that he was running an errand for her. That seemed to satisfy Nikole's curiosity.

Jamie pushed against the fatigue gripping her body. She hadn't slept well the night before. She'd gotten word that Secretary Paulson and his counterpart in the CRA had reached a tentative agreement on a meeting between Jamie and President Kaine. Anxiety surged as she heard the news. When she first proposed the trip, Jamie feared she wouldn't have the skill to pull it off. Her misgivings were so much deeper now. How could she represent a government that practiced the kind of human experimentation necessary to develop antiviral nanotechnology? Of course, she didn't know for sure how Zurich had conducted the human trials, but she had her suspicions, and Alexander was looking into it for her. What would she do if his investigation confirmed these suspicions? How could she use the technology when she now knew how it had been developed? Besides, if the CRA were planning to use the Pittsburgh Virus as a weapon, how successful would her efforts to negotiate a peace agreement be?

Today she'd be presented as Queen of the New World. It was a historic moment, to say nothing of the personal impact, and she had never been so conflicted. A public announcement that morning would be followed by a carefully crafted media interview and then a week-long national tour to introduce Raisa to the public. And all the while, Jamie would smile and show her enthusiasm for the New World.

When Jamie shared her concern about the human trials in the transport on the way home from Dr. Forrester's office, both Alora and Alexander were shocked. Alexander seemed genuinely disturbed by the thought, so much so that he volunteered to get to the bottom of it.

"How can you get information about something like that?" Jamie asked. "I would think this it's highly classified."

Alexander put on a fake New Jersey accent and said, "I know a guy." He was trying to be funny. Whenever he did that, it was either to defuse a tense situation or to keep from answering a question directly. He must have read the expression on Jamie's face because he said, more seriously this time, "I'll look into it. I do, actually, know a guy. Let me do some checking, and I'll let you know what I find. If Ashwill did this, I want to know as much as you, okay?"

That's what she needed to hear. He put his hand on the seat between them, and Jamie took it, interlocking fingers. If Alora had not been in the front seat, Jamie would have slid over, kissed him, and let him hold her. He had a way of making her feel safe, as if everything were under control, no matter what craziness was going on. And that made her love him all the more. Why had she never told him? For that matter, why had he never told her? Did he love her? He acted as if he did, but he never said it. How could he make her feel this way if he didn't love her?

Jamie squeezed his hand, and she changed her mind about what she'd do if Alora weren't in the front seat. She'd tell him how much she loved him.

The next time we're alone.

Jamie was still waiting for that moment. The night before, Alexander left as soon as they got back to the Pentagon. He didn't say how long his investigation might take, and she hadn't heard from him since.

Nikole brought in people to do hair and makeup for Jamie and had a dress custom-made for the occasion. "Classic, yet elegant," she said. "You'll look stunning, in a royal kind of way."

Stunning yet royal. Jamie wasn't sure what that meant, but it was a beautiful dress. It was a brilliant red, the same red as the highlights on the dress uniforms every soldier would be wearing.

Nikole knew fashion, and it was a good thing because she was the stage manager for this show.

The show was to take place on the steps of the old Capitol building, the place everyone was now calling the Palace. The signing ceremony would take place in the rotunda, which was now being called the Great Hall. Crews had worked around the clock for weeks to finish it in time. Jamie looked forward to seeing it in its final form.

After the signing ceremony in the Great Hall, they would move out onto the platform constructed for the occasion, and the speeches would begin. Several council members would have a chance to speak, culminating in a speech by Ashwill who would introduce Jamie as Raisa Cordova, the Council's choice to be Queen of the New World. She would give a speech, one that had been written for her, accepting the responsibilities of the first constitutionally established monarch of the nation. And then her life would forever change.

Hair and makeup were done. The dress was on. The speech was memorized. It was time to go. Lieutenants Ramirez and Penly accompanied Jamie – she still had a hard time thinking of Raven as Lieutenant Ramirez – along with Alora and her normal security detail. Still no word from Alexander. The motorcade of New World transport vehicles from the Pentagon to the Palace was the largest in which Jamie had ever been. Up to then, it was always just a couple of vehicles. Now there were a half-dozen or more, including a medical transport. That didn't do anything to calm her nerves. Despite her condition, Jamie wasn't invincible. The head of her security detail had reassured her that security personnel would be present throughout the audience looking for anything suspicious. She needn't worry.

The train of official New World vehicles zipped through parts of the city that had lost the most in the last decade. But even during the seven weeks since the vote, progress had been made in repopulating them. It was working. The neighborhoods were little rays of hope, like drooping flowers coming back to life. Closer to the

Palace, people lined the route along Independence Avenue eager to catch a glimpse of the new queen. Word had been leaked about an announcement at the signing ceremony, and people were curious. Many of them enthusiastically waved New World flags as she passed. Little girls wore plastic tiaras on their heads. The windows in the transport were clear, and when Jamie leaned forward into view and waved, the crowds responded with cheers. They didn't know her, but they loved her already.

Jamie could see the Palace ahead, gleaming white on the clear August morning. The west side lawn was already jammed with people waiting. As her motorcade neared the building, the crowds lining the road behind security barriers grew thicker. Most waved, either a greeting or a flag. Alora was giddy by the sight of all the people, the happiest Jamie had seen her since Eli's death. Her enthusiasm was infectious, and Jamie found herself unable to suppress a broad grin.

The motorcade slowed as it approached the building, and Jamie watched the people as they passed, all of them smiling and waving, except one. He was tall and thin with a bushy beard, sunglasses, and unkempt hair sticking out from under a baseball cap. He stood unmoving; his expression blank until her vehicle got closer. Then he removed his sunglasses, looking directly at Jamie.

Dad.

"Wait. Stop," she yelled to the soldier sitting in the navigation seat. "I need us to stop."

Auto navigation guided the transports, but the soldier in the pilot seat could override it if necessary. He did not. Ma'am, we can't stop here. This area is not secure."

"I need this vehicle stopped now!" Jamie twisted in her seat to look back at her dad.

"What's wrong?" Raven asked.

Everyone was looking at Jamie as her transport followed the one in front of it along the south side of the Palace, making its way around back to a secure entrance. Jamie was breathing hard and was, undoubtedly, pale. She wanted to tell Raven who she saw, but she didn't want to share that information with everyone in the vehicle. Her dad had been off the grid, hiding from Return. She realized that if he were to surface and appear to be collaborating with the New World, Return would instantly make him their very own celebrity endorsement by releasing the video they'd created. That would turn him into an enemy of the state, which wouldn't end well.

Jamie turned back around in her seat. "I'm alright. I uh . . . I thought I saw somebody." She held Raven's gaze, willing her to understand. "But it was nobody."

Inside the Palace, the Great Hall was breathtaking. The guests chattered excitedly about its transformation, and normally Jamie would have joined them in their amazement. But the image of her father filled her thoughts. As Jamie was escorted to her seat, the murmur of the crowd suddenly fell off, drawing Jamie into the moment. Everyone was looking at her. From an entrance on the other side of the hall, Council President Ashwill was also being escorted to his seat, but she was the star. No one seemed to know how to react, so they just stared. Suddenly her red dress felt like a neon sign that said, *look at me*. It was showtime.

Nikole hired style experts to coach Jamie on how to present herself in public, behavior fitting of a monarch and all that. She did her best to walk and smile just-so. A more in-depth tutorial in royal protocol would come later. But it wasn't just Jamie who would be schooled on the ways of royalty; the whole country would enroll in Monarchy 101. Public service announcements and new curriculum in schools would teach everyone what it meant to be a monarchy. This was a New World for them all.

Jamie and Ashwill arrived at their seats next to one another, at the same time. So far, the choreography was flawless. A table was set up in the Great Hall with the New World Constitution placed on it. Next to the table was a podium. In front of the table were rows of chairs facing it. Once they were seated, the ceremony began. Several people spoke about the momentous occasion, including a former senator who had served with Jamie's father and now served the New World. Everyone seemed to be saying the same thing, about how solemn and historic the moment was, although Jamie couldn't be sure because she wasn't tuned in. She didn't have a role in this part of the show, so she allowed herself to chase down other thoughts, such as why was her father here, and had Alexander found anything? She couldn't answer either one, and that unsettled her.

When the speeches ended, Jamie reengaged. The signing of the constitution was the part everyone came for anyway. Ashwill and the other eighteen council members assembled behind the table, each waiting their turn to put pen to paper. As the last council member took his sat in the chair and scribbled his name on the document, the crowd erupted in applause, and Jamie joined them. For the first time, a constitutional monarchy had been established in North America in which the queen was more than a figurehead. It was hard not to get caught up in the moment. But for Jamie, it was intensely personal. Up until that moment, her role as Queen of the New World had been contingent upon the whim of others. But no longer. The council had already signed a document naming her queen upon the ratification of the Constitution. The coronation was a ceremony with no legal significance. It was like a wedding ceremony after a couple had already gone to the Justice of the Peace and tied the knot. At that moment, standing in the Great Hall, she'd become Queen Raisa.

A wave of emotion washed over her as the applause continued. She took a tiny step, shifting her feet to a more balanced stance, and worked to control her breathing. It wouldn't look good for her to pass out just then.

The leather-bound Constitution was secured by somebody official-looking and taken under guard to wherever you would take a document like that. Jamie watched it go, and it occurred to her that she had not even glanced at it. Why hadn't she taken a moment to look it over? Not the words – she knew the words – but the document itself. It would forever change her life, and she didn't even know what the font looked like.

"Ladies and gentlemen, welcome to the New World," Ashwill said, generating another round of cheers. He was beaming. He had never looked so happy, genuinely happy. His gaze swept the room and settled on Jamie.

The signing ceremony ended as attendants ushered the VIP guests out onto the platform. Once everyone was seated, Ashwill, the Council members, and Jamie waited for their cue. It came when the New World anthem began. In a solemn procession, the eighteen Council members led the way, with Jamie and Ashwill following.

"I'm proud of you," he said as they walked side by side. "You are a woman of great courage, and you will be a great queen."

He didn't look at her when he spoke, keeping his gaze ahead, and she didn't respond. As they reached the front, Jamie took her seat in a large ornate chair. Ashwill took his. More speeches followed. Jamie plastered a look of interest on her face.

Can I go through with this? Can I lead this nation?

For the first time in a long time, she thought about the *Nutcracker*, the night her mother died.

Her father's voice echoed in her head. *"Okay. So, what are your options?"*

"I quit and let everyone down and embarrass the troupe. I go on, fail miserably, and let everyone down and embarrass the troupe."

"Or?"

"I go on and do a decent job, and everyone's happy."

"Yes. Especially you. The choice is yours, Peanut. But you need to know something – you'll get over a failure. You'll never get over quitting."

Jamie joined the applause as whoever was speaking finished, and Ashwill got up to give his speech. He began as he had closed the signing ceremony. "Ladies and gentlemen, welcome to the New World." Rousing sentiments filled Ashwill's speech, along with sweeping prose, and a grand vision for the future.

Jamie's chair sat to the right of the podium angled slightly to the left, giving her a view of the left side of the platform. Ten minutes into Ashwill's speech, a movement caught her eye. Alexander had stepped into her field of vision on the far end of the platform. Their eyes met. He looked upset, agitated even. What had he discovered? She needed to know before Ashwill finished his speech, but she couldn't very well get up without drawing attention to herself. Her eyes swept across the platform, looking for something that might provide her the opportunity. Could she find a reason to call him over? No, he was so far away. They were glued in place, unable to move. She looked back at Alexander, who was still staring at her, his lips moving. What was he saying? She shook her head almost imperceptibly, letting him know she didn't understand. He said it again, and this time she got it. "It's bad."

"Citizens of the New World, we have embarked on a historic journey, unlike anything this continent has seen before." Ashwill was nearing the end of his speech. "Our new nation is forged in the trials of the past, with a bold vision for the future, a future that you have demanded and that we all deserve. The political class has let us down. Oh, don't get me wrong, there's still a place for politicians," he said with a coy smile that drew chuckles from the crowd, "but never again can we offer our most sacred trust as a prize to those who win at any cost. Today we have replaced partisan rancor and political corruption with the honor and dignity of a constitutional monarchy. And today it is my honor, at long last, to introduce to you our queen, Her Majesty, Raisa Cordova."

The crowd erupted in cheers. Jamie looked again at Alexander, but she couldn't read his face. Maybe he was as conflicted as she was. As she approached the podium, Ashwill stepped aside and bowed his head briefly. A sign of submission to his queen. *We'll see*, she thought.

Jamie's voice boomed over the crowd as she spoke. "Citizens of the New World, I humbly accept the responsibilities that you have entrusted to me as your queen." She paused as the crowd cheered. People filled every open space as far as the eye could see — so many people. Jamie took a deep breath. The next line of her speech was loaded in her mind, ready to go, but so were the words she really wanted to say. This was her first test. Would she stick to the script, prepared for her by the council and their staff, or would she assert her authority as the head of state? By law, the president and the council answered to her. The soldiers securing the platform were under her command. But only if she embraced her authority as the Queen of the New World.

Jamie had to let Ashwill know she wasn't his puppet. She would prefer her relationship with Ashwill to have mirrored that of Queen Victoria and Lord Byron, one of trust and comradery, an older experienced statesman shepherding a young inexperienced queen. But that would never happen. Ashwill was no Lord Byron.

And so, Jamie took her first independent steps as queen. "I am not like the men and women who are seated on the platform behind me. Every one of them was elected as a governor of their state, but none of you voted for me." She could imagine Nikole frantically flipping through the speech, wondering where she was getting this. "You didn't ask me to be your queen. That's okay; I didn't vote for me either. I didn't want this job at first, I was . . . recruited. But I have come to understand the great potential of a leader who was not chosen by some and rejected by the rest. None of you voted for me, true, but none of you voted against me. Which means I am free to be the queen of every man, woman, and child in the New World."

As Jamie spoke, she scanned the crowd. It was hard to make eye contact with so many people so far away. Her eyes moved toward the front of the crowd where faces were visible. Smiles greeted her, encouraging her to continue. She was about to when a baseball cap and sunglasses on a bearded man caught her eye. She stifled a gasp. The pause became awkward. The crowd began to rustle, and she continued, trying to focus her thoughts.

"The divisions of the past nearly destroyed us." Jamie forced herself to look away. "And conflict born of that division still threatens us, as we have experienced in recent weeks. But we can live a different kind of life. We can forge a different kind of nation." Her eyes traveled back to the spot, but her father was gone. "A monarch is a unique kind of leader because the nation is his life or her life. I will protect this nation as I would protect my very own life from anyone who would do her harm. Anyone."

Chapter Twenty-One

Christmas 2075

Nate stood next to Jamie and Ben, all three wearing black. Pain touched every part of his body from the accident, but what did that matter? His wife lay in a casket, suspended over a hole in the ground. It was a clear, cold day for the funeral, nothing like the movies, where it's always raining, and everyone has black umbrellas. What a stupid thought. But that was okay. Nate allowed himself some stupid thoughts. Anything to get the image of Ella's lifeless eyes out of his mind.

The year before, there were twenty-three traffic-related deaths in D.C. Nate's attorney had told him that. Weird, since every car had an auto navigation system designed to avoid collisions. If either Nate or the other driver had been using theirs, everyone would still be alive. Nate had learned the other driver was named Gordon Wimberly. His funeral was the day before. Like Nate, Gordon Wimberly had chosen to drive his car manually, which was his right under the law. Ten years earlier, the Supreme Court upheld a driver's right to navigate his vehicle if he or she so chose. Chalk up another win for individual liberty.

Not for the first time, Nate wondered how much the two drinks he'd had that night affected him. As a senator, he afforded latitude the ordinary citizen might not get. Because the first officer on the scene recognized him, and because Nate wasn't visibly inebriated, he never checked his blood alcohol level. One of the perks of holding office in the capital, but he would always wonder.

Being a senator also meant the funeral drew a lot of mourners. The pastor led a beautiful service. Several people who knew Ella shared their memories, some of them funny, some of them poignant. People cried. Ben cried. A lot. He was ten, and he had just lost his mother, so Nate understood. But Jamie remained stoic throughout the service; eyes dry, jaw set.

The pastor was finishing and had asked everyone to stand.

"And now, to the refuge of the earth, we entrust the body of Ella Rose Corson. To the protection of God in heaven, we entrust her soul. And to ourselves, we entrust the spirit and ideals she lived by."

And it was over. Nate stepped forward and put a hand on the casket. Beside him, Jamie reached out her hand and put it on the cold metal surface next to his. She was so strong. Stronger than even she knew. She and Ben deserved better than this. One senseless, tragic moment, and their lives were changed forever. And his. How could he raise them alone? He didn't worry about Jamie so much. At fifteen, Jamie was almost grown, and she was tough. She would face her grief like an enemy to be conquered. It would not defeat her. Ben was another story. He was ten, and he needed the tenderness, and wisdom, and tough love that Ella gave him. When it came to Ben, Nate always seemed to say the wrong thing at the wrong time. He nearly always misread him. How could he possibly give Ben what he needed without Ella?

Mourners gave endless hugs and words of comfort as they filed by. When the last of them had gone, Creighton Ashwill emerged from the shade of a nearby tree and approached Nate. He paused as he got closer and Nate asked Jamie to take Ben over to their waiting car.

"It was a beautiful service," Aswhill said.

Nate didn't respond.

"Ella was a wonderful woman."

"What are you doing here, Creighton?"

"I came to pay my respects. Our differences shouldn't matter at a time like this."

"I don't know," Nate said, "Isn't this is exactly the time when we should think about the kind of people we are and the kind of legacy we will leave behind? Because that's what our differences are all about."

"Oh, I think about legacy all the time, Senator. Don't forget; I have stood where you stand now. I lost my wife, too, so I know the pain you're feeling. And let me tell you something, time does *not* heal all wounds. But you have something I don't. You have the children that your wife has given you. A legacy. Your own flesh and blood. The Pittsburgh Virus didn't just take Merissa, but also the unborn child she was carrying. My daughter. What about you, Senator? What did the virus do to your daughter?"

"Leave her out of this," Nate said. "She's as much a victim of the virus as anyone else. And this isn't about Jamie, or Ella, or even Merissa. This is about you and me. About you pressuring me to compromise what I know to be right and then turning against me when I wouldn't. Is that the kind of legacy you want to leave? You talk about corrupt politicians all the time. How are you any different?"

"I am different because what I do, I do for the country. History is my legacy, and it will never belong to the timid, Nathan. We need to take bold steps if we are going to forge a new world out of the trials of the past."

"Save your slogans for the cameras, Governor. I don't sacrifice morality on the altar of historical significance. I will never support the kind of human trials you're suggesting. I don't care what good they may produce. So, don't ask me again. As long as I am a senator, I will oppose any legislation to weaken the regulations. Now, if you will excuse me, I need to grieve for my wife."

Chapter Twenty-Two

Three-And-A-Half-Years Later - Present Day

Jamie approached her transport, with Alexander by her side and her security team surrounding her. She felt good about the speech she'd just given, even if Nikole and Ashwill might not.

Standing next to the vehicle was Commander Linch from Basic Training. "Ma'am," he said.

"Commander Linch. Shall I drop and give you twenty?"

"Ma'am, I was led to believe you were just another cadet. Had I known –"

"Relax, Commander. I'm kidding. You did your job."

The Commander relaxed his shoulders. He'd been told a week earlier, along with all the senior officers at the Pentagon, that Raisa was to be the queen. Several of them had contacted her since then, expressing their support, but this was the first time Linch had spoken to her. "It would be my honor if you would allow me to escort you back to the Pentagon," he said.

"Thank you, Commander, but Lieutenant Penly will take the navigator seat, and Ramirez and King will join me on the ride back."

"Yes, ma'am. Please know that I am at your service."

"Thank you, Commander. By the way, I'm up to fifty push-ups in a minute, so if you want me to drop and give you twenty, I can." Jamie smiled at Linch and turned toward the waiting vehicle.

Lieutenant Penly and Alora got into the front seat, while Jamie, Alexander, and Raven took the back. No senior staff. No high-ranking officers, just Jamie and the four people she depended on the most. This was her inner circle, the people she trusted more than anyone. She hadn't exactly picked them – it was more organic than that – but here they were, and she wouldn't trade them for anything.

Everyone in the transport knew about the clinical trials, so Jamie didn't hesitate to question Alexander. "It's bad. That's what you said, right?"

Alexander nodded. "Yeah. The trials lasted about a year, and there were fifteen hundred subjects tested. Over time, they infected the patients with the Pittsburgh Virus in groups of fifty. In each group, some of the patients were given the nanobots, while others were not. Then they compared survival rates. Early on, not many survived in either group. Towards the end, they were 99.5% effective in preventing the virus in the treated groups. About six hundred people in all survived the virus with the nanobots. Most of them at the end."

"How'd they pull that off? Where'd they get the people?"

"They used a research facility in Maryland that handles infectious diseases. Shortly before the trials, a firm called Cipher Technologies purchased the facility and the entire staff was relocated to other labs or fired."

Raven looked confused. "But how do you kill nine hundred people without anybody noticing?" she asked. "And what about the survivors? What's to keep them from talking?"

Alexander appeared to be uncomfortable talking about the whole incident. "Believe it or not, finding fifteen hundred people that no one would miss isn't that hard. There are still whole communities that are little more than shantytowns. Some inner cities are dead zones, filled with forgettable, powerless people. The trick is to spread it out so that no single community has too many go missing all at once."

"That still doesn't explain how to keep the survivors quiet," Raven said.

"I said they survived the virus. I didn't say they survived the trials."

Jamie gasped. "They killed them to keep them quiet?" Somehow that seemed worse than killing them in the experiment. To

188

have miraculously survived a deadly virus only to have a bullet put in your head was cruelty beyond the scope of Jamie's imagination. "How do you know this?" she asked.

"I told you. I know a guy."

Jamie began to protest, but Alexander cut her off. "That's all I can say."

"Is this Ashwill, or is the whole Council in on it?"

"I don't know."

"What are you going to do?" Alora asked.

"*We* are going to go to the CRA and do our best to make peace. And then we're going to find out who exactly did this and hold them accountable."

They rode in silence for several moments. The horror of what they'd just heard weighed heavily on Jamie. Two months ago, her biggest issue was getting her family out of town and starting life over. Now she knew an awful truth that could rip the New World government apart. Her government. How could she face this truth without destroying what they had begun? How many lives would be ruined if she didn't face it? How many if she did?

Raven broke the silence. "Hey, who was it you saw earlier on the way to the ceremony?"

"It was my father."

Jamie put her head on Alexander's chest and closed her eyes, knowing that the needs of her nation had buried the needs of her family. But why was her father there? There had to be a reason. He'd positioned himself to make sure she saw him, twice. The thought lodged in Jamie's mind like an itch she couldn't scratch.

The next several days passed quickly. Jamie's week-long tour of the nation was put on hold to prepare for the Dallas Summit. Negotiations with the CRA had moved quickly, and policy briefings and diplomacy tutorials filled every spare moment. Before the long day of meetings, Jamie had developed the habit of starting each morning with a run. Running was a chance for her to clear her head and energize her body. Her reputation as a runner with the Gamma squad was only enhanced now that she was queen. Cadets and officers alike were eager to compare their times each day to Her Majesty's time.

Once the day began in earnest, Jamie insisted that her inner circle attend the meetings with her. There was way too much information for her to absorb on her own, and she was counting on them to fill in the gaps. Of course, Secretary Paulson would be advising her, but he didn't know her – he knew diplomacy. Jamie needed a team of peers who could see through eyes like hers, young and fresh, not shaped by years of political conditioning. And so they sat through each meeting, asking questions and taking notes. Their intensity told Jamie they understood the stakes. If any of the older, more experienced professionals briefing them were bothered by the youthfulness and inexperience of Jamie and her team, they didn't show it. Jamie wondered how much respect her actions on the night of the attack had bought her.

"Negotiations on this level hinge on two things; power and relationships." A gray-haired man in a three-piece suite who used to be with the State Department was describing the art of negotiating. "The less power you have in a negotiation, the more important the relationship becomes. I hate to put it so simply, but it's important that President Kaine likes you."

"You want her to be charming," Alexander said.

"It would help."

"The fate of a continent comes down to that?" Raven asked.

"Sometimes. There's a time to press your argument, but that will mostly fall on deaf ears if he doesn't like you. Unless you've got leverage – and we don't. At least not much. The only leverage we have is the resolve of our citizens to hate the people who left us to die."

"How does that give us leverage?" Alora asked.

"It won't be easy for them to assimilate our citizens into a reconfigured United States, even if they could achieve a military victory. If the CRA were to occupy the New World, a resistance movement would make their lives hell. Their best bet was preventing the vote on the resolution. But, now that it's happened, they've got a much harder job. That's our leverage."

"Afghanistan," Jamie said.

The man in the suit nodded while the rest of the team gave her blank stares. She explained. "Larger, more powerful armies could beat Afghans on the battlefield, but they never did defeat them. Not long-term."

"Exactly," the man said, "and that's our leverage. It's not much, but it's what we've got. Still, it's all about delivery. Get argumentative, and it sounds like a threat. Build a relationship, and it's two friends trying to work things out."

"Great. Make friends with the man who tried to kill me. Twice."

"I didn't say it would be easy."

That evening Jamie found her way to the room where Lieutenant Elliot had first thrown her to the mat in Basic Training. She smiled at the memory. Most of the new class of cadets had cleared out of the training center on the first floor. There were only a few still working out when Jamie arrived. She was wearing her PT gear, so at first, no one noticed her. Two guards who insisted on escorting her everywhere she went, even in the Pentagon, stood outside the large workout room. It didn't take long, however, for the half-dozen cadets to take notice of who she was.

"Good evening," she said.

The surprised cadets offered a smattering of greetings. The problem with being a celebrity was that no one knew how to act around you. The best thing to do was not act like a celebrity.

She said, "You all are here kind of late. Don't you have an early start in the morning?"

"Yes, ma'am," one of the female cadets said, "but some of us like to get a little extra workout."

"I know the feeling. I got my butt kicked in personal combat." Empathy was good. "I could have used some extra work time. Stick with it. You'll be glad you did."

The other cadets were grinning.

"What am I missing?" Jamie said.

One of the male cadets answered. Pointing to one of the girls, he said, "She's the one who kicks everybody else's butt."

"Is that right?"

The girl nodded sheepishly.

"So why the late workout?" Jamie asked.

"This is *why* I kick everybody else's butt."

"Well, I'm glad you're here. You can do me a favor."

"Anything, ma'am."

"Show me what you've got. I'm a little out of practice, and I need a refresher."

"You want me to fight you?" The girl looked uneasy.

"Yeah. I was making real progress, but I never finished Basic, so you can help me out, teach me what you know."

The girl looked at the other cadets as if they might try to talk her out of it. When they didn't, she slowly made her way to the mat. Jamie circled, waiting for an attack. None came.

"I command you to attack me."

The girl lunged at Jamie. It was slow and predictable. Jamie struck her in the mid-section before pushing her away. That couldn't be her best effort. She motioned for her to come again.

192

Another attack was also easily defended. This time Jamie put her on the mat. "I do believe you are disobeying a direct command. I want you to attack me. I don't want you to kill me, but I'd at least like to be challenged. Take me down if you can. I won't break."

A voice echoed from the far side of the room. "She's not going to do that." It was Alexander. "And you shouldn't ask her to. She's a cadet. You're the queen."

Jamie helped the girl up off the mat. "So how am I supposed to get any better if no one will fight me? Answer me that, Lieutenant King."

"I didn't say no one will fight you, just that you shouldn't ask a cadet to."

"Oh, I see. So, do you have someone in mind for this theoretical fight?"

"Well, as far as I can tell, there are only two requirements. It must be somebody better than you, and someone who's not afraid to teach you a lesson – about personal combat, that is."

"You, I suppose?" Jamie said.

"If you insist." Alexander curtsied.

Jamie suppressed a smile, then motioned for Alexander to join her on the mat. Putting him down would be challenging but fun.

She had barely gotten herself set when he stepped forward and jabbed a fist in her gut. A soft "uhf" escaped her lips as a collective gasp came from the watching cadets. "Don't let your guard down," he said.

The pain, which wasn't nearly as bad as it could have been, sent a wave of energy through Jamie's body in a way that sitting in meetings all day never could. It reminded her that life was visceral, something she'd only recently discovered. Ever since that day in the grocery store when she was eight, Jamie had analyzed life; she hadn't lived it. It wasn't a choice as much as a reaction to the trauma. Even ballet was an intellectual exercise, not an artful expression.

Jamie smiled as the pain ignited something primal inside of her and then launched an attack at Alexander. Like him, she pulled her punches, but not entirely. There had to be an element of reward and punishment, or this would be academic, too. Sweat gathered on her skin as she took him on, using every move she'd learned. The quickness and aggressiveness of her attack seemed to catch him by surprise. For a moment, he was on the defensive. Jamie took advantage, locking her foot behind his and jabbing her elbow toward his neck. He leaned back to avoid the blow and went down hard on the mat.

The cadets signaled their approval with hoots and laughter. That would make things harder for Jamie. Alexander was a guy, fighting a girl with an audience. Even though it was a friendly fight, he had an ego to protect. Jamie could see the change in his expression. He wasn't mad, but she could guess what he was thinking. He couldn't let these cadets walk out of there talking about how the queen beat up one of her guards.

Alexander circled her and made a few moves, to no avail. She wasn't going to make it easy on him. He'd have to earn it, which he did. In a lightning-fast move, he distracted her with a swing at the side of her head. When she pulled back, he lunged low, grabbing her lead leg with both arms, his head pressed against her abdomen. Before she could react, he lifted her leg and pivoted his body using his head to pull her off balance. Then he drove her to the mat, pinning her there.

How the heck…

"Hey, gorgeous." Alexander's face was inches from hers.

A rematch was tempting, but at this point, Jamie could claim a tie. Each had taken the other down once. She could live with that. Besides, her current predicament wasn't entirely unpleasant. She closed her eyes and began tilting her head to align her lips with his when she remembered the cadets. She snapped her eyes open and looked at them. They watched wide-eyed.

Jamie patted Alexander on his chest. "Thank you for the demonstration, Lieutenant."

He got up and helped Jamie to her feet. The cadets drifted out of the room, smiling.

"Look on the bright side," Jamie said. "At least they won't be talking about how I took you down."

Alexander laughed. "Hey, I almost forgot why I came down here. Dr. Forrester wanted to let you know the results were back on the blood sample you gave her. She said you'd want to get ahold of her right away."

Chapter Twenty-Three

Five young women sat in the living room of Jamie's suite. All of them were in New World army uniforms. All of them were members of the Gamma Squad from Jamie's cadet class. All of them were newly commissioned officers. Penly was a familiar and welcome face in the group. The rest were practically strangers. Three weeks of sleeping and eating in the same room and going to the same training classes weren't enough to form lasting bonds.

Penly looked relaxed, although curious about the meeting. The other four looked nervous. None of them had treated Jamie well when she arrived a week late at Basic Training. Nothing serious, mostly attitude stuff, but still, if Jamie held a grudge, she could make their lives miserable. Lucky for them, she didn't. Even so, what she was about to tell them would be life-changing.

"Thank you all for coming. I know you didn't have a choice, but still, I appreciate it. Let me ask you a question. How many of you were recruited to be in the New World army? You didn't just sign up; you were recruited?"

All five girls raised their hands. Jamie suspected that each girl had a story like Penly's, a recruiter who took a special interest in them, found out what motivated them, and talked them into joining the army.

"I was recruited too," Jamie said. "And I think we were all chosen for the same reason."

Lieutenant Elliot spoke up. "So, this isn't about how we treated you at Basic? I mean, that's the one thing we all have in common."

"No. This is about how each of us got here and why."

"I don't get it," Penly said. "You were chosen to be the queen, so how can we all have been chosen for the same reason?"

"When I danced, there was always the lead dancer and the understudy. If the lead dancer couldn't go on, the understudy got the part."

Jamie waited as the implication sank in. "So, we're your understudies?" one of the girls, Lieutenant Ekua, said.

"Yeah, kind of, in case I didn't pan out for them. They wanted contingencies. I know that sounds crazy, but look at how similar we are. We were all born within a few months of each other. We are all physically fit, attractive, smart, emotionally-stable, strong-willed. We fit a profile, and we all ended up in the same squad at Basic. Ever wonder why there were only six of us in Gamma? A reliable source told me that six girls were being considered for this position. That's more than a coincidence."

"I have a question." This came from Lieutenant Chi. "Why are you telling us this? Assuming we're the runners-up, why tell us at all?"

"Because there's something else we all share." Jamie took a deep breath before continuing. She hadn't made them this way, but somehow, she felt responsible. "Can any of you tell me the last time you were sick?"

When the results for Penly's blood came back, Jamie had each of the girls give a blood sample that was analyzed by Dr. Forrester. All of them shared the same genetic profile. Not surprisingly, none of them could remember being sick.

Jamie told the girls about their genetic condition. Even though it wasn't exactly bad news, she felt as if she'd just told them their best friend died. After going through the same explanation that Dr. Forrester had given her, Jamie stood and walked to the window. They needed a moment to process what they had just heard. She waited. They were surprisingly quiet and much less emotional than Jamie expected. She began to think maybe her reaction to the news was an overreaction. Of course, they hadn't been abducted and suffered a life-threatening injury before finding out, so apples and oranges.

Finally, Penly spoke. "Are you sure?"

Jamie assured them she was and told them of her injury and miraculous recovery. Alora, who sat quietly outside the circle up to that point, confirmed her story. "It was miraculous," she said after describing what she'd seen.

Without a word, Lieutenant Chi stood, walked to the kitchen, and pulled a large knife out of the knife block. "Let's test this claim of yours," she said. With one swift motion, she grabbed the blade with her left hand and firmly pulled it across her palm, leaving a large bloody laceration.

The girls shrieked in protest. Jamie did not. That was exactly what needed to happen to convince them of the truth. After Chi returned to the group, her hand wrapped in a towel, Jamie fielded questions for the next couple of hours.

"How long have you known about your condition?"

"How long have you known about us?"

"How many people like us are there?"

"Can we have children?"

"Will our children be like us?"

"Exactly how long will we live?"

"Are we superheroes?"

"How did Ashwill find out about us and why the hell didn't he tell us?"

"Was he ever going to tell us?"

"What does this have to do with being queen?"

"Why are you telling us this?"

Jamie answered the questions as best she could, but some of them were still mysteries in her own mind. Some of the questions she'd never be able to answer. But there were two mysteries that she intended to uncover. *How many people are there like us,* and *how did Ashwill find out?* These were good questions that needed answers. Jamie had taken a risk in telling the other five, but they deserved to know, and she could use their help. These ladies were smart and highly motivated to get some answers.

"I'm assigning all of you to my staff," Jamie said. "Alora will work out the details, but I need you to help me get some answers. If there are six of us who fit our profile, I'm willing to bet there are more out there with this condition. We need to find them and help them."

"How are we going to find them?" Lieutenant Holloway said. She was petite with olive skin, dark hair, and dark eyes.

"Why don't you ask President Ashwill how he found out?" Ekua asked.

President Ashwill. Ekua still respected him. That made sense. After all, he was in her chain of command. Jamie weighed the risks of asking them to keep him out of the loop, and finally decided to take a chance.

"As Queen of the New World, my duty is to the people of the New World. I serve them, and you serve me. I know this is a lot to ask of you, but events are moving quickly, and you're going to have to trust me. We can't ask President Ashwill or anyone under his direct authority about this. We need to keep this information in a tight circle for now." She added, "I need to know that you are with me and that you will follow my orders."

The room was quiet for a moment. Jamie glanced at Alora, who looked worried. If they didn't trust her, this could go very badly. Ashwill was a known political figure. He'd been in the public eye for years. Jamie was new on the scene. First instincts would say go with the known and tested over the unknown and untested. They might have, but at just that moment, Chi unwrapped the towel from around her hand, revealing a bright pink line angling across her palm where the cut had been. It was nearly healed. Open mouths and tear-filled eyes told the story.

"We're with you," Lieutenant Chi said.

Jamie had never been on an airship before. She'd been on a plane, but this was different. Because of their expense, airships were used primarily by the military. But for fast, secure travel, they couldn't be beaten, according to Secretary Paulson. Three of them would be used to transport Jamie and her entourage to Dallas.

The final arrangements had been made a couple of days earlier, but Paulson was not optimistic about a favorable outcome. He was under the impression that President Kaine had agreed to the summit out of curiosity over the new young queen as much as anything else. He was certain that Kaine would not have agreed to meet if it had been Ashwill making the arrangements. If that were true, it only reinforced what the man in the three-piece suit had said; personality and relationships mattered.

Don't forget to be charming.

The airship was not large compared to some airplanes, but it was big enough for Jamie and her team to move around. With her was Secretary Paulson, who looked as if he had aged significantly in the last week. Besides, Alexander, Lieutenants Ramirez, and Penly and several other security officers went along. The other airships carried staff from the secretary's office, more security forces, a doctor, and a couple of spare pilots. Alora stayed behind to get the four other girls set up. Jamie didn't want Nikole asking too many questions about why she had added them to her staff. They had come up with a plausible cover story, but she needed Alora to manage it. Before leaving, Jamie had named Alora as her personal secretary. In an American administration, she would have been called her chief of staff.

An hour into the two-hour flight, Jamie ended her conversation with Paulson reviewing the goals of the trip and settled into a seat next to Alexander. The time for prepping was over; she needed to relax. Her dad had participated in a couple of debates for his Congressional and Senate seats. They weren't on the same level as a presidential debate, but they could be nerve-wracking anyway. He would always say at some point, "If I'm not ready now, I never will be," and he'd go watch a baseball game or take a nap, anything to unwind. That was the right move, Jamie decided, now that she was feeling the pressure. She leaned her head on Alexander's shoulder and listened to the low hum of the engines at work. She slipped her hand under his jacket and ran it along his chest. She could feel the small lump of the device that had been implanted under his skin. The device that would protect them from the virus, should they be exposed. The device that cost fifteen hundred people their lives.

Each of them had one of those devices, including Jamie. Ashwill argued that even with her unique genetic condition, they didn't want to take any chances with her. Besides, he said, if she were the only person without one, her team would begin to wonder why.

The device was barely visible under bare skin. A small lump and a faint blinking light were the only evidence of its presence. The light, which showed through the skin, blinked green until the device was activated and virus-fighting nanobots were released. At that point, it would blink red. Most shirts or blouses would conceal their presence altogether. If everything went according to plan, they'd never be seen or needed.

It seemed like no time before Alexander was trying to get her up. "Wake up, sleepyhead," he said.

Jamie opened her eyes, her head still resting on his shoulder. An image of her father standing in the crowd at the signing ceremony faded as she emerged from a dream. Again, she wondered, why had he been there?

"We're about a half-hour out. Time to get your game face on," Alexander said.

Paulson had worked out the protocol for their arrival with his counterpart in the CRA and briefed the group before they left.

"Apparently, they think the New World is a petri dish of viral infections," he said. "They are insisting on a biocontainment protocol when we arrive. It's not as bad as it sounds, but it is highly insulting." He turned to Jamie. "I apologize for not being able to get this demand dropped, but since we're the ones who insisted on the meeting, I didn't have a lot of room to negotiate."

"That's the least of my worries, Mister Secretary. Tell us what can we expect."

"I'm embarrassed to say that when we land, a biohazard team will meet us at the airfield. They'll escort us to a facility at the landing site where they'll draw blood and check our vital signs. Once they confirm that we are virus-free, everything changes, and we'll get the royal treatment, pun intended."

Everything went as Paulson had described. A professional and polite team of scientists met them wearing protective gear. They were escorted to a specially constructed room in a hangar at the base where they had landed. The makeshift lab was no more than an area in the hangar which had been cordoned off with heavy, clear plastic sheets that acted as its walls. Through the clear walls, medical equipment was visible. It was large enough for all of them to enter, and they were invited to do so. Once inside, someone quickly drew their blood and labeled it before taking it to a piece of equipment for analysis. Jamie and Alexander talked about the danger of letting the CRA take a sample of Jamie's blood, but they couldn't think of any way around it without raising suspicion. It was unlikely that anyone would think to analyze her DNA.

Comfortable seats, arranged throughout the makeshift lab, were offered to them after their blood was drawn and vitals were taken. As the samples were tested, the staff offered Jamie and the others something to eat or drink. A table had been set up with fresh fruit, finger foods, and various beverages. Jamie declined, but some of the rest of the team took them up on their offer. Every detail seemed to indicate the utmost care had been taken to make them feel welcome.

It didn't take long for the scientists to get the results from the blood tests. Once all the tests were completed, they conferred for a moment and then began removing their protective gear. One of the scientists, a lady probably in her fifties, approached Jamie with a broad smile and an outstretched hand. She was tall and big-boned, with the initial hints of gray in her hair.

"Your Majesty, I am so sorry for the inconvenience, but everything checks out, just as we knew it would. It is an honor to meet you. I am Dr. Wallace, the chief scientist for the Department of Infectious Diseases."

"Thank you," Jamie said. "I appreciate the care you've taken with me and my team."

Outside the makeshift lab, an official-looking man had arrived with several subordinates. It wasn't always clear what made someone look official, but whatever it was, this man had it. Dr. Wallace guided Jamie out of the lab to meet the man who was waiting for her.

"Your Majesty, welcome to the Constitutional Republic of America. I am Christopher Woodhouse, Deputy Secretary of State. It is my pleasure to escort you to your hotel and help you prepare for an official welcome from President Kaine."

At the hotel, the entire floor of penthouse suites had been cleared for Jamie and her team to use, as well as the floor below it for security purposes. Arriving at the hotel was like arriving at a fortress. The drive from the airbase gave Jamie a good view of the flat, wide-open topography of Texas. The sky really did look bigger there. The people also seemed to be better off there than they were in the New World. Or maybe it was that the people in Dallas were better off than the people in Washington, but it was probably true across the country. These people hadn't experienced the devastation a viral epidemic could unleash on society. And apparently, they were patriotic; every street displayed the CRA flag. *For real or a show*, Jamie wondered.

Arriving at the hotel, Jamie had two hours to get ready for the official welcome from President Kaine. Thank goodness for the wardrobe attendants. Picking an outfit and getting it on would have been nearly impossible without some help. Jamie emerged from her suite's bedroom wearing an elegant white off-the-shoulder gown. Off the shoulders, but not so far off that her implant was visible. Members of the entourage waiting in her suite voiced their approval, but Jamie only cared about one opinion. Alexander smiled. He didn't need to say anything; it was written all over his face.

Twenty minutes later, Jamie was helped out of the car by Alexander, who looked dashing in his dress uniform, in front of an impressive mansion – the White House of the West. Pictures didn't do it justice. According to Paulson, plans for the building were conceived when the government moved temporarily to Dallas. It was built with private money by a consortium of rich Texans who wanted to preserve Texas identity, as the union began to fall apart. When the dust settled, and it was evident that Texas would be the heart and soul of the CRA, it was given to the government as the official residence for the President. It looked a lot like a cross between the White House and a Texas ranch house.

Waiting for her outside the car was a short, fit man with close-cropped gray hair and intense blue eyes. He wore a traditional black tuxedo. His skin was tanned but not leathery. He had an air of vibrancy about him, youthful energy, even though he was well into his forties.

"Your Majesty." He approached with both hands extended in greeting. "I would say at long last, but with our two countries being only about two months old, it just didn't seem to fit. Even so, it feels as if this day has been long in coming. Welcome to the Constitutional Republic of America."

"Thank you, President Kaine. It is a great honor to be here as your guest. I speak for everyone in the New World when I say that we are optimistic about our future as neighbors sharing the continent."

"Yes, of course, but let's leave the diplomacy for tomorrow. Tonight is about getting to know one another, and maybe even enjoying ourselves."

Kaine turned toward a bank of photographers smiling broadly and guided Jamie to do the same. As he had said, the first night was not about diplomacy. They would enjoy a state dinner, giving her time to be charming. It also gave Kaine a media event to show the world how welcoming he was. Too cynical? Maybe? Time would tell. He put her arm in his and led her up the short flight of stairs. Alexander and the rest of her entourage trailed behind.

Chapter Twenty-Four

The state dinner was a big success according to the only gauge that mattered – Jamie's relationship to President Kaine. As it turned out, being charming wasn't hard to do, because Kaine was so personable. He was a genuinely nice man. As a bonus, he was a student of history. What could be more fun than arguing history with someone who knew something about the past? Their common interest created an instant rapport. Not so much that they both liked to talk about history, but they liked to argue about it. Formality soon gave way to familiarity. In no time, she was Raisa. He was Thomas.

Alexander didn't seem to be enjoying the evening nearly as much from across the table. Jamie was seated next to Kaine, with Secretary Paulson next to her on the other side, and then his counterpart in the CRA along with his wife. Alexander wound up several seats away on the other side of the large round table. Jamie had no idea who was on either side of him, but he wasn't going out of his way to talk to them. He seemed more interested in watching her and Kaine. If Jamie laughed at something Kaine said, Alexander's expression would change. Was he jealous? Of President Kaine? If so, that was ridiculous. Kaine wasn't married; his wife had died ten years earlier. But he was old enough to be Jamie's dad.

On the ride back to the hotel, Secretary Paulson was oblivious to the tension between Jamie and Alexander. His take on the evening was about as optimistic as he got. "That was a good start," he said, "better than I expected, but the real work starts tomorrow."

It was not exactly a pep talk, but considering the source, Jamie took it as a word of encouragement.

"You haven't said two words since the dinner," Jamie said to Alexander once they were alone in her suite.

"It's been a long day."

Fine, don't talk about it.

"It has been a long day, and I have another long day tomorrow, so I need to get some sleep. I'll see you in the morning."

Alexander moved as if to leave, but then suddenly he turned to her. "You were flirting," he said.

"I was charming, as instructed."

"But you were enjoying it."

"Yes, I enjoyed it. We hit it off. Isn't that what I was supposed to do, make him like me?"

"I just didn't expect you to be so good at it."

"It was a state dinner, Alexander, not a date. We were both putting our best foot forward, trying to build some a connection so that we can avoid a war. It's not like you to be jealous."

"I'm not jealous. Okay, maybe a little, but more than that, I'm worried. I don't want you to get hurt. Kaine was very disarming tonight, but that could be a tactic to get you to let your guard down, to take advantage of you in the negotiations. You're trying to prevent a war. Are you sure that's his objective?"

Jamie realized he'd made a good point. If she were trying to get Kaine to like her so that she'd have an advantage in the negotiations, wouldn't he be doing the same? Could somebody who tried to kill her twice be that nice? Jamie, who had changed into sweats and a t-shirt, plopped down next to Alexander on the couch. His head was back, and his eyes were closed. It was his way of dealing with stress. She took his hand in hers and lifted it to her lips, kissing his palm. His eyes didn't open, but a faint smile crossed his lips.

"This is exactly why I brought you," she said. "I need to know how this all looks to you."

"It's not just me. Penly and Ramirez agree."

"That Kaine might be trying to manipulate me?" she asked.

"Yeah, and that you were being flirty."

• • • • •

The following morning, Jamie prepared for her first session with President Kaine. She wore a suit that said, "I'm all business," rather than an outfit that said, "I'm window dressing." If she were going to be more than a figurehead, she had to act and dress like it.

The meeting was scheduled to be forty-five minutes long and would take place at the executive mansion where they had been the night before. Paulson explained that the first meeting would be short to prevent Jamie from getting in over her head. They would discuss a few preliminary issues, and then it would be over. She would then debrief with her team, and they'd help her craft responses based on what they had said. A second, longer meeting would follow after lunch. Nice and slow.

When Jamie arrived, she was greeted by Kaine's chief of staff and escorted to a room that appeared to be designed for one-on-one negotiations. It was a comfortable size, but not large. A few people meeting together wouldn't feel swallowed up by it. It was definitely a workspace, though. A desk made of a reddish wood sat on one end. It was beautiful and looked as if it had been handcrafted. Behind it sat a leather chair. Across from the desk on the other side of the room was a sitting area. Two wingback chairs angled toward the desk with a round table between them. A portrait of Abraham Lincoln hung on the wall above them. Was that on purpose? After all, Lincoln had committed the country to war to preserve the Union. Was Kaine giving Jamie a subtle hint about his intentions? Below the painting, a large area rug covered the wooden floor. On the table was a pitcher of water and two crystal glasses.

Jamie sat in one of the chairs and waited. It wasn't long but long enough to feel she'd been kept waiting. When President Kaine entered, he walked over to her confidently, a steward in tow. He wore a dark gray pinstripe suit that matched his hair.

Jamie stood.

"Your Majesty, it is good to see you again. I'm sorry I kept you waiting. Can I get you anything before we start?" He motioned to the steward with him.

"No, thank you."

Forty-five minutes. Nice and slow.

Kaine dismissed the man and sat down, unbuttoning his coat. "I like this," he said without any preamble. "Two leaders sitting down to talk, one on one. No advisors. No lawyers. They're useful, don't get me wrong, but they don't bear the responsibility for leadership as we do. The decisions we make can be the difference between life and death. It's a very exclusive club."

This was not at all how Jamie envisioned the meeting would begin. There was no small talk or warming up to the issues. Nothing that she had prepped for.

"You're familiar with the Cuban missile crisis?" he asked.

"I am."

"I imagine that the whole mess could have been avoided if Kennedy and Khrushchev had sat down face to face. I hope that our meeting will help to prevent a similar crisis. I don't want a war."

Nice and slow was not happening. Jamie looked at President Kaine, searching for any sign of guile, but found none. It was time to decide if she could trust him or not. "If you don't want a war, why did you attack us?"

Kaine looked genuinely surprised. "That was retaliation," he said, "for the biological attack at the border. We targeted the naval station because it was the closest military installation. We assumed that the New World would stage a military attack from there once the border had been compromised from the virus."

Jamie could feel her cheeks flush red. She knew nothing about a biological attack at the border. Had Ashwill instigated an attack against the CRA using the virus, and kept her in the dark? And if the New World had released the virus across the border, how had CRA contained it? Why wasn't there an epidemic running amok? She couldn't ask Kaine because that would expose the fact that this was news to her.

Instead, she tried to distract him. "You've made some pretty strong statements opposing the New World and vowing to preserve the Union. They could be interpreted as a threat of war."

"I suppose they could," Kaine said. "What's happened to this country breaks my heart. We were the greatest nation in the world, and we let it slip through our fingers. I would do just about anything to get it back if I thought we could. But I'm a realist, Your Majesty. A war would only destroy what's left of America. I made some threatening statements, but they were before the vote, a last-ditch effort to keep it from happening because I knew that once the Senate voted, we would never undo it. My goal now is to preserve what America was, in the CRA. I can't do that if we're at war with the New World."

"And targeting the White House? That wasn't a military installation." Butterflies filled Jamie's stomach. She hadn't planned on confronting him so directly about the attack.

"That was directed at Creighton Ashwill. We've had intel for a while suggesting he was planning an attack. When it happened, we felt justified in targeting him."

"He wasn't living in the White House," Jamie said. "I was."

He bowed his head as he spoke. "I know. I found out after the fact. I'm glad you weren't in residence that night. Truly. But I need you to tell me something, Raisa." He sat on the edge of his chair and looked directly at her. "Did you know about the biological attack at the border?"

Jamie hadn't hidden her surprise as well as she thought she had. "I did not. This is the first I've heard of it."

"I didn't think so. That's why I agreed to meet with you. If there is going to be peace between the New World and the CRA, you and I will have to broker it. But you've got to understand that Ashwill may not be on board with it. He's a powerful man; this will put you in a vulnerable position."

Any plan Jamie had for this conversation had become obsolete. It was time to trust her gut. "With all due respect, Mr. President, I haven't agreed to anything yet."

"I understand. This is probably a bit overwhelming. It's easy to forget you're only eighteen." He leaned back in his chair, assuming a more relaxed posture.

"Why did you attack me at the Palace? Pardon me, the Capitol Building."

"We didn't. We heard about it, but that wasn't us. Probably Return."

"Aren't you supporting Return?"

"We are, but only as a contingency, and to get intel from them. We aren't providing that much support. Only enough for them to keep the communication channels open. We had nothing to do with that attack."

There should be something more to ask, something more to press him on, but there wasn't. Either everything Ashwill had said about him was misleading, or President Kaine was lying through his teeth. One of them was playing her and Jamie had a good idea which one.

"One more question." Jamie pointed to the portrait of Lincoln and tilted her head as if you say, *What's up with the portrait?*

"It's a reminder to both of us of how costly the last war was on this continent."

More searching. Still no sign of deception.

Kaine continued. "Normally these kinds of talks take a lot of time to develop," he said. "Diplomacy is all about dancing around the issue until you get what you want without giving too much away. But I think we can both get what we want. Let's make history by putting together a treaty that will preserve what's left of America in your nation and mine."

This was too easy. But why shouldn't it be? If two people were pursuing the same goal, why should it be hard?

"There's still a lot for us to put out on the table," Kaine continued, "but let's not waste time with needless meetings. Let's get our teams together and hammer something out. It's time for action."

"I don't know about your team," Jamie said, "but if I go back to my guys and say we're ready to put a treaty together, they may have a collective heart attack." She stood and extended her hand to Kaine. "But I'm willing to take that risk."

Chapter Twenty-Five

Jamie wore a Dallas Cowboys baseball cap, sunglasses, a baggy t-shirt, and jeans. Alexander dressed in an equally nondescript way. He instructed her security detail and the rest of the team not to disturb her in her suite for the next several hours. If they needed anything, they could contact him, via his com.

"Oh, that's great," she said. "You know what everybody's gonna think!"

"It can't be helped. If you want to do this, the two of us have to be out of commission for a while. There's no other way."

After returning from her meeting with Kaine, Jamie spent hours with her team going over the details of her conversation. She left one detail out, the revelation about the biological attack. That wasn't something that could have happened without Paulson's knowledge and consent, and she wasn't ready to let him know that she knew.

"Why'd they attack us if all they want is peace?" Raven asked.

That was a natural question to ask, and Jamie was ready with an answer. "They said they felt threatened. It was preemptive." Judging by the looks she got, no one was satisfied with that answer.

"That doesn't make any sense," Raven said.

"It will have to do for now," Jamie said with a look that said, *drop it.*

When the briefing was over, and Paulson left with his staff, Jamie closed the door and turned to her inner circle. "Ashwill used the virus in a biological attack across the border. That's why they attacked. It was defensive."

Alexander hung his head. "How's it possible that he's stooped even lower than we knew?" He looked up at Jamie. "We've got to make this work, or we are all screwed."

After the debriefing, Jamie's team arranged with Kaine's group to meet the next morning at ten and begin crafting a treaty. Both she and Kaine would attend. She had instructed Paulson and the rest of his team to put something together that could serve as a starting point for them. She'd review it later that evening. At the moment, she wanted to take advantage of being so close to one of the most tragic scenes in American history.

Alexander guided her out the front of the hotel and onto the street. Downtown Dallas was busy as people hurried past them. Several of the men wore cowboy hats, just like Raven thought. Jamie smiled. They walked west on Commerce for a couple of blocks, and then cut over to Main Street and continued west for several more blocks until they came to Dealey Plaza, the spot where President Kennedy had been killed nearly one hundred, fifteen years earlier. Jamie stopped when the Plaza came into view. She had come alone with Alexander because she didn't want a VIP tour where she was the center of attention. She wanted to see this historic place like everyone else.

The rest of the city had changed in the century since then, but not the Plaza. It was a scene she knew well. She sucked in a sharp breath at the sight and fought back tears. Jamie had been to Ford's Theater in D.C. more than once, but somehow this was different.

"You alright?" Alexander asked.

"Yeah, sorry." She wiped a tear from her cheek. "I don't know what's wrong with me. I think I've read every book on John Kennedy and his assassination. But seeing it in person is just a little overwhelming."

As they neared the site, Jamie looked up at the sixth-floor window in the corner of the red brick building that bordered the plaza. She imagined the barrel of the rifle of the assassin extended through the open window. They walked down the sloping street to the grassy knoll and stopped at the spot where Kennedy had died. She could see the grainy images of the Zapruder film and hear the faint shots. Bang, bang. His head snapping back. Jamie's throat tightened, and her heart began to race. The sound of traffic and pedestrians faded. Bang, bang. *She* was in the limo. Bang, bang. *Her* head was snapping back. She couldn't breathe. Jamie reached out and grabbed Alexander to steady herself. Her knees wouldn't hold her up, and she lowered herself to the ground, sitting in the grass.

"What's wrong?" Alexander asked, leaning over her. "Jamie?"

Tears began to flow down her cheeks, and she openly sobbed. Alexander sat next to her, putting his arm around her. He had enough good sense to say nothing. He just held her.

After the sobs stopped, Jamie said, "Thank you." She took a deep breath.

"Was this not a good idea?" Alexander asked.

"I keep forgetting I'm not just a teenager anymore. It's like I've been playing a part, but it's not me. Like I can step in and out of being the queen any time I want. Coming here, thinking about President Kennedy, I realize that I can't do that any more than he could. This is who I am. And these are the kinds of threats that I'll live with for the rest of my life. I guess kids that grow up in a royal family figure that out early." She stood, brushing the grass off her jeans. "It's time for me to stop sneaking out and take responsibility for who I am. It probably wasn't a good idea to come here alone. I'm surprised you agreed to it. You should call for secure transportation back to the hotel."

Alexander smiled as if he had a secret. He spoke into his comm and security materialized around them as if out of thin air. "Glad you won't be sneaking out anymore. This is a lot harder to arrange."

That night Jamie reviewed the treaty stipulations Paulson and his team had developed. It included what the New World was willing to stipulate, as well as what they would require of the CRA. It was written in broad terms and included six major stipulations. First, the CRA would officially recognize the sovereignty of the New World and its borders as defined in the document. The New World would reciprocate. Second, The CRA would not cross the border of the New World without consent. Again, the New World would reciprocate. Third, they would each respect the other's right to international commerce. This included unrestricted shipping lanes.

The fourth condition, that the CRA would pay reparations for the attack at the border and on the White House, made no sense. Why would Paulson include this if the New World initiated hostilities with a biological attack? It would only put the issue on the table.

"Maybe he felt he had to," Alexander said as he reviewed the document with Jamie.

"What do you mean?"

"Well, if there were no biological attack, he'd be expected to include something like this because the CRA attack was unprovoked. So if he doesn't include it, that's him admitting to the attack right up front."

"But if they challenge it, he'll have to admit to it, or lie about it," Jamie said,

Alexander shrugged. "Not necessarily. He could offer to drop the stipulation, without admitting to anything. It would be a concession that wouldn't cost him anything."

"Hmm. You're good at this."

The fifth stipulation dealt with the navigation of the Mississippi River, which served as a natural border, and the last one dealt with travel between the two countries.

Jamie read the document carefully several times, mulling over each stipulation, and determining her position on each of them. She supported all of them in principle except one; number four, the payment of reparations, had to go. But that meant confronting Paulson about the biological attack. That was no problem if he could be trusted, but Jamie had no idea where his loyalties lay. Instead, she would move that particular stipulation to the bottom of the list, pushing it to the end of the negotiations, which would buy her some time to figure out how to deal with it.

The morning was clear and warm as Jamie went for an early jog around downtown Dallas. She had a full security detail with her this time. She wasn't recognized as a public figure yet outside the New World, and it was early enough that her security team didn't object to the outing. This would be, without a doubt, the most important day in her young life. She needed to have a clear head, and nothing did that for her like running.

Half a mile from the hotel was a large sculpture commemorating nineteenth-century cattle drives in Texas. Raven, who was the most excited about being in Texas, suggested making that a stop on their run. The site was so stunning that Jamie stopped to take it in when they arrived. Forty-nine larger-than-life bronze steers and three trail riders made up the work of art on about four acres of land. A manmade limestone ridge and stream created a dramatic wilderness effect. Despite all the monuments and statues in D.C., Jamie had never seen anything like this. This was one part of history that she hadn't studied much. She made a mental note to read up on cattle drives of the old west when she got home.

"Pretty awesome, isn't it?" Raven said.

"Yeah. Pretty awesome." Forty-nine steer and only three cowboys. Those steer could go anywhere they wanted if they had the mind to, and the cowboys couldn't do a thing about it. But they didn't. The steer went where the cowboys guided them. Not in a straight line of course, but the cowboys got them where they were going. That was the power of leadership, Jamie thought, the power to influence others, to guide them to a specific destination. But Jamie couldn't figure out if she was the cowboy or the steer. Ever since Kaine's revelation about the biological attack against the CRA, something felt off to Jamie. Why would Ashwill offer so little resistance to this trip, knowing that she'd find out about the attack? Jamie couldn't shake the feeling she was being manipulated, herded to follow a certain path. But where did the path lead? That she did not know.

Having arrived at the executive mansion for the third day in a row, Jamie was getting comfortable with the surroundings. This time she and her entire team were escorted to a large conference room. One wall was composed of glass French doors that looked out on a courtyard. Jamie and the principal players on her team were seated on the side of the table that gave them a view of the courtyard. The rest of her team sat in chairs against the wall behind them. Shortly after they were seated, President Kaine's team filed in and took their seats. And, finally, President Kaine himself arrived.

"Good morning," he said. He wore a dark blue suit and stood behind his chair as he addressed the group. "And welcome. I realize, as does Her Majesty Queen Raisa that we are proceeding at an unprecedented pace in these treaty negotiations. But these are extraordinary times. It is my hope ... No – it's my belief that we will forge a relationship between our two nations today that will not only bring stability to North America but will set the standard for international relations on the continent, for generations to come. History will judge us for what we do here today. Let's make sure she smiles on us."

As Kaine sat down, Jamie said, "Thank you, President Kaine. The New World looks forward to a peaceful and prosperous relationship with the Constitutional Republic of America."

Everyone at the table had a document in front of them that listed in parallel columns the stipulations sought by each side. The document was designed to compare and contrast those stipulations. Thankfully, there was a lot of agreement, and only a few differences. One of the most glaring differences was the reparations sought for the attack on the New World. Jamie feared that she had made a strategic error in not confronting Paulson about this before the meeting.

"Why don't we get to work," Kaine said. He shuffled the document in front of him. "If no one objects, I'd like to start with the points of agreement, and I am pleased to say there are many. The most important, the foundation for these talks, is the stipulation that each party must recognize the right of the other to exist as a sovereign nation." He put the document down and looked directly at Jamie and her team. "I can say without equivocation that the Constitutional Republic of America is willing to recognize the New World as a sovereign state with the right to exist and defend itself." He smiled at Jamie. "We welcome you as our neighbor."

Jamie thought she heard a low grunt from Secretary Paulson next to her. If so, it was low enough to be meant only for Jamie to hear. She ignored him.

"Thank you, Mr. President. And, of course, we reciprocate," Jamie said, using the language Paulson had suggested. "We are pleased to recognize the sovereignty of the CRA."

A team made up of members from both delegations would hammer out the language and draft the final document, but the real work was being done right there, right then. Jamie couldn't keep a smile from finding its way to her lips. It wasn't just that this treaty would lay the foundation for a peaceful relationship with the CRA, but she had been able to form a personal alliance with President Kaine.

She was about to say something about establishing embassies in their respective capitals when Secretary Paulson interjected. "Forgive me, Mr. President, but can we so easily agree on this point when there has been such a recent attack that we have yet to address? Reparations would be a tangible indicator that you are serious about respecting our sovereignty."

Before Jamie could speak, Paulson's counterpart from the CRA responded. "Reparations are only appropriate when one party has wronged another party, unprovoked. We were not unprovoked. Our actions were in response to a biological attack perpetrated by the New World. We were acting in self-defense."

"How many people died in that attack?" Paulson asked.

Jamie looked sharply at him. Was he admitting to it?

"I'm sorry?" Kaine said.

"How many people died? Not fifty-eight million, I assume. Isn't it true that you were very successful in containing it."

Jamie was suddenly off-balance. What was Paulson doing? Had Ashwill sent him to sabotage the talks? She felt that she had to jump into the conversation. "I think what Secretary Paulson is saying–"

Paulson cut her off. "*What I'm saying* is that is it hypocritical for you to act as if our actions were unprovoked. When the Pittsburgh Virus first began to spread, your states effectively sealed us off from the rest of the country and left us to die."

"That was nearly twenty years ago," Kaine said. "We're here to start a new chapter in our relationship."

Paulson raised his voice. "Not until you admit that what you did was wrong."

"That's enough, Mr. Secretary," Jamie said.

A stunned silence hung over the room.

Jamie looked down at the document in front of her, searching for a way to redirect the conversation. In her lower peripheral vision, she caught sight of a blinking red light under her blouse. At first, she didn't realize what it was. But then it dawned on her. It was the warning light from her implant.

Chapter Twenty-Six

A blinking red light could mean only one thing – Jamie had been exposed to the virus. But she refused to concede that Ashwill had been right about Kaine. It made no sense that he would try to infect them with the virus. If he had, everyone in the room would be infected, including Kaine himself.

"Would you excuse me for just a moment?" she said.

"Of course," President Kaine said. "Let's take a fifteen-minute break."

He undoubtedly thought that Jamie needed a break to work through the reparations issue with Paulson. She stood and motioned for her team to follow her. Once they'd stepped out of the room into an adjacent hallway, she said to Alexander, "Did your implant activate?"

He pulled back his collar to check. Shaking his head, he said, "It's green. Did yours'?"

"I think so, but that doesn't make any sense."

She had everyone from her team check their implants — all green.

"We need to get you out of here," Alexander said.

"No, wait. Maybe it malfunctioned. It's not unheard of for people to get a false positive when being tested for the virus. Maybe it misread something in my blood. These talks are too important to walk away from because of a technology glitch."

Jamie checked her implant again and saw that it was now blinking green. She tapped the lump under her skin with her finger, but it remained green. "There you go," she said as if that explained everything.

Alexander looked less than convinced, but he didn't verbalize any objection he might have had.

"What do you think Paulson's up to?" Jamie asked.

"Like I said, anyone over thirty is going to have a hard time forgiving and forgetting. I suggest you and Kaine have a little sidebar and talk it through before we start up again. My guess is that he will have a compromise that will satisfy both sides enough to move on."

Jamie took Alexander's advice and sought out Kaine as she entered the room. They stepped away from the others for a private conversation. "I apologize for Secretary Paulson's comments," she said. "We still have some issues to work out, as you can see."

Kaine waved off her apology. "He's right, you know. So many of us were afraid, and we let that fear control us. Your people died when we could have helped. We were wrong, and there's no way around that."

His admission warmed Jamie, but she wasn't surprised by his transparency. Her admiration for the man was growing. "I appreciate you saying that, Thomas. But you can't say that at the table, can you?"

"No. In a different context, it might do some good, maybe even start the healing process, but not here. If someone like Paulson hears that, he'll use it to gain a political advantage."

Jamie was pleased that he didn't think of her as someone like Paulson.

"Here's what we can do," he said, "the CRA can *invest* in the New World. Reparations are out of the question, but Paulson has a point. This isn't about what happened twenty days ago, it's about what happened twenty years ago, and we share some responsibility for that. We had a part in your past. Let us invest in your future."

"Do you think that will work?" Jamie asked.

"I do if you suggest it."

They moved back to their respective seats. Everyone else took their cue and did the same.

Once everybody had settled in, Jamie took the lead. "President Kaine, members of the delegation, there is much that has divided us in the past. If we choose to, we can enumerate those divisions and drag them from the past to the present. But I believe there is more that unites us than divides us if we look to the future." Jamie went on to lay out the proposal suggested by Kaine. After an hour of discussion, they agreed to the plan. The CRA would invest in the New World without ever raising the issue of who was ultimately to blame for the recent attacks. Paulson did not object.

The rest of the day flew by as stipulations were discussed and agreements reached. The longer they worked, the more at ease Jamie felt, as if an impending danger were disappearing over the horizon. The treaty was good for her country, but it also gave her leverage with Ashwill, and she planned to use it. No longer was she just the girl he'd picked to be queen. Now she had something of her own to claim, a diplomatic victory that averted a war. She could not have scripted a better outcome. If only her dad could have been here to see it.

The thought of her father brought a pang of guilt. The life she had chosen to embrace didn't include her father. She thought back to his bearded face in the crowd, listening to her. Was he proud of her then? Would he forgive her for choosing her country over her family? It was what he had done, and she wasn't sure that he had forgiven himself for that.

Leaving the executive mansion, Jamie appeared before photographers standing next to President Kaine.

"Smile," he said quietly, "You've earned it."

She did.

• • • • •

The motorcade that would take them to their airship had been summoned and was waiting. President Kaine kindly offered to escort Jamie and her team. He rode with her, and the rest of the team filled the remaining transports.

"Now's when the real work begins," he said. "Creighton Ashwill is a brilliant man, but I don't think he ever got over the death of his wife and daughter. You're going to have to press this with him.

Legally, he may not hold the authority you do, but he has an awful lot of political weight to throw around."

"You knew him before his wife died?"

"Yes, I was just out of college looking for a job in Washington. He was a freshman congressman who was hiring, and I ended up in his office. I was with him for three years before the outbreak. I was out of town when . . . I never went back."

"Maybe we can arrange for you to visit the New World soon." Jamie thought for a minute, and then added, "I'm inviting you right now to my coronation."

Kaine smiled at that and then coughed, wiping his mouth with a handkerchief from his coat pocket. "I would like that very much, but I'm not sure Creighton would be as pleased to see me as you would. Early on, when we first learned about the epidemic, he wanted me to find a way to get his wife out. As I said, I was away when it happened. The border between infected and uninfected states began to form, and crossing it became more difficult. He asked me to do whatever was necessary to get her out, bribe someone, whatever. I tried, but I couldn't make it happen. Then his wife got sick, and he lost her and the baby. He blames me as he blames everyone who turned a blind eye to what was happening. After that, I think he pinned all his hopes on his stepson. At least that's what I hear from some of our mutual friends."

"Stepson?" Jamie asked. "He never mentioned a stepson."

"His wife was a single mom with a young boy, maybe two when they got married."

"Whatever happened to him?"

"I don't know. He was about three the last time I saw him. That was just before the outbreak. I've lost track. Creighton and I haven't talked about anything but politics in years, and only when necessary."

Kaine tried to clear his throat, coughing into his handkerchief. He grabbed a bottle of water from the stash in the transport and downed half of it. "All the talking we've done today is getting to me." He coughed again.

As they entered the airbase, the three New World airships gleamed in the bright Texas sun, pilots standing ready next to each one. The sight of them with their blue and red emblems filled Jamie with pride. Seeing the New World colors so far from home stirred an unfamiliar longing in her. Jamie found herself eager to be back, to tour the cities she couldn't visit before she left. Many of them she'd never been to before, and now she couldn't wait to see them. Having won the favor of President Kaine, Jamie couldn't wait to win the hearts of her people.

Alexander helped Jamie out of the car and then stepped aside as President Kaine said goodbye. "I know it's not protocol to hug visiting dignitaries, but I wonder if you would allow me, Your Majesty. I think we've found something special here, and a handshake doesn't feel quite right."

Jamie hesitated a moment. "Don't read too much into it," he added, "I'm old enough to be your father. Besides, I've seen the way the young lieutenant looks at you."

Jamie stepped forward and hugged President Kaine, to the gasps of those watching. Jamie could even hear an, "Oh, my" from Nikole. Kaine then took a step back and with his hands to his side, bowed his head.

Jamie turned to her team and said with a broad smile, "Let's go home."

Jamie's euphoria gave way to pleasant exhaustion. Nikole joined her for the flight back to talk about the coronation, but Jamie had no energy to make plans. Besides, she wanted to enjoy the moment before thinking about the future. She watched as conversations on the airship petered out, and realized that her team must be as tired as she was. But it was a good kind of tired. The kind of tired that felt like a reward instead of a punishment. The kind of tired that says, *congratulations, you've worked hard and have done well, now rest.* Her head was swimming with thoughts, replaying moments from the past three days. Jamie wanted to relive them all, but she couldn't fight back the fatigue that had her in a bear hug. Alexander already had his head back, and his eyes closed. She snuggled next to him with her head on his chest and closed her eyes. Sleep overtook her without resistance.

A warning alarm woke Jamie from her deep sleep. She forced her eyes open. Everyone else was up and moving toward the cockpit where the alarm was sounding. Alexander was leaning in. "What is it?" he asked.

The pilot, Captain Deeson, was furiously pushing buttons and checking displays.

"A group of three CRA combat airships is headed this way fast, and they've locked on to us with their weapons system."

Just as Jamie stood and began to make her way to the front, the ship lurched to the right, throwing everyone off balance in unison. The sound of an airship streaked by outside. She could hear her pilots communicating with pilots of the other New World ships.

"Stay in formation. We're just over two hundred kilometers from New World airspace." A pause. "Negative, do not initiate hostile contact."

"How long have we been in the air?" Jamie asked.

Alexander looked at a display on the bulkhead. "Just about an hour."

"Ma'am," Deeson said, "they're instructing us to return to the airbase under their escort. They have orders to fire on us if we do not comply."

"I don't understand. What happened?"

"We're getting a transmission. Putting it through now."

A monitor on the bulkhead in the cabin came to life, and an image of the vice president of the CRA filled the screen. Jamie had met him at the state dinner, but she hadn't talked to him much since then. He hadn't been part of the negotiations.

"Do you have no shame?" he said. "We welcome you to our nation in good faith, and this is how you repay our hospitality?"

The Vice President was older than President Kaine by more than ten years, making Jamie feel as if an angry teacher was scolding her."Mr. Vice-President, I don't understand. Tell me what's happened?"

"Don't insult me, Your Majesty. Your charm might work on President Kaine, but it will do you no good here. You and your team will return to the airbase and face the consequences for your actions, or we will shoot you down."

"Please," desperation strained Jamie's voice, "tell me what's happened."

The vice-president leaned into the camera. "If you have any honor at all, you will not deny that you infected President Kaine with the Pittsburgh Virus."

Behind her, Jamie heard gasps and swearing from the rest of the team.

"What is he talking about?" Raven asked. "We didn't infect anybody."

"Mr. Vice-President, are you telling me President Kaine has contracted the Pittsburgh Virus? How is that possible?"

"That question will top the list in our investigation. You will submit your airships and your team to our investigators upon arrival. We will figure out how you tried to kill our president."

Alexander reached past Jamie and deactivated the monitor. "I don't know what's going on, but we need to get to our airspace. We cannot let them take you."

"We may not have a choice," Captain Deeson said.

Out of the front of the airship, Jamie could see several CRA combat ships hovering in their path. Deeson brought their ship to a stop, hovering in front of them. The other two New World ships did the same.

He put his hand to his headgear, listening. "They're telling us to turn around and return to the airbase." Deeson twisted in his seat and looked at Jamie, "Ma'am?"

"What do you think, Captain? Can you get us home?"

"Not easily. We're close, but if we make a run for it, they could shoot us down. The bad news is that they've got a lot of firepower. The good news is that we have better maneuverability. I give our odds of making it at one in four."

"If we go back, I give our odds of making it as zero," Alexander said. "I don't know what happened back there, but they think you tried to kill President Kaine. Think about what they will do to us if he dies."

Jamie was about to make a decision when Penly shouted a curse. Jamie turned and saw that Penly had pulled down the collar of her uniform tunic, revealing her implant. It was blinking red. The rest of the team pulled their collars down, showing a blinking red dot in each case.

Jamie turned back to the captain. "Get us home. Now."

Chapter Twenty-Seven

Captain Deeson began changing the settings on the panel in front of him. He was more than willing to respond to her request to get them home quickly. "Yes, ma'am. I need everyone to sit down and strap in." He gave brief instructions to the other New World ships and then replied to the CRA airships blocking their path. "Copy that. Executing course change to Bush Airbase."

The ship tilted as it made a slow turn to the left, and Jamie assumed the others were doing the same. Without any windows in the bulkhead, her only view was out the cockpit window. From her vantage point, all she could see in front of them was open sky. Jamie had the sense that they were moving forward slowly. Then she heard Captain Deeson say, "On my mark; three, two, one," and without warning her stomach pushed up into her chest as the forward view changed from open sky to fast approaching ground. She would have screamed, except that she couldn't push enough air out of her lungs to make a sound. Her body pressed back against the seat and then lurched to the left against the harness, as the airship pulled out of its dive and banked to the right. The metal frame of the ship protested with loud creaking, and Jamie wondered how much stress the ship could take. Fear had plastered itself on the faces of the team strapped in around her, and she had no doubt that her expression mirrored theirs.

Pulling out of the turn, Captain Deeson accelerated, pushing her back into her seat again. They were close to the ground now, with the landscape whizzing by below them. He touched something on the panel in front of him, and a virtual display appeared on the forward window, overlaying their view. It highlighted roads, buildings, and natural contours of the land on the ground in front of them. It also showed them how far it was to New World airspace. Alarms sounded in the cockpit, and Deeson took evasive action, turning their flight into an unwelcome rollercoaster ride.

Jamie could see a missile as it flew past the ship, thankfully missing its target. The numbers displayed on the front window were rapidly counting down the distance to home. This felt like some sort of crazy VR game Jamie had played with Ben. Only the stakes were a lot higher than bragging rights. She began to wonder about her decision to make a run for it. Everything happened so fast; she didn't have time to think. The truth was, Jamie didn't have any idea what was going on. Nothing made sense. How had Kaine been infected and why had their implants been activated? Jamie realized that she hadn't checked her implant. When she did, it was blinking green. All clear.

What in the world is going on?

The ship veered to the left, and Jamie grabbed Alexander's hand, squeezing it hard. At the same time, Deeson's copilot worked feverishly to contact New World command, to no avail. "They've jammed our communications," he said.

"Our friend is back at six o'clock," Deeson said as he initiated more evasive maneuvers.

Jamie hated being stuck in a metal can with someone shooting at them and not being able to see what was going on. Six o'clock meant a CRA ship was behind them, but how close? Were they seconds away from being blown out of the sky, or was there some way to shake them before they got to the border? As if on cue, a loud explosion erupted behind them rattling their ship and shoving it forward. Jamie thought they'd been hit and apparently so did Raven who started saying the Hail Mary rosary, or at least what she could remember of it from her days at church.

It wasn't until Jamie heard Captain Deeson yell, "Yes! One down," that she realized the CRA ship chasing them must have been shot down. Everyone on board cheered, but was that something to cheer about? Their chances of getting home just went up, but so did the chances of an all-out war. Just a few short hours ago, she'd been sitting around a table with CRA leaders working out a peace treaty, and now they were shooting at each other. Someone had sabotaged the peace process, and Jamie had a good idea who, she just didn't know how.

The numbers on the forward display sped below one hundred kilometers counting down the distance to New World airspace. If they could survive for another ten minutes, they would make it home. Deeson zig-zagged above the terrain, making them an uncooperative target.

"Now that we have the advantage, I'm guessing our other two ships will try to engage the enemy and buy us time to get home," Alexander said.

The enemy. They weren't supposed to be enemies. They were supposed to be allies, sister nations mending a common wound. Together she and Kaine would set an example for peace in North America. Together they would ensure its security and prosperity. She would invite him to her inauguration, and he would learn to admire the New World as she had learned to admire the CRA. She could see it all there right in front of her. But just as she was about ready to grab it, someone snatched it away.

The ground in front of them exploded as a shot from somewhere above narrowly missed the ship. An alarm sounded from the cockpit, and Captain Deeson pulled up sharply to a dead stop, out of the path of a burning airship hurling toward the ground in front of them. It was one of theirs. It hit the ground in full view, bursting into a ball of fire and coloring the interior of their ship with its orange glow. Nikole cried as Deeson shoved the controls forward, accelerating through the flames. On the forward display, a grid-like wall approached, indicating the New World border. Ten kilometers.

Another explosion rocked the ship, this time to their right. Jamie waited for Deeson to react with a triumphant expression. Instead, he was silent as he guided their ship to the border. If it had been a CRA ship, he would have said something, right? At least a fist-pump. She looked at Alexander, whose face betrayed the same thought. Had they lost their other ship? Was the rest of the team dead?

Jamie's words rushed back to her mind: *Get us home. Now.* Why had she said that? Why hadn't she gone back to the airbase? She had a connection with Kaine. She could have convinced him they had nothing to do with his infection. But that was just it. She didn't know. There were too many unanswered questions. How could she say anything with any conviction at all? With so much confusion, going back was suicide. As it turned out, so was going home.

The forward display showed two kilometers to the border.

Jamie leaned her head on Alexander's shoulder. "I'm so sorry."

"This isn't your fault," he said. "You made the right call. Someone doesn't want peace, and they've made sure it would never happen."

"But how?"

"The implants. It has to be the implants."

"I don't understand how –"

An explosion rocked the ship, and the sound of twisting metal filled Jamie's ears. It was an awful sound like a monster in agony. Multiple alarms sounded, and smoke began to fill the cabin. The ship shook violently as Captain Deeson warned them to prepare for impact. The last thing Jamie could see through the smoke was the countdown at zero. They were home.

The next few minutes were chaotic. The ship crashed in a wooded tract of land, clipping the tops of trees before slamming hard into the ground and flipping over. Jamie found herself suspended in the air, held in place by her harness. Orange emergency lights had an eerie glow through the smoke. People were coughing and moaning. Jamie's head pounded.

"We need to get out of the ship." It was Captain Deeson's voice. "Follow the emergency lights to the hatch."

Someone opened the airship's hatch, letting in a scant amount of light at dusk. It was enough to give Jamie a sense of direction in the orange darkness, however. She pulled her harness release and fell hard to the ground. Alexander had already dropped from his seat and helped her stand. As they moved around the darkened cabin, they checked on others. Raven was out of her seat and dazed. Nikole couldn't release her harness. Jamie helped her with it, and Alexander eased her to the ground. Penly hung limp in her seat, not speaking or moving. Lieutenant Spikes, Deeson's copilot, was already working on getting her down. "Her buckle's jammed. Give me a hand," he said as he pulled out a knife and cut the straps of her harness.

Once she was down, he carried her out of the ship, navigating carefully through the upside-down hatch. Outside, he laid her on the ground. She began to stir, letting out a low moan. Spikes knelt next to her and pulled out a penlight, checking her eyes and a large gash on her forehead.

"How do you feel?" he asked.

Penly moaned, "Like I might throw up." When she opened her eyes fully and looked at the man kneeling next to her, she added with a slight slur, "But not on you. You're gorgeous."

He ignored her. "I think you have a concussion, and you're going to need some stitches for your forehead. Lie still, and we'll get you some help as soon as we can."

As he wrapped Penly's wound, Jamie approached Deeson. "What happened?"

"We were shot down, but we can talk about that later, ma'am. Right now, our priority is getting you to safety."

"We crossed into New World territory before we crashed. Won't the military send a rescue team?"

"They will," the Captain said, "but they won't know where to look. We were way off course, and the CRA jammed our frequency once they saw we weren't going to cooperate. As far as I can tell, we're somewhere in Kentucky." He looked at the growing bump on Jamie's head. "Has someone checked you out?"

"No, but I'm fine."

"With all due respect, you need to have someone look at you; we need to make sure you're okay. Lieutenant Spikes trained as a medic," he said, pointing to his copilot. "Let him check you out."

Jamie didn't know how to tell the Captain about her condition, that her injury would be healed soon, so she agreed to his request. As Lieutenant Spikes examined her, she asked the Captain, "How do we get out of here?"

"I'm afraid everything electronic in the ship has been fried, so we'll need to find another way to contact the command center. I didn't see any lights as we came down, and since it's dark, we'll stay here tonight and explore our options in the morning. We can salvage enough supplies to camp out for the evening." He motioned to Alexander and Raven. "Collect some wood and let's start a fire. I'll get what I can from the ship."

Jamie kept Penly company while everyone else set up camp. Ironically, the two with special healing qualities were the only two injured in the crash, and in the hour since then, Penly's condition had improved considerably. The gash on her head was disappearing fast.

"It will be nearly gone by morning," Jamie said. "Not sure how we'll explain that to Lieutenant Spikes."

"Did I really call him gorgeous?"

Jamie didn't answer. She knew what Penly was doing; trying to take her mind off of the fact that they'd lost two ships that night. It's what a friend would do, but Jamie didn't want to take her mind off the situation. Those ships went down because of her.

With the camp established, the rest of the group joined Jamie and Lieutenant Penly around the fire, eating emergency rations. The collective mood was somber. Jamie could sense the weight of what they had experienced settling in, now that they no longer had the busyness of setting up camp to distract them.

For a few long moments, no one spoke, and then Nikole asked with a shaky voice, "Is everyone else dead?"

It was more of a statement than a question, but Jamie didn't blame her for not wanting to say it outright. Deeson didn't answer with words, but his face told them all what they already knew – the CRA had destroyed the other two ships, and they were the only survivors from the delegation.

Jamie pulled her knees to her chest and wrapped her arms around them. If she could have willed herself into a state of unconsciousness, she would have. This was her delegation, and she was responsible for their deaths. How could she live with that? She'd been so full of herself, convinced that she could change hearts and minds. And now all but seven of them were dead. Jamie put her chin on her knees and closed her eyes.

"There's nothing we could have done differently," Captain Deeson said, "It went south the minute they discovered Kaine was infected. We did what we had to."

"They're still dead," Jamie said.

"And I want to know why," Deeson answered. "How in the world did we get exposed to the virus, and why do they think we infected Kaine?"

Jamie looked at Alexander, remembering what he'd said on the ship just before they crashed. "Because we did infect Kaine," he said. "At least she did."

Every eye turned to Jamie, but she locked her's on Alexander. Why did he think she was the one? She furrowed her brow in a questioning look, and he tapped the implant beneath his collar. She felt the lump beneath her skin as her mind put it all together. Her implant had been used to deliver the virus. She'd been turned into a living, breathing biological weapon. The very thought made her feel violated. Had anything Ashwill said to her been genuine or had she been a Trojan horse all along?

What a fool I've been.

"It was me," she said.

Captain Deeson and Lieutenant Spikes were the only two in the group who didn't know about Jamie's condition, and she had no option but to explain how the virus had changed her DNA. She avoided the term *conditional immortality* and instead said, "I have an extraordinary immune system, and I heal very fast." Jamie could see the confusion on their faces, so she added, "I am immune to viruses, including the Pittsburgh Virus. It doesn't make me sick, but I can carry it and transmit it to others."

"Raisa wasn't the target," Alexander said. "She was the weapon. It's the only thing that makes sense. Think about it; her implant activated when we were with the largest group of CRA leadership at the talks. But the truth is she doesn't even need an implant. She's already immune to the virus. It wasn't protecting her; it was infecting her so that she would infect everyone else."

"If you don't need an implant, why did you agree to get one?" Raven asked.

"Dr. Zurich said if I were exposed, it would prevent me from carrying the virus and transmitting it to others."

"But what if that wasn't the reason?" Alexander said.

Jamie nodded. "He also said nanobots could deliver the virus. What if they loaded my implant with nanobots carrying the Pittsburgh Virus? I wouldn't have any symptoms, but I'd be deadly to anyone around me."

"So why didn't we all light up at the talks when your implant activated?"

"Maybe it takes a while for the virus to replicate itself enough before I become contagious. I did ride to the airfield with Kaine."

"We need to slow down here," Captain Deeson said. "What you're suggesting would involve a massive conspiracy."

"Yes," Alexander said, "but it's the best explanation for how we were infected and how Kaine was infected. If you think about it, it's a brilliant plan, who else from the New World would have direct access to the leader of the CRA but the Queen?"

"Okay," Lieutenant Spikes said, "just playing devil's advocate here, who's to say it wasn't your plan? You all are a pretty tight-knit group. With all due respect, Your Majesty, I was told this mission was your idea."

He was right. It had been her idea, or she thought it had. And they *were* a tight-knit group. To some, they might even seem secretive and exclusive. Even then, at that very moment, her inner circle bunched together on one side of the fire, while Deeson, Spikes, and Nikole were on the other.

"Well, we'd be stupid to spill the beans at this point, wouldn't we?" Alexander said. "Besides, we didn't develop the nanotechnology, and, up to three weeks ago, Raisa didn't even know about her condition. No, someone has been planning this for a long time."

"Such as?"

"Creighton Ashwill."

Nikole let out a gasp.

"Wait a minute, Lieutenant. You do realize that's treason? And even if it were true, how would you know that?" Deeson asked.

"Because he's my step-father."

Chapter Twenty-Eight

Jamie was on her feet before she realized it, hot tears stinging her eyes. She backed away from Alexander. "You knew? All this time you knew because he was your father?"

Alexander stood and took a step toward her, but Raven got to her feet in front of Jamie, standing between her and Alexander. "Let me explain," he said. "It's not what you think."

"You know what I think? I think ever since that man showed up and took me from my home, from my family, nothing in this world has been mine, really mine, except you and this mission." Jamie let tears stream down her face. "But you're *his* son, and this mission is all a part of *his* plan. And now my own body doesn't belong to me. It's *his* weapon!"

Captain Deeson and Lieutenant Spikes sat silently with stunned expressions. Her diatribe must have been an earful for them, but Jamie didn't care what they heard about Council President Ashwill. He had taken everything from her.

"Yes, all of that's true, except I'm not his son. I'm his stepson, and he hardly knows me. I grew up in boarding schools and military academies. But I know him. I've spent my life trying to get him to pay attention to me, trying to make him proud. So, when he asked me to work with him on this . . . this project, I didn't ask too many questions. I regret that now. But here's what I know about my step-father; he never got over the death of my mother, and twenty years of hatred and grief can twist a man into something ugly, and dangerous."

Alexander had a desperate look on his face. Two days ago, that look would have touched a tender spot in Jamie's heart, a place that allowed her to be vulnerable, trusting, and forgiving. But that place was gone, or at least buried so deep she didn't feel it anymore. The innocence she'd clung to over the past seven weeks, despite everything, had been ripped from her grasp, leaving her wounded and angry and defeated. "I can't trust you, Seth. And I won't." Jamie used his real name to drive her point home.

"Seth?" Raven said with a sneer.

"Yes, my name is Seth Bridges," he looked at Jamie, "and I told you that because I wanted you to know me. You can trust me because you know me. Jamie, look at me. You know me."

"No, I don't."

He took a step forward, and Raven put a hand out to stop him. "I wouldn't do that if I were you, *Seth*."

Captain Deeson stood up. "I don't know what's going on here, but Lieutenant King outranks you, Ramirez, and we will follow the chain of command."

"Lieutenant King is relieved of his commission," Jamie said without hesitation.

"What?" Alexander said.

Jamie watched Captain Deeson. Would he challenge her, or would he submit to her authority? She had a pretty good idea, but she needed to be sure. Relieving Alexander of his commission was as much about testing Deeson as it was about punishing Alexander.

"Yes, ma'am," he said. "Lieutenant King, I'll need you to give me your sidearm."

Alexander stared at Jamie as he handed his gun over. "This is a mistake."

She ignored him. "Captain, the CRA believes we have attacked their president, and they will retaliate. We need to find a way to communicate."

"Agreed, but if President Ashwill is behind this, and that's a big if, wouldn't he be ready for retaliation?"

Jamie shook her head. "You don't understand me. I'm not suggesting we contact Ashwill. We need to communicate with the CRA. Where are we right now, Captain?"

"We just barely made it to New World airspace, so we're somewhere in Kentucky near the border."

"Will the CRA still be looking for us?"

"I think we can count on it."

"Good. Is there a way for us to blow up the ship and create a huge fireball, maybe put us on their radar?"

Suddenly, from the darkness, two floodlights blinded Jamie as they lit up the camp.

"That won't be necessary," a voice said behind the light. "I need everyone to face away from the lights, and get on the ground, face down with your hands above your heads. And just in case you're wondering, there are more of us than there are of you, so don't be stupid."

Jamie turned her back to the lights and got on the ground with the rest of her team, face down. She could hear footsteps approaching. She felt hands checking her for weapons. Then they secured her wrists in restraints, and she pulled her feet along with the others. The floodlights were extinguished, and she found herself looking at two armed CRA airmen in the glow of the campfire. Pilots.

"I lied," one of them said, "there weren't more of us." He was young but presented himself with a confidence that bordered on cocky.

"You violated New World airspace," Captain Deeson said.

"Yeah, and you tried to assassinate our president, so don't get all self-righteous."

"He's still alive?" Jamie said.

"Last we heard. But he's dying, thanks to you."

"Listen to me, you're right. I infected President Kaine. I didn't know I was carrying the virus, but I can save him. You need to take me back to Dallas. Right now. I can save President Kaine."

"Lady, I don't know what you are talking about, but you *are* going back to Dallas per my orders."

"Fine, but I need to talk to the vice president right away."

"You may be a queen in your country, but not in mine. Right now, you're my prisoner, so you don't give orders."

"Listen to me, Captain," she leaned forward to see his name plaque in the dim light, "Detweiler. I'm not asking you to violate your orders, but I am asking you to consider that something is going on here that you might not fully appreciate at the moment. And if you will just put me in touch with Vice President Pearson, you might end up being the hero."

Jamie could see that she had gained a little ground with the captain. He was at least considering her request. Good. She only needed him to trust her long enough to put her in touch with the vice president.

He turned to the other pilot. "Let's get 'em back to the ship."

As they lined the prisoners up to start walking, the crack of a rifle and the flash of a muzzle came from the darkness of the woods. Jamie didn't react to the first, but when a second shot sounded, and both pilots fell to the ground, lifeless, she panicked. *No! I needed them alive.*

A group of two men and a girl emerged out of the woods, guns at ease, but ready. The oldest was probably in his sixties and the youngest, a girl in her late teens. Father, son, and granddaughter most likely.

"We're unarmed," Captain Deeson said.

"I can see that," the older man said. "That's kind of why we helped you out. We don't need CRA soldiers coming in here and taking our people, now do we?" He nodded to the other two who produced knives and started toward them.

"Wait," Jamie said. "You don't want to get near us." She didn't want to tell them the whole story, so she offered a slightly altered version. "There's a chance we've been exposed to a virus." It was likely that no one in the group was contagious except Jamie. The antiviral nanobots everyone else had received should have destroyed the virus before it could replicate. But that was way too much information for three people who had walked out of the woods. "Toss the knife, and we'll get ourselves free."

As Captain Deeson cut Jamie free, holding the knife behind his back, she asked the older man in the group, "How did you happen to find us?"

"We have a hunting cabin a couple of miles that way, and we saw your ship go down. We figured you might need some help. We got here about the time these two showed up. So, we decided to sit back and see how things played out. I don't know what started all this, but it became pretty clear that they were fixing to take you folks out of here, and we couldn't let that happen." He paused a moment and then added, "You're Queen Raisa, aren't you?"

Jamie rubbed her wrists and then used the knife to free Deeson. "Yes, and thank you. Your service to your country will not go unrewarded." She was angry that they had killed the pilots instead of capturing them, but she stuffed her anger down for the moment. "Right now, we need to get to their ship. You don't happen to know where it is, do you?"

"No," the older man said. "We never saw them land. You all made a much bigger show of it."

Alexander stepped forward and stood next to Jamie. "What about your cabin? Our comms don't work out here without a ship to sync to, but you've got to have a way to communicate, right?"

Jamie stepped away from Alexander, a move very much intended to send him a signal. "That would be very helpful."

"Yes, ma'am," the younger man said, "but won't that put us at risk, having you all come to our cabin? We want to help and all, but I've got my daughter here to think about."

Jamie smiled at the man, trying to look reassuring. "I'm going to need you to trust me on this. It's a long, complicated story, but in reality, I'm the only one who might be contagious. Everyone else has some technology preventing them from getting the virus, so I'll keep my distance, and I won't come into your cabin. Sir, I need to know, do you trust me?"

"Yes, of course," the older man said. "Follow us."

It took nearly two hours to hike the two and a half miles to the cabin. As they followed the three men through the woods, Deeson walked alongside Jamie. "How can you save President Kaine?" he asked. "You told the CRA pilot back there you could save him. Is that true?"

"I don't know. I was hoping a transfusion of my blood might be enough to pull him through. It's a long shot, but it was the only thing I could think of."

"So that's a real thing, with your DNA?"

Jamie nodded.

"Is it contagious?" Deeson was smiling as if he thought that was funny.

With an unpleasant edge to her voice, Jamie said, "Have you ever heard of someone's DNA being contagious?"

"Well, Lieutenant Penly seems to be healing remarkably well, so I was just wondering."

Jamie looked back at Penly who had removed her bandage. Jamie explained, "She has the same condition I have, for the same reason. She should be completely healed by morning."

He nodded his head but kept whatever thoughts he had to himself. Jamie sensed that he had quite a few.

"Captain, you do know this is all because of Creighton Ashwill, don't you?"

"That's quite a statement," Deeson said. "How sure are you that President Ashwill is responsible?"

"The device you're wearing to protect you from the virus was first tested on fifteen hundred human subjects. Some of them survived the virus, some didn't, but none of them survived the clinical trials. So, I know that he's ruthless." Jamie stopped walking and faced Deeson. "President Kaine told me that Ashwill holds him personally responsible for the death of his wife and child. So, I know that he's got a personal vendetta to settle. He kidnapped me from my home and manipulated five other girls with the same condition I have to join the military, and then he put them all in the same squad at Basic. So, I know that he has a plan that involves someone with my condition. And lo and behold, while we're in the CRA, President Kaine comes down with the Pittsburgh Virus, and the implants protect everyone in our group. Either that's one heck of a coincidence, or President Ashwill has been executing a very well-thought-out plan. And I need you to decide which one you think it is before we reach the cabin."

Jamie told Deeson the truth, hoping that his honor would compel him to act on it. Somebody had to hold Ashwill accountable for his crimes, and she wasn't sure she'd ever get that chance. As Jamie trudged through the woods, her clothes doused in smoke and blood, she felt small. Weak. A part of her screamed inside her head to get as far away from Creighton Ashwill as possible. That made sense, right? A teenage girl couldn't stop a killer like Ashwill. He'd controlled her like a maniacal puppeteer from the start. She'd been played by someone who knew the game far better than she did, and people were dead because of it.

Run far away.

The power of the monarchy was an illusion; that was the lesson she'd learned. The power to make a difference was something Ashwill allowed Jamie to believe in so that he could use her. She was a puppet who thought she was something more. She was Pinocchio.

But how could an illusion feel so real? You did spread your wings. You flew.

No, falling is not the same thing as flying, even if it feels like it for a while.

The cabin probably wasn't anything special as far as hunting cabins go, but it looked like a little slice of heaven to Jamie. Set near a pond, it was quiet and calm, and everything her life had not been since her father moved them to D.C. A generator with solar cells was used to power a few appliances and their satellite link for communication. A fireplace and kerosene lamps took care of everything else. A large porch stretched across the front of the cabin, adorned by two rocking chairs. That's where Jamie sat, away from the rest of the group, looking out on the pond. Raven joined her as everyone else went into the cabin.

"There are only nine people in the world right now who know where I am," Jamie said, "and eight of them are in there."

"Your point is?"

"I could walk away, disappear into the night, and be done with all of this."

"And probably get eaten by a bear," Raven said. "So, what's your real plan?"

"To get my father and brother, and then walk away. I need to hit a reset, start over without Ashwill and the New World in my life."

"You're gonna quit? Just like that? Then Ashwill wins."

"He's already won. How can you not see that?"

"Do you remember why you wanted us to come on this trip? It was to make sure you didn't change into somebody you're not. You're not a quitter."

"And I'm not a queen either. People are dying, Raven. I can't live my life afraid that every decision I make will kill someone else, or worse, that it's all part of Ashwill's grand plan."

"I know," Raven said, "but you can't just walk away either. People are counting on you. You might be the only one who can stop Ashwill."

"My father and my brother were counting on me, too. A lot of good it did them."

As Jamie mentioned her father, an image of him in the crowd during her speech flashed through her mind. There he stood, looking at her wearing that cap. He wanted her to see him – she was sure of it – but why? Why there at the Capitol? It was as if he had something to tell her, but he gave her no signals, he didn't try to communicate with her in any way. If he had something to say, why didn't he try to say it? Jamie thought about all the times he had taken her to the Summerhouse because he had something important to say to her.

The Summerhouse!

Just then, Captain Deeson came out of the cabin. "The satellite link is activated. I'm guessing, based on our conversation earlier that President Ashwill is not going to be your first call."

"No," Jamie said, "I need you to get in touch with my secretary. Her name's Alora. She's at the Pentagon."

Chapter Twenty-Nine

July 4, 2078 - Six Hours Before the Vote – Summer house

As Nate approached the Summerhouse, he saw Jamie sitting on one of the benches inside waiting for him, early as usual. He took off his coat and loosened his tie.

July certainly puts the summer in Summerhouse.

He stopped outside, just before entering. It was probably the last time they'd rendezvous here for one of their father-daughter talks, certainly the last time he'd be Senator Corson. After tonight's vote, he'd simply be Dad again. Nate was looking forward to that. This job had taken its toll on their family, even before Ella died. After the accident, he felt as if they were barely hanging on, and he knew the strain it put on his daughter. Maine was so far away and so cold, but it was a small price to pay for a new start.

"Hey, Peanut. Ben still at home?"

"No, dad. He's at school. Remember?"

"That's right," he said with a smile, "It's Monday. They still making kids go to school on Monday?" Nate tried to cover his embarrassment with a joke. How had he become so disconnected from his family? He knew Jamie could see right through his jovial smile.

"Yeah. They don't cancel school for Mondays, and they don't cancel it for earth-shaking political votes either, although they probably should."

The smile left Nate's face. "It is earth-shaking, isn't it?" He sat on the bench next to her.

"Yeah. You're gonna be famous."

"Great. Not exactly what I was hoping to be known for. It irks me that in the future nobody will talk about how the states amended the Constitution, allowing the Senate to take this vote – that was an act of cowardice, by the way. But nobody will remember that. But they *will* remember my resolution to end it all."

Jamie looked at her hands without saying anything. She was probably used to his habit of thinking out loud, Nate thought. It was his way of processing things. He didn't expect a response. After a moment, he shrugged off his concern and looked at Jamie.

"I didn't ask you here so I could talk about me. You've got a birthday coming up. A big one. Eighteen. Even in the best of times, turning eighteen can be a challenge, but these aren't the best of times, are they? And I haven't been the best of fathers. I know that, and I'm sorry. I'm sorry about a lot of things. I'm sorry you have to become a woman without your mother around. But I want you to know that you are an extraordinary young lady, and you will grow into an extraordinary woman in ways you can't imagine."

Jamie's eyes widened, and she sat up at Nate's words, like a wilted flower getting watered. How long had it been since Nate had talked with his daughter like this? Not just giving her information – he did a lot of that – but sharing his heart? Too long.

It pained Nate that his daughter seemed so hungry for his attention. "I was going to record this and give it to you on a data dot, but I thought this would be better."

Jamie nodded.

Okay, now what? Nate questioned himself.

He hadn't decided how much to tell her. He wanted her to know about her condition, but she was under so much stress. Adding that bombshell didn't seem like a good idea, so he'd wait until they got settled in Maine. But he could tell her the rest.

"You know you're special. Right?"

Jamie smiled. "You have to say that. You're my dad."

"No. I say it because it's true. You're gifted, and you can't let your gifts go to waste. You have so many days in front of you, and you need to seize them, make them your own, and fully experience the life you were meant to have." *His words would make more sense if I could tell you the whole story.*

"Jamie, you can't spread your wings if you're taking care of Ben and me. I'm kicking you out of the nest."

Before Ella had died, their family had watched a nature show together on television one night. They were mesmerized by the program, watching a mother bird push her offspring out of the nest, forcing them to fly. One by one, the not-so-little birds were eased out of the safety of the nest, only to discover the freedom of flight. Ella had started stretching her arms, declaring that she would start pushing her baby birds out pretty soon. Everyone had a big laugh at the time, but Jamie seemed stunned by Nate's words then.

"You're kicking me out of the nest? Where will I go?"

"Harvard." The school had weathered the epidemic better than most. The administration was ahead of its time in establishing protocols for a biomedical disaster. They did what the border states had done, secured the campus, admitting only medically cleared people. The idea had come from a research virologist on the faculty who feared the U.S. might face a catastrophic epidemic.

Jamie's mouth fell open, but she quickly closed it. "Harvard? University?"

"The president, Jonathan Teague, is a former Senate colleague. He assured me that you'd have a spot in the fall. That's my birthday present to you."

Nate was surprised to see Jamie's face cloud over. "Dad, don't get me wrong, I'd love to go to Harvard, but not because I'm Senator Corson's daughter. I want to make my way on my own."

"That was part of the deal," Nate said. "John can't afford to let someone in who couldn't hack it academically. But with so many schools shut down, there are more people qualified to go than they can possibly take. I just made sure your name was noticed among the sea of choices. You'll do the rest."

Nate watched as Jamie considered this. It took a moment, but a smile of delight replaced the contemplation of a furrowed brow. "You did that for me?"

Nate nodded; happy he had pleased his daughter.

"Who will take care of things here?"

Nate knew the real question was, *who will take care of you and Ben?* He wanted to say that he was more than capable of taking care of himself and his son, but he didn't. He had allowed grief and alcohol to shape his life for three years, and he wasn't sure how he would function, facing the one without the other.

"Ben and I will learn to take care of each other. Our world is changing, Jamie, and we need bright young minds like yours to be able to lead the way. You can have an impact for generations to come. But you can't do that looking after Ben and me."

"You and Ben are everything to me, Dad. I'll go, only if you promise me that the two of you will be all right."

"I promise."

Chapter Thirty

Eight Weeks Later – Present Day

It took a couple of hours to hear back from Alora. Jamie instructed her to go to the Summerhouse and look in the notch in the wall for a message from her father. He'd communicated to her once that way already – maybe he'd do it again. There was no guarantee that Alora would find a note there, but if she did, Jamie needed to know what it said. There was something about her dad's eyes when they drove past, and he pulled off his sunglasses. It was as if he were willing her to read his thoughts, to sense the weight of his burden. Nikole fussed at her for wasting time on a harebrained idea when they could already be back in D.C., but Jamie wasn't going to make a move until she knew if her father had tried to contact her.

Finally, Alora came back on the video link. The Sawyers, the family that owned the cabin, stayed inside, but everyone else gathered around her on the porch. Alora's complexion was pale, and tight lines formed across her face.

Jamie was impatient for information. "Did you find a note?"

"Not exactly," Alora responded cryptically.

With a flash of temper, Jamie said, "Yes or no?"

"It's a data dot, with a message from your father." Alora held up the tiny circular disc. "We've uploaded it for you."

Jamie eyed the team standing around her. They all nodded at her and gave her space to view the message alone. "I'm ready," she said.

An image of Jamie's father replaced Alora's.

"Hey, Peanut," he said. Jamie's heart broke at seeing her dad. He looked old and tired and not entirely sober. "Look at us. Who could imagine that we would have ended up where we are; a U.S. Senator in hiding and an eighteen-year-old in charge of the country? The truth is, I'm afraid you're not really in charge. I know Creighton

Ashwill, and I know he's just using you. But you're smart enough to know that already. That's not why I made this video. It's about Ben. The last two months have been hard on him. Losing you was like losing his mother all over again. He's become angry, and he's been looking for a way to express his anger. Return offered him away. They've taken him in like family and are training him to fight. He thinks I'm weak for letting Ashwill take you, so he's just as mad at me as he is at him, but I'm worried that they're turning him against you, too."

That last statement caused Jamie to catch her breath. How could Ben ever turn against her? She had been his anchor after their mother's death, and, in many ways, he'd been hers.

As if reading her mind, Nate's next statement answered her question. "Jamie, we know that on the night the White House was attacked, you were out dancing with a bunch of New World soldiers, including the one who took you from our house. That didn't sit well with Ben. He thought you were being held against your will, that you didn't come to him because you couldn't. Turns out that wasn't true. When he hears about the speech you gave today, I'm afraid it will convince him all the more that you've become one of them."

Nate paused to collect himself, tears welling up in his bloodshot eyes. When he did, Jamie could make out the sound in the background. Someone's voice was amplified over a sound system. It was the woman who had sung the New World anthem after Jamie's speech. Suddenly, details of the video in front of her began to flood Jamie's vision, like the brick wall behind her father. He was making this video in the Summerhouse, just after she spoke at the signing ceremony.

"I thought I should tell you," Nate said. "I know how much he means to you." And then, with a heavy sigh, "I can't see how this will end well, Jamie. Please, contact me. Jimbo can make it happen."

The video ended abruptly, and Jamie began to weep. She had the foreboding sense that she was losing what was left of her family

– her father to hopelessness and the bottle, her brother to bitterness and maybe violence if the resistance ever got organized.

After a moment, Alora returned to the link. Jamie spent the next few minutes talking with her, making plans. She watched her team watching her. They were too far away to have heard the video or her conversation with Alora, but, no doubt, they could see the aftermath on Jamie's face.

Alexander approached her first. Jamie was surprised that Raven didn't try to stop him. How had he sweet-talked his way into her good grace? "You okay?" he asked.

She wanted to brush him off, but she was too emotionally exhausted to be rude. "My little brother, Ben, joined Return and most likely hates me. He was the one thing left that Aswhill hadn't managed to take from me, and now I've lost him." Hot tears found the way down her cheek again.

Alexander sat in the rocking chair next to her, but he didn't try to touch her. Part of her wanted the familiar comfort of his touch, but she knew better than to expect it, and she wasn't ready to give up being mad at him. She had to hate someone for everything that had happened, and he was the closest thing to a target she had.

"What are you going to do?" he asked.

"I don't know, but somehow I have to save my family." Jamie could taste the tears as they ran to her lips. As angry as she was, a larger shadow loomed in her heart: sadness. How could she have abandoned the most important thing in her life? It was the answer to that question that saddened her most; despite what Jamie told herself, her family wasn't the most important thing in her life. If they were, she'd still be locked up somewhere, making life hell for Ashwill. She had justified her cooperation by choosing to believe he would hurt them if she didn't, but the truth was, she wanted this. Even before Dr. Forrester told her about her condition, Jamie felt drawn to something more. She'd never regretted the years spent taking care of Ben and her father, but there were times she had felt like a bird in a cage, wanting to fly. And, at the first opportunity, she spread her wings and left her family behind.

Alexander said, "You know what I want? I want to make Ashwill pay for what he's done to all those people he experimented on, and what he's done to Kaine, and you."

"I can't afford revenge right now. Ashwill has controlled my life for the last two months, and I'm done with that. Revenge puts me back in his orbit. I don't want to be there." Even as Jamie said it, she questioned it. Could she walk away?

"Maybe getting out of his orbit is part of the revenge?"

"That sounds too subtle, and not nearly painful enough, to be called revenge."

Alexander was silent for a moment. Then he said, "I'm not saying it's everything, but it would be more painful than you think. He's been planning this, all of it, for the last twenty years, and you're a big part of his plan. Walk away now, and you'll put a stop to it. Trust me that'll hurt."

"I'm listening."

"Good, but first we need to make sure President Kaine doesn't die. If he dies, I'm not sure anyone can stop Ashwill."

Questions filled her mind, but she focused on the most urgent one. "How can we save Kaine?"

She discovered that while she'd been watching the message from her dad, Jamie's team had been discussing their best options. Although none of them were geneticists or doctors, for that matter, they all agreed that using Jamie's blood wasn't their best idea.

"It might work," Alexander said, "but we don't know for sure. What we do know is that *our* blood is teeming with virus-killing nanobots."

"Yes," Jamie said, wiping the tears from her cheeks. The thought of saving Kaine buoyed her hope. "And Dr. Zurich said they would last for weeks once they're released into the bloodstream." She stood and headed toward her team, putting a hand on his arm as she passed. "Did anybody think of a great way to find the CRA ship?" she said to the group. "Because without it we've got no way to get your blood to Kaine in time."

"I've been thinking about that," Deeson said. "The CRA could tell us exactly where their ship is, assuming the pilots didn't deactivate their transponder. And I can't imagine they would do that in enemy territory."

"I guess that means we'll have to ask them."

Jamie used the satellite link to connect with Vice President Pearson. In the ten hours since she'd seen him, he'd only grown angrier. He unleashed a verbal barrage on Jamie that left little doubt where the CRA stood; they were pissed, and they were going to make the New World pay. When Jamie explained their plan, that she and what was left of her team would return to try and save the president, Pearson laughed out loud. "If you want to return to the CRA voluntarily, we won't stop you, but you will be held accountable for what you've done here."

"I understand that. But our group will only come if we're able to give President Kaine and anyone else infected a blood transfusion." It took forty-five minutes of stating and restating the plan, explaining how everything had unfolded in the first place, and promising that this wasn't some sort of clever trick before Pearson reluctantly agreed, albeit with a list of consequences that would occur if Kaine didn't recover.

"Oh, and there's one more thing," Jamie said. "We need you to send us the coordinates of the ship that followed us into New World airspace."

That was good for another verbal explosion and thirty more minutes of arguing. Jamie debated whether to tell him that the pilots were dead, but opted for the truth on the chance that an honest admission might buy her some credibility. It did. They received the coordinates, and Captain Deeson loaded them into his comm unit. He set off with the younger of the Sawyer men for the ship. Everyone agreed that the two of them could make better time without the rest of the group in tow. They estimated they'd reach the ship in an hour.

As Deeson and his guide disappeared into the woods, Lieutenant Spikes approached Jamie. The team had also decided that before she went anywhere, he needed to remove her implant. If the implant was the source of the virus, it should come out. She should also be the first recipient of a nanobot-filled blood transfusion from one of the team members, to ensure she was completely virus-free. Jamie didn't disagree with the plan but questioned how the lieutenant would accomplish this in the woods in the middle of the night. Spikes assured her that all he needed were supplies from a medkit, which he had salvaged from their airship, and a sharp knife that the Sawyers provided.

Lieutenant Spikes sterilized the knife with some whiskey from the cabin and had Jamie lie on a picnic table by the pond. The floodlights used by the CRA pilots provided illumination as he made a small incision below the collarbone, exposing the implant. Getting to it was the easy part. Getting it out without rupturing a major artery was another matter. As he worked, the lieutenant explained everything he was doing, something Jamie didn't appreciate. Because the implant was just under the skin, the pain was manageable, but the play-by-play was nerve-racking.

"Would you mind talking about something else?" she said.

"Sorry. Bad habit. I talk through things I'm working on."

"Not a problem, but let's change the subject."

"Okay, to what?"

"You pick." Jamie couldn't believe she had to talk him through proper bedside etiquette.

"So, tell me about Lieutenant Penly."

Spikes gently pried the implant from beneath the skin as she gripped the sides of the picnic table.

"You've got to be kidding me," Jamie said through gritted teeth. "That's what you want to talk about?"

"Yeah. Probably not the right time."

Three small tubes extended from the implant leading deeper into the tissue of her chest. Deeson decided that instead of removing the tubes, he'd cut them from the device, leaving them where they were. Someone else, with more experience and better tools, could remove them later. Using the knife, he cut the implant free, placed it in a plastic bag, and sealed it. That was a smart idea; if it still contained virus-carrying nanobots, there was no sense in risking exposure for anyone else.

After bandaging her wound and getting her into a chair, Spikes was off to collect blood from someone else in the team.

A few minutes later, he returned with a bag full of the dark red life-giving liquid. "Using the one needle for two patients is generally discouraged," he said, "but my med kit only had one IV set. So…"

"Well, I'm getting their blood, so I don't really think it's an issue."

"Good point. I was lucky to find someone with your blood type."

Spikes started the IV and tied the bag to an old broomstick suspended in the branches of a tree above her. "This is going to take a few minutes, so just relax," he said as he headed back toward the cabin.

While she waited, Jamie closed her eyes and leaned her head back. The serenity of that place, the cabin and the pond and the woods, pushed against the despair forming in her heart. It had not always been there, and she couldn't let it become a permanent resident. She thought about Ben and the bitterness that had begun to frame his heart, turning him into an angry thirteen-year-old boy. No, not thirteen – his birthday was weeks ago. He was fourteen now. Jamie had forgotten his birthday. What kind of person forgets her little brother's birthday? An added layer of guilt settled on her like a fresh coat of paint.

"A New World credit for your thoughts."

Jamie opened her eyes to see Alexander standing next to her, holding a piece of cotton to the crook of his arm. So, it was his blood. "I'm not in the mood," she muttered.

"I'm sorry about your brother."

Jamie ignored his apology. "You owe me an explanation. Earlier you said that getting out of Ashwill's orbit could be a form of revenge. What did you mean by that?"

"Killing Kaine is only part of his plan. I think what he's after is preserving the legacy of my mother."

Jamie shook her head. That didn't make any sense.

"Look at it from his point of view," he said. "He lost his young wife and unborn daughter. As far as he's concerned, it's Kaine's fault and the fault of all those states that closed their borders. So, what does he do? He sends you to infect them with the very virus that killed his wife. It's poetic justice, very Ashwillian. But revenge is small potatoes. Immortality is a much bigger goal."

"Well, I'm the one who's immortal here, not you," Jamie said. "And immortality is not contagious."

Alexander tilted his head. "You and your descendants . . ." He stopped, letting Jamie fill in the blanks on her own.

"And Ashwill wants my descendants to be your descendants, too," said Jamie slowly as her mind grasped what he was saying. *Of course. That was why he chose Alexander*. Once again, Jamie was just a puppet in Ashwill's scheme.

"And my descendants are my mother's descendants. So, the woman who died in her prime lives on through offspring with superhuman lifespans. Again, it has a nice poetic ring to it. And what better way to preserve someone's life than through a line of descendants who rule as a royal family. Especially if you happen to be obsessed with monarchies."

"He told you that?"

"Not in so many words. But he never got over losing my mom, and he never failed to remind me that I was the only link he had to the greatest love of his life. Our entire relationship revolves around my mother. I'm more of a surrogate than a son."

"That's twisted," Jamie said.

"Agreed, but that's why walking away will hurt him. Everything he wants is wrapped up in us. If you disappear and we never get together, he gets nothing. If Kaine survives, he gets double-nothing."

That seemed more like a consolation prize than revenge, but it had the advantage of allowing Jamie to stick it to Ashwill while retreating, a scorched earth strategy of sorts.

"He'll replace me," said Jamie.

"Maybe, but the Council won't give him the same leeway he had before. They trusted him with that decision once. If you quit, they'll want to know what went wrong; there will be investigations and inquiries. It'll be a serious blow to establishing the throne in the New World. Besides all that, he knows how I feel about you. He can't possibly hope that I'd fall in love with the runner-up."

"When did you figure this out?"

"I started putting the pieces together after I learned about your condition."

"And you went along with it anyway?"

Alexander didn't answer, and Jamie didn't push it.

Jamie thought about the logic of Alexander's plan and said, "It seems to me that if I want to hurt Ashwill, I should kill you."

Alexander smiled wryly. "That would do the trick."

Chapter Thirty-One

The familiar hum of an airship broke the stillness of the pre-dawn hours. Its bright lights transformed the darkness into day, revealing dense woods surrounding the cabin and illuminating the small pond. Jamie thanked the Sawyers before joining her team as they made their way to the airship, which had landed in a clearing fifty yards away.

Captain Deeson approached her. "They've informed us that once we pass into CRA airspace, they will take control of navigation and guide us to the airbase. Are you okay with that, ma'am?"

"Wouldn't you do the same?"

"Of course, but I don't like not being in control of my ship. It's your call."

"I don't think we have a choice, Captain. We're not in a position to make demands."

"All right then. We need to load up and get underway."

"I'm not going with you," Jamie said.

"What? You can't stay here," Penly said. She nodded toward the cabin. "They've been helpful and all, but we're not leaving you out here in the middle of nowhere with them."

Jamie opened her mouth to respond, but Captain Deeson cut her off, "With all due respect, ma'am, she's right. Your safety is our first concern."

"And you think taking me to the CRA right now is the best way to keep me safe?"

"That can't be helped if we're going to save President Kaine. It's a risk, but leaving you here is not an option."

Jamie was glad to hear the *thud-thud-thud* of an approaching helicopter.

"I won't be staying here. That's for me." She motioned toward the sound.

"A helicopter?" Nikole said. "Who uses helicopters anymore?"

"Smugglers," Alexander said. "How'd you manage that?"

"I needed to get back to D.C. without Ashwill knowing about it. Alora got a hold of Jimbo Haynes, and he made the arrangements."

"This is a bad idea," Alexander said. "You shouldn't be traveling alone and especially not with friends of Jimbo Haynes."

"I'm not traveling alone," she said to him. "You're coming with me." Her team was staring at her as if she'd grown a third eye. That was why she hadn't shared her plan with them earlier. She didn't want to spend an hour defending her decision. "You can't use my blood," she explained, "and Alexander can't afford to give anymore. You don't need us, but my family does."

The helicopter grew louder until it circled overhead before landing. The pilot, a tall, scruffy man with a gray beard and a gun tucked into his pants, got out and approached the group. He eyed the CRA airship and the New World soldiers suspiciously. "Someone here named Jamie?"

"That's me."

"Jimbo said you needed a lift to D.C."

The man looked skittish with so many uniforms standing around, but he didn't ask any questions. Jamie guessed that people dealing with Jimbo were used to not asking too many questions. He kept his distance from the group as if to ensure a quick getaway if needed.

"That's right. He gave you the coordinates?"

"I got 'em, but if you want to go, we need to go now."

Despite the stunned looks from her team, Jamie hugged each of them before insisting they board the airship. As they did, she wondered if she would ever see them again. Once they had left, she held up one finger to the helicopter pilot and said to Alexander, "We need to change clothes."

A few minutes later, the tops of the trees passed in a shadowy blur below the helicopter. Jamie leaned against the seat, trying to let the tension drain from her body. She and Alexander had boarded the helicopter after borrowing clothes from the Sawyers. Jamie had changed into a pair of jeans that mostly fit, and a pink camo shirt. Not exactly a discreet outfit for D.C., but she didn't have many options. She was roughly the girl's size, and Alexander was not quite the father's size. He had to hitch up his pants with a belt to keep them on. She hoped a Kentucky Wildcats baseball cap would help conceal her identity.

Jamie closed her eyes. She realized this was the first time in a long time that she was doing something for her family. She had told her father she would only leave him and Ben if he were sure they'd be all right. But they weren't all right. Not even close. Maybe if they had gotten to Maine and her dad had started teaching, and Ben had a chance to adapt to a new life, maybe it would have been okay. Harvard was only a couple of hours away from where her father had taken a teaching job. That might have worked, but not whatever this was. This life as Queen of the New World was destroying her family.

So why was it so hard to give up? Why did she feel as if she was finally spreading her wings? "I like being queen," she said softly.

Alexander was strapped into his seat across from her, wearing jeans and a plain blue shirt, sound asleep. She admired his ability to compartmentalize. Her mind was too active. She couldn't stop thinking about what would happen next, and those concerns were too pressing for her to have any hope of sleep. She didn't have a plan as much as a goal – get her family back and get away from Ashwill. If Raven had her way, Jamie would single-handedly take him down. But that was a fantasy and Jamie had spent enough time in the last couple of months living in a fantasy. It was time to return to the real world, and step one was to find her father.

That's where Jimbo came in. He had arranged for the helicopter to take her to a secluded spot in Virginia outside D.C. From there, a car would take her into the city to the place where her father was hiding out. It was all very clandestine, and she was glad not to be alone.

Alexander had agreed to come, without any idea of what her plan might be. Did that mean he trusted her judgment, or was he concerned for her safety? Maybe a little of both, Jamie realized, and she was okay with that. She watched him sleep and considered the rollercoaster of a relationship they'd had over the last couple of months. She did a quick calculation; it had been fifty-two days since she'd first seen him standing outside her bedroom. So much had changed since then. His deception had wounded her, but only because she loved him so deeply. He would never betray her to Ashwill. She knew that. But the mere possibility that he could be somebody other than the man she fell in love with had frightened her. Still, wasn't that always the risk with love? Jamie decided it was, and that Alexander was worth it.

"Why did you come with me?" she asked his sleeping form. "I'm gonna ruin your life right along with mine."

"But at least we'll be ruined together," Alexander said without opening his eyes.

"How long have you been awake?"

"I've been dozing on and off." He opened his eyes to slits.

"I'm getting my father and my brother, and we're leaving. I'm not coming back. If you come with me, you'll be done with the New World, your career, everything."

Alexander ignored her concern. "Where will you go?"

"I'm hoping Kaine will give us asylum."

"What's your plan B, in case, I don't know, the CRA puts you on their most-wanted list instead of giving you a medal?"

Jamie didn't answer. She was trying not to consider that the team in Dallas wouldn't succeed, or that Kaine wouldn't be sympathetic to her need.

Alexander nodded. "You don't have a Plan B."

"I have one plan. It's the plan I had on the night of the vote, and I should never have given up on it. I should have . . . done something to stay with my family that night."

Sadness touched the features of Alexander's face. Jamie hadn't considered how her words would sound to him. She no longer thought of Alexander as the guy who took her from her home. Based on his reaction, he still thought of himself that way, though.

You've got to learn to think before you speak. "I'm sorry, I didn't mean that," she said.

"I'm the one who's sorry," Alexander said.

Jamie smiled. "I'll accept your apology if you accept mine."

Alexander slid from his seat and knelt in front of Jamie. "I accept your apology." He leaned forward and kissed her, lingering long enough for both of them to let out a low sigh.

Jamie rested her arms on his shoulders. "I thought you and I were supposed to be over, you know, to stick it to Ashwill and all that."

Alexander smiled at her. "I thought you were supposed to kill me, you know, to stick it to Ashwill and all that."

"Looks like *we* need a Plan B."

Alexander moved to the seat next to Jamie and turned serious. "Are you ready to give it up?"

"What choice do I have? If I don't leave, Ashwill will continue to use me, he'll threaten my family, and my brother will hate me for the rest of my life. I can't live with that."

"What about us?"

"What about us?" she said.

"Our relationship is part of his manipulation. It serves his purpose. Can you live with that?"

"That's how it started, but we've made it more than that. And it serves a greater purpose now. It's our choice, not his. Why is it so important to you that he doesn't think we're together?"

"Because I don't want him to win." Alexander's voice rose as he spoke. "I don't want him to have the satisfaction of knowing that any little bit of his plan succeeded. He used me, and he used you, and he killed a bunch of people to fulfill some sick fantasy. I want him to end up with nothing at all."

Jamie had never seen Alexander so angry. Through gritted teeth, he continued. "He's the only father I've known. All my life I've tried to please him, to make him notice me, to make him proud of me. And yet, when he looks at me, he doesn't even see me. I don't like the thought of giving him anything."

Jamie put her hand in his. "I don't like the thought of losing you just to settle a score."

"Yeah. Me neither."

The helicopter landed in a field near a road. No words were exchanged between the pilot and his passengers as they disembarked. They had barely gotten their feet on the ground when he pulled his mechanical bird back up into the sky.

Nothing like customer service.

A car sat just off the road, with a driver leaning against the hood, arms crossed. He didn't move as they approached. "Jimbo said, one passenger."

"And now there are two," Jamie said. "Things change, get over it."

"He hired me to transport and protect one passenger. If I've got to protect two of you, I'll need to raise my fee."

"Okay, so raise your fee."

"How do I know he'll pay it?"

"Have you ever known Jimbo Haynes to shortchange anyone?" Jamie asked. "He's good for it."

"You better be right," the driver said as he opened the door.

Jamie didn't know if she was right or not, and she didn't care. She needed to get to her father. Jimbo could hash it out with his hired help later.

Once they were on the road, she asked, "Why are you driving? Wouldn't it be easier to protect us if you let the car auto navigate?"

"This is part of protecting you," he said. "The GPS has been disabled so no one can track us."

The ride was quiet until the driver said, "Don't I know you from somewhere?"

Of course, it made sense that Jimbo didn't tell anybody who she was. The fewer people who knew, the better.

"I just have one of those faces." Jamie pulled the cap down over her brow a little more.

"No, you don't. You're that girl they made the queen."

Crap.

"But here's the strange part," he continued. "You're supposed to be dead."

Dead?

The driver activated the monitor in the dash, which was streaming the latest news. A talking head was explaining how the CRA attacked Queen Raisa and her delegation on their way home from a diplomatic mission. According to the news anchor, the queen was missing and feared dead. The woman reading the news was then replaced by a picture of their upside-down airship in the woods. It looked more damaged than Jamie had remembered.

"That's all they've been reporting for hours," the driver said.

"Yeah, well obviously I'm not her. She's dead."

"So, you're just a couple kids flying in on a helicopter in the middle of the night who need a ride to D.C." The driver stared at Jamie in the mirror. She didn't answer.

"Don't worry about it. I'll get you to where you need to be."

Jamie wasn't sure if the coverage on the news was a good thing or a bad thing. On the one hand, if they were supposed to be dead or at least missing, no one would look for her in Washington. On the other hand, the government-controlled the news outlets, so if this was the big story, there had to be a reason. Jamie could only think of one reason: Ashwill wanted a war with the CRA. What better way to fire up the country than to tell them that the CRA brutally attacked their pretty young queen had on a mission of peace. Pictures of a burned-out airship didn't hurt either.

Alexander was thinking the same thing. He leaned over to her and whispered, "If he thinks his plan to kill Kaine failed, he'll use the attack on our airships as a reason for war."

"How would he know his plan failed?" Jamie said softly.

"Someone in the delegation was a part of the plot. Whoever it was must have activated your implant remotely when the time was right. I thought it was secretary Paulson, but I think there's a more likely candidate."

"Nikole?"

"Yeah. Think about it: how did they find our ship?" Alexander asked, pointing to the news feed. "We were there for more than ten hours, but just after Nikole boards the CRA airship, rescuers find our wreck?"

Jamie kicked Alexander's words around in her mind, following his logic. "The commlink," she finally said.

"I think so. Like the rest of us, she had no way to contact anyone without a ship that would sync to her com. My guess is she sent her coordinates as soon as she got close to that airship."

Something wasn't right about Alexander's scenario. "If Nikole sent the coordinates like you say, then the New World forces would have been led to the Sawyer's cabin, and they'd know we're alive. So why the story about us missing and feared dead?"

"Are you kidding? Ashwill gets the drama of a possible assassination *and* a miraculous rescue all in one. Gandhi would go to war after that."

Chapter Thirty-Two

The car pulled in front of a church and stopped. The sign read "St. Andrews." Although the sun was up, it was early, and there was little activity on the wide suburban street in Reston, Virginia. "We're here," the driver said.

Jamie didn't see any cars in the parking lot or any sign of life in the church. "This is it? A church?" Jamie had never heard of St. Andrews, and her dad wasn't particularly religious, so it didn't make sense that he'd arrange to meet them there.

"This is where Jimbo told me to bring you. He said you should go around back, find the green door and push the button."

"That's it?" Alexander asked.

"That's it."

"No passwords or secret code or anything?"

Jamie rolled her eyes. "Come on."

The green door wasn't easy to find, but maybe that was the point. It was tucked into an alcove on the backside of the building. Alexander tried the handle, and it was locked. Next to it was a black panel with a button and a tiny camera — strange security for a church. Jamie pushed the button and waited. When nothing happened, she removed her baseball cap and let her blond hair fall to her shoulders. A moment later, the door clicked. Alexander tried it again, and it opened.

As they stepped inside, the faint smell of incense tickled Jamie's nose. The church was dark, but the dim light of the still-rising sun offered them enough to see. They were in a hallway that had several doors on the right and only two doors on the left, one at either end of the hall.

Alexander opened the first door on the left, revealing the church auditorium. They were at the front, next to the stage. The room looked as if it could seat about three hundred people, but Jamie couldn't imagine that many people showed up each week. No one she knew went to church. After the virus devastated the region, most of the churches had been torn down or refitted for some other purpose. In that part of the country, the virus had killed more than just people.

Jamie stepped into the auditorium to find it empty. The room was long and narrow with wooden pews on either side of a center aisle. Large stained-glass windows ran along the walls. Each window depicted a scene that Jamie assumed was from the Bible or maybe church history. The artwork was exquisite. She imagined how vivid the windows must be in full sunlight.

One scene toward the back of the room caught her attention. She walked down the aisle to get a closer look. It showed a girl wearing a crown, not a halo as she'd seen in pictures of Mary. The girl was dressed in colorful robes and was facing a man who also wore a crown. A king and his queen, Jamie guessed, although she didn't know which king and queen they might be. What made the scene unusual was a third man in the background of the picture. He was dead, having been impaled on a pole. What kind of story was this? Jamie looked more closely at the queen. She seemed to be smiling.

Alexander interrupted her thoughts. "Do you think we're supposed to find your dad in here somewhere?"

"Not in here," a deep accented voice said from behind them. A tall man in a clerical collar stood in the doorway they had come through. He was black and appeared to be in his seventies, with a slight stoop in his back.

"Forgive me. I didn't mean to startle you. I am Father Aasir Jabari. Your father is downstairs."

The priest spoke with an African accent, although Jamie couldn't place it. He waved at them to follow as he led them out of the auditorium and back into the hallway. Along the hallway were a couple of offices, a storage room, a bathroom, and a door labeled *Mechanical Room*. It was locked. Father Aasir unlocked it, revealing a stairway that led down into a large basement. It was musty, dimly lit, and partly filled with what appeared to be junk like a large nativity, old computers, stacks of folding chairs.

Jimbo Haynes stood at the far side of the room wearing a bright Hawaiian shirt and aqua shorts with sandals. He smiled when he saw Jamie. "Your majesty," he said with a slight bow. "Delivered safe and sound, as promised."

She had to admit, Jimbo had come through for them. Maybe she needed to change her opinion of him.

In the corner next to him, sitting on the edge of a cot, was Jamie's father. He looked every bit as haggard as he had in the video, but when he saw Jamie, his eyes brightened. He stood as she rushed to him, embracing him. He held her tight, tighter than he had since her mother died. For that moment, she was his little girl again, lost in his protective arms. She thought she was there to rescue him, never considering that there was something in her that needed rescuing. Jamie had grown up in ways she could never have imagined since leaving her home, but deep inside was a girl who needed the reassuring love of her father. No matter how old she got, that would never change.

As Nate released Jamie, he spotted Alexander, who had been partially blocked by Father Aasir. "What's he doing here?"

"It's okay, Dad," Jamie said. "Alexander's not a problem. He's with me."

"Like hell, he's not a problem. He came into our home and took you by force. I consider that a problem."

To his credit, Alexander kept his mouth shut and stayed on the other side of the room. "Why don't we all sit down," Jamie said, "and I'll explain everything."

Thirty minutes later, Jamie had summarized the last two months of her life. She chose to leave out Alexander's true identity, fearing it would complicate the situation. At the moment, she needed her father to focus on their next steps.

"We need to get Ben, and then we need to get as far away from here as possible," she said, thinking only about what was best for the family.

"I'm not sure Ben is willing to go with us," Nate said. "And even if he is, where would we go?"

"I'm hoping the CRA will take us, but we'll have to see." Jamie didn't want to consider that she might not be welcome there. "Wherever we decide to go, I think Jimbo can get us there."

"I'll do my best," Jimbo said with a smile. Jamie was beginning to think that Jimbo took on these shadowy jobs because he liked the adventure of sticking it to whoever was in charge.

"Maybe you shouldn't go anywhere," Father Aasir said. Up to that point, he'd been quiet, sitting outside the circle of discussion, listening. Now everyone turned to look at the old priest. "Perhaps your place is right here in the New World."

"My place is wherever my family can be safe. As long as they are here, they are in danger."

"I understand the danger you face. But I'm not sure that you do."

Jamie felt her cheeks flush with anger at being lectured to by someone she'd never met. "I appreciate you protecting my father, but you don't know me at all or what I need."

Jimbo stepped into the conversation. "Father Aasir grew up in Sudan and Kenya. Both of his parents were killed in a government-backed massacre that lasted two days and wiped out most of his village. When he was a young man, before he became a man of the cloth, the CIA used him in covert anti-government operations in Africa. He's seen a thing or two, so why don't you hear him out?"

The priest never took his eyes off of Jamie. She felt as if he were studying her, sizing her up to see if she were worthy. Finally, he spoke again. "The scene in the window you were viewing upstairs is of an ancient queen named Hadassah. But she wasn't always a queen. She was a girl who was taken from her home to be made the wife of King Xerxes of Persia. This was not her choice, but it was her destiny. You see, Hadassah was not Persian. She was a Jew who was living in exile. As it happened, a very powerful man in the government had determined to kill all the Jews. Of course, he did not know of Hadassah's heritage, or he would never have pursued such a reckless policy. When the queen found out about his plot, she used her influence to stop this evil man, and she saved her people."

"He's the man on the pole," Jamie said, letting her flash of anger subside.

"Yes, the very same pole on which he planned to impale Hadassah's adopted father. So, you see, you may be able to save your nation *and* your family."

As she let her defenses drop, Jamie was drawn to the old priest. He had a gentleness in his dark eyes, and he talked like her father used to, as an idealist. Jamie wanted to be that kind of person, full of the hope that, if you do the right thing, everything else will work out. But those dreams had gone down with the airships from her delegation. The most she could hope for now was saving her family, and she wasn't sure she could manage that.

"That is a compelling story, Father, but I'm just a girl. Ashwill is the most powerful man in the New World. What can I possibly do to him?"

"You are the queen," the priest said with passion in his voice. "You can do what Mr. Ashwill cannot. You can win the hearts of the people, and you can speak the truth."

The truth. How would she get anyone to believe the truth about Creighton Ashwill? "There's no guarantee speaking the truth will work, is there?"

"No, there is not. Hadassah took a great personal risk to expose the plot against the Jews. It was more likely she would have been killed than succeed."

Father Aasir stood and made his way to the stairs leading out of the basement. Jamie wondered if he would add something positive before he left, maybe "I believe in you" or "I know you'll do the right thing." He did not.

"What's the pole?" she asked.

"What do you mean?" he said, turning around.

"In the picture, the bad guy was impaled on a pole he had set up to kill someone else. So what's the pole, for Ashwill?"

"Perhaps you are."

Jamie sat in the auditorium of St. Andrews alone, letting the others finalize the details of the plan. She sat below the colorful window displaying Queen Hadassah. Father Aasir had given her a copy of the Bible and showed her where the story of Hadassah. It was a book called *Esther*, and it was short, not more than a few pages. She read it twice. As a student of history, Jamie wanted to know if the account was history or fable. When she asked, Father Aasir only said, "Would it be more instructive for you if it were true?"

Jamie considered the question and determined that it would not. The story was compelling because it reached from the ancient past and spoke to her in that moment, real or not. Jamie felt a kinship with Hadassah. She thought about the choices made by this ancient queen in light of the decisions she had faced, and that thought gave her strength.

Once again, her eyes drifted to the figure skewered on the pole. "It took some guts to do that," she said to the stained glass woman, "Now it's my turn."

Jamie had made up her mind. Creighton Ashwill had turned her into a biological weapon, so a biological weapon she would be. He would be impaled on the pole he had made. Father Aasir had suggested Jamie should stand up to Ashwill by speaking the truth. She would do more than that; she would let the truth play out in front of a live audience.

Chapter Thirty-Three

Raisa's stomach tightened as the moment approached. Everything hinged on getting this right. Inside the Great Hall, she could hear Ashwill welcoming guests, oblivious to what was about to happen. Raisa stood in the darkened interior of a nearby room, waiting for her cue. Her thoughts drifted to her dad and Ben and Victor, wondering if they had landed in Dallas yet. She looked forward to being with them again. Ben was still angry, especially considering how they had gotten him. Raisa needed to be with him, to explain things to him. Soon. It hadn't been easy to arrange transport for them, but Jamie made it clear that the plan would not go forward until her family safe, so Jimbo made it happen. That was one of a thousand details hammered out over the previous five days.

As the old priest ascended the steps from the basement, Jamie realized that she had been of two minds since the day Ashwill had taken her from her home. Part of her, the part she had embraced as the real Jamie, longed to protect her family. That part took over when her mother died, and her father retreated into his sadness. Like a superhero's alter ego, that Jamie masked a deeper, hidden part of her. She had buried that deeper reality for so long that she forgot it was there, until Creighton Ashwill showed up, with a young second lieutenant, and took her from her home.

Alter ego Jamie was furious. But somewhere underneath the fury, a deeper part of her was . . . what? Intrigued? Curious? Liberated? That part of her now had a name, Raisa; and a power, conditional immortality; and a love, Alexander. How could she deny all of that? She couldn't. But she couldn't deny her family either. Jamie and Raisa lived in the same body. One had wings, and one didn't. One was meant to save her country, the other to save her family. The question was, could she be both?

281

Father Aasir had persuaded her that she should try. Convincing her dad she should confront Ashwill took some doing. Originally, he just wanted to get Ben and get out of there. Alter ego Jamie understood that; lie low, don't make any waves, survive. But to Raisa, that kind of thinking was like a heavy blanket smothering her. She needed to face the tyrant. She knew the risk, but she feared regret more than she feared failure.

On the other hand, Jamie wasn't willing to put her family at risk. If Jamie was going to let Raisa confront Ashwill, she had to know her family was safe. That was the deal she made with herself.

Of course, Jimbo was onboard. Jamie guessed it was for the sheer adventure of the occasion. Alexander quietly nodded his agreement, saying only that they had to have a plan. "No more winging it," he said. Jamie couldn't imagine how conflicted he was. Even if Ashwill was every bad thing they thought he was, he was still Alexander's only family.

They spent the next hour brainstorming what it might look like to take Creighton Ashwill down. Everyone agreed that simply accusing him wasn't an option. Without proof, Aswhill could easily silence Jamie. Even her virus-laden implant couldn't be tied directly to him. And they couldn't expect Ashwill's co-conspirators to blow the whistle, at least not publicly, because they feared Ashwill more than they feared Jamie. The Council would have no choice but to remove Jamie if she made such an outlandish claim.

Killing him outright was also rejected as a viable option. Forget the logistics; the political fallout alone would be catastrophic for the newborn country, leaving it in worse shape than it was with Ashwill at the helm.

Alexander was adamant on this point. "Even if we succeed, it will ruin you," he said to Jamie. "If you have any hope of fulfilling your constitutional duty as queen, you can't be a part of the assassination of the president of the council."

When he put it like that, it seemed so obvious. "We're brainstorming," she said defensively. "There are no bad ideas."

"Yeah, there are."

Jimbo said, "Too bad we can't kill Ashwill with the virus, the way he tried to kill Kaine. That's the kind of drama I like."

Jamie looked at Alexander, who had been waiting to hear something on his comm from the team in Dallas. He shook his head. Still nothing. As of that moment, they didn't know if Ashwill had succeeded in killing Kaine. If he died, Raisa would lose a valuable ally, making it harder to stop Ashwill. She shuddered to think that he had turned her into a weapon. If Kaine survived, would he ever want to see her again? Or would seeing her be like looking down the barrel of the gun after being shot?

That's it. "Why can't we?" she said.

Alexander asked, "Why can't we what? Use the virus? Have you lost your mind?"

"Queen Hadassah impaled her enemy on the pole he made. Father Aasir said I was the pole. Don't you get it? I don't need to accuse him of anything. I just need to show up with my implant blinking red." She held it up, still sealed in plastic.

"Yeah, and kill everyone around you, starting another epidemic." Alexander waved his hands emphatically. "They put people away for stuff like that."

"That's the beauty of it."

On the table next to Jimbo was a handgun he carried for personal protection. Jamie snatched it with one quick motion and turned her back to the group. She depressed the magazine release, allowing the ammo clip to move down less than an inch. Jamie then worked the slide, making sure there was no round in the chamber. She knew, however, it would sound to everyone else as if she was loading a round. With the clip disengaged, preventing any ammo from automatically loading, she turned around, pointing the gun at

Jimbo. His eyes went wide, and he ducked as she pulled the trigger three times. *Click, click, click.*

"She has lost her mind!" He grabbed the gun, bumping the clip into place with the palm of his hand. He tucked it in the waistband of his brightly colored shorts.

"Ashwill turned me into a deadly weapon," Jamie said. "But a weapon doesn't have to be loaded to make a man flinch."

A torrent of overlapping conversation followed fifteen seconds of silence as everyone else in the room caught on. Jamie wouldn't have to prove a thing. She'd let Ashwill incriminate himself. As long as he thought she was lethal, she could get him to flinch, and that was all she needed. Her implant had been an evil stroke of genius on Ashwill's part, and now Jamie would use it to take him down.

In the minutes following Jamie's epiphany, details began to flood her mind. This wouldn't be easy. At the moment, all she had was an idea, a thought, really. She needed a plan. How would they get her father and her brother out of the country? That was non-negotiable. Who would re-implant Jamie's device, or at least one that looked like it but was, in fact, harmless? Spikes had left a mess when he took it out, and they needed someone who knew what they are doing. Where would this drama with Ashwill play out? How would they make sure it was seen and understood by enough people to make a difference? How would they make the implant activate when it was supposed to, with its blinking red light? The answer to that one was not hard to get, but they'd have to kidnap Dr. Zurich. Jamie suspected that, with the right motivation, he would tell them everything they needed to know.

She threw her questions out in rapid-fire succession. Alexander had begun to write them down, ranking them in priority, when his comm activated. Halfway through her dictation, he stopped, touched the tiny device in his ear, and listened. His face didn't indicate what he was hearing, but his foot did. Jamie had learned that Alexander reacted to stress the opposite of most people.

Nearly everybody she knew got fidgety when they were under duress. Alexander got calm, almost placid. He started to fidget when the stress was relieved. At that moment his foot was tapping like someone sending Morse code.

Chapter Thirty-Four

"Mission accomplished."

The words sent a wave of relief washing over Jamie. She didn't realize how much tension had built up in her muscles until it started to recede like unwelcome floodwaters. Cheers erupted from the others in the room. They needed the CRA if they had any hope of success. But more than that for Jamie, she wanted Kaine as her ally. She wanted to preserve the bond they had formed in Dallas. Like a madman with a knife, Ashwill had tried to sever that bond and nearly succeeded. But his plan didn't work. Saving Kaine's life was the first step in pushing back against Ashwill's maniacal plot. It felt good.

An hour after Alexander had received the good news from Deeson, they were able to secure a video link with President Kaine. He looked tired and gray.

Jamie took the initiative, starting the conversation. "Mr. President." Her voice broke. She took a breath, determined to get through this with poise. "I cannot tell you how sorry I am for what has happened to you and the others who were infected. I wish I could report that the attack was carried out by some rogue operative acting on his own. The truth is, it came from the highest levels of our government."

Up until then, Kaine's expression had been flat, not revealing his frame of mind. His mouth turned up at the ends in a smile. "But not at the highest level, Your Majesty."

"No, certainly not."

"I must say that I was relieved to hear that your people were returning, and not just because they promised to save my life. I didn't want to believe you could do such a thing. But having said that, I'm in a difficult position. We've been attacked. The New World tried to assassinate me, and members of my administration. As you might imagine, I am under a great deal of pressure to retaliate."

"I understand, but President Ashwill's actions do not reflect my policies toward the CRA. I meant everything I said in Dallas."

Kaine looked sad as he spoke. "Raisa, I'm afraid you're a leader in name only. Creighton used you. It's a rookie mistake, but the people in my government do not have confidence in you."

Kaine's words crushed Jamie. "How about you?" she managed to say.

"I like you. We could have worked together, but my hands are tied. We can't let this go unchallenged."

That doesn't sound like confidence. "There has to be a middle ground, Thomas. Something other than all-out war."

"You sent your people back to save me, and for that, I owe you. But short of delivering Ashwill's head on a platter, neither one of us can stop this war."

"Then I guess that's what I'll have to do."

Finding a venue for their plan turned out to be the biggest challenge, only because they had no control over Ashwill's schedule. They needed the attack to be at a public event, preferably with TV coverage, but certainly with a live audience. Alora gave them a list of Ashwill's upcoming events to consider. Two stood out as possibilities. One was a speech to be delivered at the American University commemorating fifteen years since the reopening of the school. Students, faculty, staff would attend along with invited guests. It wasn't a big media draw, but since the New World controlled the press, anything Ashwill did in public got some coverage. The problem was that the event was in two days, not enough time to make the necessary arrangements.

On the day of the speech, Jamie and the others watched it on a government access feed. Ashwill took the opportunity to make a case for war against the CRA, using Jamie's untimely demise for all it was worth. He vowed to find Queen Raisa and to avenge the attack on her delegation. A resounding ovation signaled widespread approval.

The other option for their plan was a party, a gala actually. It had been scheduled months in advance to celebrate the New World's entrance onto the world stage. Everybody who was anybody would be there. The New World Council would be there along with other dignitaries, foreign and domestic, and hundreds of Ashwill's closest supporters. Raisa had been scheduled to be the guest of honor before her disappearance. She imagined that Ashwill would use her absence as another opportunity to beat the war drum. If all went well, he'd never get a chance. The gala was in five days which was barely enough time, but Kaine had made it clear that if they hoped to avoid a war, they had to produce Ashwill soon, to stand trial in the CRA.

With the time and place nailed down, the next big question was how to get Ben away from Return. Jamie said, "Jimbo, what connections do you have that could help us find Ben? Somebody has got to know where they're hiding out."

"That won't be necessary," Nate said. "I know exactly where he is."

That drew raised eyebrows.

Jimbo said, "I'm impressed. How'd you manage that?"

"Victor joined Return with him. He's been in communication with me ever since Ben left."

"Victor's been spying on Return?" Jamie said. "That sounds dangerous." He wasn't even her dad's chief of staff any longer, and he was still taking care of him.

"It was his idea. After you left, Ben confided in him. Victor was the one person he wasn't mad with. He knew he couldn't talk Ben out of joining Return, so instead of alienating himself, he went along and joined up. He figured it was the only way he could protect him."

Jamie always had like Victor, but her respect for the man now reached new heights. If everything went according to plan, she would make sure he had a place in her government, or at least on her staff.

With this revelation from Jamie's dad, the only question was how to get Ben back. With Victor's intel, they all agreed that snatching Ben was the best option. They were running out of time, and any other option like trying to reason with him would take too long. He'd be mad if they took him, but he'd be safe, and that was Jamie's priority.

"I'll set things up," Jimbo said. "Just put me in touch with Victor, and I'll make it happen." Everyone stared at him with disbelief. "I know a guy," he said.

"You *are* a guy," Alexander answered with the hint of a smile. That was the second kidnapping of this operation, but nobody objected. It was what had to be.

After their first night in the basement, Jamie decided she needed to go for a run. There was a connection between body, mind, and soul. It had only been a couple of days since her last run in Dallas, but already she was feeling it. Her physical and mental reflexes weren't sharp. Jimbo offered to get her some running clothes, and she took him up on it. Alexander wasn't crazy about her being out on her own, but Jamie needed the time. Besides, it was a suburban neighborhood in Reston, and no one knew she was there. With her hair tucked into the Wildcats baseball cap and a pair of shades on, she'd be just another runner to anyone who saw her. Normally, she'd love for Alexander to join her, but it was Alexander and her future as the queen that she needed to think about. Kind of hard to do that when he was pounding the pavement next to her.

Jamie headed south from the church. Every step was an effort; her stressed body not yet receiving the benefits of the run. That would come later when her muscles released the lactic acid and endorphins found their way to her brain. At the moment, putting one foot in front of the other was a matter of willpower. Two blocks of houses gave way to a small shopping district with a main-street feel. There were a lot of empty shops, but some new businesses with *Now*

Open signs in a few windows. One of them was a coffee shop. Jamie made a mental note to stop and get a cup of coffee on her way back.

As air filled her lungs, her mind cleared. Jamie depended heavily on the advice of those around her, but she needed time to process their advice without anyone saying anything. She needed to hear her own thoughts without distractions. Jamie had never ascribed to the *follow your heart* way of thinking, but this was close. It was a gut check. What was her gut telling her? She had more or less committed to a course of action, but no one had pulled the trigger yet. She could still change course if she wanted to. So that was the question, what did she want? When was no one else telling her what she should want or what her duty was, what did she want?

Alexander.

Every version of the future that Jamie imagined included him. She'd never told him that, probably because she hadn't realized it until then. The thought had probably been kicking around in her subconscious mind, but the rhythm of her legs pumping against the asphalt brought it to the surface.

She wanted Alexander in her life, that much she knew. And she wanted to be queen. No, that wasn't right. She *was* the queen. That was the problem. She had never embraced her new identity, not fully. She'd always had one eye on the exit, even in Dallas. That had to change. If Jamie wasn't all-in, she needed to get out.

As she reached the forty-five-minute mark, sweat covered her body. It was time to reverse course and head back to the church. The run back yielded no thoughts that changed her mind as she continued to probe her conscience. With every step, her resolve only deepened. As she approached the coffee shop, she slowed, allowing her heart rate to come down. Inside she ordered a cup of ice coffee.

The guy behind the counter made the drink and told her how much it would be. It was then that Jamie realized she didn't have any money. Her cheeks reddened. "Uh, funny thing," she said, "I left for my run without any money."

The counter clerk didn't appear sympathetic.

"I got it," a voice behind her said. Jamie turned to see an older man standing behind her in line, shoulders stooped and hair white. He wore an old Greek fisherman's cap that was complemented by his ruddy complexion. A warm smile lit up his face. "It's been a while since I bought a pretty girl a drink."

Jamie was going to protest, but why rob the gentleman of a small pleasure? He probably didn't have too many. She flashed a big smile. "That's very kind. Thank you."

"It's my pleasure," he said, pulling a few credits from his pocket, putting them on the counter. "What's your name, young lady?"

That's the question, isn't it? Who am I? "I'm Raisa," she said.

"That's an unusual name. The same as our queen."

"Yes," Raisa said, "and it's spelled the same way."

"That poor girl. I hope they find her. And if they don't, I hope they make the people who did this pay. We can't have people treating our queen that way."

"Yes, sir. I have a feeling everything will work out the way it's supposed to."

• • • • •

Later that evening, Raisa waited in a room, not far from the Great Hall, for her cue that it was time. She was wearing the evening gown Alora had picked out for her. Thankfully, she trusted Alora's sense of style. She had to since she couldn't exactly show up at her Pentagon apartment suite and put together an outfit. She tugged at the dress for the thousandth time. It was a nervous habit, but she couldn't help herself. She needed some way to expel the energy building up in her body. Music and the soft chatter of conversation from the Great Hall made their way to the room where Raisa waited for Commander Song to tell her it was time.

Alexander stood next to her, wearing a tuxedo. He said, "You know, Ashwill was right about one thing. You do look great in a dress." And then with a smile, "You don't need to adjust a thing."

Alexander slipped his hand into hers and held it tight. She let the warmth of his touch make its way up her arm and fill her with serenity. Raisa stopped tugging at her dress.

They waited down a corridor from the Great Hall, which had once been the Capitol Rotunda. The room they were in was inaccessible to guests since it was in a yet to be renovated area of the Palace. Song said it would be a safe place until they were ready. So, they waited alone, holding hands.

"I've never met anyone like you," Raisa said.

"I'll take that as a compliment."

"You should. I feel completely safe with you. No, safe is not the right word. At home. Content. Complete."

He said, "Wow. It sounds like you got the hots for me, bad."

Raisa punched him in the arm with her free hand. "I'm trying to be serious. We're about to do something that will either succeed or fail momentously. Either way, our lives will change forever again. So before we go in there, I need you to know how much I love you."

"I know," he said, his tone turning earnest. "I love you too."

"Do you?" Raisa asked.

"Of course." Alexander looked slightly offended by the question.

"Then marry me."

"What?"

"Promise me that when this is all over, you'll marry me." Raisa could feel her heart beating wildly in her chest. She was sure Alexander could feel her racing pulse in their clasped hands. Raisa looked into his eyes, awaiting his response.

"It's time," Commander Song's voice came from the doorway of the room, interrupting the moment. "You wanted to know when Ashwill was about to address the guests. Well, it's right now." Song looked in the direction of the Great Hall and then back at Raisa. "I put my neck on the line for you, Your Majesty, so I hope you know what you're doing."

"Me too," Raisa said, her eyes still locked on Alexander's. Then she let go of his hand and made her way out of the room and toward the Great Hall. It was time to find out if she could make Creighton Ashwill flinch.

Chapter Thirty-Five

Raisa entered the Great Hall from the south corridor, opposite a platform which had been erected on the north side of the room. That's where Ashwill stood, addressing the crowd. For the moment, everyone was facing away from Raisa, listening to the speech. As she entered, she was stunned once again by the beauty of the newly-renovated hall. The tiny lights shining through semi-translucent marble created a fantasy-like atmosphere that was only enhanced by the beautiful men and women dressed for the occasion. The overhead lights were dimmed, intensifying the effect of the starry floor.

The spotlight on Ashwill was not dimmed. He stood out, larger than life, in the brilliance of the beam. Raisa was nearly one hundred feet from him on the other side of the room. She realized that, with the lights dimmed and a spotlight in his eyes, he couldn't see her or Alexander who stood just behind her. She had not anticipated this, but it wasn't a problem. If anything, it would only heighten the drama about to unfold. The brief moment of anonymity allowed Raisa to take in more of the scene than she would have otherwise.

She could see Lieutenants Penly and Spikes quietly entering from the west entrance as Captain Deeson and Raven did the same on the east side. They had returned from Dallas just that morning. Nikole didn't make it to the gala, however. A check of her comm unit confirmed their suspicion that she had alerted Ashwill to their location at the cabin. She was currently in the basement of St. Andrews. When Raisa last saw Nikole, Father Aasir was telling her the ancient story of a woman named Rahab who, according to the priest, was smart enough to side with the winning army. The not-so-veiled suggestion was that she had picked the wrong side. Behind the platform was the west entrance into the Great Hall. Raisa knew Commander Song was waiting there, even though she couldn't see her yet.

It hadn't been easy getting Commander Song to agree to the plot against Creighton Ashwill. She was intensely loyal. It was a risk even telling her. But Raisa was counting on something she saw in the commander the day she toured the Palace, basic decency, and honesty. When Alexander briefed Song on the details of the clinical trials, she wanted to know more. He told her what he had not yet told Raisa, that he'd learned the details of the trials from Ashwill himself. Creighton told Alexander, probably not realizing how strong his attachment to Raisa was, or not believing she could do anything about it. Whatever the reason, he felt safe, confessing his crime to his stepson. Commander Song was visibly disturbed by the report. When they told her about the plot against Kaine, she said she needed to think about it. But Raisa knew she would not support someone who had done those things.

Ashwill's speech was quite good. Raisa might have enjoyed it, had it come from a better man. He spoke extemporaneously, giving a brief history of how the New World came to be, and what their future would hold. It was nothing this crowd hadn't heard before, but like stories from their favorite storyteller, they loved to hear it again.

For the previous five days, the news had focused twenty-four seven on the tragic loss of Queen Raisa. Of course, search efforts continued, but hope was fading that the young queen would be found alive. Ashwill reminded the faithful of the bigger picture. They had overcome insurmountable odds before, and they would do it again. They would have a glorious future free from the aggression of the Constitutional Republic of America. "For too long," he said, "they have held us down. No more. We are rising from the ashes, and we are strong."

He was just getting to Queen Raisa's tragic end, and how the New World would avenge her death when Raisa made her move. She began to walk toward the platform. She walked with the steady confidence of a woman on a mission, not looking to the right or the left. She didn't hurry, but let her forward movement build momentum like a wave sweeping through the room. As she passed people who had had their backs to her, they slowly recognized her, whispering her name to one another.

The whispers turned into a murmur that grew loud enough to capture Ashwill's attention. At first, he tried to continue his speech, not knowing why a ripple was making its way through the crowd. Soon though, he stopped and shielded his eyes from the spotlight. Raisa smiled as his search of the room brought his gaze into contact with hers.

"Hello, Creighton," she said.

He didn't respond. A panic momentarily touched his expression, but it didn't stay long. As expected, Ashwill recovered quickly from the shock.

"As I live and breathe," he said. "Ladies and gentlemen, I am rarely speechless, but rarely have I witnessed a miracle." He looked at Raisa. "My dear, you, here tonight, are a miracle." He looked back at the crowd. "This is a stunning development. As you might imagine, Her Majesty and I have much to discuss. If you will excuse us –"

"Actually," Raisa interrupted, "I thought we could stay here. We're among friends Creighton, and I have so much to say."

Raisa's gown featured a plunging neckline, leaving exposed the spot below her collarbone where her new implant had been inserted. She wasn't sure if he had noticed the solid green light showing through her skin, but she was certain that he saw it turn red and begin to blink. His face drained of color as he abandoned any effort to hide his trepidation. Raisa, who stopped at the midway point across the room, resumed her progress toward the platform, followed by Alexander. Spikes and Penly mirrored her movements on the west as did Raven and Deeson on the east, each group closing in on the platform like a tightening noose. Ashwill stepped back as if he might make his way to the steps leading off the stage, but Commander Song blocked his passage. She had moved into place when she heard her cue, Raisa's voice.

"Commander," Ashwill said, looking confused. "I need you to escort me to my car."

Commander Song didn't move. Raisa and the others continued to close in.

"Are you okay, Creighton?" Raisa asked. "You don't look well."

The crowd's uneasiness crescendoed as people shouted out questions, asking what was going on. Raisa was almost to the platform. She turned to the guests. "Ladies and gentlemen, I know this is all very unusual, but if you will be patient, everything will become clear."

She made her way up the stairs, watching Ashwill with every step. The man liked being in control, and Raisa didn't know how he'd react to the sudden shift in power. He moved to the opposite end of the platform, trying to appear casual. He kept his gaze on the red blinking light. Once she was on the platform, Raisa stopped. It looked as if she might stand there when she took a quick step forward as if she were about to close the gap between them. Creighton Ashwill flinched.

"Our young queen has been through a traumatic ordeal," he said in an unsteady voice. "I think it would be best if she were taken somewhere where she could rest." He motioned to one of the soldiers assigned for his protection to escort her out. Raisa shook her head at the young man. The soldier hesitated. He appeared conflicted about whose order he should follow.

"Don't move, Lieutenant," Commander Song said, and the young soldier immediately stood down.

Raisa stood motionless where she was. Ashwill was nervous. No point in pushing him over the edge just yet.

A tall, distinguished man in the crowd approached the platform. "What in the world is going on here?" he said. It was

Johnson Tate, the governor of New Jersey, a member of the New World Council.

"Governor Tate," Raisa said before Ashwill could respond. "As you've heard, the CRA attacked my delegation on our return from Dallas. But they only did so because we infected President Kaine and members of his administration with the Pittsburgh Virus."

That set off a cacophony of voices expressing shock, disbelief, and anger. "Wait, you need to hear the whole story," Raisa said over the crowd. "It was President Ashwill who initiated the attack. He used me as a weapon to deliver the virus."

Another wave of shock rippled through the room.

"I don't believe you," a voice called from the room.

Ashwill held out his hand in a gesture to calm the restless gathering. "Please, our queen has suffered a great ordeal, and she is confused. But let's not forget, it was the CRA who cut us off from the world and left us to die. I'd say having to deal with the Pittsburgh Virus is just punishment, no matter how it happened."

"You're saying you have no idea how Kaine was infected?" Raisa asked.

"None at all. But you are a patriot for avenging the New World."

Even from the other side of the platform, Raisa could see beads of sweat glistening on Ashwill's forehead. She turned her attention once again to the crowd. She noticed that the other Council members had joined Governor Tate near the platform.

"I have a genetic condition which makes me immune to the Pittsburgh Virus, but I can be a carrier," Raisa said, "and President Ashwill knew that. That's one reason he chose me to be queen. He wanted someone who could get the virus close to President Kaine, without raising suspicion. It was payback for the death of his wife, Merissa."

Ashwill's nostrils flared at the mention of Merissa, but he remained silent. Anyone who knew Creighton Ashwill knew better than to broach the subject of his wife. It was not a topic open for discussion or comment.

She continued, "Right now an interview with Dr. Sidney Forrester is streaming on all the major media outlets. She is a geneticist who has studied my case. She is discussing my condition and particularly my immunity to viruses, including the Pittsburgh Virus. Look for yourselves."

People throughout the room began reaching for their comm devices, verifying her claim. Raisa could hear Dr. Forrester's voice coming from dozens of tiny speakers across the Great Hall. She noted that none of the council members were looking at their comms to verify her claim.

They already know.

Of course, that made sense, didn't it? Ashwill had used her conditional immortality as a selling point with the council. It made her special, unique, a rare find for a royal post. She wondered if they knew there were other girls just like her.

"We've come a long way since Native Americans were given smallpox-infested blankets at Fort Pitt, but that's essentially what Creighton Ashwill did. I went to the CRA in good faith to negotiate a peace treaty, but Ashwill never had any intention of supporting peace."

"How could he possibly turn you into a weapon?" Governor Tate asked, but not accusingly. He wanted to know.

"Creighton, would you like to tell them?" she asked.

Raisa had always hated Ashwill's arrogant posture, but never more than tonight. It was as if he thought he could control the outcome of any situation by sheer force of will. But not this time. Raisa began to close the gap between herself and Ashwill. He focused again on the red blinking light of her implant, his eyes shifting to Alexander long enough to deliver his disgust with a look. He held his head high, refusing to admit defeat as she drew closer. Thirty feet. He even managed a smile, although it was less than convincing. Twenty feet. Another five feet and he looked over the edge of the platform as if judging his chances of successfully jumping off.

When Raisa was within a dozen feet, he yelled, "Stop. It's true, she's infected with the Pittsburgh Virus, and she has probably infected everyone in this room."

Chapter Thirty-Six

No. No. No.

The room exploded with screams and shouts and the sound of rushing feet as men and women in suits and gowns fought to be anywhere except near Queen Raisa. Silver trays with glasses of champaign crashed to the floor, knocked from the hands of waiters caught in the stampede. People slipped and fell, cutting their hands on the broken glass. Most of the guests in the room had been alive twenty years earlier, and they knew what the Pittsburgh Virus could do to the body. They didn't want any part of it. Raisa tried to yell above the din, but to no avail. She looked back at Ashwill in time to see him throw Song to the floor and leap from the back of the platform. He had not been in his prime for years, but he was still in good shape for a man his age. He disappeared in a run behind a backdrop hung for the occasion. He was heading down the north corridor toward what had been the Senate chamber.

Alexander turned to Commander Song, "We've got to contain these people. We can't let them leave thinking we've got another epidemic on our hands."

"Already on it," she said, getting to her feet and accessing her comm.

"And let's jam all private communication while we're at it. Keep it tight. Official business only." He touched the comm unit in his ear and informed every soldier at the Palace that, despite what they had heard, no one had been exposed to the Pittsburgh Virus that night.

Raisa kicked off her three-inch heels, darted to the back of the stage, and jumped where Ashwill had leaped a moment earlier. Alexander called for her to wait, but she ignored him. Ducking behind the backdrop, she saw Ashwill disappear down the corridor on the other side of the small Senate rotunda. Raisa followed. She had never run in a dress, and it was more restrictive than she thought it would be. She stopped long enough to rip the skirt up one side. *That's better*; now she could move.

Raisa lost sight of Ashwill when she looked up. He hadn't made it down the corridor to the Senate chamber, which meant he'd turned off before then. *Where did you go?*

Out of the building? No. Too many variables, especially with the panic he'd caused. Ashwill preferred settings that he had carefully orchestrated. Although there were no members of the media in the Great Hall during the event, the reporters were outside covering the comings and goings of VIPs. Ashwill wouldn't run the risk of having to talk about what happened tonight on camera, not until he found a way to control the story. His best bet was to stay in the building until he could arrange for secure transportation. She didn't see a comm in his ear so he was probably cut off from the outside until he could find a New World official. That suited Raisa since he had run into a part of the building that was unfinished and mostly empty.

She hurried to the spot where she thought he might have disappeared from the corridor. To her left was a series of offices that had not been touched by the demolition crews yet. It was unlikely Ashwill would have gone there. To her right was the old Senate chamber used by the Senate in the late nineteenth century. Raisa paused to peer into the room. It had been gutted and partially renovated as a reception hall in the Palace residence. Motion on the far side of the room caught her attention. A door swung shut. Raisa sprinted fifty feet to the door and burst through. She found herself in a hallway on the other side.

She swung her gaze to the left a half a second before she heard footsteps to the right, heading up a nearby staircase. Raisa followed the sound of steps. They took her down one level. She was in better shape than Ashwill, which meant she was gaining ground on him. She paused at the bottom of the stairs, listening for his footsteps. They trailed off to the right. Raisa had been down here before with her father. It was the basement level that ran under the Great Room. She realized it was the best way for Ashwill to get on the other side of the building, without having to encounter any of the people that came that night. But why? Where was he going?

Are you heading to the dome?

That was the only thing Raisa could think of. On the south side of the main level, just outside of the Great Hall, was an unobtrusive door. Behind the door was a series of stairs between the domes. They led to the interior and exterior walkways encircling the rotunda. The first interior walkway was just above the frescoed frieze designed and partially painted by Italian artist Constantino Brumidi. The stairs continued to a second gallery walkway at the top of the rotunda, nearly two hundred feet above the floor. They concluded at another door that led out to a walkway on top of the iron dome.

When she had toured this part of the Capitol with her father, Raisa learned that there were two domes. The exterior dome was a nearly nine million-pound cast-iron structure sitting over the smaller dome made of sandstone. It was the smaller dome that had, until recently, displayed the Apotheosis of Washington. Between the exterior and interior domes, a tight space contained a stairwell with three hundred, sixty-five steps leading to the top. The space between the domes looked more like an industrial building or the interior of a ship, with iron trusses crisscrossing one another, rather than the stately government building it was. But why would Ashwill go there? He'd be trapped.

The virus. Of course. He believed Raisa was contagious and, by then, probably a number of the guests as well. He was isolating himself from any chance of becoming infected. Ashwill probably didn't know that Raisa was following him since her bare feet made no sound as she ran. But still, it was a strange place to go. There were plenty of spaces on the main floor to hide.

She raced up the second set of stairs, back to the main level, and found the door. Pushing through, she could hear Ashwill's heavy footsteps above her on the metal steps. She followed them to the first interior walkway, about halfway up the dome. That would lead to another door and another set of stairs.

When Raisa stepped out onto the walkway that ran along the circumference of the rotunda, she spotted Ashwill a quarter of the way around. He was in a full run. Below, the starry floor was aglow, littered with trays, broken glass, napkins, and handbags – the debris of a frightful exodus.

"Ashwill," Raisa yelled.

He stopped for a moment, looking back at her, his eyes wide. Raisa had startled him. Good. He hesitated long enough for her to gain ground. It wasn't much, though. He resumed his flight, racing toward the door halfway around the walkway. Raisa's legs pumped and her heart raced as she closed the gap, but he reached the door and disappeared through it before she could get to him.

As she reached the door, Alexander called from behind her, "Raisa. Wait."

"No time," she said, pulling the door open. Behind the door, she found herself, once again, between the two domes. Fifty feet away, a staircase stretched up to the top, zigzagging back and forth from landing to landing. Near the top, the stairs transformed from a zigzag pattern to a spiral. Ashwill was already a third of the way up, taking two steps at a time. He was talking into a hand-held comm device, but Raisa couldn't hear what he was saying.

Alexander came through the door behind her as she reached the stairs. Together they scaled the steps. Above them, Ashwill disappeared as the spiral staircase led him out of view. They could hear and door open, then close.

When they reached the top of the stairs, Alexander put his hand against the door before Raisa could open it. "What do you plan to do?" he asked. "He can't go anywhere, and there's no one left to hear his confession."

"I'm here, and I need to hear him say it."

"What makes you think he will?"

"He's got nothing to lose," said Raisa. "And he'll want me to know it was him."

Alexander moved away from the door, allowing Raisa to open it. At nearly thirty stories high, the view was breathtaking, and more than a little unnerving for someone who didn't like heights, even with its waist-high barrier wall. Below, scores of emergency vehicles surrounded the Palace, responding to the events of the evening. Stepping out onto the narrow walkway, Raisa knew that she was at the base of the Tholos, a structure of twelve columns encircling a lantern that had been used to signal when Congress was conducting an evening session. Raisa imagined it would now be used to signal when the queen was in residence at the Palace. Above the Tholos was the Statue of Freedom, which Raisa couldn't see from that angle. Below them was the iron dome. Ashwill was nowhere in sight.

Alexander followed her out the door. Together they made their way around the walkway until they saw him. Alexander was right; he didn't have any place to go, so he waited for them, with his gun in hand. He always carried one, but Raisa had never seen him draw it.

As they rounded the bend, he said, "Stop there. I don't intend to die from the Pittsburgh Virus."

Raisa and Alexander stopped. Raisa had no intention of telling him she was not contagious. Not yet.

Ashwill spoke with a calm voice, despite heavy breathing from climbing the stairs. "Well, you've made a mess of things, Your Majesty. I knew something was wrong when we couldn't find you after your ship went down, but I didn't think you'd show up here tonight. At least I wasn't sure," he added. "It was a bold move, but in the end, a foolish one."

"Kaine's alive," Raisa said, "thanks to your nanotechnology."

Ashwill didn't speak for a moment. He seemed to be considering this bit of news. "As I said, you made a mess of things."

"Aren't you even curious about how we managed to stop you?" Alexander asked.

Ashwill didn't answer.

"I'm curious about something," Raisa said. "How did you know I'd go to the CRA and negotiate a treaty in the first place?"

"I didn't, at least not without some prompting. I hoped you would, but I thought I'd have to bait you with more than just the possibility of peace. As it turns out, you are more of an idealist than your father was."

"My idealism paid off. We negotiated a treaty."

"It doesn't matter. Nothing will change."

"Everything will change," said Raisa. "There's no war, and you've been exposed. Everyone saw your reaction to me tonight. They'll ask questions. The Council will investigate, I'll make sure of it."

"You don't think they might be preoccupied with why you would show up to a crowded room of dignitaries carrying the Pittsburgh Virus?" He gestured to her implant. "That's what I'm curious about. Why in heaven's name would you save Kaine only to start another epidemic in your own country?"

As the last words left his mouth, his expression changed. Creighton Ashwill didn't like being played. As the realization that Raisa had deceived him crept into his mind, he said, "Of course, you wouldn't. I must say I underestimated you." He nodded his head briefly as a sign of deference. "Be assured, that won't happen again."

The sound of an approaching airship pulled Raisa's attention away from Ashwill. It appeared to be heading directly toward them.

Ashwill looked at the airship as it approached. "I don't ever leave myself without options. As I said, nothing has changed. I will have my war, and Alexander will marry the queen. The only difference is, it won't be you." Ashwill raised his gun, pointing it at

Raisa. "By the time they recover your body, it *will* be infected with the virus; I'll make sure of it. Everyone will believe you came to kill me as part of some twisted plot concocted by the CRA because that's what I'll tell them."

Raisa's heart pumped at a furious rate, creating a lighted-headed sensation. The panic of an eight-year-old girl crept back into her skin. The gun in front of her at that moment was aimed squarely at her face, and she had no doubt Creighton Ashwill would pull the trigger. She remembered the words of Father Aasir that Queen Hadassah was more likely to have been killed than succeed. Raisa clenched her fist and raised her chin. If her life ended here, she would know she'd died for something that mattered.

"There's a flaw in your plan," she forced out through shaky breaths. "If you kill me, you will lose Alexander too. Isn't that a part of your plan, an heir for Merissa?"

At the mention of his wife's name, Ashwill's head bobbed to the side, as if Raisa had pushed a button that caused an involuntary reflex. But he immediately bounced back and said, "The problem with Alexander is that he's too sentimental, but that works to my advantage. If he doesn't marry the girl I choose, I'll kill her entire family. You can't live with that on your conscience, can you, son?"

Alexander didn't respond, but Raisa could feel that he had put his hand on her back, grabbing a fist full of her gown.

Ashwill said to Raisa, "It could have been you, but you were too smart for anyone's good."

As the last word escaped his mouth, two things happened simultaneously. Ashwill lowered his head enough to line up the shot and pulled the trigger. At the same moment, Alexander yanked hard on Raisa's dress, throwing her to the floor of the walkway.

Raisa hit the concrete hard. Her head ached, and her ears rang from the deafening explosion of the gun. Lying on her back, she felt her forehead. It was wet. She pulled back her hand and saw blood, a lot of blood. It must be a nasty gash. Rolling over and putting a hand against the column, she pushed herself to her feet.

In front of her, Ashwill stood with the gun still pointed forward. Raisa instinctively put up her hands in a defensive motion, expecting him to turn it on her and fire again. But he did not. He was unmoving, as if in a trance. Raisa pivoted to look behind her. Alexander lay on his back, blood staining his shirt.

Chapter Thirty-Seven

Raisa froze. She expected Ashwill to break from his trance at any moment and fire again. But she couldn't just stand there waiting while Alexander bled out. She broke from the fear that held her in place and knelt by his side. Pulling the comm from his ear, she shoved it into her own. "Lieutenant King is down. I need medics now! We're at the top of the Palace dome."

It would take forever to get medics up there, and that was assuming they could find their way up. Not everybody knew about the stairway between the domes. By then, it might be too late. She looked back at Ashwill, who had lowered his gun. His face had drained of color. He was a man who prided himself on being prepared for every contingency. But it didn't look as if he had prepared for this one. He dropped to his knees on the hard walkway. If Raisa hadn't known better, she'd say he looked like a man who'd never taken a person's life before.

The airship Ashwill had summoned was close enough now that Raisa could see the pilots through the windshield. She stood and waved at them. They'd been coming to rescue Ashwill, but she needed them to rescue Alexander. The ship moved to the level of the Tholos and held in place. Unlike the helicopter that Raisa had been on a few days earlier, an airship could hover in place with no movement at all. From the back, a gangplank was extended to the walkway. Two soldiers ran down, guns drawn. They looked at Raisa and Alexander, and then at Ashwill.

Seeing the soldiers seemed to break Ashwill from his trance. He shook his head and opened his mouth to speak, but no words came out. Without hesitation, he raised his gun, put it under his chin, and pulled the trigger. Raisa screamed, turning away from the gruesome sight. The soldiers stopped their descent momentarily at the sound of the gun and then hurried to Raisa's side.

"Do you know who I am?" she asked.

"Of course," one of the soldiers said. "What's going on here, ma'am?"

Raisa waved off the question. "I need you to get us to a hospital. Now."

Since the airship wasn't a medical ship, they had no stretcher, so the two soldiers grabbed Alexander by his arms and legs, carrying him on board, laying him on the floor. Raisa dropped to her knees next to him as the ship began to move. She checked Alexander's pulse. It was weak but steady, at least for the moment. His eyes fluttered open, and he focused on her.

"Yes," he said softly.

"Yes, what?"

Blood trickled from the corner of his mouth. "Yes, I'll marry you."

His image blurred through the tears. "Okay. But we've got to get you fixed up first." Raisa bit her bottom lip to keep from losing control. She couldn't lose Alexander. Not now. Not like this.

His eyes closed, and his breathing became shallow. Raisa fought the urge to hyperventilate. She put her hands on either side of his face. "Alexander. Alexander!"

She looked up to one of the soldiers. "Do you have a med pack onboard?"

The soldier opened an overhead bin and pulled the pack out. Raisa tore it open and found the IV kit. It had only one needle. There wasn't time to fill a bag and then give him a transfusion. But with only one needle, she had no other option. She connected the needle to the tube, and then the tube to the bag. With a shaky hand, she tried to find a vein in her arm, but she'd never done it before. One of the soldiers put his hand on hers and took the needle from her. He tied a band around her upper arm and inserted the needle. "The New World Army requires soldiers to train in multiple disciplines. I'm a medic," he explained.

Raisa nodded her thanks.

"May I ask why you want to draw your blood?"

"I have a special condition that enables me to heal quickly from serious injuries."

The soldier didn't mask his curiosity. Or was it doubt?

"He needs my blood, but I don't think we have enough time to fill a bag and get it into him." Raisa couldn't contain the tears any longer. "He saved my life. I have to save him."

"If he needs your blood, then let's do a direct transfusion," the soldier said.

"But there's only one needle."

"Only one per pack, but we have two packs." He stood and retrieved another pack from the overhead compartment. "We'll create an end-to-end anastomosis and transfer blood directly from your body to his." He talked while he tore the pack open. "From your artery to his vein. Piece of cake."

He sounded more confident than he looked, but Raisa willingly leaned back, stretching her arm out. What choice did she have? As the blood flowed from her body into Alexander's, Raisa closed her eyes and willed him to live. With Ashwill dead and her family safe, he was the only thing she still needed. Her life had been interwoven with his. She couldn't imagine reigning without him by her side. Until he lay prone on the ground, blood seeping from his chest, she hadn't known that. She knew she loved him, but she didn't know how much she needed him. If he died, part of her would die too, a part she had only just discovered. Raisa would die.

Epilogue

One Year Later

Raisa's hand reached out to the space next to her in bed. It was empty. She hated waking up to an empty bed. So much in her life had changed since that day atop the Palace dome. At nineteen, she bore the responsibility for a nation, albeit not alone, and for that, she was grateful.

With Ashwill dead, the truth began to emerge with an uneven cadence. It took weeks to sort out what happened, but the Council was satisfied that they had discovered the full depth of Ashwill's plot. He hadn't acted alone. Three other council members were privy to his plans and aided him in carrying them out. They were each prosecuted and convicted for treason. Special elections were held to fill each of the vacant seats. There had been civil unrest for a time, especially with the rumor of another viral outbreak that Ashwill had started, but the government quickly restored order. The New World came through the crisis bruised but not broken. Leading her nation through such an upheaval nearly broke Raisa, but like her nation, she had endured and was stronger for it.

During the investigation, new leadership emerged on the council. At least it was new to Raisa. Governor Tate of New Jersey took a leading role and was later chosen by the Council to serve as President, advising the queen in directing the day-to-day affairs of the government. He proved to be a valuable resource and a capable tutor. His honor and integrity stood in stark contrast to the previous council president, but Raisa wouldn't make the same mistake she'd made with Ashwill. President Tate would not act as her sole liaison to the rest of the Council. She would communicate with them directly, as would her staff. Ashwill had gotten as far as he had by keeping everyone in the dark. Raisa was determined to drag the affairs of state into the light. President Tate was all too happy to comply. With the full backing of the Council, Raisa was ready to lead the New World past its first few faltering steps into a steady stride alongside the nations of the world.

She rolled out of bed and put on a robe. An attendant pulled back the curtains, causing the room to become awash in the morning light and laid out the clothes Raisa had chosen for the day. Out the window, she could see the Summerhouse off to the right. Straight ahead was the Peace Monument on the Palace grounds, and beyond that in the distance, the Washington Monument. Raisa was still getting used to life in the Palace, but so far, the view from her bedroom was still her favorite. Commander Song's vision for a royal residence had turned into a beautiful reality. There was still construction going on in other parts of the Palace, but the residential wing was completed, and it was a work of art.

After getting dressed, Raisa moved to a small adjacent office for breakfast and a morning calendar review. She always took her breakfast in that room. It was richly appointed, with antique furniture. Her father's Senate desk stood out as the central piece in the room.

Alora reviewed the day's events while Raisa finished her breakfast. There were several items on the day's agenda, but only one that caused Raisa to look up from her grapefruit and cottage cheese. "At ten, you meet with the Pittsburgh Virus Genetics Commission to hear their findings."

Before she left for her diplomatic mission to the CRA, Raisa had asked the five other women from the Gamma Squad who shared her genetic condition to find out how Ashwill knew about them and who else in the New World might be like them. Were there others who would live beyond the normal life expectancy, immune to the normal aging process? It was months after the events of that dramatic night before Raisa was able to follow up with the team to find out what they'd discovered. Their report was incomplete. They had discovered that Ashwill found the other five through random genetic testing of populations where the viral outbreak had been the worst. The testing was done under the guise of anti-viral genetic research. Thousands were tested, and from those, he had found his five contingencies, in case Raisa didn't work out.

What they couldn't say was how many more of them there were. That's why the Pittsburgh Virus Genetics Commission had been formed. Raisa charged the commission was with determining how many people in the New World had the genetic condition known as conditional immortality. Were there twelve, or two hundred, or two thousand? Nobody knew. After the interview with Dr. Forrester went viral, the term "conditional immortality" became a familiar one, not just in the New World, but globally.

To determine how many people might have the genetic condition, the commission set up strategic testing centers throughout the nation. Since they knew the age of those most likely affected, they tested a sampling of young adults registering for military service. Then, using a specially written algorithm to analyze the data, they calculated the number of New World citizens who likely had the condition. The commission would deliver the report that morning.

Alora ran through the rest of the day's schedule and then said, "We have set aside some time this afternoon to visit the cemetery."

Raisa looked away. "Has it been a month already?"

"Yes, ma'am. You said you wanted to go every month, but we can change that if you'd like."

"No. That's fine," Raisa said.

The rest of the morning seemed to drag, but ten o'clock finally rolled around. The commission meeting took place in one of the Palace conference rooms. Raisa and the other five women with conditional immortality sat on one side of the table, while the director of the commission, Dr. Forrester, and three of her assistants sat on the other side. She explained again the process they had followed to come to their conclusion, although it wasn't necessary. Raisa waited patiently for the bottom line. Penly wasn't as long-suffering.

"Sorry, Doc, but we know all of this. What we don't know is how many others there are?"

Dr. Forrester looked down at the report in front of her as if she needed to check for the answer. "We estimate ten thousand."

Gasps erupted from the six women facing her. That was a small percentage of the population, but still, it was more than Raisa had imagined. The ramifications of this news began to flood her mind. How did a society change when one in every, what – four hundred people? – would live indefinitely? What were the economic, social, and political implications? Raisa didn't know how the other girls were processing this, but she was filtering it through the mind of a queen. There was a new minority class in her nation, and she was a part of it.

Dr. Forrester sat quietly for a few moments, apparently letting them process the new information. Then she said, "Your Majesty, you do know what the next step must be."

Raisa nodded her head.

Dr. Forrester explained, nonetheless. "This is like a pregnancy; you can hide it for a while, but not for long. In sixty years of so, it will become evident that there are those among us who are not aging like the rest. That will create problems, to say the least. We need to identify who these people are and help them prepare for a new kind of life. We also need to make sure the New World is ready to deal with the fallout. There may be people who take exception to the fact that some among us will live forever."

"It's not forever; just a very long time," Raisa said.

"That nuance will be lost on someone dying of cancer at seventy-five."

"Of course." She looked at Alora. "Let's authorize the commission to identify citizens with the genetic condition."

Alora nodded her agreement. "I'll contact President Tate and work out the details."

The group spent the next forty minutes talking through the implications of the commission's discovery. There was a lot to work to be done, and they were only beginning to understand the issues. Raisa let the others talk. There were things she had to work out in her mind. Her first instinct was to count this as a burden, but that wasn't right. It wasn't a burden; it was a privilege. But it was more even than that. It was her purpose. Introducing a monarchy in North America had been revolutionary, but this was something altogether different. It would take somebody who understood the implications on a personal level to navigate the rough seas ahead. Raisa imagined this issue would define her reign more than any other. Time would prove her right.

The rest of the day passed quickly, leading to Raisa's four o'clock appointment at the cemetery, sooner than she would have liked. She thought about canceling the monthly ritual, but it was a necessary reminder of what mattered most in life, painful as it might be. Her transport arrived at the front of the Palace, complete with a security detail. As she slid in, she was happy to see her brother Ben in the vehicle.

"You decided to go this time?" she asked.

"Yeah," was all he offered.

"Well, I'm glad. I think you'll be glad too."

After he was taken from Return, loaded on an airship and flown to Texas, Ben had been angry. Although there was plenty of indignation to go around, he seemed to focus most of it on Victor who had lied to him and betrayed the cause as part of the extraction effort. He hadn't spoken to Victor since that night. Raisa caught some of the heat as well, as did their father, but that changed after what had happened to him in Texas.

The motorcade wound its way through the streets of the capital; no one called it Washington anymore. There had been talk of officially changing the name. Raisa thought it would happen eventually.

The New World

The cemetery was small but well-manicured. Although there was room for many more graves, at that moment there was only one. Over the simple headstone stood a hexagon-shaped brick structure that was designed to look like the Summerhouse, only smaller. Raisa and Ben exited the transport and made their way along a gravel path to the grave. The headstone within the brick walls read:

Nathan Andrew Corson
Beloved Husband & Father
United States Senator
2033-2078

Raisa held back as Ben approached the headstone alone. It was his first time at the grave since the funeral, even though Raisa invited him every month. She understood why it was so painful. Ben blamed himself for their father's death. After Ashwill's suicide, the events unfolding in the New World were the leading news story around the globe. News agencies in the CRA began digging more deeply into Raisa's identity. It had not been hard to uncover that she was Jamie Corson, daughter of Senator Corson. The same Senator Corson who had authored the resolution to dissolve the union, a resolution that was unpopular in what had become the CRA. His popularity plummeted further when rumors surfaced that his daughter had tried to kill President Kaine, a rumor that the president put to rest, but not after one vigilante decided to take justice into his own hands.

One evening, after they'd gone to Texas, Ben and Nate got into a heated argument, one that ended with Ben storming out of the hotel where they were staying in Dallas. It was evening on the streets of downtown Dallas, and Nate, probably worried that something might happen to his son, followed. Coverage of the events in the New World was nonstop, and much of it featured pictures of Nate, mostly his official Senate portrait. He had become a highly recognizable figure in the CRA. Later, Ben told Raisa that he didn't know their father had followed him that night until he heard the scuffle a block behind him. When he looked back, he saw a man with a knife stab their father twice and run away, leaving him to die.

It didn't take the CRA long to find the man, convict him, and put that man to death. Raisa appreciated the swiftness of their justice system, but nothing could bring her father back. The attack stirred up tensions between the two nations, which were already nursing tender wounds. Those tensions lingered longer than they should have. Raisa and President Kaine had a bond that could not be easily broken, but it was a bond that many of their citizens and many within their governments didn't understand. In hopes of calming unsettled nerves, Raisa sent an envoy to Texas a week earlier. She had learned that nothing could replace face-to-face conversations. The envoy and his team were due back that day. Raisa eagerly awaited their arrival.

At the cemetery, she allowed Ben a moment alone with their father. Then she joined him, putting her arm around him. He'd grown so much in the past year that he could barely lean his head on her shoulder without stopping, but he did his best. As she ran her fingers through his hair, he cried. Raisa knew it was long overdue. She had arranged for Ben to see a psychiatrist to work through everything that had happened. He resisted for a long time but had finally started seeing him. It seemed to be helping. She had not seen her little brother this emotional since before the night she was taken.

Maybe there's still hope.

It didn't thrill Raisa that Jimbo Haynes had become Ben's surrogate father. But she had to admit, the man had come through for them, and Ben needed a strong male figure in his life. Raisa had reluctantly agreed, allowing Ben to live with him, but she had put a security detail on them, to be safe. The security team had strict instructions to contact her if they witnessed anything suspicious. They had called several times, mostly reporting Jimbo's questionable behavior.

As the day drew to a close, Raisa was impatient to return to her residence. She still had a hard time thinking of it as home, but she was working on it. Entering her bedroom, she slipped off her heels, leaving them where they lay. Before she reached the bed, where she planned to flop on her back in exhaustion, she saw a bouquet of bluebonnets in a vase on her dressing stand. They were the state flower of Texas. Her special envoy to the CRA was back. Raisa searched the room for any other sign of his return. Thankfully, she found several; a coat on the chair, a crinkle in the bedspread that hadn't been there when she left, and a closed bathroom door. Raisa followed through with her plan, flopping loudly on the bed, a smile plastered on her face. The bathroom door opened.

"You're home," Alexander said, emerging from the room, toweling water off of his face.

"And so are you. I haven't had a foot massage since you left." She raised her foot, pointing her toes at him.

"Oh, really," he said, playfully tossing the towel onto the bathroom floor. "This is the first time we've been apart since the wedding, and you want a foot massage? That's not what I had in mind."

He pounced on the bed with exaggerated enthusiasm, attacking her neck with kisses. Raisa's joyful laughter came from a deep place in her heart, and she was sure it could be heard throughout the Palace.

Acknowledgments

No book is the product of one mind or one set of eyes, and *The New World* is no exception. Without my wife, Linda, I don't know if Jamie and Alexander would have come to life as they did. Her encouragement, support, and feedback were invaluable.

Many people helped with getting my manuscript ready to publish. My editor, Wendy Thornton, was a valuable resource. Who knew there were still so many typos, even after I proofed it! I can't forget my friends who were willing to preview *The New World* and offer their honest assessment: Sarah, Rachel, Wayne, Ryan, and Lance. Their input helped me polish the story and make it even better.

I am also grateful to the staff in Congressman Ted Yoho's office for arranging a private tour of the Capitol Building that took me to the top of the dome. It was a great experience and invaluable research.

The cover of the book was designed by an incredible graphic artist and friend, Matt West. I knew when I asked him to work on this project that it would be good; I just didn't know how good.

My mother, Sandra Felton, has been a constant source of inspiration to me, teaching me by example to reach beyond the familiar and find new adventures in life. As a best-selling author, she has shown me what is possible when you go for it.

Finally, I would like to thank the Lord for giving me a mind with which to create. Everything I do is because of Him and is for His glory.

About the Author

Doug Felton is a husband, father, pastor, and, most recently, an author. *The New World*, his debut novel, has opened a new vista for him in the world of fiction – creating it. Doug has degrees in political science and theology as well as a Doctor of Ministry degree. He lives in Florida with his wife Linda, and his two grown children, Ryan and Haley. Two dogs round out the family. Doug's greatest pleasure in writing is creating stories his wife enjoys. This will continue to be the greatest measure of his success. You can connect with Doug at his website, dougfelton.net, or on Facebook.

A Word from the Author

Writing *The New World* as my debut novel was a transformative experience, in big and little ways. One of the pleasant surprises along the way was learning about things of which I was previously unaware. Two features in this book, the Foxo gene and the two domes of the Capitol building, were among those bits of knowledge I picked up while doing research.

The Foxo gene regulator protein is real and behaves in the way I described it in the book. When activated, it delays aging and fights age-related diseases. Currently, scientists are working to develop medications to activate the Foxo gene and extend lifespans. However, these drugs do not change the genetic structure, and they have negative side-effects that make them impractical. Making genetic alterations along these lines is possible today. But, the finetuning necessary to generate the benefits without creating other maladies is not yet in reach. Maybe someday.

The other bit of information I gathered in my journey shed light on the structure of the Capitol dome. I gathered a great deal of interesting and historical knowledge about the Capitol building and grounds. (As a side note; if you are ever in Washington, stop by the Summerhouse on the Capitol grounds. It's worth a short visit.) It turns out, as I describe in the book, that the Capitol building has two domes.

The first, smaller dome was part of the original building. It was originally wooden and then replaced by a sandstone structure. When you stand in the rotunda and look up at the Apotheosis of Washington, you are looking at the interior of this dome.

Seated above and around this dome is the iconic iron dome for which the Capitol building is best known. It was added when the Capitol was expanded to include the wings on the north and south sides where the Senate and House of Representatives meet, respectively. The smaller dome was too diminutive for the expanded building, so, Congress approved a second dome, one of the most ambitious undertaking in American architecture, with unprecedented speed. The result is a fascinating feature of the Capitol building; space between the domes.

As described in the book, stairs lead from the main level to the top of the dome. Along the way, you can view the floor of the rotunda from an interior walkway about halfway up. As you continue to the top of the first dome, you encounter a second interior walkway just below the Apotheosis of Washington, one hundred, eighty feet above the floor. From there, stairs take you to a door that opens on a narrow walkway encircling the top of the dome.

The Tholos (the circular temple-like structure on top of the dome) is directly above this walkway with the Statue of Freedom above that. From on top the dome, the view of Washington, D.C., is worth checking out if you ever have the chance.

To learn more about the Capitol, visit the website, *Architect of the Capitol*, at aoc.gov. You can also check out my blog, *A View From the Top*, at dougfelton.net. If you love history like Jamie, you'll be glad you did.

An Excerpt from *The Ten Thousand*

Book Two in *The New World* Trilogy

Once they were seated, the Russian czar leaned over to Raisa and spoke in a low voice. "Is it true, these stories we've heard about you? That you cannot die?"

About time, Raisa thought. Most people didn't wait that long to quiz her about her genetic condition. She had answered the question so often; she could recite it without thinking. "Not exactly," she said. "My condition prevents me from aging like other people, or getting sick, and I heal very quickly. So, chances are I will live for a very, very long time. But I can die. I need to eat and breathe just like everyone else. I need my heart and lungs and brain to function. So, a knife to the heart or a shot to the head would do the trick."

"Let us hope that never happens."

"Agreed," said Alexander, who had leaned in on the other side of Raisa to join the conversation.

"May I ask another question? I hope I'm not too forward."

"Of course," Raisa said.

"I understand there are others like you?"

"Yes."

"But Prince Alexander is not one of them?"

"No," Raisa replied, knowing what his next question would be.

"So, he will live a normal life span? You cannot change him to be like you?"

"No. He'll live a normal lifespan." Raisa put her hand on Alexander's. Whatever their differences, she loved him more than life itself. "We don't know how to alter a person's DNA. We know what the virus did to me, but we don't know how."

"Your media has reported that there are ten thousand more like you. Is this true?"

"It is."

"*O Gospodi!* How do you manage ten thousand immortals in a society of mortal men and women?"

Raisa knew precisely what Viktor was asking her. Since discovering the ten thousand several months earlier, she'd thought about little else but the issues that might arise from announcing the presence of so many immortals among them. Even though they represented less than one one-hundredth of a percent of the New World population, ten thousand was enough to raise serious concerns. Would people fear them? Would they resent them or idealize them, or maybe demand to know who they were? Raisa had wanted to explore these questions on her terms, but the New World Media Group made sure that it was no longer an option.

"Trust me when I say we've been asking ourselves that same question. I'll let you know when we figure it out."

The czar leaned in and lowered his voice. "If you will permit me, a word of advice. You must determine who you are first, an immortal who is queen, or a queen who is immortal. I think you will find they are two very different things."

Made in the
USA
Columbia, SC